Praise for Patricia Murphy

"Brilliantly imagined and gripping story from the heart of the 1916 Rising, based on meticulous research" *Joe Duffy, broadcaster and author of* Children of the Rising

"A fascinating story with a compelling young girl at its heart . . . a beautifully written and accessible read for all ages" *Nora Twomey*, Cartoon Saloon (award winning animation studio)

"An excellent book for parent and child to read together before bed" *Children's Books Ireland*

"An invaluable insight into what it is like to be caught up in violent political upheaval – as relevant today as ever" *Historical Society*

"Murphy, an award-winning documentarian and children's author, nails this character's voice and, importantly, doesn't patronise the intelligence of her youthful target readership (9-12 years)" *Sunday Independent*

"*Molly's Diary* by Patricia Murphy is an exciting non-stop adventure" *Scotsman*

"Poolbeg are offering a very exciting way to enjoy history. The books tell the story in such a way that the details stick" *Evening Echo*

"Throughout the well-researched narrative, Murphy raises contemporary questions such as violence being used for political motives, sectarianism, and even the GAA ban on foreign games. Young readers will be enthralled by the exhilarating adventure story while gaining a great understanding of the complexities of Ireland in the 1920s" *In Touch Magazine April 2016*

The
Irish Civil
War
1922-23

Ava's Diary

PATRICIA MURPHY

Published 2017
by Poolbeg Press Ltd
123 Grange Hill, Baldoyle
Dublin 13, Ireland
E-mail: poolbeg@poolbeg.com

Typesetting, editing, layout, design, ebook © Poolbeg Press Ltd.

1

A catalogue record for this book is available from the British Library.

ISBN 978-1-78199-882-3

About the Author

Patricia Murphy is the bestselling author of *The Easter Rising 1916 – Molly's Diary* and *The War of Independence 1920-22 – Dan's Diary*, both published by Poolbeg.

She has also written the prize-winning *The Chingles* trilogy of children's Celtic fantasy novels. *The Irish Civil War 1922-23 – Ava's Diary* is her most recent novel.

Patricia is also an award-winning Producer/Director of documentaries including *Children of Helen House*, the BBC series on a children's hospice, and *Born to Be Different*, Channel 4's flagship series following children born with disabilities. Many of her groundbreaking programmes are about children's rights and topics such as growing up in care, crime and the criminal justice system. She has also made a number of history programmes including *Worst Jobs in History* with Tony Robinson for Channel 4 and has produced and directed films for the Open University.

She grew up in Dublin and is a graduate in English and History from Trinity College Dublin. She now lives in Oxford with her husband and young daughter.

Dedication

For my mother Betty, nephew Henry, niece Muireann
and my daughter Rosa

The Battle of Dublin July 1922

THE BLOCK

ROTUNDA HOSPITAL
ROUND ROOM
PARNELL STATUE
THE GRESHAM
THOMAS LANE
HAMMAN HOTEL
TRAMWAY OFFICES
O'CONNELL STATUE
O'CONNELL BRIDGE
COLLEGE GREEN
TRINITY COLLEGE
SACKVILLE ST
NELSON'S PILLAR
MOORE STREET
BARNELL ST
GPO
LA SCALA PICTURE HOUSE
HA'PENNY BRIDGE
MERCHANT'S ARCH
TEMPLE BAR
CAPEL ST
RIVER LIFFEY
REBEL HQ
PUBLIC RECORD OFFICE
FOUR COURTS

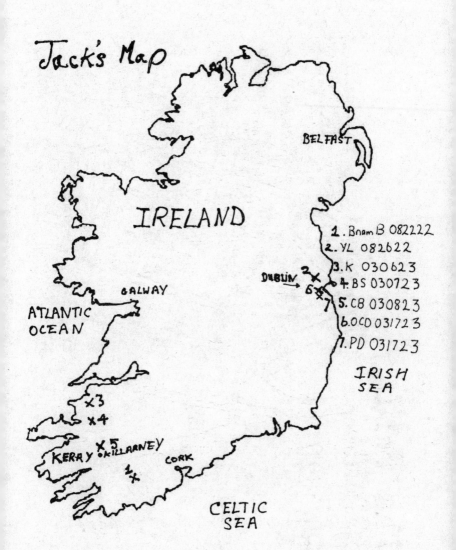

List of Characters

Present Day

Ava – 12-year-old Irish-American girl, newly arrived in Dublin

Mal – her 14-year-old neighbour, who grew up in Northern Ireland

Ava's mother – newly separated from her father

Ava's father – lives in the United States

Honey Belle – Ava's former American nanny

Nora – friend of Ava's mother, lives in Killarney

Betty – semi-retired schoolteacher and Ava and Mal's friend at the library

Karen – local librarian

Rachel – Mal's cousin and jewellery designer

Patrick – research mineralogist and Rachel's boyfriend

Irish Civil War

Molly – 18-year-old medical student

Jack the Cat – her brother who is a circus performer in the United States

Dan – their 13-year-old cousin

Sanjay – correspondent of Molly, lives in the United States

Anto – Jack's former best friend, anti-Treaty supporter

May – Anto's sister

Nancy – Anto and May's mother and former charlady to Molly's family

Chapter one

My Diary

KEEP OUT or you might read something you don't like!!!

June, Year One of My New Life, Dublin

"Ava honey, welcome to Ireland," my mom said as the plane touched down from New York. "The past is behind us. Ireland is our future. This is our Year One. A fresh start."

Outside the window all I could see was black greasy tarmac and a curtain of grey mist.

The swirling mist seemed to follow me around Dublin, creeping under doorways, fogging the windows of our dingy flat and even my brain. I thought it was never going to lift. Until this morning when I discovered we have a haunted chimney in our home! And even more freaky, it's like an answer to my prayers.

But let me tell you about myself first. Have you ever been split in two? I have. Only a few months ago I was Ava, skinny and mousy and small for my age. Just another normal twelve-year-old kid in New York. I lived in an apartment near Central Park with my mom and dad. I wore braces and had two best friends and a nanny. I liked school and even had a pet rabbit called Floppy.

I'm still skinny and mousy and titchy and wear braces. But now I'm an alien in Dublin with a funny accent. I only have a mom and we live in our pokey four rooms near a cold and rainy and, of course, misty seaside. I hate my new school and I have no friends. Since we couldn't get a passport for Floppy, she went to live with a neighbour. Oops! I nearly wrote "neighbor". I keep having to remind myself not to use American spelling.

Now the nearest I have to a pet is sweet little Robbie Robin. He perches on this creepy tree outside my bedroom window and I leave crumbs out for him on the window ledge. I couldn't do that in our New York apartment, which was on the seventh floor. See, I'm trying really hard to look on the bright side.

Especially as my big mouth gets me into trouble. When I stupidly told my new teacher, Miss Moran, that history was my favourite subject because I couldn't think what else to say, she had this great idea: write a history essay during the vacation about where I live to help me settle in!!

Gee, thanks, Miss Moran. I mean, history isn't the cheeriest subject. "And then they all died." It never has a happy ending.

But then the totally weird thing happened that was like a gift from the ghost of Christmas Past.

This morning I was mooching about tidying up our doll's size house when I saw some rubbish peeking out of the chimney. I stuck the poker up and got soot all over my face. Then these old papers floated down, blackened and scorched at the edges. I could just about read one in swirly old-style writing in purple ink.

Feb 1922

Dear Sanjay,
It's hard for me to continue my medical studies with Ireland on the brink of civil war. Even former best friends Harry Boland and Michael Collins are quarrelling. It all began over the Russian Crown Jewels, would you believe. Collins said they were bloodstained and threw them back at him . . .

Strange, huh? A History Mystery right there in my fireplace. Though the Civil War may as well have been between the fairies and the leprechauns, for all I know about Irish history.

What were Russian Crown Jewels even doing here? Sounds like Mr. Boland and Mr. Collins, whoever they were, were spoiling for a fight. Best friends falling out is something I do know about. Cleeter and Cookie, my best buddies in New York, haven't replied once to any of my postcards. Since Mom can't afford phones or computers, and I'm not online any more, it's like I'm dead.

Mom only dragged me here from New York because my parents are having their own *un*-civil war. We don't have much money because of something complicated to do with frozen bank accounts. The hope about Ireland being a fresh start has already gone a bit stale on her. She was born here but, since we arrived, all she does is lie in bed and cry. At least in Ireland you can't see her tears for the rain.

To tell you the truth, even though we lived in foreign countries before when I was little, I'm finding it hard to fit in. I miss my huggy bear of a dad. I miss my nanny Honey Belle – she's from Texas and calls me "Li'l Peanut". But . . . well, I don't want to talk about it. My fun gran has gone travelling around the world. Mom's brother Uncle Keith has just moved back to London. Turns out all Mom's friends have left too.

But I'm not a quitter. So I'm going to nail my summer project with the help of my mystery message. And I'm starting right here in my own backyard. Even though I don't have one. Our new "fun-size" home is on the top floor of a narrow three-storey building, squashed between two others.

When the landlady came to collect the rent later this morning, I asked her if the house was real old. She's this old woman called Lil with false teeth and wiry dyed-blonde hair. But she was more interested in grabbing the envelope with the dough.

My face fell when she said it had been built by her late husband Benjy in the 1990's.

She clicked her teeth and took pity on me. "If you're interested in history, there are lots of old books and things in the attic that my husband kept. He was a terrible hoarder." She tried to peer over my shoulder into the mess of the "kitchenette". "He renovated this old house around the corner and they came from there. It's a load of old rubbish. I keep meaning to chuck it all out."

"Had they anything to do with the Civil War?" I asked her.

"Yes, there was some famous fellow lived in the house who was in that. And Bram Stoker, that fellow who wrote *Dracula*, lived there before him."

"Wow! He must have had a real creepy childhood round here to come up with that!" I was thinking he was now maybe a ghost up our chimney! Though I didn't tell her because she'd start charging extra rent.

Old Lil gave me a stern look. "Nothing creepy about our desirable properties near the coast. Now can you give me the rent like a good girl?" She snatched the envelope and vamoosed.

I chased after her. "Can I take a look in the attic?"

"That young lad from downstairs that always wears the hoodie – Mal – has the key. He's storing some things up there. He's a couple of years older than you."

"Ah yes, I've seen him around." So Mal was the name

of Hoodie Guy who ducked out of sight every time he saw me.

I ran back into the flat and stuck the poker up the chimney again. This time I banged against some little shelf thing and dislodged something. A large paper came fluttering down in the same handwriting as the previous one.

After three years of guerilla war against the British, a truce at last. But Collins was right when he told us the Treaty giving Ireland some freedom from the United Kingdom would cause ructions. Merciful hour, as Nancy our old cleaning lady used to say. De Valera and he were always fighting but now it's a proper divide. The oath to the king literally sticks in Dev's throat. He wants a republic of the whole island. But many Protestants in the Northern counties, like my Great-aunt Bessie's family, are loyal to the King – down to her red, white and blue underwear, my father used to say. But hundreds of poor Catholics have been murdered by bigots. Thousands forced out of their jobs and many more burned out of their homes.

My big fear is that the arguments over the Treaty will only be settled with bullets.

Friends are even . . .

The page was torn there. But too weird, right? I really do live in a house with a spooky chimney. It's like instead of sending a letter up to Santa Claus for presents, he's sending me some useful letters back. I got to work with the poker again, hoping to dislodge some more ghostly messages, but no go. I was hooked now and couldn't wait to rummage around the attic. That guy Collins sure knew how to pick a fight. What with that darned Treaty as well as the Russian Crown Jewels!

At least I'll get to meet my neighbour Hoodie Guy. *Mal* means *bad* in French. Maybe I'll find out if he also has a head under that hood.

It will take my mind off missing my dad and worrying about my mom who used to be so cool. It just breaks my heart to see her so lonesome. I don't want to take sides. But even though I'm pulled in both directions, I can't really split myself in two.

Chapter two

Just after breakfast my mother gave me a heart attack by getting out of bed.

"I have an appointment," she announced, snuffling into her handkerchief, as she came into the kitchen.

I was so pleased to see that her legs still worked I didn't ask any questions and gave her a big hug. I hoped she was going to see a counsellor. She used to be one. But she can't really look in the mirror and counsel herself.

"You'll be okay on your own for a few hours," she said as she went out the door.

I nodded. *Sheesh!* I've been a regular Orphan Annie since we came here!

While I was goofing around, trying on her make-up in her bedroom, I heard this *thump thump* up the stairs and this loud knock on the door.

There was ole Death Head Mal dithering on my doorstep. He gazed at his scruffy trainers.

"Lil said I'm to help ya," he grunted. His voice was croaky, like he wasn't used to talking, and his accent was strong.

"It talks!"

He ignored me as he lurched towards the rickety staircase opposite our flat that led to the attic.

"Where are you from?" I asked.

He turned back. *"Norn Urlan,"* he grunted.

"Where's that? The Moon? The Gobi Desert?"

"Very funny," he said.

It sounded like *verra funna,* He said it in a flat voice that meant the exact opposite.

When he spoke again, it was more distinct.

"Belfast."

"Oh, that place with the bombs," I said too eagerly, as I closed the door and came out onto the landing.

He sighed and put on an affected British accent as if he was a newsreader. *"Where the Catholic natives and the Protestant settlers have been killing each other for centuries. Now held together in a fragile peace."* He gestured towards the attic. "Are you coming?"

I followed him up the staircase and he opened the black door with a huge rusty key, I swear, like a prop in a horror film.

"Watch out! Dracula's daddy came from round here!" I said, laughing like a nervous loon.

The door didn't budge until Hoodie Boy put his shoulder to it. He was surprisingly strong for a string bean. He took a torch from his pocket and sent a shaft of light into the gloom.

I caught a glimpse of a moth-eaten rolled-up carpet, a broken chair, and a teetering tower of old books. We

9

crept forward. Ropes of old spiders' webs dangled from the ceiling. A floorboard creaked. Hoodie Boy lurched to the right.

There was a terrible clatter. *"Ouch!"* He had dislodged the pile of old books. He flashed the torch while I bent down to look. One of them was a dog-eared manual called *Delorme's Book of War Surgery*. It weighed a ton! Smelt of damp and looked as if mice had been nibbling it. I dropped it back on the pile.

The torchlight died in that instant. It was pitch black in the attic now. Maybe there was a light switch – we hadn't looked for one. Duh!

A door banged somewhere in the house.

Then *CREAK!*

Followed by a low, gurgling moan like a wounded animal in a trap.

"Okay, you can stop goofing around," I said nervously. *"Ma-a-al,"* I bleated like a sheep.

Something spiny brushed my shoulder. A bat's wing, I was sure! I screamed. A tap on my arm made me jump out of my skin. I spun round.

A hooded creature with a skull-like face loomed out of the darkness.

"Maaaallll! It's Dracula! Back from the dead!" I screamed. Then next minute I was gulping for air. Like I was being suffocated.

"Take my inhaler." Mal dropped the torchlight from under his chin and passed me an inhaler.

"Easy – one, two, three, four." His voice was softer

now, easing my panic.

I inhaled deeply, pushing the air into my lungs. After a minute or two I was all right.

I handed him back the inhaler without a word. I was real sore with him.

But he was having problems of his own.

"*ACH-HOO!*"

The torchlight flickered around in crazy arcs as Mal dissolved into a massive sneezing fit.

I groped around near the door and found a light switch. A faint murky light illuminated broken old vacuum cleaners, a rusty old fridge, a yard sale's worth of old clothes. Mal had sneezed his hood off. A hank of greasy black hair hung down over his eyes. But I saw a few teenage pimples and a bit of bum fluff on his upper lip. So basically your average teen pin-up. NOT.

I handed him my handkerchief. He blew his nose loudly like a train hooting into a station. Then he smiled at me and he had really good teeth for an Irish person. His eyes were green under long eyelashes. Emerald green.

"You're welcome." I smiled sweetly.

Before he knew it, I decked him with a big ole pillow I found over by a couple of rusty bicycles. He unbalanced, laughing, then grabbed another pillow.

Soon we were having a full-on pillow fight. Feathers burst out and dusted us like snowflakes.

"Hey, stop, Asthma Girl!"

"Sure, Allergy Boy!"

I ducked.

His pillow collided with a big plank that toppled over and bounced against the wall.

"*Woah!*" he said.

He went to lift the plank up but something on the chimney breast caught my eye. A brick had sprung out. It was hinged like a little door.

"Look, Mal!"

"Wow."

We leaned in for a closer look.

Mal pushed at another few of the bricks next to the first one and a couple more sprang out. He shone the torch in.

"It's a hidey-hole, in the chimney breast," he said. "There's a sort of little shelf."

"Are there any papers in there?" I craned to have a look.

He pulled out a few burnt scraps. "There were – but they got burnt over the years."

"Gee, some of those fragments came down to my room!"

I told him about the notes from the Civil War but he was too busy investigating the hidey-hole to listen.

He shone the torch in again, put his hand in and fished out a solid bronze key.

We scoured the room and pulled back some old tarpaulin. Underneath was an enormous storage trunk like a treasure chest.

We tried the key and it worked!

Inside was a ton of old stuff. Some tiny dolls, a teddy bear with its arm in a sling, a set of tin soldiers with the paint peeling off and larger ones wrapped in faded yellow chamois leather. Some moth-eaten very old long skirts, tweed trousers and jackets. There was also a belt from a uniform. Some kind of old Boy Scout outfit. A faded embroidered shawl.

I pulled out a beaten-up leather pouch with animal and geometric symbols on it which looked Native American. It was quite large. I opened the tatty drawstring but there was nothing inside. It smelt like it had once contained tobacco.

There was also a load of old medical stuff – bandages, first-aid kits, splints, even a woman's white apron with a red cross on it.

"The person in the letter I found was studying medicine. Maybe this is her stuff?"

Mal pulled out a battered old typewriter. The sort they had in the olden days before they invented screens – with keys you had to strike that go straight onto paper. He thought that was really neat.

Towards the bottom was an old leather satchel, covered in mould. The buckle was rusty. I found a spanner in a toolbox and pried it open. Jammed inside was a mildewed school copybook with hand-drawn anatomical drawings and piles of old papers. Including a newspaper dated 1922 with a big headline saying "CIVIL WAR!" I checked the flyleaf of the copybook but there was no name.

"Okay – I'm going to take this stuff downstairs – I'd like to have a proper look," I said.

"Right you are."

Mal locked the box and shone the torch into the gloomy hole to put the key back. "Wait a minute. There's something glinting down there." He pushed his hand back in. "Ah, my fingers are too big to grasp it."

"Let me try."

I pushed my hand in and my fingers brushed a sharp object.

I fished it out and held it between my thumb and forefinger. It was sort of a diamond-shaped brooch, the metal bashed in and tarnished with age. But with the sweetest little smooth green stone in its centre.

"*Wow!*" both of us exclaimed at the same time.

The stone was smooth like a glass pebble. Mal shone his torch on it. It reflected back the light – a pure green colour, like a dewdrop on a blade of grass, or an oak-leaf in midsummer. Or the colour of Mal's eyes.

"It looks like an emerald, my mom's birthstone," I said. "Hey, you don't think it could be a Russian Crown Jewel? In those pieces of paper up my chimney, these two guys were fighting over them."

Mal looked at me like I'd suddenly turned into a nut-job. "A Russian Crown Jewel, how are yeh! Did you just come down in the last shower?"

I laughed. "You mean was I, like, born yesterday?"

He smiled and tapped the stone with a bitten fingernail. "Och, maybe it's just glass."

"The old guy Benjy, Lil's husband, must have hidden it there," I said.

Mal's nose started to twitch again. "Let's get out of here."

"I guess since old Lil thinks it's all rubbish, she won't mind me taking the brooch and satchel?" I said.

"Guess not."

He handed me the brooch and replaced the key behind the brick, springing it back into place. I picked up the satchel of papers and we left the attic, locking the door behind us.

Before going back into my flat, I hesitated, eager to talk about our find. But Mal had already turned to leave.

"I gotta go," he said.

"But don't you want to talk about the gemstone, the papers?"

"I know someone who could help us with that tomorrow," he said. "Knock on my door in the morning at eleven."

As he walked down the stairs he hitched up his trousers. He was wearing some kind of bracelet around his right ankle. Well, shoot! What was that about?

In my mother's bedroom, I caught sight of myself in the mirror. My mom's purple lipstick had gone all over my face during my asthma attack. I looked like a deranged clown. I would have to start carrying my inhaler with me. But I didn't want to tell Mom, to add to her worries.

I cleaned off the make-up. Then I cleared all the take-

15

out cartons and pizza boxes off the table, dumped a million tissues from Mom's bedroom and sorted garbage for recycling.

The landlady came up to tell me my mom had rung to say she was going to be late. I showed her the brooch, without mentioning the hidey-hole, and asked if I could keep it and the papers.

She wrinkled her nose. "Ugly-looking yoke. Throw them all in the bin for all I care," she said. "No use hanging onto the past. That's what I always told Benjy but he never listened."

I closed my hand protectively around the brooch. How could she call the emerald ugly, just because the metal around it was twisted and tarnished?

I reheated another pizza and watched a stupid crime drama on TV. But there was one thing that struck me. The master criminal was let out of jail but he had to wear a tag around his ankle. Like that bracelet Mal had around his ankle. Just my luck to share a house with a possible serial killer.

Chapter three

I was back in our New York apartment, looking out over Central Park, the treetops plump as pillows, the slash of the lake. I could hear my mother singing in the kitchen. An angry howl of a song. The four walls started to close in, the tendrils leaping off the floral wallpaper. My father came in wearing a hood, like a monk. He had no face. I screamed but no sound came out. He handed me a bundle and his hands were blood-red. It was the satchel from the attic. It burst into flames.

I awoke screaming, back in Dublin, the duvet wound around me. Beads of sweat on my forehead. My mother was at my bedside, mopping my brow with a tissue.

"There, there," she said, like when I was a little kid.

It was the middle of the night and I fell back into a fitful sleep as she crooned "Molly Malone", her favourite song about "Dublin's fair city".

When I awoke in the morning I went to my mother's room. She was in a deep sleep, her dark hair tumbling about her on the pillow, her face grey and slack. She must have taken a sleeping pill.

I ate my cornflakes in a blur. Recalling my nightmare, I decided to put the satchel and its papers back in the attic. Half fearful, I held it in my hands. But in the daylight, dusty and hard with age, it looked innocent. I thought I should at least go through the papers before I put it back.

The papers were a jumbled mess. It looked like they'd gotten wet and then someone, probably Benjy, had tried to dry them out by a fire. But the ink just got faded and the pages burnt and scorched. Some were blurry typewritten notes from an old-fashioned typewriter. There were fragments of handwritten letters. Also a file of press cuttings, mostly adverts for medical products, and a couple of torn photographs – black-and-white. But they were too damaged to see the faces clearly. Just a bunch of people in old-style clothes. I looked at some of the dates of the newspapers: 1922 and 1923.

I glanced through some of the torn papers and could pick out an odd word here and there. They mentioned the war and a treaty, just like in the other fragments! I picked out a couple of names: Mr. Field and Mr. Woods.

Then I had an idea. All I had to do was sort through these old papers by date and find some kind of order. I'd solved my summer project already! It was fate after all, stuff coming down the chimney like that. Should take me a morning, tops! Then I could find some stuff on the Internet to pad it out.

And then I got lucky. There was a clump of torn pages but they all fitted together. The handwriting was exactly the same as that in the fragments from the chimney. It was even the same purple ink.

Our old friend Anto, who I rescued during the Rising, is all for a republic. I think my brother Jack would be itching to get mixed up in it too. So please think of any reason, however flimsy, to keep him in the States! He is with the circus for now but I think he also does some hush-hush jobs on behalf of the Irish Provisional Government. Though I am relieved he kept out of that business with the eggs between 'Mr. Field' and 'Mr. Woods'!

He dined with Mr. Boland and de Valera in the United States. They all hold him in high regard for his exploits as 'Jack the Cat', gathering together all the funds for the Widows and Dependents Fund in 1916. But he is a daredevil and inclined to acts of sheer madness. His promise to me to never fire a gun will not protect him from stray bullets!

Maybe he could try to find those other jewels? You must tell him all about them! It might occupy him and keep him out of harm. Though I'm not sure the Russian master spy would be a good influence! But do keep me posted. Jack is not one for writing and I count myself lucky if he sends me a postcard now and again. My parents, who are extending their stay in Florida because of my mother's ill health, seldom see him as he moves around so much with the circus.

At least Dan, my young football-mad cousin, is back at school. He no longer wants any part in this war after our recent meddling in politics at the Treaty negotiations in London. He is content to trounce people only on the pitch.

With respect, always,

Molly

P.S. Thank you for the beautiful embroidered Mexican shawl. A HUGE surprise! And, by the way, I am following Michael Collins' practice and keeping a carbon copy of my correspondence in case it goes astray. One doesn't know who to trust any more!

Now this really was something. Pleased to meet you, Molly! Gee, hope you don't mind us rifling through your storage trunk! That tatty old thing must have been her beautiful shawl once upon a time.

Just before 11 o'clock I knocked on Mal's door, jigging from one foot to the other, with my bits of the letters in a project folder and the brooch in a small plastic bag.

The door opened abruptly.

Mal was wearing an enormous overcoat – all ready to go out.

I showed him the scraps of the letters. He read them, then shrugged as usual, but his eyes were ablaze with excitement.

"Could I use your computer or your phone?" I asked him. "Maybe I could find out a bit more if I did a search. We haven't got them yet."

"Neither have I," he said.

"So how come we're the only two kids in Dublin

without a phone or a computer?"

"I know a place with access to thousands of files." He looked at his watch. "If we're quick, we'll fit it in. Have you got the jewel?"

He sounded like a secret agent.

"I have it here." I handed him the brooch in the plastic bag and he put it in the inside top pocket of his overcoat.

"My cousin Rachel is a jeweller," he said. "She said she could see us for a few minutes if we're there at one o'clock on the dot."

I tucked the fragments of the letters back in my project folder and we set off straight away.

I'd felt cold since we left New York and was wearing my Yankees baseball sweatshirt. But even I thought his huge coat was over the top. Especially as he was also wearing his hoodie pulled up over his head.

As we walked along the busy road, I asked him what exactly was going on in Ireland in the early twentieth century with that guerilla war and treaty and all.

"All I know is England and Ireland have been fighting for about eight hundred years." He sighed. "You see, I went to school over the border. That's actually part of the United Kingdom, Yankee girl."

"*Mal-chance*," I said. "Bad luck in French."

He gave me a brief smile. "So you can talk rubbish in French as well, can yeh?"

I laughed. "When I was seven we lived there for a year. My dad's a manager on scientific projects. We moved around a lot."

21

"So how come you've ended up in this dive?"

I gazed at my toes, which were squashed into my sandals. I needed a bigger size. "My parents have split up. And you?"

"Let's just say my dad's not very good with money when he isn't off working abroad. He's a mining engineer." He changed the subject. "Must be strange for you living here?"

"Suppose so. Hey, what did you guys do with the sun? Why is everything in black and white?"

"Ha, ha, ha," he said in a cold voice.

I was getting on his nerves now. I noticed that he didn't say anything about his mother so, not wanting to pry, I didn't ask.

We turned the corner and Mal's big centre of connection was . . . *TA-DA!* The library!

I used to love the library in New York, reading on plump beanbags in the kids' section. So it sort of felt like coming home. It was even heaving with old folk and moms with pushchairs, just like where I came from.

The librarian, a young woman of around thirty I guess, beamed when she saw us.

"Hey, Mal," she said.

He grinned and gave her a thumbs-up – kind of goofy for a cool kid like Mal.

Several old ladies and a tramp gave him friendly waves. He was obviously something of a regular.

The librarian, who said her name was Karen, was a real pretty lady with orange-red hair and freckles. She led us to a bank of computers in the centre of the floor.

"Now if there's anything you need, just call me." She turned to Mal. "And maybe you'll finally join up and get your library card? I know what you get up to!"

He turned red, I swear, under the ratty old hood.

Karen went back to help some swarthy guy in a beanie hat. He thanked her in a heavy Russian accent, like a Bond villain.

The computers were maybe five years old. Jurassic. The server was as feeble as some of the customers. It kept crashing when I searched for 'Mr. Field' and 'Mr. Woods'. But then we hit gold.

"'*These were code names of rebel leaders Michael Collins and Harry Boland during the Irish War of Independence 1919-1922,*'" Mal read.

"Like in the letter! So that's another war before the Civil War! Sounds like there was a lot of fighting way back then."

"Well, it all began with the Rising in 1916, I think," he said.

"Was that something to do with bread?" I guessed it was some old rebellion but I was just winding him up.

He rolled his eyes and tapped 1916 into the computer. "This wee group declared a Republic and there was looting and shooting in Dublin. Lots of people at the time thought the rebels were nutters. Hundreds died and it only lasted a week. But when the British executed the leaders, the tide turned and that led to the War of Independence." The computer froze again.

Mal went off to help an old lady get a book down from a high shelf, like he was a regular Boy Scout. I tagged after him and two little bratty kids with their mother grabbed my place at the computer.

"Ah, now I won't be able to find out why Collins and Boland fell out so badly," I fumed.

Mal's friend, a youthful-looking old lady, smiled sympathetically at me. She had a lovely face framed with silky dark hair, and bright nut-brown eyes. She introduced herself as Betty, a semi-retired history teacher.

"I couldn't help but overhear," she said. "Maybe I can help. I'm guessing neither of you know a whole lot?"

We both nodded like two dumb nodding dogs at the back of a car.

She smiled. "My class wrote a rap poem. I've heard it so often I know it by heart. I can recite it if you like?"

Mal rolled his eyes but I could tell Betty was real proud of the poem so I nudged him and we both said yes.

She coughed and began, shy at first but then giving it all she was worth, getting into the rhythm.

"When Pearse, Connolly and Clarke
Lit the revolution spark
In Easter 1916,
An independent Ireland was just a dream.
But when Britain executed the leaders,
Making them martyrs,
The people said 'No more,
We want a Republic now for starters.

Your Empire might be fighting
A world war for power and glory,
But you being here for seven hundred years
Is no longer our story.
Only the guys in the North disagreed,
Because they followed the Protestant creed.
So between 1919 and 1921,
Ireland was under the rule of the gun.
Collins 'the Big Fellow', head honcho and star,
Led assassinations and bombings in a guerilla war.
De Valera the President,
A teacher and a scholar,
Went to the USA
To get support and dollars.
The British sent cruel Auxies
And then the Black and Tans.
But the Irish fought back harder,
For the freedom of their land.
It ended in a stalemate,
So Collins tried negotiation.
But got a 26-county Free State,
Not a 32-county nation.
Plus the Free State had to swear
An oath of loyalty to the King.
Seventy-five per cent voted yes
Hoping peace it would bring.
But De Valera cried, 'STOP!
This Treaty is a flop.
I'm not swearing any oath!'

> *Losing six counties gets my goat.'*
> *Some dudes like Boland*
> *In the Republican Army*
> *Didn't think he was totally barmy.*
> *So friends became foes,*
> *To add to Ireland's woes.*
> *And that's how the Treaty*
> *Split the new nation.*
> *And led to Civil War,*
> *A vicious conflagration."*

Well, ole Betty really nailed it, chopping the air like a regular rapper. I liked the rhythm of her Irish accent. So I burst into spontaneous applause and had to be shushed by Karen. Even Mal clapped Betty on the back. She smiled modestly and blushed a deep red.

She soon got her breath back. "But it was personal too between Collins and Boland who took the anti-Treaty side." She shook her head like they were two naughty boys in her class. "They also fell out over a woman – Kitty Kiernan. She ditched Boland in favour of Collins."

"That's sad," I said. "My best friend Cleeter has become better friends with my school buddy, Cookie, and I'm like history too."

Betty glanced at Mal. "I'm sure you'll make new friends."

I took out the fragments of the letter to show her.

"Hey, look what I found in our house. They also had some quarrel over Russian Crown Jewels."

Her eyes widened in amazement as she read it. "This might be of great historical importance! And how interesting about the Russian Crown Jewels. I must learn more about that. Let's show this to Karen!"

But Karen was still talking to the swarthy guy with the beanie hat.

I waved to Mal and he came over to us.

"Why are they going on about eggs if it's a war?" I asked Betty.

She closed her eyes briefly as if she were scanning her brain. "'Eggs' was a code word they used for guns or ammunition. They must have been smuggling arms."

"Of course! Eggs – short for explosives!" I said. "I thought Field and Woods were mad farmers!"

"Did you ever hear of a medical student called Molly?" Mal asked. "Or her brother Jack the Cat?"

She looked blank and said it was unusual for women to study medicine back then.

I started to say "We even found –" but Mal glared at me and I shut up.

He pulled me by the arm. "Come on. Sorry, Betty, we're meeting someone in town. See you soon."

He almost dragged me out the door.

Someone in even more of a hurry pushed past us at the entrance. The swarthy man with the beanie hat. I wrinkled my nose. He had a very distinctive smell, like the allspice you put in Christmas cake.

As soon as we were out of sight of the library, Mal grinned and opened his big overcoat. In the inside pocket was a slim volume. He pulled it out and showed me. *"Top Facts of Ireland's Road to the Republic."*

"That's stealing!"

"I'm temporarily borrowing what is legally mine to borrow," he said evasively.

"Well, I'm not reading it," I said.

"Suit yourself," he sniffed, then added sarcastically, "But I suppose that won't stop you seeing my cousin about the brooch?"

I nodded and hurried after him as he swept off in a huff.

Mal was hungry and bought a bag of chips in a curry shop. He offered me a few, so I thought we were friends again.

"Hey, why didn't you want Betty to see the jewel?" I asked.

"If it really is a Russian Crown Jewel or even a precious stone, do you really want to flash it about in a library?"

He surged ahead of me and I trotted after him.

"Why don't you get a library card like normal people?" I asked when he slowed down to cross a road.

"Why do you ask so many questions?"

"I know some kids think it's okay to do bad stuff," I said. "I think it's stupid."

"You're not very cool, are you?" he jeered.

"Just leave me alone if I'm not 'cool' enough for you. *I don't care!*" I must have shouted the last bit because a few kids and their moms passing by looked at me in surprise. Tears sprang to the back of my eyes.

Mal walked on but I stayed where I was, my legs wobbly.

Then he turned back to me. "Come on. Let's go see my cousin and show her the stone."

An uneasy truce between us.

We didn't have enough money for the DART, the local commuter train, so we walked into town. Mal stormed ahead on his long legs like he was invading a country, while I lolloped after him, trying to keep up. Just before Connolly Station, near the centre, I stopped by a wall, gulping for air. Mal's expression softened as he turned back to me.

"I'm sorry," I blurted out. "I know I'm a bit of a goody two-shoes. But that's just how I am."

Hot tears ran down my cold face, salty into my mouth. He handed me a crumpled tissue. I blew my nose.

"Come on, Saint Ava," he said. He shot me a goofy grin, deliberately sticking out his teeth like a bunny rabbit. Like my old Floppy.

We cut down through the busy shopping precinct of Talbot Street and stopped at the corner of Earl Street and O'Connell Street, before the thin silver needle of the Spire. He pointed towards the large stone hulk of the General Post Office – the GPO – that occupied a whole block.

We went and stuck our heads inside the door. It was a bustling old-fashioned post office with a high ceiling, wooden desks and counters with people milling about buying stamps.

I saw someone hunched at one of the desks writing a postcard. He was wearing a beanie hat.

"Hey – Mal – see that guy over there – with the beanie pulled down low? I just saw him in the library. He nearly ran us over on the way out. That's a coincidence."

Mal shrank back into himself, pulled his hood down over his eyes and lit out of there like his feet were on fire, me on his heels.

We skirted around the back of the GPO past a Luas tram track, then came out by the River Liffey. Mal grabbed my arm and we hurtled over this cute iron humpbacked bridge called the Ha'penny Bridge. We ducked into the alley in front of us, which was thick with gawping tourists.

Breathless, we stopped at a doorway with a security lock. Mal pressed some numbers, then yanked me inside, pulling the door shut.

I wasn't sure if he was playacting or really spooked.

"Mal, are you on the wanted list?" I gasped. "Cos all we ever do is run from one darn place to the next!"

He mimed shooting at me. "Come and meet my cuz Rachel."

We went up a winding, creaking wooden staircase that smelt of wax. Her jeweller's studio was at the top. It had a large glass dormer window and was flooded with golden light.

Rachel was sitting at a wide wooden table crowded with instruments and waved us in with a broad smile. She was maybe thirty. Her hair was dyed a rainbow of colours.

Her studio was so cool. Along one wall was a workbench with a few big lamps illuminating her work in progress – half the beads threaded onto a bracelet, different sizes of rings beside an engraving tool. A range of instruments, hammers of different sizes, pliers, wire-cutters lined the wall. Lots of drawings were pinned on a corkboard.

I was so busy taking it all in I didn't realize Mister Beanie Hat must have slipped in behind us.

He had made a beeline for Rachel. Together they were inspecting a glass case filled with glinting jewels. He muttered to her in his guttural voice, his bulky thickset body vibrating as he jabbed his fingers at the case. His face was tanned and pock-marked like a golf ball, with a scar down his left cheek, and when I glanced at him he glowered at me under thick black eyebrows. I turned to look for Mal who had shrunk into the shadows and when I spun round to look at the man again, he was gone.

"Who was that?" I heard Mal's croaky voice ask Rachel.

"A customer who wants to order a special commission for his mother," she said. "He's Russian or from somewhere in Eastern Europe. His English isn't very good."

"She must be about a hundred, because he ain't no spring chicken," I said.

Rachel laughed. "You must be Ava. Mal told me all about you."

I wondered what he could have said.

Rachel beckoned us over to the glass case, which was alongside another bench littered with swatches of fabric, buttons, silver, gold and copper wires. I admired the beautiful array of gemstones in the case, and read the nametags: *Beryl, Amethyst, Quartz.*

"They're just semi-precious," Rachel explained. "The really expensive ones are safely under lock and key."

While she and Mal chitchatted, I examined another

cabinet of her amazing work. Swirly Celtic designs of metal birds, flowers and fish were studded with gems. Some were spiky and punky-looking. There were also several framed photographs on the walls, of models wearing Rachel's jewellery in the kind of magazines you'd see on a newsagent's rack – *Vogue, Vanity Fair.* So, pretty high class! The price-tags made my eyes swim. There was nothing under €1000!

Cleeter would have loved Rachel. He wanted to be a designer when he grew up. But who cared about him.

Mal handed her our gemstone in the plastic bag.

"Hope you came by it legally," she said playfully.

Mal glared at his grungy trainers.

"We found it in our attic," I said.

She took out the diamond-shaped brooch with a tweezers and held it up to the light. Then, she put a magnifying glass to her eye and examined the sweet little green stone, about the size of a little pea, peering at its surface. It looked so lovely, like a present from a fairy.

"Oh, it looks like an emerald!" she said. "I'll have to run some tests to find out if it's genuine. There are some very good synthetics out there. Can I hang on to it?"

"Sure," I said.

Her phone rang – she said she'd be in touch and went to take the call.

"She's very clever, my cousin," Mal said proudly as we descended the staircase. "Trained as a designer in Milan. It was my granddad's job too. My dad's father. This used to be his studio."

"Talented family. What happened to you?" I asked.

He gave me another one of his Death-eater stares, so I clammed up.

"Guess you won't talk to me on the long trudge home," I said as we crossed the Ha'penny Bridge.

He flashed me a wicked grin and held up a twenty-euro note.

"Present from Rachel," he said. "We'll get the DART."

When I got back to our ratty flat, I rushed in to tell my mom about my adventure but she was lying in her room dozing. I felt a bit deflated, like a balloon at the end of a party. I really wished that I could talk to her about my fun day like I always used to. But she looked so tired I couldn't bear to wake her.

That night, I was too worked up to sleep. I couldn't wait to go back to the library! Just like old times in New York. And that made me think of my dear old dad and how he loved to talk to me about books. It was like a sharp pain in my stomach. But I counted about ten thousand old sheep and eventually I fell into a stupor.

Chapter Four

On the way to the library the next morning, I was feeling kind of chipper again. I had something to do. It wasn't raining or misty. Mal was my buddy – sort of. So, I was pretty good until I spotted the mean girls from my class across the road. I saw the halo of blonde curls around the head of chief tormenter Suzy shake with laughter when she eyeballed me. I tried to duck behind Mal.

"*Woohoo! It's the two weirdos!*" she called over.

Mal stood stock still, and gave her a thousand-yard stare.

She crossed over to us with her pack in tow and smiled sweetly.

"Hey, Yankee Doodle Dandy – say something funny." She rolled her eyes at Mal. "She cracks us up in class."

"Why are you so hostile?" I asked, plucking up my courage to impress Mal.

"What hostel? Like that stinky little place you losers live in?" Suzy roared.

Her friends all exploded into cackles.

"Sorry, 'hostel' is how we say it in America." I blushed to the roots of my hair.

"It's hostile to rhyme with 'vile'," Mal said calmly in his cutting accent. "You can think of Suzy and her Banshees to remind you."

The smirk died on her face. She took a step towards us – real hostile, whatever way you say it. "You're just a –"

Mal shocked her by clicking his fingers in her face. She and the others turned tail and ran back across the road.

"Can't wait until you go to prison!" she shouted over.

"Run along now with your coven and go pull a few legs off toads!" He dismissed them with a wave of his hand.

We walked on.

"Thanks, but they'll just torture me even more back at school," I said.

"You don't have to put up with them," he said.

"Have you noticed how itty-bitty I am? My only hope is to grow longer legs and become a fabulous star and get my revenge in interviews."

We reached the library.

Mal held the door open for me.

"Well, at least there's no chance of those boneheads following us in here," he said.

Betty was thrilled to see us. "I've dug out some information for you about Harry Boland and the jewels."

She explained to us that when Boland was in the United States he got to know the Russian Bolsheviks. They had set up as a new country, the Soviet Union, after the Russian Revolution and the execution of the Tsar, Nicholas the Second. Like the Irish, they wanted to be recognised by the United States.

The Bolsheviks wanted to fund more revolutions around the world but they had no money. However, they did have lots of jewels. The Irish had raised plenty of funds from Irish emigrants in America. In exchange for a loan of $20,000, the Bolsheviks gave Boland some of the Russian Crown Jewels until they paid back the loan.

"My dad told me about the Bolsheviks," I said. "They believed in equal shares in everything. But killed anyone who didn't agree with them and put millions of people in camps."

Mal asked Betty what kind of jewels were given to Boland.

She checked her notes. "Four items in all. A 16-carat diamond cluster and three sapphire-and-ruby brooches or earrings. Though another report said they were just diamonds and topaz and part of a crown. Some claimed they were later valued as worthless imitations."

"But no mention of an emerald?" I asked.

She shook her head. "Before Boland died in the Civil War he left instructions with his mother and sister to keep the jewels safe until de Valera came to power and established a Republic. So they remained up Mrs. Boland's chimney until the 1940's when de Valera was leader of the country. The family handed over the jewels, the Soviet Union paid back the loan and the jewels returned to Moscow."

I was aching to tell Betty about our find, but Mal flashed me a warning look.

We left the library, both feeling quite excited. Mal of course didn't want to show it.

I was jumping for joy!

"Our brooch might be an actual Russian Crown Jewel!" I was tingling with the thrill of it.

"I don't know," Mal said. "The loaned jewels were rubies, topaz, sapphires and diamonds. We found an emerald."

"But maybe there was an extra jewel nobody knew about?"

Mal pursed his lips. "Could be. Molly's letter did say 'other' jewels. And there is the link with the old Boland family home where the stuff in our attic all came from. But let's not get carried away just yet."

Boland's old address, Marino Crescent, was on our way home. It was tucked in from the main dual carriageway behind a little park. I had expected a ramshackle mansion, since it had once been home to Bram Stoker, but the house was in a classy-looking terrace. It had three storeys and a bright red door. Way fancier than the dump we lived in. And not a bat in sight.

"Funny to think of Russian Crown Jewels ending up in a Dublin house," I said.

Mal twisted his mouth sideways, a habit of his when he was thinking. "Hmm, there are still a few unanswered questions. Let's wait and see what Rachel comes up with."

We didn't have long to wait. Back home, as I was fixing a peanut-butter sandwich, there was a loud knock on my door.

It was Mal.

"My cousin rang. The emerald is real. She thinks it's exactly the kind of thing that might have belonged to the Russian royal family, the Romanovs!"

Chapter Five

We had enough money to pay for the bus fare into town, which was a relief as it was raining. Again. Have I mentioned the rain? It drips, it drizzles, it sozzles, it soaks. It cascades, it floods. It's soft, hard and comes down like cats and dogs – maybe even like crocodiles and elephants. (Miss Moran told me before I needed to use more colourful language.) That day puppies and kittens were drowning all over Ireland. Towns were sinking into the bog. Somewhere, somebody was building an ark. Okay, I exaggerate. But only a little. No wonder the Emerald Isle is so freakin' green.

At the studio, the big hulking Russian was there again inspecting the jewels in the case. Today he was wearing a yellow waterproof hat jammed onto his fat head, like Paddington Bear. Mal bristled, wary as a cat. Bond Villain glanced quickly at us – then, with a nod to Rachel, he disappeared down the stairs.

Rachel ushered us over to the microscope. She placed the jewel on the clear glass mount.

I looked down the lens. It was like gazing into a far-off galaxy. The colour was the most beautiful pure green, glowing like a light was shining through it. Almost fiery.

"It's a genuine emerald, as green as a meadow after rainfall," Rachel said. "Do you know that in this state it's more precious than a diamond?"

We gasped.

"The name comes from a word meaning 'green gem' in Greek," she continued. "But it's a fragile beauty, easily chipped or broken."

I moved aside to let Mal take a look.

Then Rachel projected the images onto a computer screen.

"The nature of the fine marks within the gem gives a clue to exactly where it comes from," she said, pointing to it. "But I'm not a gem expert. With your permission, I'd like to send it off to a laboratory."

Mal and I looked at each other – unsure. We didn't really want to hand our prize over.

"There's something else about this," she said. "It isn't a brooch. It's been wrenched or damaged – my guess is by force. It must have been part of a larger piece. A necklace or a tiara. Look at the fine swirls. It may have been studded with diamonds."

Mal reached to take it back. "Thanks, Rachel. We'll think about it."

But she stopped his hand. "Mal, where did you get this? You must tell me the truth. You don't want to endanger –"

"*Shut up!*" Mal interrupted her, anger flaring. He faced her like a gladiator.

I stepped back. "We truly did find it in the attic of our apartment block and the landlady said I could keep it," I blurted out. "There was a letter about Harry Boland and Michael Collins falling out about Russian jewels. I swear."

Rachel listened with a frown of concentration.

"It might belong to the State," she said. "Those are major historical figures. But we should find out a bit more first. And there's one other weird thing – there's some chemical damage on it. Like salt damage."

"How could you figure that out?" I asked.

She smiled. "I've been experimenting with distressing stones and metals."

Mal was still looking thunderously at her.

"Mal, just reassure me you came by it legally."

Mal actually blushed this time. "I swear. Miss Ava here doesn't tell lies to save her life."

Rachel looked thoughtful. "Look, my new boyfriend Patrick is a research mineralogist in a lab at Trinity College. He's really trustworthy. He could take a second look. At least I can keep it safe and not in a plastic bag."

Mal and I both nodded. Rachel took some more photos. She let me angle the light to help her. My dad used to let me do that in his office.

"Are emeralds bad luck?" I asked her, thinking of Harry Boland's sad end and the row about them being bloodstained.

"The opposite. They're considered to have healing powers," she said. "The ancient Egyptians used to believe they would give them eternal life. They are supposed to ward off evil spirits."

"So they'll come in handy against Mal."

Mal grinned. "Superstitious rubbish. Watch it, small fry."

Rachel went into her inner office. I watched her place my precious jewel in a big safe hidden behind a picture of a rose.

We said goodbye and left reluctantly.

As we walked down the staircase, I saw a dark shape, the man in the ugly rainhat, scurry ahead. Yellow was so not his colour.

"Did you see that guy? He's still coming and going every place we are," I said to Mal, breathless.

Mal shook his head. "It's weird all right. We'll just have to keep an eye out and see what he's up to."

I was burning to find out why Rachel was so nervous about Mal being involved in illegal activities. But I didn't dare risk winding him up. I was walking a tightrope with him. A bit like with my mom and dad when they were fighting.

Back in the bustle of Merchant's Alley, I forgot about the strange man and squealed with delight. "We really do have a regular mystery!"

Mal broke into a broad smile. "Let's go visit the museum at Collins Barracks – are words I thought I'd never say. We might as well learn what we can while we're here."

We walked up along the Liffey as the rain cleared and a shy sun peeped out from behind the clouds. We crossed the bridge near the brewery where they make the famous beer, Guinness. You can smell the yeasty odour for miles! I looked around a few times but there was no sight of Russian Bond Villain in his interesting range of headgear.

The museum was housed in a massive stone building that used to be a barracks for soldiers. It was built around a central courtyard. Inside it had been all dickied up with steel, chrome and glass into a proper swanky museum. But when I looked at some of the instruments of torture, guns and cannons it gave me the heebie-jeebies.

Mal got super-excited when he saw the special-agent-type stuff they used during the War of Independence.

There was even this book with the middle hollowed out that was used to smuggle documents. As we stared at it, something popped into my head.

"That *Delorme's Book of War Surgery* that we found," I said. "It was kind of heavy for a book. Are you thinking what I'm thinking?"

We left the museum, raced back to the house and straight up to the attic.

We found it where we'd left it, on the pile of books beside the trunk.

Mal picked it up. "It weighs a ton."

"I wonder why it wasn't in the trunk?"

Mal gazed around at the mess of the room. "I guess Benjy went through all the stuff and didn't put it back."

We examined it under the light. The first eighty or so

pages were like a normal book. There were reams on bullet wounds, dressings, and parts of the anatomy. But from Page 87 the pages were glued together. We shook it. But no dice.

Mal looked at his watch. "Look, you take the book. I have to be somewhere."

He turned tail and ran out of there like his pants were on fire.

So I closed everything up and heaved the book downstairs. I shook it again, desperate for inspiration. Then I saw it – a thin wire, the merest thread, poking out from the bottom of the spine. I got my mother's tweezers and fiddled around in the spine, hoping there was a spring mechanism. But nothing budged.

I shook it again in frustration. The book flew out of my grasp and fell to the floor.

"Oh no!"

But the fall had dislodged something and it sprang open. Inside was a cavity and in it was tucked a thick roll of papers. I took them out and peeled off the first sheet. This one was a letter typed on heavy paper. It smelt faintly of limes and had a *Crowne Plaza Hotel* watermark when I held it up to the light! I had often walked by that high-class old hotel overlooking Central Park in New York. The letter connected me to home.

Chapter six

12th March 1922

My Dear Molly,

I have traced the other set of jewels! It really was true that two sets were smuggled to America by the notorious Russian master spy Borodin.

I was able to get to the bottom of it through family connections. I had even met him several times at my cousin Roy's house in Mexico City – Roy was living there in exile after he was thrown out of India for opposing the British.

Borodin looked exactly like you'd expect of a dangerous revolutionary. He had shaggy black hair brushed back from his forehead, a thick beard, deep-set eyes, and a face like a mask. The Bolsheviks' mission is to spread armed revolution around the world. But they have no money so wanted to sell the Crown Jewels to pay for it.

This Borodin smuggled one consignment of jewels to America sewn into the bottom of a suitcase. These were passed on to the Russian Ambassador, Martens, in New

York. They are the sapphires and diamonds (rumour has it) that your leaders Boland and Collins have quarrelled over.

But I found out Borodin travelled by boat from Mexico to New York with a second set of jewels: a beautiful emerald necklace that once belonged to a Grand Duchess. When the boat was in New York harbour, it was boarded by a Customs patrol. In order to avoid arrest, Borodin threw the necklace in a wooden box over the side, with a lead weight. He boasted that it was right under the nose of the Statue of Liberty! He told my uncle that if anyone was brave enough to retrieve it, they could keep it!

Here in the United States everyone is obsessed about Russian jewels. You would not believe the wild stories circulating – jewels smuggled out of Russia in coffins or buried in the Gobi Desert.

So if you are looking for a wild goose chase to divert your brother, searching for jewels in New York harbour fits the bill. Jack is beyond excited!

The end of the page was too damaged to make out the rest.

When Mal came back we pored over the letter together. He pointed to very faint blue lines here and there and a bluish sheen on the whole paper.

"Maybe these dents and marks are from carbon paper like Molly said she was using," he pointed out. "I wonder if Molly is all she seems? She appears to know a lot about espionage for a humble student."

"And Sanjay has some shady connections too," I said.

Mal carefully unpeeled the roll of papers. We sorted them into what we guessed were separate letters and laid them out on our kitchen table in the order in which we'd unrolled them. There were at least fourteen letters, we thought, some of them very long, roughly dated 1922-23. They seemed to be in sequence as far as we could tell. Some of the pages were as thin as tissue paper. Others were crisp and woven and looked expensive. There were a few on lined paper, maybe torn from school copybooks. But none of these remaining letters were in plain English. Some were in a foreign language. Others were in some sort of code. A few were just strings of numbers and letters. It was like a big jigsaw with lots of pieces but where we'd lost the picture we were supposed to assemble. It really was a puzzle.

A few were typed. Others were in tiny writing to cram as much as possible onto a page. Many of the pages had the telltale blue sheen from carbon paper. It was difficult to tell if they were by the same person or several correspondents.

"Some of them must be from Molly," I said. "And others replies from Sanjay."

"Assume nothing," said Mal. He frowned in concentration, reminding me of his cousin Rachel.

"These might be Greek and Hindi," I said, pointing to a couple. "We learned how to say 'hello' in all these different languages when I was in first grade. *'Efaristo'* in Greek looked like that. And *'Namaste'* in Hindi looked like that squiggly one there."

"We can find out about Borodin when the library opens on Monday," Mal said.

Mal didn't stay long as he and his dad were going to Belfast to visit relatives. He'd wanted to take some of the letters to work on the codes but I was worried that he might lose them. We agreed to work on them when he came back.

"My dad wants me to stay for a couple of weeks," he said, cool as you like.

I felt downcast at his news. Why was everyone always deserting me?

But Mal was reassuring. "Don't worry. After one day my aunt and uncle will be begging him to take me home! They are the most house-proud people you ever met!"

After he left I tidied away the letters into the cavity of the book and put it under my bed. Then I moped around the house a bit and left out some crumbs for Robbie Robin.

That night, when I was paying for my curry at the takeaway, I had a brainwave. Parvati, the pretty teenager who served there, was always very friendly. I asked her if she knew Hindi and if she could read a letter for me. She said she could. I hurried home and fetched it from under my bed. She confirmed it was Hindi and said to leave it with her to translate.

Mal came back next day as he predicted, saying his aunt and uncle couldn't stand the smell of his feet. He blushed when I told him Parvati was going to translate the Hindi letter for us. But, when I asked him if he liked her, he glared at me so I let it drop.

Next day, when we googled Borodin at the library loads of stuff came up. He was a real-life spy all right, just as Sanjay described. A mysterious character who had flitted about, smuggling jewels for the Bolshevik government and trying to start rebellions. In his photograph he was just as scary as Sanjay had described!

Roy too was a genuine Indian politician. M. N. Roy to give him his full title. He started off being a regular guy who believed in peaceful protest but ended up supporting violent revolution under Borodin's spooky spell.

We called back to the curry shop on our way home from the library. There was a big queue. But Parvati called us round to the back where they kept huge vats of cooking oil and vast bags of chipped potatoes and vegetables.

"The handwriting was tiny so it was difficult but I managed to translate it," she said, tucking her glossy black hair back under her hairnet. She glanced shyly at Mal under her long eyelashes. Mal turned beetroot.

"What can we do to repay you? We don't have any money," I said.

"I loved doing it," she said.

But then her father called to her in Hindi. From his tone, he didn't sound very happy with her.

She dashed back into the shop, leaving us to let ourselves out by the side entrance.

"I think I know now why you're so fond of curry and chips," I teased Mal. "Is it something to do with the charming service?"

He blushed under his ever-present hoodie.

"For the record, I think Parvati likes you too," I said.

"Do you think so?"

"But I'd forget her. It would be like Romeo and Juliet. Her father wouldn't approve."

Mal shook his head. "Who asked you, small fry?"

"You did actually."

He frowned. "Come on, let's hurry up so we can read the letter."

We went to the little park in front of Marino Crescent. Iron railings and a high hedge surrounded it and we felt hidden away in a lost world.

Mal read the translation aloud: "*Dear Molly, if you are reading this then your Indian friend, the engineering student, has managed the translation! J is now determined to dive for the jewels in New York harbour. He is very much the headstrong boy that you told me of, running all over Dublin with tin soldiers in 1916!*"

"Tin soldiers!" I interrupted. "There were heaps of them in the trunk! That trunk definitely belonged to Molly's family. I wonder what he was doing with tin soldiers in the Rising."

He shushed me and read on: "*It was a mercy you got him smuggled out on that ship to America. He has spent a lot of time here with interesting people. With Native American tribes, circus performers, Buddhist monks from China! Even the great Houdini himself from whom he has learned how to escape from locks and chains underwater. He showed me and I thought I would explode with worry as he wriggled free from a* lock in an underwater tank. He hasn't performed the trick in public yet as he's trying do it in less than two minutes and make it even more dangerous! He charms and captivates everyone he meets. I can see why you love him so and for your sake, dearest Molly, I love him too. I may call you that, Molly – may I? But even if you scold me I will be glad. For you are most pretty when the colour flushes your face and you toss your flaming hair.'"

"I think Sanjay is in love with Molly," I interrupted. "Like you are with Parvati."

Mal glared at me. "If you don't shut up, I'm going to run off with this letter."

I clamped my mouth tight shut.

"And I hope Sanjay finishes too with this nonsense!" he added and then read on. "'*But now, I must attend to the hire of a boat, the purchase of a diving suit and the invention of a good cover story for our escapade. If the coast guards intercept us we will all end up in chains! No, that last bit was a joke. Jack said we could just say he is practising his trick! Your fondest friend, Sanjay. P.S. Jack said to tell Anto that he wishes him well at his wedding. And someday would love to meet the bride.*'"

"Anto. He was their old friend who was a hardliner, who didn't like that Treaty one itty little bit, according to Molly," I said. "These letters must hold the clues to what happened."

"I'm sure I could crack those cryptic codes," Mal said. "Those ones with numbers are ciphers – substituting symbols for letters."

"At least we know Molly had the engineering student to help translate Hindi for her," I said. "I don't expect they had Indian takeaways back then."

We went back home and took the roll of letters out of Delorme's book.

The next two letters were pages and pages long and were on such thin paper we were scared we'd poke a hole in them. The flimsy tissue paper was covered in this tiny crabbed writing.

"That's Irish," Mal said. "As I'm from the North, too bad, I never learned it."

We decided to see if Karen at the library could help us.

I went back to the flat to get my things. My mother was up, still in her dressing gown, sitting at the table with a cup of coffee, staring into space. I started to gabble about Molly and the interesting letters that I'd found and how it was helping my history project.

She looked at me blankly. I told her I was going to the library with Mal. She just nodded.

Even though I liked my new-found freedom, I was a bit puzzled. Before she would have asked me a thousand questions and didn't like to let me out of her sight.

She began to clear away some of the rubbish on the table.

"We'll have to stop buying so many expensive takeaways," she said abruptly as I put my jacket on.

I wanted to ask why Dad couldn't send us some money but I didn't want to upset her.

"And I'm starting a new job," she continued.

"Cleaning." She looked down at my sandals. "I think you're having a growth spurt."

I felt bad about costing her money. My arms ached to give her a hug. But I was afraid if I did she'd start crying again, so I quickly ran out the door.

Karen suggested we ask one of Betty's friends, from the book group she ran, for help with the Irish translation. She was mooching around the library and her name was Bríd. She was wearing a scarf on her head, which maybe I stared at too long. We showed her the letter and asked if she could help. I told her I was doing a history project and we'd found these old letters in the attic.

"It would be a pleasure," she said. "Do you just want me to translate the pages orally right here? There's rather a lot – maybe you'd like me to do a written translation? I'll type it out for you. But I'd have to take it home as I must leave now."

We agreed.

"I'll try to do it as quick as I can," she said. "I'm having some hospital treatment. But this will help take my mind off it!" She gave me a big smile.

I was super-pleased that Irish people were so kind, just like my mom always said they were.

Bríd had one of those soft Irish voices that made me think of lambs skipping in spring. I felt a pang in my heart because I guessed she had cancer. One of my mom's friends lost all her hair when she had chemotherapy and always wore a scarf like that.

The next morning a large crisp white envelope was in the pigeonhole for our flat, addressed to "*Ava*". Mal and I carefully opened it.

Chapter seven

27th June 1922

Dear Sanjay,
Please excuse my delay in responding to your letter. I hope your Irish friend at the university won't find this too difficult! (My Irish is basic so I asked the fiancé of a friend for help. He is a Quaker and an Irish scholar. I trust him completely.)

But what news! It's all-out war now over the Treaty!

The first I knew about it was when Nancy, our old charlady, came to see me in my rooms in Rathmines at Dr. Dorothy Stopford's.

Nancy has nine children and both her oldest son, Jemsie, and her husband fought in the Great War. Her husband, Joe, suffered nerve damage in Flanders and cannot work. Jemsie, the apple of her eye, has joined the Free State Army. He doesn't care a fig about politics but he can't get any other job. But Anto, her second son, Jack's friend, has joined the anti-Treaty side which has occupied the Four Courts! Nancy wanted me to speak to him because she thinks I have a special influence over him. She dictated a letter to me, as she cannot write. "Exactly the way I say it," she insisted. "So he gets the sharp end of my tongue!"

I must confess I smiled here and there, at Nancy's lively expressions.

It went like this:

"Anto, you big eejit,

If you don't come home, I'm coming in there to kill you meself. Would you ever get some sense into that thick head of yours and realise the Republic is a lost cause? And don't be mindin' yer one, even if she is your wife. I know her father died in 1916 and you want to show her you're a big hero. But I tell yeh, it wouldn't be long before she'd wish you'd rise from the grave.

Your lovin' mother

Nancy

(And don't forget to say your prayers like a good boy)"

I took my doctor's bag to the Four Courts when I went to deliver the letter to Anto first thing the next morning. I also took some medical supplies and a basket of oranges as they spend so much time holed up in tunnels and dugouts they don't get proper food.

So I rushed through streets bombed and scarred with six years of war, the fine 18th century buildings, the heaving slums riddled with disease. And yet the sun still warmed the grey stones, promising a pleasant summer's day. Outside the gates of the Four Courts, which faces onto the River Liffey, the air was thick with expectation. Onlookers gathered in little huddles as if awaiting a parade while pro-Treaty officers in their khaki-green uniforms brooded from the opposite side of the quays.

When the Republican sentries saw the Red Cross on my arm, they waved me in cheerfully as if I were going to a dance.

But I was lost! The Four Courts is actually a collection of buildings occupying a large area — built in grand neoclassical style. It's vast! There are three separate entrance gates leading up to courtyards. There is also a Public Record Office at the rear, housed in a separate building. The rebels have made their Headquarters in a larger building beside it. As there are fewer than 200 rebels, I have no idea how they hope to defend this sprawling complex.

The hub of the main building which faces the river is a round hall with several corridors leading off to the wings. The huge central dome is surrounded by high columns. Everywhere statues of stern lawyers in wigs and gowns look down in disapproval.

Eventually I found Anto, nestled in the pantry in the bowels of the main building. A former grocery-delivery messenger, he was in charge of provisions. They were well provided for. Tins of bully beef, loaves from bakeries, bottles of milk.

He was pleased to see me but even more so the oranges. He fingered the tissue paper around them with tenderness. I handed him the letter from Nancy, which he read slowly. Joy, worry, a flash of anger registered on his face. He folded the letter and put it in his breast pocket.

"Tell my mother I'm doing it for a noble cause. The Treaty is wrong, Molly. It splits Ireland."

"But a majority of people voted in support of the Free State," I said. "It's the legitimate government."

"But we fought for the all-Ireland republic that was founded in 1916," he said. "The politicians have fooled the public."

"But your family, Anto. Your wife, Sinéad. She is too young to be a widow. You might have children."

"It's for our chiseler I am doing it. Sinéad is expecting."

I caught his hand. "A baby! Oh, congratulations! But you must leave now!"

"I can't and I won't."

I looked him in the eye. "But occupying

buildings didn't work in 1916 during the Rising. And now you're fighting your former friends!"

"We don't want to fight our comrades. We want to provoke the British into restarting the war so we can bring down the Anglo-Irish Treaty. Then we can unite the Volunteers against the old enemy."

I shook my head. "Anto, you are living in cloud cuckoo land. Many of your comrades have followed Collins and support the Treaty. Besides, two thirds of the population in the North are Protestants and want to *stay* in the United Kingdom."

Anto spat. "Collins — I loved the man, but he has betrayed us."

His words filled me with dread.

"How's your foot?" I asked him, to change the subject. Dr. Ella Webb had to amputate his big toe during the 1916 Rising after Jack dragged him to safety and left him in a doorway on Crown Alley. I had found him and called an ambulance.

"These oul' hobnail boots are giving me gip," he said, wincing.

I bid him show me. His poor feet had many sores and chilblains and his old wound was scabbed where the shoe chafed his foot. I dressed his wounds as best I could.

"At least you'll be safer here chopping vegetables than out on the roofs like our Jack in 1916."

Anto bristled. "I've had five years of war, Molly, while Jack has been fooling around in a circus. I'm as good a shot as he is now."

I recoiled from him with a cold feeling that I immediately tried to control.

"Anto, my old friend, who will write poems now?"

"Kids' stuff," he said. "But let's not part on bad terms." He held my hand tight.

As I tidied up my bandages and tinctures, he fumbled in his pocket and took out a locket. He showed me the photos inside — him and Sinéad on their wedding day. A smile on her delicate heart-shaped face.

"If anything happens to me, Molly, will you see the new baby gets it?"

I took it wordlessly, fighting back the tears.

Someone shouted his name and he left abruptly.

I was told their temporary hospital was at the rear in the building they'd turned into their H.Q.

As I cut through a courtyard on my way, I passed by one of their leaders, Ernie O'Malley, a former medical student and a legend for the number of times he has escaped imprisonment and recovered from bullet wounds. He was rushing around giving orders about a consignment of arms.

I asked O'Malley if he knew where Harry Boland was. I said I wanted to meet him to talk about the Russian Crown Jewels.

O'Malley looked at me like I was mad. "Girl,

do you think as we face total ruin he's worried about Russian jewels!" Then he told me Boland was out in Blessington gathering together the reinforcements they hoped would come into the city.

He turned to one of his men and I heard him say that the weakest point was the north-west section at the back of the complex, which was defended by the Fianna Éireann boys — the young scouts in Countess Markievicz's troop. Some of them didn't look like they were even shaving.

Everywhere you looked, these young Fianna boys were crisscrossing the courtyard carrying piles of books from the Public Record Office and barricading windows with medieval records — priceless old manuscripts and leather journals.

Seán MacBride was in another courtyard, supervising allocation of guns. His father John MacBride was executed in 1916 as one of the leaders. Seán, who is about my age, has seen a lot of action. He used to be rather full of himself but war has knocked the edges off him.

He smiled briefly when I waved to him but went back to supervising the job.

Rebels were also running in and out of the Public Record Office with mine cases and grenades. One of the Tipperary boys told me that they were storing all their ammunition and explosives there. Doesn't seem very wise to me, among so much paper.

I ended up staying most of the day as one of

the young Fianna boys shot himself in the foot and there were numerous other minor injuries to attend to.

The rebels had been told to evacuate at midnight by the Free State government. I saw no sign of it happening.

I left towards early evening on this bright June day. As I passed out the back gate, I was distressed to see Free State snipers placed on the roof of Saint Michan's church and Jameson's Distillery in Bow Street. I'd heard rumours that the Free State had got an 18-pounder from the British. That's a big class of gun they used in the Great War. Now former friends in the Free State Army and the anti-Treaty side are playing a terrible game of cat and mouse.

I hope to God I get some sleep tonight. I am staying in a nearby hotel where May, Anto's sister, is a chambermaid. I'll go back to the Four Courts to dress some of their injuries tomorrow. May has just started the job. The owner is a fierce Republican — a die-hard. May doesn't like it but she can't find any other work and the pay is good.

Always,
Molly

Bríd had affixed a Post-it note to the end of the letter to

say that she would drop the next section of the translation in to us in the morning. And that she loved doing it.

When my mother got back, plum tuckered out from her new part-time cleaning job, I tried to interest her in the project. But she was too tired and just stared at the pages. As I was about to go to bed, the landlady came up to say there was a phone call.

My mother came back into the room dead-eyed. But the tip of her nose was red, like she was ready to cry.

I had come out of the bathroom in my onesie with my toothbrush in my mouth. "Who was it?" I asked.

"Your father," she replied. "He wants to file for divorce."

My mouth dropped open.

"He's asking to speak to you." My mother blew her nose in her hankie.

I felt the anger rise up like heartburn. "Tell him to go to hell."

Chapter eight

Of course that completely ruined my sleep. How could my father do this without consulting me? Didn't I get a say? It was like he was deciding he didn't want to be my father any more. I was so upset I nearly forgot to leave crumbs out for Robbie Robin. But he didn't stop by. I hoped he hadn't deserted me as well.

Later in the morning Mal knocked on my door with a new crisp envelope.

"Latest instalment, thanks to Bríd," he said, unusually chirpy for him.

I didn't even smile.

"Something up?" he asked.

"I don't want to talk about it."

"Fine by me. Come on – grab your coat and we'll read the next instalment in town."

So we took the wheezy old bus into Dublin's city centre. I looked out the window as dreary suburban streets gave way to traffic-clogged city roads. But in my head I was cycling to school with my dad along a buzzing New York sidewalk. Now I would never do that again. We sat in silence. I was relieved that Mal wasn't the nosy type. He spent the time reading his "borrowed" library book, *Road to the Republic*.

He hit me lightly on the head with the book.

"Is there life on Planet Ava?"

I ignored him.

We walked along the Liffey and stood outside the Four Courts. It was a large hulking building, a bit like a Greek temple in grey granite. It had several columns at the front and a round stone building topped by a green dome looming up from the middle that Molly said was the hub. The building stretched all around the corner of the next street.

At the entrance, a sign said the courts were sitting but visitors could enter to the public areas.

A bustle of lawyers in wigs and black cloaks rushed up the steps into the building like a swarm of bats. One of them, a woman, gave Mal a piercing look then a thin smile as if she recognised him.

He stood back as if electrocuted.

"Is she someone you know?" I asked him.

"Come on!" He pulled my arm. "We can see the dome much better from the other side of the river."

We crossed the bridge over to the south side. Mal led me to a shop where we bought two ice creams. In front of the great big slabs of the square Corporation building, we perched on a stone flowerbed wall. We had a good view of the green copper dome of the Four Courts perched on the circular drum.

Traffic streamed past, clouds raced in the sky.

Mal took the crisp white envelope containing the translation printout out of his backpack.

It was as if Free State soldiers had risen from the grave in their khaki green and we were transported into the heart of the Civil War.

⌘

30th June 1922

Dear Sanjay,

Miraculously, I got your telegram saying that you have retrieved the jewels! Doctor Dorothy had it forwarded to the hotel. I am amazed that, apart from some salt-water damage, they are intact. But please don't let Jack come here with them. There is no chance of him getting near any of the leaders now.

It was a terrible night when the fighting began. I had only slept a few hours when May ran in.

"The Free State soldiers are bombing the Four Courts, Molly!"

It was seven minutes past four o'clock in the morning. We listened to the low rumble. Then the clatter of returned gunfire. A boom, then a retort as if the earth was erupting.

"You've got to get to safety," I told her

and the staff, as the wall rocked from the blasts.

But the owner, Mrs. Mulligan, stood her ground. "We'll stay here. We have enough food. It's more dangerous out there and we've nowhere to go."

I dressed quickly, grabbed my medical bag and, counting the time between the cannon's fusillades, made a run for it to the nearest First Aid station. It was not far from the back entrance of the Courts. Judging by the far-off booms, some of the shells were landing way off their mark. Clearly some of the soldiers of the Free State were inexperienced.

It struck me then. Oh Lord, have mercy! We really were in a state of civil war!

The noise went on all day. But it felt unreal. The Free State troops scurrying about in their ill-fitting uniforms looked like raw recruits.

As daylight broke, the mad Dubliners lined the streets on both sides of the Liffey. The police held them back, as if it was a Lord Mayor's show. What is wrong with the people of this city? Soon we had a steady stream of casualties into the First Aid station. Shrapnel and bullet-wounds among civilians, some of those very same gawkers. But others were unfortunates who had failed to get to safety. There were scores killed in the crossfire.

All day, people came in with snippets of

news. Four hundred Free State troops had surrounded the whole building. The anti-Treaty side had planted mines. General Dalton, only twenty-five years old yet second in command to Collins, had to man the gun himself for three hours. He was the only one available who knew how to use it.

Around nightfall, I do not know the exact time, the bombing died down. I decided to seek some rest at the hotel. But, as I came near, I saw Free State troops posted outside. I hoped May was safe.

I shrank into the side of the building and decided to go back to the First Aid Station and seek to rest on a mattress. But the cries of a child stopped me in my tracks.

A little fellow of about ten, his face streaked with dirt, came out of the foggy gloom. The air was heavy with dust from the bombing, like a filthy snow globe. He tugged at my skirt and pointed at a dim hallway.

"Please, me mam is having a baby!"

I rushed with him to his home above a legal bookshop opposite the Four Courts side entrance. The family occupied a few cold, cramped rooms in the attic. I found the mother on a bed in the main room which had a dormer window in the low roof, looking out onto the street.

I moved her and the little boy, Davy, into a back room, out of the line of fire. She was feverish but I hoped that if I watched over her she would survive. Her name was Maggie and she was brave as a lioness, biting the pillow to stop herself crying out. When I asked about his father, Davy whispered that he was in heaven, dead from "coughing" — tuberculosis, I bet. I settled him down to sleep in an old armchair by his mother's side.

I had to go to the main room to boil water on the fire. I was nervous about delivering the baby. Even though I had attended births, I had never brought a child into the world on my own.

Each time I went into the main room, I peeped out at two snipers playing cat and mouse across from each other. A Republican on the Four Court roof faced a Free Stater sheltered behind a chimney across the street. I was at a safe distance out of the line of fire. But even so, the conflict was nerve-wracking. Bullets peppered the rooftops at intervals. A terracotta chimney pot shattered and fell to the street below.

Towards dawn there was a lull in the fighting. Curiosity got the better of me and I looked out again. Suddenly, across the way, the cap of the anti-Treaty soldier appeared above the parapet. Shots rang out. The rebel's cap fell and tumbled into the street below.

A little point of light flared in the early dawn. The Free State soldier was lighting a match. He stood up, thinking the coast was

clear and looked down at where he thought his
opponent would be lying. But too late he
realised his rival had played a trick on him.
It was only the cap that had fallen, not the
soldier.

The crack of a rifle! A shout of pain! The
bullet had found its mark and the Free State
soldier, his rifle flying from his grasp, fell
like a sack of potatoes to the street below.

There was no way he would survive that fall,
if the shot hadn't killed him already.

The Republican sniper crawled off the Four
Courts roof. Soon after, in the early-morning
haze, I watched him flee from the Four Courts
and make his escape. All was still in the
street below. He limped as he crossed the road
and picking up his rival's gun darted down a
laneway. He barely glanced at where his fallen
enemy lay in the gutter a few yards away.

My heart pounded in my chest. I knew by the
cut of him. Anto!

I blessed myself. He had lived to fight
another day but at someone else's expense.

Even though there was little hope the Free
State sniper was alive, I had to make sure.
Maggie's birth pangs were more regular now but
I didn't think the baby would come for a while
yet. The little boy was pale with hunger and
there was no food that I could see. I decided
to risk the street. After I checked the soldier
I could get food for them at the hotel.

As I gained the street and checked the coast was clear I saw someone else running towards the fallen sniper.

May! She turned back and the look of horror on her face will haunt me to my dying day.

"Jemsie was up on that roof!"

I ran to the soldier, awkwardly slumped by the pavement. Saw the red hair peeking out from the Free State cap, so like his brother's. The red stain of blood flowing from his head wound. I pulled back the cap and saw the bullet hole. So it was Anto's bullet that killed him, not the fall. He was a good shot. I'd give him that.

May cradled her brother, her eyes wild in her white face. I felt for the pulse in his broken, lifeless wrist, knowing it was a lost cause.

"Oh Jemsie, Jemsie!" she cried. "To survive the Great War to die in your own back yard!" Then a look of anger came over her. "Where's the gun! I want to kill the murdering coward that shot my brother."

The name Anto nearly flew out of me but my hand stopped my mouth. I couldn't tell May what I had seen. Brother had killed brother.

"The other fellow took the gun," I said.

I held her by the shoulders as she shivered.

"Did you see him?" she persisted. "The shameless, godforsaken coward! May he too die like a dog in the street. I curse him!" She

71

screamed then, like a fury from hell. Her grief, a living thing, escaped from her core.

"Shush, May, don't," I tried to calm her. "Don't let the war kill your good soul."

My own soul was torn apart. Oh Anto, what have you done, I thought. But then I remembered me jeering at him about being safe peeling vegetables. Did my thoughtless joke goad him into savagery?

As two Saint John's Ambulance men made their way to pick up the body with a stretcher, I did what I could to comfort May. She quickly wiped her eyes and removed a photograph out of Jemsie's breast pocket. It was of his mother Nancy.

"I will go and let Ma know," she breathed, her voice unsteady, her eyes dead. "Jemsie was delicate as a child, you know. They thought he was dead when he was born blue. But she willed the life back into him." She sighed and choked back the tears. "For this!"

We clung to each other for a long time. Then she was gone.

I begged the ambulance people to return to take Maggie to the Rotunda Maternity Hospital with little Davy. There were no neighbours around to mind him. It was nearly noon when the ambulance returned. I confess my mind went blank during that time.

I settled the woman and her son in the back of the ambulance and it sped off. There was no room for me.

Soon after, sniper fire and shelling erupted again and split the air. I went back up to Maggie's rooms and fell into a dead stupor.

I must have slept for a long while for next thing I knew there were voices roaring in the street. I peeped out the window.

A Free State soldier was calling out, *"You better make a run for it! We're going to storm the Four Courts!"*

I gathered my things and ran down the stairs. I looked back towards the Four Courts. About thirty Free State soldiers were advancing at speed towards the back gate. I ran in the opposite direction, my heart thumping in my chest. I stumbled up the streets, fleeing through back alleys and shortcuts. Blindly toward Sackville Street.

I came to a halt in a doorway. I caught sight of five shimmering Mollys in a fractured plate-glass shop window. I saw my red hair, my tense white face. It was as if I was that innocent twelve-year-old girl again who had plunged into the madness with one thought only: to save her brother Jack. Then I saw my doctor's coat, my Red Cross armband.

A curious mood came over me. I touched my own face. My cheeks, my nose, I gazed at my own battered hands. I was still here. I could still walk the earth. I had survived the Easter Rising, the War of Independence, prison even. Had spun around in the chaos.

Live through this, I told myself. At least Jack is safe.

I looked back, the pounding echoing in my ears. There was a sudden calm. But it was only a lull in the storm. For then an almighty explosion nearly knocked me off my feet. The great green dome of the Four Courts rose atop a column of smoke and was blown to smithereens!

An ominous black mushroom cloud rose from the building, like some satanic apparition. It hung over the city like a fiend, darkening the noon sun.

The acrid smell of smoke filled my lungs. Only pure terror fuelled my body as I stumbled blindly towards Sackville Street. At the corner of Abbey Street and Capel Street, I heard a rushing sound behind me. As if heavy boots were thudding on the pavement and a whole army of Free Staters was coming to hunt down the escaped rebels.

My heart pounded in my ears. I lunged into a doorway and flattened myself against the door. Men from the Citizen army, rebels to a man, peeked out from Dobson's public house, their slouch hats pulled down low, their weapons cocked at the ready. Their faces took on a look of surprise.

But it was no army coming towards us but law books bounding along the road, as if a giant was flinging them like pebbles. The sight was frightening and unsettling.

A cloudburst of paper fell on the city like snowflakes. A million paper airplanes, twisting in the breeze. Documents fluttering in the sky like a flock of paper seagulls. All the contents of the Public Record Office blown sky high! Several hundred years of history carpeted Dublin as far as the eye could see. A hard wind took up the papers.

The snowstorm of paper must have gone right out to the Hill of Howth and the Sugar Loaf Mountain in Wicklow. A thousand years of keeping accounts — the marriages and the deaths from every parish in the land, scattered to the four winds. All those dead souls were once recorded in ledgers. Now not even their names were left behind.

There was an eerie silence. But that was not the end of the fighting! I crouched down, got my bearings. Through the pall of smoke, small platoons of men skirted along the streets and over rooftops, heading for Sackville Street. They were the Republicans, fleeing from the Four Courts. Ragged groups of men, and here and there a single shadow, fleeing from trouble into further mayhem. I hugged the buildings, feeling trapped in my own city.

I caught sight of myself full length in the mirror of a dress-shop window. A ghostly apparition stared back at me. I was covered in chalk dust from the explosion, my face a mask with only my two red eyes glowing in my face. I tried to wipe it off with my coat cuff but that was also dusted white, like sugar sifted on a cake.

I crouched for a long time in that doorway. Clutching my doctor's bag, steadying my nerves. I prayed and thought. How would Anto feel when he found out he'd shot his own brother? I remembered the happy-go-lucky boy he used to be — pulling my pigtails, getting into scrapes with Jack. It would destroy him. I made a vow never to tell him or any other living soul.

"Please, Miss!"

The sound made me jump. It was another ghostly fiend calling me from across the narrow road. I squinted. A youth of maybe fifteen had flattened himself into the narrow porch of a shop entrance. I watched in horror as he stumbled out into the street. He came to a shuddering stop in front of me.

"Miss, which way to the Hammam Hotel? We're continuing the fight." His voice, croaky and exhausted, had the lilting tone of Cork. His face like mine was coated with plaster dust, but there were two runnels down his cheeks, the tracks of his tears.

"Sackville Street will be flattened too," I said.

"I've just got out of the Four Courts," he said.

"Then run for your life! The Free State soldiers will arrest you."

He pulled his gun close. "My brother was killed

by the Tans. Our cottage in Cork was burned in a reprisal." There was a catch in his voice. "B-b-but . . . I didn't think it would be like this."

I was roused out of my daze. Suddenly it became very important to save this boy.

"What's your name?"

"Patch. From Macroom. In County Cork." Fresh tears streaked down his face. "My friend was shot. His stomach . . . They should pay." He choked back the tears.

He tried to cock his gun. For a terrifying second I thought he was going to shoot me. But he aimed vaguely up the street and his hands trembled so much the weapon clattered to the ground.

He was wracked with sobs, snot and phlegm choking his throat. "It was like the butcher's. Blood and guts like tripe . . . the smell . . ."

"Quiet . . . there's a good boy," I said softly.

"I could never abide the slaughterhouse — I don't even eat black pudding." He crumpled to the ground, cradling his own stomach, the gun by his side.

"You need medical attention for shock. There's a group of the Citizen Army in Dobson's pub. We'll see if we can find some brandy for you . . ." I gestured towards the pub.

He nodded gratefully. We both struggled to our feet. My left foot had pins and needles but

I guided him down the street, inch by inch, hugging the sides of buildings like shadows.

Near the pub, a sudden throb of an engine on its way up to Sackville Street set the hearts crossways in us. But it was an ambulance — a Rolls Royce Silver Ghost, one of the Fire Brigades fleet. It slowed down and the driver pulled up alongside me.

"I thought it was you, Molly!"

It was P.J. Cassidy, someone I knew well!

I snapped out of my quagmire and put Patch in the seat beside him.

"They've surrendered up in the Four Courts," he told me. "Quite a few have been arrested but most have legged it. Some are off to the mountains and others to Sackville Street for the last stand."

I couldn't help wiping away a tear as I told him about Jemsie. He handed me a handkerchief — good man that he is.

"Here's something that might cheer you up," he said. "You know Maud Gonne McBride, Seán's mother? She's set up a Women's Peace Delegation to convince both sides to a truce. The Lord Mayor said I am to drive them around. They want a medical orderly — a woman if possible."

"I'll do it!" I said immediately. "But after you drop us, please take Patch to Sister Dymphna at Saint Vincent's Hospital. He's a severe case of shock. Tell her to get him on the first train back to Cork." I handed Patch my emergency twenty-pound note.

P.J. nodded assent and gave him a Red Cross armband to protect him.

I got into the back of the vehicle. Even in my dazed state, my nerves raw, I was openmouthed. There, seated in regal splendour and clothed in a great deal of black drapery was Maud Gonne, the lady the poet Yeats has written famous poems about. And Charlotte Despard, the sister of the former Lord Lieutenant, Lord French, who had thrown her lot in with Ireland.

Charlotte Despard made room for me on the wooden bench. She was a small vivid lady of about seventy-five with a strong face and a forceful voice. She wore a Spanish black mantilla.

Maud Gonne had a curious-looking little puppy on her lap who she stroked lovingly. "There there, Wuzzo Wuzzo," she said. She thrilled her 'r's as I imagine the Continentals do. Her musical voice was just like a songbird that had learned to talk.

She was also as beautiful as everyone says and carried herself like a painter was about to paint her portrait.

"We were told Seán has surrendered alongside the leaders at the Four Courts," she said. "I thought he might be in Mountjoy Gaol but the governor said no."

I thought of Nancy who would never see Jemsie again.

"I saw a friend shot dead," I said. "By a Republican soldier." I sniffed loudly.

Madame Gonne MacBride fished a bottle of *eau de cologne* out of her handbag, daubed a handkerchief and tenderly wiped my face.

"That is why we must bang all their heads together and have peace," said Charlotte Despard firmly.

We pulled up outside the College of Science on Upper Merrion Street where the government had its H.Q. during the fighting. P.J. immediately continued with Patch to St. Vincent's Hospital.

I managed to clean myself up a bit in a ladies' room before we went into the meeting with the Free State government.

As well as Maud Gonne and Charlotte Despard, there was Hannah Sheehy Skeffington, the wife of dear Francis who was killed in Easter week. She is a severe woman but strong and determined and not easily frightened. And also Louie Bennett, a refined, well-educated lady who is secretary of the Trades Union Congress that supports workers' rights. She is a noted pacifist.

"Irish nationalism is too much in love with the gun," she said as we waited to be led into the meeting.

Mrs. Sheehy Skeffington frowned. "We would never have got freedom without 1916. I believe in a Republic but not through civil war."

"Dear Hanna, all they want is that we knit

socks and bear sons and, if we can't do that, we'd better get out of the way," Louie replied. She turned to me. "Keep studying, Molly. Every exam you pass is a victory for women!"

Inside the meeting room, Collins bounded forward to shake our hands.

He shook his head when he saw me. "Molly, always in the thick of the action! Have you come to tell me off again?"

I blushed and said I was there to accompany the senior women.

Griffith looked dreadful. An old and broken man. Cosgrave, a small dull man who is the senior minister in the government, was very disdainful and hard-faced.

Louie Bennett spoke first. "People are suffering and in a really desperate condition. Don't you think Ireland has seen too much fighting?"

"The Republicans started it," Cosgrave said coldly. "We are the elected legitimate government of the Free State."

"It doesn't matter who started it. Will you agree to a truce?" said Mrs. Despard in her crisp way. Then, when he turned his back on her she said loudly, "I see I will have to address your honourable posterior."

Collins snorted with laughter.

"The anti-Treaty rebels must give up their arms," said Griffith.

He looked so wretched I thought at one stage

I would have to administer him a powder.

"But you know they will not give up their arms," cried Maude Gonne. "Would it not be better to let them go than to cause more destruction!"

"I don't know why the Republicans don't just go home with their guns now," said Collins. "There is nothing really to stop them."

Maud Gonne was scornful. "And what then? You know the fighting will just start again without an honourable truce."

She appealed to President Griffiths.

"Dear old friend, have I not just been in Paris trying to gain support for you? Why are you intent on killing our own, now that you are armed by the British? Please listen to me as a mother as well as a dear friend."

Griffith's temper flared. "If one of them was here, they would not hesitate to shoot us or any member of the Free State!"

"And most of the women in Cumann na mBan — those unmanageable revolutionaries — have joined the anti-Treaty side," sneered Cosgrave.

We left the meeting feeling very despondent.

"There is little point in talking to the Republicans if the Free State side won't compromise," said Charlotte Despard.

Louie Bennett spoke. "We must. It would be unfair not to. We should show them there are at least some women who want peace."

P.J. was back and he drove us over to Sackville Street and around to the back of the

Hammam Hotel on Marlborough Street. We passed tanks and army cars. Gunfire rent the air. A sentry from the Republican side challenged us and we were led into a kind of outhouse full of men and petrol tins, bicycles, stepladders, boxes and general rubbish. It was chaos. Doctors and nurses, soldiers and messengers dashed in and out all the time. The men were mostly in civilian clothes. They all had big revolvers in holsters and military belts.

Some looked dead tired. All of course were untidy and unshaved. After waiting a while, the Commander in Dublin, Oscar Traynor, was fetched to us, and Hanna and Miss Bennett tackled him. He was young and handsome, in a semi-military dark suit, with a revolver in a belt, and the Sacred Heart badge in his buttonhole.

"You will have to surrender your arms," Hannah Sheehy Skeffington said.

"We have offered to evacuate but not to surrender arms, of course, to those people," he said. "We're digging ourselves in here, and if they attack us we'll defend ourselves."

"Why don't you just make a run for it and melt away with your arms?" I blurted out. "Collins himself suggested that earlier!"

He shook his head in disbelief. "I believe in the Republic. I don't put any faith in anything Collins or those people would say. He would hunt us down."

Those people. I felt our good intentions melt away, flimsy little things in the face of war. There was no way out but through a sea of blood.

As I made my way back to the ambulance I saw an old friend, Nurse Linda Kearns, who was carrying in an armful of towels. We were in Mountjoy Gaol together, she for gun-running, I on the trumped-up charge of giving medical attention to a rebel. After we escaped, she threw in her lot with the Republicans.

I thought she looked thinner — tougher too. With the same grim look as Anto.

She put down the towels and flung her arms around me.

"Are you one of us? Do you know they're calling us 'Irregulars' now?" she said. "Like we're some sort of disease."

I shook my head. "I'm on the side of anyone who needs a bandage or a splint."

"Even so, I could do with a medic here, Molly," she said. "There are a lot of gunshot wounds and head injuries from falling masonry."

I was nervous but I agreed to stay. They had turned that section of Sackville Street into something they are calling 'The Block'. It included the Gresham, the Hammam Hotel and the Tramway Office.

Was it really only six years ago that Jack and I used to clamber on the roofs, to look at

the bathers in the Hammam Hotel all snuggled
up in towels taking Turkish baths?

❦

It broke off there, as if there was a page missing or maybe
something had happened to interrupt Molly.

As I looked up from the letter, I was almost expecting
to see the Four Court in ruins. They'd done a pretty good
job of rebuilding it. But must have been much harder for
the people caught up in the battle to forgive and forget.

We left our perch on the flowerbed wall and caught
the bus on Dame Street near Trinity College, both locked
in our own thoughts. I was thinking, if I got caught up in
a war zone I would never see my mom and dad again.

When we reached O'Connell Street the bus got held
up by a demonstration not far from where the rebels had
got holed up in "The Block". A stream of people
marched by carrying banners. One said: **"Stop the Civil
War in Syria."** Another said: **"Half a Million – 1 in 10
Syrians Dead or Wounded by War."** There was a
terrible image of a dead child. This snapped me out of
my own troubles.

"That's a lot of people," I said to Mal. "How many
died in the Irish Civil War?"

He thumbed through his borrowed library book.
"Nobody has ever calculated the precise figures. One
estimate is around 1,700."

I whistled. "That pales in comparison to S

even the American Civil War that left three quarters of a million dead."

"It's not a competition," he said quietly. "It's all suffering. And the Irish Civil War was savage, with former friends killing each other."

The image of my father flashed through my mind. Even though I was mad as hell, I still didn't want him dead.

The demonstration moved on. Below us the posters swayed like the sails of boats in a rough sea. Millions who had left the country. Millions needing humanitarian aid.

I wondered if any of those children caught in the war had pets. Did all those fluffy rabbits, cute dogs and fur-ball kittens sense danger and start trying to leave before the humans? Or were they abandoned or dead in the fog of war? I was glad my old rabbit Floppy was living with Mrs. Babbitt and hoped she was getting along just fine with all her cats.

As we stopped at the traffic lights near the Financial Centre, I gazed out the window. I could see into an empty lit office on a level with the top of the bus. Among the rows and rows of desks, a hunched figure concentrated on wiping clean the computer screens. Just another worker doing a crummy job. Except the curve of her back was as familiar to me as my own face. My mother. She turned as if sensing someone was staring at her. But I cowered in my seat. Not wanting her to see me. Not wanting her to know I was ashamed.

When we got back to the house, Mal and I agreed to meet in the morning. I was beat. And felt kind of lonesome with my mother working late. Before, my dad would have fixed my supper, talked to me about my day. Maybe explained Syria to me, why people have civil wars. I had that torn-in-two feeling again.

I made a sandwich and I stared out the bedroom window, the sky turning pink in the setting sun, the tree silhouetted against the sky. But there on the window ledge was Robbie Robin, pecking at his crumbs. I could have sworn that he nodded thanks to me before he took wing and flew off back into the tree.

And later that evening Mal pushed a note under my door. His cousin Rachel wanted to see us first thing the next day.

Chapter nine

We met in the laboratory where Patrick was conducting research at Trinity College. It was housed inside the Geology Museum, the coolest old place you can imagine. It looked quite fancy from outside – a rectangular building of light grey stone with arched windows and high chimneys. It was like the bottom tier of a giant wedding cake. But inside it was a riot! There were different kinds of stone with lots of rich carvings of animals and flowers. Tiles zigzagging everywhere in crazy patterns. On a plinth there were also the skeletons of these giant Irish deer, one with huge antlers. He had a cute smile for a skeleton.

The lab was upstairs, reached by a marble staircase, and even though the room was full of fancy stonework the equipment was totally modern. There were industrial-sized microscopes, stainless-steel tables, test tubes and charts with the names of chemicals on them.

Rachel's boyfriend Patrick wore a white coat and thick black-framed glasses. But he wasn't a nerd. He was tall and athletic and Rachel told us with pride that he was a champion kickboxer.

He demonstrated some of his moves when I asked him. And like – he was ferocious! Even Mal was impressed. You wouldn't mess with Patrick!

He led us over to this large microscope where the emerald was placed on a glass with light shining through it. A screen was attached to the microscope and there was a camera rigged to it to capture digital images. He projected 3D images of the gem onto the screen.

"It's from Muzo in Colombia – the most prized place for emeralds in the world," he explained, zooming in on the tiny flecks invisible to the naked eye. "They were brought back to Europe by the Spanish Conquistadors in the sixteenth century and made into exquisite jewellery for monarchs like the Russian Tsars."

Now that was way past cool.

"It's a 'cabochon', which means a shaped and polished stone. It hasn't been cut because it's of such pure quality," Patrick said. "The Bolsheviks had been planning to sell many of the Crown Jewels to raise money."

"Is it worth a lot?" Mal asked.

Patrick smiled. "At the time, the cheapest item in the collection was valued at a million dollars. Even a fragment like this would be worth a lot. But, because of the Romanov link, it's priceless."

Rachel's eyes were sparkling. "It was probably made by the famous jewellers called Tiffany. They made many of the Crown Jewels of Europe, particularly necklaces."

"So what makes you so sure it's linked to the Tsars?" Mal asked.

"They recently found a rare photograph of the Russian Crown Jewels in 1922 in a forgotten book in a geology library in the United States," Rachel explained. "A bracelet, a crown and an emerald necklace went missing and have never been found."

She showed us an image of a faded old brown photograph. It showed three rows of what she said was the emerald necklace encrusted with precious jewels. She told us that all the drop-stones and the gems in the diamond-shaped settings were emeralds. The nine diamond shapes and the eight swirling links were all encrusted with diamonds. It must have been dazzling!

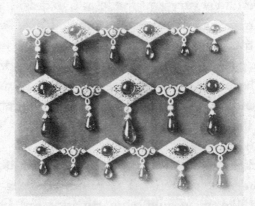

We looked at our emerald in its battered metal setting. It was so beaten up, it was hard to believe it belonged with the shiny complete ones in the photograph.

"Your setting looks like it's wrenched apart from the

main necklace. And the drop-stone has disappeared."

Patrick focused in on the torn edges of our setting. In giant close-up it resembled a jagged mountain range.

"Now look what happens when I superimpose my photos of the piece you found onto a blow-up of one of the large diamond-shaped settings of the Russian Crown Jewels. It looks like it was wrenched off and mangled. It's a miracle the gem is still intact."

The dimensions were an exact fit, like playing cards in a game of Snap.

"We can contact that American library where they found the photos, and maybe the Russians," I said. "Maybe there's a reward."

Mal frowned. "No. I don't want to do that."

"Why? Oh, I forgot you're an international spy!"

I noticed that, instead of laughing at my stupid joke, Patrick and Rachel exchanged a look.

"If you do that, I won't help you with deciphering the letters," Mal said in that mean, deliberate way of his.

"I'll get other people to help," I said stubbornly. "Jeez Louise! Why all the top-secret mystery act, Mal?"

He gave me his slitty lizard-eyes.

"I'll ask our metallurgists to run some experiments," Patrick said, breaking the tension between us. "They study the physical and chemical behaviours of metals. That will help us work out what caused the damage to your piece. We'll find out if Rachel's hunch about it being salt damage is right."

"Let's see what else you learn from the letters before

we take it further with official channels," Rachel said.

That satisfied both of us.

As we went to leave, Patrick voiced the one question on all our minds. "If there's this one piece, I wonder where the rest of the necklace is?"

When we got back to the flat we decided to make an incident room in the attic. Mal produced some old whiteboards and I had a load of stationery and thumbtacks. We had fun clearing up the debris – the old broken vacuum cleaners, the pile of old newspapers and bags of clothes. Mal replaced the murky bulb with a better one. He was very secretive about a box of his own stuff hidden under some tarpaulin. But after our spat at the lab I knew better than to pry.

We began to assemble our story. We had one board marked: **THE MAIN PEOPLE**. Mal drew some impressions of what he thought Molly, Jack the Cat, Anto, Sanjay, Dan and May looked like and we put them on the board. They were pretty good in a cartoonish sort of way. Then pictures of the leaders – Collins, Boland, de Valera. We added Maud Gonne, Charlotte Despard, Ernie O'Malley and Seán McBride. I put together a pretty okay map with the main locations of the battle of Dublin. Mal said I'd aced it even though I was a new girl in town! We even had a go at a timeline – the dates of the letters and the dates of the main events. We assembled another board about the jewels.

We looked through the letters and laid out the dates in

sequence. I glanced at the next one in date and saw it was in Greek script. It began: Παρακαλώ συγχωρήστε.

"Why don't we ask Stavros at the kebab shop for his help?" Mal suggested.

I risked a joke. "Shame he doesn't have any beautiful daughters. Only that old guy chopping onions. Then you'd eat more kebabs."

Mal fixed me with his lizard look.

So we visited Mr Stavros. He was a short, kindly man with a large wobbly belly. Probably ate too many of his own kebabs. But he shook his head sadly when we showed him the letter.

"I grew up here so my Greek's a bit shaky," he said in his broad Dublin accent. "But you're right, it's definitely Greek. And I know a man who can translate it." He gestured to the wizened old man working in the kitchen, his face as lined and brown as the bark of a tree. "Me da – old Stavros. Came here as a teacher of Greek, you know."

The old man limped to the counter and we showed him the letter. He flashed us a grin, showing his yellow false teeth, tears streaming down his face.

"Give me a couple of hours and I'll even type it out for you on my new MacBook Pro," he said in a heavily accented voice. "Chopping onions bores me to tears!"

When we went to hang out at the library, I suggested to Mal we could try Google Translate next time. But old International Man of Mystery Mal was reluctant.

"It's not very secure," he said.

"Why are you worried about cyber-security?" I asked. "You don't think the Russian will hack the computer here, do you?"

He shrugged. "Stranger things have happened. He is following us after all. Besides Google Translate turns everything into gobbledygook."

So, a couple of hours later we went back to old Stavros who, proud as punch, handed us a printout smelling faintly of onions. Young Stavros even gave us two kebabs.

And there, in a kebab shop in Dublin, we read it together and entered Molly's time machine to the heart of Ireland's Civil War.

Chapter ten

8th July 1922

Dear Sanjay,

Please excuse the break in letters. I have been through such a lot. I asked a college friend to translate this letter into Greek, which I know you understand.

Sometimes I feel that I am caught in a nightmare from which I am trying to awaken. Being trapped in the Gresham with the anti-Treaty forces was one of those times.

The rebels had occupied the entire block of terraced buildings on the north-east end of Sackville Street from the corner of Little Britain Street to Earl Street. These included the Gresham Hotel, the Hammam Hotel, the Tramways Office and Lipton's Tea House. The fighters had burrowed holes between all the separate buildings, creating a corridor. So it was possible to move from Lipton's in Earl Street to the Gresham Hotel without being seen from the outside.

As I was sorting out mattresses for casualties, a young student I knew by sight, Todd Andrews, arrived. He is a tall lanky fellow with a wide grin and sticky-out ears. My cousin Dan knows him better and told me before that he was a good sort.

"What are you doing here?" I asked him. "I thought you'd have the good sense to stay out of it."

He took me aside and whispered, a look of sadness in his eyes, "I tried. I went up to Cavan to see about smuggling arms to the Catholics in the six counties in the North. They're outnumbered at least two to one by Protestants loyal to the Crown. But we won't be able to help them, now that we are fighting each other."

"Were you in the Four Courts?" I asked him.

"No, I went looking for some of my pals. This whole Battle of Dublin is a suicide mission. Makes no military sense. But I believe in the Republic, Molly, and I want to join my friends. I don't like the way the Free Staters are trying to stamp down on those they don't agree with."

He helped me carry bandages to the First Aid station in the old Tramways Office. He was also grappling with a rifle and a newfangled-looking shotgun.

"What's that yoke?" I asked him. It was a cross between a handgun and a rifle with a circular drum in front of the trigger.

"A Thompson gun. It's an American sub-machine gun. It fires a continuous stream of

bullets as long as the trigger is held down."
He tapped on the drum and held the gun against
his hip. "I can fire fifty bullets without
stopping to reload."

I regarded it with horror. A more efficient
way to kill even more people.

"Harry Boland brought them in from the
United States." He dropped his voice, "I'm not
really sure how to use it."

"Did you know he brought in Russian Crown
Jewels as well?" I asked him.

He laughed bitterly. "Fat lot of use they
are!"

The Tramways Office was in a corner site
with a complete view of Sackville Street as far
as Westmoreland Street. Nelson's Pillar
towered over the building.

There were about twenty or thirty lads
there, all members of the 4th Battalion. There
were also a few young Cumann na mBan girls.
They were led by Kathy Barry, the sister of
Kevin Barry. He was the medical student
executed during the War of Independence — the
one they wrote the famous song about. She was
a glamour puss, even here in the grime and
filth of battle, wearing lipstick with her hair
bobbed.

"Look at you, training to be a doctor like
my brother!" she exclaimed. "I am lucky to make
tea and Bovril. Cathal Brugha, our hero of
1916, won't even let us fill sandbags."

I showed them quickly how to make a sling
for a broken arm. They were full of energy and

fight. Far more than the men.

Some of the soldiers knocked out the glass and barricaded the windows, using the tightly packed records and old ticket stubs of the Dublin United Tramway Company. Not much use in stopping a bullet! The place smelt fusty.

Todd looked at the wads of paper. He laughed. "Some of these are for passenger journeys taken between Drumcondra and Nelson's Pillar thirty years ago!"

Kathy and a couple of other Cumann na mBan girls set up a little comfort station for the troops. There were deep mattresses and thick blankets from the Gresham. Even fresh pears and apples! My eyes fell on them.

"Here, have a pear!" Kathy Barry said to me.

I bit into it. The juice dribbled down my parched throat. I tried to eat slowly at first. But then I devoured every bit of it, even the skin and core.

I thought I would faint when one of the girls produced a box of chocolates.

Linda joined us. "Go on, have one, Molly. No reason why only the quality should have the best."

I felt full after my pear so took a toffee and a Turkish Delight and wrapped them in a handkerchief for later.

It was quiet that first night. I went back to the billiard room in the Hammam Hotel which had been set up as a hospital. A hole had been knocked through to the lobby in the Gresham. The wounded were stretched out on the tables, their red blood staining the green baize covering. The only food I had was the toffee in my pocket. I saved the Turkish Delight for later.

I snatched some sleep towards dawn in a bedroom set aside for the use of the First Aid workers. But I was awoken by the sound of sporadic gunshot. It came from the Ballast Office on the corner of Aston Quay, just over O'Connell Bridge. The men in the Tramways Office and the Gresham returned fire, shooting out all the windows.

At one stage Madame Markievicz strode in and volunteered for sniper duty. She was dressed in breeches and jacket, like a man. Tall, stooped but as precise as a whip.

The young rebel at his post was surprised to see her.

"Young man, move aside," she insisted. "I have not only seen more action than you, I am a crack shot!"

As the morning continued, a sizeable crowd of spectators gathered at O'Connell Bridge, the eejits craning their necks to see what had happened. I watched them through my field glasses. I even saw a couple of people stroll down Sackville Street like a bunch of goms.

"Go home!" I shouted at one middle-aged woman in a smart suit. But she ignored me. As did an elderly gentleman in a top-coat. But he jumped when a sudden shot rang out. I feared I would have to make a mercy dash into the street. More shots were fired. Dust rose in the

air like puffs of clouds around the head of Nelson's statue on his pillar. Todd Andrews was taking potshots with his rifle at Nelson!

"That's for not being nice to your wife!" he called out, laughing.

For indeed, Nelson was famous for running off with another woman.

Downstairs later, I saw de Valera trying to lift Kathy Barry bodily across the lobby of the Gresham. "You and the other women must leave!" he urged her.

But as soon as he turned his back she ran off and hid.

The first real attack came late in the evening when an armoured car pulled up at the corner of Henry Street. They fired belt after belt of machine-gun bullets into the buildings.

I watched Todd Andrews grapple with his Thompson gun. Bullet after bullet firing out in a horrible rat-a-tat. Todd reeled back in surprise. He scrunched his face in a disappointed expression like a schoolboy.

"I missed the armoured car."

I was relieved.

The next day shooting was more frequent. Under cover of darkness the Free Staters had crept into the Metropole Hotel next to the GPO. They were now only about fifty yards away on the opposite side of the street.

They continued to close in. Someone said there were at least two armoured cars stationed outside and several machine guns in the building opposite. I went back up to the Tramways Office, by the back stairs, away from the line of fire.

I crouched down beside Todd Andrews at the window.

"We're in a hopeless position," he confided in me.

A hail of fire burst through the window. We jumped! Bullets were now raining through the building. Some penetrated the flimsy barricades of the Tramways records with short bursts of flame. The battalion commandant, Dowling, called out, *"We're doomed!"*

There were a few priests there and they started to say the Rosary. The response was taken up by the entire company, most of them crouching under the windowsills.

"Hail Mary, full of grace . . ."

The terrible sound of a bullet hitting a stone flag.

"The Lord is with thee . . ."

The tinkle of shattered glass and the powder of brick dust.

"Blessed art thou amongst women . . ."

The hum of prayer like the buzz of bees massing outside a beehive. The rage of guns broke over us like a wave.

I tried to join in. But I was too busy fixing a bandage on the shoulder of a young lad from Wicklow who'd been struck by falling masonry.

As we picked our way through to the Gresham the

following morning, collecting the walking wounded, a frightening scream rang out. It was a young man hit in the head by a bullet. I rushed up to him with my medical bag.

By a fluke, it was just a flesh wound above his ear and needed only a bandage. His name was Coughlan.

"Are you related to Frank Coughlan?" asked Todd Andrews who was nearby.

"He's my cousin — but he's with the Free Staters," he said.

Todd Andrews gasped and then swore under his breath. "He is . . . was my best friend. I didn't think he would support the Treaty." His eyes filled with tears.

What a terrible war! Would Todd and Frank Coughlan end up trying to kill each other like Jemsie and Anto?

The main lobby of the Gresham, all polished marble, chandeliers and plush sofas, was filled with dust and disarray. I too was covered in plaster dust. I was kept going with cups of tea from the Cumann na mBan girls. There were so many wounded in our billiard-room hospital that we set up a First Aid Station outside it in the Gresham lobby to deal with less serious injuries.

I saw some of the big people hanging around: de Valera, Oscar Traynor and a weary Cathal Brugha. They looked like wraiths at the gates of hell. Shook, hopeless, unimportant even.

Todd, who had come back down to see how Coughlan was getting on, practically spat. "I

don't know which of them is responsible for
this military blunder of occupying buildings
and making us sitting ducks. But I don't care."
He left me to go back to the Tramways Office,
looking like he couldn't care less if he got
shot.

That night the buildings were once more
under attack. The gunshot now felt like normal
background noise.

The stream of wounded was still being
brought to the billiard room and First Aid
station. I saw the leaders huddle in corners
in the lobby, trying to piece together a way
out of the mess.

As I went to get some rest sometime in the
middle of the night, I had a terrible shock. I
saw Patch, the boy from Macroom, filling
sandbags.

"What in God's name are you doing here?" I
demanded.

"I snuck out of Vincent's hospital." He
stuck his chin out in defiance. "I have to do
my bit, Molly. I can hold my head high now."

"Well, don't hold it too high, you fool, or
it will get shot off you!" I was mad at him and
strode off.

But then I felt bad about it. You never know
when you will see someone for the last time. I
went back and gave him the Turkish Delight that
I still had in my pocket. He looked like a ten-
year-old boy who'd been given a gold coin.

The following morning we were told of the
plan.

"The ordinary soldiers who are not currently on sniper duty and all of the women must leave the building," Oscar Traynor commanded, his voice croaky with exhaustion.

That would leave only a few fighters. The game was up.

The troops slipped away in ones and twos to try to escape down the back alleys and warren of streets.

But, to my amazement, the girls walked out the main entrance, heads held high, into the centre of Sackville Street. I watched them from the safety of a corner. You'd think they were going to catch a tram home. They were oblivious to the rifle and machine-gun fire.

The Hammam Hotel had come under heavy fire So we had to move the hospital to another room further up 'The Block'.

"What are you still doing here?" Cathal Brugha said to Linda and me when he saw us moving medical supplies.

Linda glanced at me. "I'm going nowhere," she said.

Another female doctor came in, helping a soldier who was bleeding from a shoulder wound. She was a slight woman of about fifty but with such dignified bearing she made a strong impression. We immediately attended her as she cleaned the young boy's wound. It was superficial — there was no bullet.

She nodded to Brugha and introduced herself as Dr. Ada English.

"He wants us to go," Linda told her.

"As long as the fighting continues, there will be casualties. I think that settles the matter," she said.

Brugha knew better than to argue. He nodded and left.

She explained she was the assistant director at the lunatic asylum in Ballinasloe. I would have loved to talk to her but we were in another version of a madhouse.

An air of despondency, thick like a fog, descended on remaining troops in the half-destroyed building. We were indeed sitting ducks.

Later that afternoon, a single armoured car, a Lancia, snaked down the street. It was an ugly snub-nosed vehicle, gun-metal grey with slits for gun-holes and a moving turret. It opened fire on the Tramways Office without cease, battering it with bullets like a hailstorm.

A fellow from Tipperary arrived with a terrible leg injury. The ligaments and bones were so badly smashed I feared it would have to be amputated. Then another young man came in, his eye bloody and mashed. There was no hope for it. He would lose the eye. We had them stretchered out to the Mater Hospital.

A few minutes later, the Tramways commander, Dowling, staggered in bearing the weight of a tall man, his face a mess and blood spouting from his arm. It was Todd Andrews. He looked stunned, his face pocked and pitted like a pepper canister had been shaken over it. He moaned softly.

105

"A hail of bullets caught his firing slit and blasted sand from the sandbags in his face," Dowling explained.

Doctor English examined him.

"No major damage," she said briskly. "It's a large bullet splinter lodged in your forearm." She threw iodine over it and fished the splinter out with a tweezers.

"But I can't see!"

She looked at his eye.

"Is there any distilled water left?" she asked me.

I shook my head. "It's over with the supplies in the office."

But there was firing near the windows and it was too risky to fetch some.

"Hold his head still," she instructed me.

I did as she asked. She bent over him and licked out the sand from his eyeball.

"Get him to the Mater! He'll need an operation to clear out the bullet wound," she instructed and moved on to tend to an older man with a terrible stomach wound.

"Can you see anything?" I asked Todd.

He nodded his head, relieved. "It's a bit blurry. But I can see you, Molly."

I was glad at least that he was going to the Mater. But the casualties must have been piling up there!

Soon after that, the magnificent chandelier in the ceiling lobby tinkled. The room vibrated and plaster angels dislodged from the ceiling and were smashed to the floor. I watched it all with dawning realization. There was a deep rumble from the bowels of the earth. A mighty explosion shook the room, nearly knocking me off my feet.

"*They planted an incendiary bomb under the building!*" someone shouted out as thick smoke and the smell of burning filled the air.

"*We're surrounded!*"

There were now very few of us remaining in 'The Block'. De Valera left with one party and Countess Markievicz too made her escape. I went to find Patch and told him to leave. But, when he saw that Cathal Brugha was staying put, he stubbornly refused.

Soon, the Free State soldiers were right outside. The last ragged group of rebels including Kathleen Barry was led out by Art O'Connor, one of the First Aid officers. He took off his Red Cross armband and led them out with a white flag. They were arrested almost immediately. I tried to drag Patch with me but he ran off through the smoke and hid. I could not leave him.

"He can't have gone far and he'll have a better chance with me," I said to Linda Kearns who had also stayed behind.

So I tied a kerchief around my mouth and searched for him down corridors blurry with smoke, glancing into rooms thick with plaster-dust with the ceilings caved in. Back on the ground floor, I found him crouching in a cloakroom. I managed to drag him before Brugha who was finishing his confession to a Capuchin friar in his distinctive brown habit with the pointy hood. The friar left straight away.

Cathal Brugha looked at Patch sternly. "Do you not know the punishment for a soldier who disobeys orders is to be shot?" he said. But then he softened. "Would you go for love of me?"

Tears sprang to Patch's eyes. He saluted and, choked with emotion, agreed to leave with me.

The place was burning all around us — Linda, me, Cathal Brugha and Patch. We heard the scream of fire engines. Smoke billowed towards us.

We kept moving to escape the smoke until we reached the back door.

"Cathal Brugha means to go out fighting!" Linda whispered to me. "He intends to be a martyr and die in battle! 'Tis cracked he is surely."

She turned to him.

"Are you wise going to your death?" she asked him.

He paused there, in the burning building, and he spoke like Joan of Arc going to the stake.

"I feel that if it put a stop to the Civil War, it would be a death worthwhile," he said.

My heart knocked sideways. It was like listening to Patrick Pearse all over again in the GPO. He wanted to be a sacrifice as if he was a new Christ come to save the world. But it was a strange notion. For Jesus never fired a gun.

The heat was becoming intolerable. We had to move.

We lost sight of Brugha behind the black smoke and dust. But Linda went back to him. I wasn't sure what she was thinking. But I stuck to Patch, determined to get him out of there. He still had the Red Cross armband in his pocket that P.J. had given him. I made him put it on in the hope it might save him from arrest.

I held up an improvised white flag, a Gresham Hotel napkin tied to a broom handle. We went out into Thomas Lane but in the confusion Patch melted away. Some Free State soldiers were about to arrest me, but their officer saw my armband and I was left alone.

I looked back but couldn't see Linda.

Cathal Brugha then came out. He emerged from the smoke, his face blackened with soot. He had a revolver in each hand, and he kept on shouting: *"NO SURRENDER! NO SURRENDER!"*

The Free State soldiers aimed low. I got the impression they didn't want to kill him, just to hit his legs to bring him down. He cried out as he buckled to his knees then collapsed on his side. Then all at once there was a scene of utter chaos. It flashed before me like a newsreel in the cinema.

The shooting must have stopped. Linda, who was at the exit, immediately ran to Brugha.

She tore off the leg of his trousers. "His femoral artery is severed!" she cried out. She held the artery together with her bare hands.

Then in a flurry of white coats and uniforms other doctors and the St. John's Ambulance surrounded him. They moved him to the side of the lane near a telegraph post.

He was still alive — just — as they stretchered him to the ambulance.

I later went to the Mater to see what had happened to him and his comrades. And all around the side streets little children were playing war games between Republicans and Staters. Barefoot urchins in ragged clothes sang:

"What's the news, what's the news,
De Valera pawned his shoes,
To buy ammunition for his men!
They were eating currant buns,
When they heard the Free State guns,
And all the dirty cowards ran away!"

When he arrived at the hospital, Brugha had been taken into theatre. But he had lost so much blood his life was hanging by a thread.

I was so dog-tired I went back to my digs on the other side of the city and fell into a stupor.

Brugha only lived for another two days.

A few days after, I went to the Mater to see him lying in state. He was such a small man they could only find a normal-size uniform to bury him in and he looked dwarfed in it. His hair looked blacker than I remembered it.

With him was the body of a boy shot outside Mountjoy Gaol. Another forgotten casualty of war.

I saw Todd Andrews in one of the wards, surrounded by fussing visitors. His arm was in a sling. He'd had an operation to remove the bullet fragments but was otherwise well. Although his eye was bloodshot, he had not lost his sight.

But others were not so lucky. Beside him was

the soldier who lost an eye and the other whose leg could not be saved. They are all to be moved to convalesce in Portrane. The Free State Army is so disorganised, nobody had thought to arrest them. I have heard other Republicans, including Ernie O'Malley, were let escape by former comrades.

There were around eight dead after the week of bloodletting. Yes, Mr. de Valera, the streets ran with blood. Among them innocents caught in the crossfire.

It should be the end of the Civil War in Dublin at least. But there are awful rumours that the war is to continue down south. I am too exhausted to do much else for now. I have come down with a bad cold. I will nurse it and hope to return soon to my lectures.

Yours, always,

Molly

P.S. I have just received your telegram. I cannot believe it! Jack is coming back and with more Russian Crown Jewels to deliver to Harry Boland! I will make haste now to seek out Linda to find out where Boland might be. I assume Jack will first make contact with him. Molly

Chapter eleven

So Jack was coming back with the jewels! Just as the whole country was tearing itself to shreds. What a story! Our translator old Stavros sure was wasted chopping onions. We went back to the attic and took out the next letter, eager to unravel its secrets.

This letter was just a random series of triangles and arrows. It began:

⇋⇨⇨△ ∪⇕ʚʚ◢⇂
⇉ ↩⇨⇨△ ◀↑↓▽ ʚ⇨◀◀⇨△ ▷↓ʚʚ △⇨⇨↑
◢⇕▶

Mal took the page and furrowed his brow in concentration. "It's a cipher. Each symbol is substituted for a letter. I just need an 'in' to break it down."

I looked closely at the paper. There was "The Crowne Plaza Hotel NY" watermark again.

"Mal, this letter is from New York – it must have been written by Sanjay."

Mal looked like he was doing Math in his head. "Okay, the date August 1922 is written normally as usual. We can assume the first two words of the cipher are 'Dear Molly'. That gives me the first clue to crack the code. It has exactly the same number of letters and my guess is the last pointy-down symbol is a comma."

I peered at the code. "So the first symbol must be a capital D. And the second is an 'e' and so on?"

Mal smiled at me and ran his eye over the text. "Good work, Watson! That symbol of the arrow pointing right – the one with the heavier line – gives us another anchor. It's about twenty per cent of the whole text. It confirms it is an 'e', the most common letter in the English language. The second plainer arrow is an 'a'. Don't get them mixed up!"

He got a pencil and paper and it took him about half an hour to work out which letter went with which symbol. I was well impressed but I didn't like to tell him in case he got a swelled head.

Finally we had a translation which Mal typed up on the old-fashioned typewriter we'd found in the trunk.

∞◎∞

23rd July 1922

Dear Molly,
I am sorry I have failed you and Jack is back in Ireland. I can only hope that I can help if either of you need to get to the United States.

Only this morning I read in the newspaper that people do not understand, after the long battle for Irish freedom, why the country is tearing itself apart in a civil war.

And this has had an effect on Jack. I think he has some mad plan about bringing peace to Ireland. That emeralds are a healing stone. And if he brings the new jewels to Boland, he can try again to present them to Collins as a peace offering.

He has had many talks with me about Mr. Gandhi and passive resistance – when a whole country refuses to co-operate with an alien power. But his time with Native American tribes has given him other ideas. He tells Cherokee stories about the good and bad wolves inside us and the need to feed the good wolf with acts of love big and small.

Jack has learned about the peace pipe and has mastered the dances of peace to the sun. He jokes that if he cannot bring an end to war in Ireland, maybe he can make it laugh at its folly. When I asked him if he intends to put on an acrobatic or a magic show, he said he has friends who can help him arrange a performance. I don't know how these wild ideas will work in your land in a civil war!

Your faithful friend,

Sanjay

P.S. If you are reading this, I assume you got the separate telegram with the clue to the code. Just as well Jack and you loved doing puzzles when you were children!

∽৯৹৶ঔ∾

"Quite an ingenious idea sending the clues in a separate telegram," Mal said. "Well, it certainly isn't among the papers we found. Could it be in the trunk? Did we miss it?"

We rummaged around in the trunk but there was no trace of it. Then we searched the attic – but it was impossible to find anything in that bombsite.

The telegram must have disappeared long ago.

We moved on to the next letter. It was again in a mystifying code, like Egyptian hieroglyphics.

The first couple of lines looked like this:

"Maybe Sanjay also included this code on a separate telegram," Mal said.

I started to yawn, so Mal turned into my big brother and told me to go to bed. We'd sort it out in the morning.

I went back to my flat with a happy feeling. We were on the trail of the jewels now. And it was Red Alert – Jack was in town!

But my mood was ruined when I caught sight of the letter that the landlady must have shoved under our door. It had an American stamp with the head of a Native American chief. I was struck by the coincidence.

My hands were trembling as I opened it. It had been forwarded by our lawyer. It was from my dad. He said he missed me so much and hoped we would see each other soon. He hadn't wanted us to leave. But respected my mother's decision. I would always be his precious daughter. Yada, yada, yada.

Then he tried to explain that there was nothing between Honey Belle and him while she was my nanny. They only got together after he and my mother split up. Honey Belle was an important part of his life and he hoped I would eventually accept her as part of the family.

Honey Belle part of the family? I slumped down on my bed. Sweet homely Honey Belle. The nanny who I used to pretend was my big sister was going to be, like, my step-mom? The words made no more sense than the symbols on the pages of Molly's and Sanjay's letters. How was I supposed to be happy that we were stuck in this dingy flat in Dublin while he made a new life? Now that he loved Honey Belle more than Mom and me?

I read on. He said he hoped we'd see each other real soon. He was very busy (there's a surprise) but he offered to fly me over and take me to the Harry Potter studio in Hollywood in California.

He and Honey Belle could hang out together with me and pretend to be a happy family. Except he'd stabbed my mom in the heart. And if that wasn't bad enough . . . the real kicker was we could even do some kind of fun kid's stuff with my two so-called best friends, Cookie and Cleeter. Well, yeah, that would be the icing on the cake of the visit FROM HELL!!!!

In a fit of anger I tore the letter into a million tiny pieces and flushed it down the toilet. I didn't want Mom to find it.

Before I knew it I was pounding my pillow and was so

crazy I triggered an asthma attack. I pawed around trying to find my inhaler. I heaved into it. Then I let out a scream. *"I hate you all!"*

I caught sight of myself in the mirror. My face was distorted like a mad lunatic. My chin crumpled and I started to cry.

A knock on the door caught me off balance. I answered it before I could clean myself up.

It was Mal. He stood there, his eyebrow raised.

"Telly on a bit loud? Or were you murdering someone?"

"It isn't funny," I sniffled into my hankie.

He gazed down at his grubby trainers.

"Do you want to talk about it?"

I shook my head.

"Good," he said. "Don't you hate all that caring and sharing nonsense that adults think is so important?"

He grinned at me. I could only manage a weak smile.

There was an awkward silence then.

"Good news," he said eventually. "I think I've cracked the next cipher. If we work steadily I reckon we could translate all these mysterious letters." He touched me lightly on the shoulder. "Try to rest, kid. We need your sharp mind on the case." Then he turned me round and closed the door on me.

His kindness helped me push my father's betrayal out of my mind. Roll it into a tiny ball and toss it in the wastepaper bin in my mind.

And it was Mal's belief in me, wanting to work shoulder to shoulder, that helped me go to sleep.

Chapter twelve

Next morning, Mal had already deciphered a good bit of the letter and had started typing it out on the old-fashioned typewriter! *Ching-ching*!

We worked on finishing it in the attic together. Mal wrote out the principles of the cipher on the white board and we took a page each. The sideways ℘ symbol that looked like a 6 and a 9 was an "a". The ☐ was the letter "o" It was fun. We were like two medieval monks transcribing the Book of Kells. Except we were really two kids in a junk-filled attic in Dublin that smelled of damp and old clothes.

I was eager to try out the old-fashioned manual typewriter, a model called Underwood. A lot more bulky than a laptop! It was fun. Mal showed me how to load the paper into the cartridge and make sure the ribbon with the ink was straight. The keys sprang up and down and the letters made a satisfying clatter against the paper when you hit them. Then a bell went off at the end of the line and you had to clank the carriage return. It took some getting used to but I kinda liked the way the words stacked up on the page.

I hadn't been this excited since reading *Harry Potter*. And this was even better because it was for real. I didn't need to go to a stupid theme park.

∽✍✍✍✍✍✍✍✍✍✍✍✍✍✍∾

August 1922

Dear Sanjay,

I wish I could telephone you. But the telephone lines are tapped.

I waited at my digs for days and days in the hope that Jack would contact me. But when there was no sign of him, I gave up my vigil and ventured out.

Sackville Street, the beating heart of the city, is in ruins again. The chemical smell of burning. Rubble at my feet. Bloodstains on the grey stones.

I went to visit Nancy, our old char. I was banking on Jack seeking out his best friend Anto. I also had the locket to give to Anto's wife. His mother would know where to find her.

In my grief over Anto's shooting of Jemsie, I had been avoiding seeing Nancy and May. Afraid that I would betray something. Aside from you, Sanjay, I have vowed not to tell a soul about Anto firing the fatal shot.

Nancy had moved back into their old Moore Street neighbourhood, where Pearse and the leaders of 1916 surrendered. Her rooms above a butcher's shop were better than her previous ones. She had a fine old dresser with some bits of crockery, an iron bedstead and even some photographs on the wall.

I was let in by her younger daughter Alice who is about ten years old. Nancy was hunched in a shawl in the iron bedstead under a worn coverlet. She had taken to her bed in her grief. She clutched a photograph in her arthritic hands. Her face was lined and seemed sunken in. She is no more than fifty but looked about seventy.

When she saw me she rallied briefly and smiled, showing me her few front teeth. I ran to her and wrapped my arms around her. A sudden sob escaped from the depths of her suffering. But after a moment she pulled away and raised her poor knobbly hands to tidy her hair.

"Oh Molly, forgive me lyin' in bed. Me oul' legs are playin' up. I'm not long for the knacker's yard meself!" She laughed then. But it was a faint rattley laugh, the ghost of the old spirited Nancy.

I looked at the photo on her lap. Jemsie, handsome in his uniform, wearing his medal from the Battle of the Somme.

"He was a good son, Nancy. You can be proud of his memory," I said.

She smiled then. A mother's tender smile. "He was a fine boy. The best. He and Anto were always fightin' as kids. And I'd let a roar at them. 'One of these days you'll end up murtherin' one another!'"

My heart stopped. She had spoken so near the truth.

I must have betrayed something because she said to me: "I hear your mam and dad are havin' a nice time in Florida. But your mam's health isn't too good. Tell them never to come back to this stinkin' hole full of corpses livin' and dead." She almost spat the words.

I told her that Jack was back.

"Oh, God save us, no," she said.

"Have you had any word from Anto?" I asked her, almost afraid to say his name.

Her face took on a worried expression. "He's on the run again."

Her body shook with a wracking cough. I didn't like the sound of it. I took out my stethoscope and listened to her chest. I got her to breathe deeply. She said that she'd only had the cough for a week. But her chest was wheezy and I judged her lungs to be inflamed.

"You have acute bronchitis," I said. "I will make you up a cough mixture to help you bring up the phlegm. But it would get much better in the fresh air."

At that moment May came home from work in the hotel, her face ashen. She didn't give me her customary smile.

"I've lost my job," she said flatly. "The hotel can't afford to keep me on."

I saw her mother's face crumple.

May hid her worry. "Would you believe, Clery's are having a summer sale? They're selling off all the stock in their temporary premises in that warehouse in lower Abbey Street, before moving back into their restored shop on Sackville Street. They've only been waiting for the fighting to stop."

"You might get some bargains," I said with forced enthusiasm.

"No, I was thinking they might need some staff," May said. "With so many hotels destroyed there will be too many other hotel workers around to get a job in the ones still standing."

I felt terrible. Here was me thinking of spending money when poor May was worried about feeding her family. But

May saw my embarrassment and came to embrace me.

We held each other for a long time.

"You were a little divil when you were a girl but now I think of you as our guardian angel, Molly!" Nancy called from the bed. "It's a comfort to me that you and May were near Jemsie at the end."

"But I couldn't save him, Nancy."

Nancy sobbed but then laughed, her chest convulsing. "Now don't be getting' notions, young wan. I said you were an angel not God himself!"

We all smiled to see the old Nancy rallying.

"Have you seen Jack or had word from Anto, May?" I asked.

May shook her head. "Nothing."

I asked for the address of Anto's wife. May told me she'd called to see Sinéad but the neighbours had said she'd gone back to her people in Tralee in County Kerry.

"Mam and Sinéad quarreled," she said to me quietly. "They don't see eye to eye about Anto siding with the anti-Treaty forces."

May sighed and went to a small mirror on the wall to tidy her hair. "There's only one thing for it," she said. "If the men can't sort things out, us women need to try. Out of that bed now, Mammy, and we're off to the Rotunda for the Women's Peace Rally."

So we headed off to the Round Room, which is just up around the corner at the top of Sackville Street, passing the Rotunda Hospital which is on the same site. We had to dash to avoid a sudden shower that fell from the heavens.

Inside the Round Room, the most beautiful circular room in these islands, it was a sea of hats of every colour: violet, red, rose, pink, sky-blue. There were also women with shawls on their heads beside bright young things with daring bobs and lipstick. All talking and arguing at great volume, enough to make the brilliant chandeliers tinkle. None of them apparently much keen on peace. There was much catcalling and jeering between the different sides in the Civil War.

Louie Bennett stood at the lectern on the stage before the crush of women. She was the chairwoman. Mrs. Despard and Maude Gonne MacBride were among the speakers. The Lord Mayor Lawrence O'Brien, a fine-looking man with a bushy moustache, was also present in his large red cloak and chains of office. The huge room hummed. It soon became muggy as steam rose off our rain-spattered clothes.

Louie Bennett began in a loud clear voice, "We are here today to show the fighting men that the women of Ireland want peace!"

Someone shouted out, asking why was the Lord Mayor there. Louie Bennett answered that he was a great supporter. And peace-loving men were just as welcome.

Nancy provided a wry running commentary. "The state of that Lord Mayor smirkin' at us – isn't he a slum landlord himself?" she said loudly.

Maud Gonne McBride spoke movingly about the heartbreak and sacrifice of mothers.

"Look at yer one Maud Gonne Mad herself! Wasn't she trying to divorce the ould bamboozler MacBride before he became a martyr? And now suddenly she's proud to bear his name!" was Nancy's verdict.

Mrs. Despard gave a speech about the folly and uselessness of war in her clipped voice and made a great impression on Nancy.

"That poor 'oul wan Charlotte Desperate is right. Isn't she great giving them what for?"

At one stage someone went out to quieten a couple of shouting Free State women in the hall who had got it into their heads that all the speakers were Republicans.

Then some fools started singing a hymn to the Queen of Heaven. It all ended in uproar and confusion. I do not know if the Women's Peace Rally will achieve its aim. But it certainly gave Nancy a lift!

As we came out of the meeting, I pressed May to find out if she had really heard nothing of Anto.

She bent her head close to mine. "One of his old battalion told me some of the Fianna boys were holding out in the Wicklow Mountains."

"I'm surprised no one has seen my brother," I said.

She dropped the peace leaflets she was intending to pass out on Dublin's streets. As she bent down to pick them up a necklace escaped from under her blouse. It was a vivid blue sapphire like her eyes. She straightened up and saw me staring at it.

She quickly concealed it back under her blouse.

"Where did you get that?" I asked her.

"I can't tell you so don't press me, Molly." She was flustered and looked down.

"Have you an admirer, May?"

She blushed. Then we smiled in unison and she put her hands to her mouth.

"Just tell me he's the very best sort," I said.

"The best. I know in my heart you would agree." She laughed. "Now don't press me."

She was looking quite beautiful. She has dark curly hair and those striking blue eyes in a fine-boned face. From some angles she is unremarkable. Her hands, like mine, are a fright with bitten nails and blotches. But when she smiles, which she does often, her eyes are filled with such sparkle she could light up the world. Kindness radiates out of her. You could warm your hands on her at the best of times. But now she was like a sun. May was in love, I realised. I treasured this news as if I'd found that sapphire in the dust myself.

Otherwise, good news is in short supply. The Republicans plan to concentrate the war in the south of Ireland, where their support is more solid. But I was still none the wiser about Jack's whereabouts, even though I asked several women at the meeting to keep a watch out for him.

Then I decided to try Linda Kearns to find out if Jack had been in contact with Boland. She is close to the Republicans. But also has friends on all sides.

She confirmed that Collins and Boland had a row over Kitty Kiernan and over jewels.

"Now Boland is on the run from Collins. He fears him especially."

"Does he still have the jewels?" I asked.

"I would imagine so," said Linda. "He probably has them somewhere for safe keeping."

"I must speak with Boland. I think Jack will try to contact him," I said.

"Meet me after Cathal Brugha's funeral," she whispered. "Boland is in hiding but he might be there. They won't arrest him at a funeral."

I missed most of the funeral on the day. I was attending a busy dispensary in Westland Row with Doctor Dorothy and we ran late.

As I drew near to Glasnevin Cemetery, I waded against the

tide of people coming back. Linda had parked her motorcar inside the entrance. She was standing there with a middle-sized man in his thirties who had his hands in his pockets, his hat brim cocked back on his broad face. He was sharing a joke with her and I guessed he was Harry Boland. You could tell even from ten paces away that he had a sunny nature.

Linda introduced us and he seemed glad to meet me. We walked a little way off and stood behind a tombstone.

I took a deep breath and told him I was seeking my brother.

A look of recognition dawned on his face. "Ah, Jack the Cat from the circus! I thought he was close to Collins but he has kept himself out of it. Is he solid for the republic?"

"I have not seen him in six years, sir – I don't know how he thinks," I said.

"And you?" he asked me.

"I am a medical student and my mother was a Quaker. I am drawn to her faith which preaches non-violence."

"Perhaps we should listen to you so," he said.

"I believe Jack may be in Ireland and has something to deliver to you," I continued.

A shadow passed over his face. "Eggs, butter, planks of timber?"

He meant explosives, arms, and guns.

I whispered. "No, sir, Russian Crown Jewels."

His face darkened. "Those jewels have already caused enough trouble."

"These are different ones that have been rescued from the sea. I believe Jack will try to contact you about them."

"There's a war on, girl. It's no time for games and fantasies." He was stern now.

"But . . ." I began to protest but stopped when he shifted

from foot to foot and wrung his hands, suddenly nervous.

Two men in uniform had entered the graveyard from the entrance near the Botanical Gardens.

"Mick Collins won't leave me alive for long," Boland said. "I know too much about him."

He left me abruptly and hurried towards Linda who was now waiting outside the main gates with the engine of her car running.

I ran towards the car as he jumped in.

He stuck his head out the window. "If your brother really has something to deliver he'll know how to find me."

The car sped off and I was left standing in the pall of exhaust fumes.

His words about Collins troubled me. Surely Collins was working towards peace? Yes, he had led an assassination squad. But he had changed since negotiating the Treaty. Hadn't he?

As I cycled back to my digs through the ruins of Sackville Street, I felt angry with my brother. I had spent so much of my childhood running after Jack. Covering for him. Risking my own life to make sure he was safe. Had he ever shown a similar regard for me?

But I pushed down those thoughts. Jack was a good brother. He treated me as an equal. Without him I would never have become a medical student. If Harry Boland was to be believed, he had listened to me when I asked him to stay away from the conflict.

All I could do was wait and go back to my studies.

As it was summer recess, I was asked to take on some practical training in a ward and was assigned to St. Vincent's Hospital.

I worked with the nursing nuns and attended Dr. St. John Gogarty on his rounds. He is very close to both Collins and Griffith. A Free Stater to the core.

I saw much agony and suffering. Last night I heard one boy from Cavan with a mutilated leg call out in such pain that he asked the surgeon to put an end to his life. And a young Free State soldier grabbed the anaesthetic from the doctor's hand and pressed it closer to his mouth so he could pass out more quickly before we changed his daily dressing on a seeping stomach wound. When I hear people say lightly that someone was "only wounded" it makes me quite mad!

As the days and nights ticked by with no word of Jack, I decided to ask my cousin Dan to go visit Mrs. De Valera with a message for her husband. He took the tram out to Greystones where they live. When he returned, his face was shining.

"I saw Jack!" he exclaimed.

My hand flew to my mouth.

"Are you sure? How did he look?"

"Amazing!"

"Can you tell me more than that?" I was hungry for details.

"He looks like a Yank, Molly," he said. "He's tanned and his hair is very blond. He was wearing a check suit and two-tone shoes."

"Did he give you a message for me?" I asked.

Dan handed me a tin soldier like the ones Jack used to play with as a boy. Inside was a note.

"Molly, my dearest sister, I will try to see you as soon as I can. Do not look for me. Your fondest brother, Jack."

I stared at it for a long time. Jack was back in Ireland but who knew what he was up to?

On Sunday evening, I went into St Vincent's Hospital to work on the wards. Things were tense, but we did not expect a busy night as the fighting had largely finished in Dublin.

At around seven o'clock on Monday morning we were told someone important was being admitted. He'd been shot on the north side of Dublin. An hour later a man badly wounded with gunshot was stretchered in, accompanied by Free State Officers.

The House Surgeon Dr. Kennedy and I were doing ward visits and were summoned to come immediately by the matron, Sister Dymphna.

To my horror, I recognised the patient as Harry Boland! He was in a bad way. Gunshot wounds to his abdomen and back. But still alive. He had been shot about six hours before in a hotel in Skerries, which was about twenty miles from Dubin.

"He was wounded when resisting arrest," the young stretcher-bearer said. "He was unarmed but tried to rush an arresting officer for a gun and in the scuffle was shot."

He was bleeding profusely. It was astonishing he was still alive. Dr. Kennedy examined him. The bullet had passed through his stomach, tearing at his spleen and liver. It was still in his chest.

"We need to operate immediately to remove it," he said.

But Harry Boland was still conscious, as white as a sheet, his skin like parchment. "No, I want to see my sister Kathleen and . . . the chaplain before facing the knife."

"Molly, can you do as he says?" Dr. Kennedy instructed me. I fetched the chaplain who said he would take a jaunting car to get Kathleen who lived out in Clontarf. He took Harry's wallet with him to give to his mother.

I was with Harry Boland, helping a nurse give him a drink of water, when his sister Kathleen arrived. She was a sensible-looking woman with glasses. She rushed up to the bedside, but her face drained when she saw her poor brother.

"You'll get over this, Harry!" she said with forced conviction.

"Ah no, Kit, I don't think so," he said faintly as she leaned in close to hear him.

"Who fired the shot?"

"I'll never tell you, Kit," he said. His breathing came hard. "Only that it was a friend who was in Lewes Gaol with me. I forgive him and want no reprisals."

She looked like she might faint. I found her a chair and she drew it up alongside him.

"I want to be buried in the same grave as Cathal Brugha," he said.

Around midday, we prepared him for the operation. Dr. Kennedy extracted the bullet. But there wasn't much hope.

His mother came into the hospital and she sat with her unconscious son the whole time. She was grateful to me for making sure she had cups of tea.

"Molly," she told me, "if you ever need a favour, come to me."

A steady stream of visitors started to arrive at the hospital but we kept them out. A small crowd had even gathered outside.

The next morning, Harry Boland opened his eyes.

"I want to see Gerry," he said.

His brother Gerry had been imprisoned in Mountjoy Gaol after his arrest at Blessington with another group of Republicans.

As Kathleen and her friend left to see if the governor would let him out to visit his dying brother, the officer in charge of the military guard came up to her.

"I'm warning you. We have orders to shoot Boland dead if there's any attempt at escape."

Kathleen looked like she might hit him. "Can't you see he's dying! Is Mick Collins so far gone in his hatred? It's not so long since he was hiding in my mother's attic. Shame on you!"

The officer backed off, shamefaced. "Sorry. There will be no guard placed over him."

She came back about an hour later, looking like a ghost. "They won't let Gerald out!"

They were standing a little way off from the bed so Harry couldn't hear them.

"Gerald!" Harry called from the bed, trying to sit up.

Kathleen went to him. "They won't let him out, Harry."

He lay back down on the pillow. His face white, his chest heaving with the effort of breathing.

"Kit, I want you to hold on to the Russian jewels until de Valera is in power." He clutched her hand. "If ever a Republic is declared, you can hand them over to him."

Kathleen nodded.

"Promise me!" His breath rasped in his throat.

"I will consider it a sacred trust."

My ears perked up. I hesitated, debating if it was right for me to interrogate a dying man about my brother. But I dithered too long. For a group rushed in, including several priests.

Boland's suffering was terrible. The end did not come until ten past nine on Tuesday evening, the 2nd of August, after forty-three hours of struggle.

It was a close and stuffy night. I felt I couldn't breathe. When my shift ended I went out onto the top balcony near the roof to catch some late-night air. I heard people calling and crying outside. Perhaps news of Boland's death was spreading.

I stood out there for the longest time watching the city I loved, lights coming on, occasional shouts, the sound of armoured patrol cars roaring in the street. The stars still twinkling in the heavens. The night closing in.

Just as I was about to go back in, I heard the scrape of a heel on slate. There was the blur of something or someone in the corner of my eye. My heart stopped. But not from fear. It was a familiar presence.

"Jack!" I called out. "I know it's you!"

And then, as if stepping out of my dreams, there he was. My brother. As familiar to me as my own shadow.

We embraced and held each other close. Then he held me by the shoulders and looked into my face in the moonlight.

"Molly, *mo chroí!* You look different but exactly the same!"

I looked at him, my eyes filling to see his dear face. He was gleaming in the moonlight. Older now, more solid but still lithe as a cat. He smiled and his teeth caught by the moonlight seemed whiter in his tanned face.

"And you've turned into a Yank!"

We gazed at each other a long time with great joy, smiling from ear to ear.

A bell chimed in the distance.

Jack finally spoke. "We have so much to talk about! But first I need to speak to one of your patients, Harry Boland. It's urgent."

But he caught my sad expression before I could speak.

"I'm too late!" He swore under his breath. "God have mercy on his soul."

"He has entrusted the jewels he has to his mother," I told him. "Only to be handed over when de Valera declares a Republic."

Jack closed his eyes and held his hand to his temple. "I have a second set of jewels. I had hoped they would bring about a reconciliation between the two sides in the Civil War."

"He died not trusting Collins," I continued. "What will you do, Jack? You must return to the States."

Jack looked at me from under his fringe, which kept flopping into his eyes. "It might still work. Emeralds have healing properties. They can bury the hatchet and smoke the pipe of peace, like the Native Americans do."

"But you don't want to get sucked back in, Jack. These are dangerous times. Why are you hiding in the shadows?"

"I don't want to run the risk of arrest," he said. "People don't know me here any more. They want to know what side I'm on."

"And which side are you on?"

"Same side as you, Molly. Peace. I had my fill of war in Easter Week."

We grabbed each other's hands then, glad that we at least were at one on this.

"But why the rooftops, Jackie Boy?"

"I'm still the Cat! And old habits die hard."

"You're not telling me the whole story," I persisted.

The wind rustled in the darkness.

"I was there, Molly, when Boland was shot in Skerries," he said. "I went out to the hotel, hoping to meet him. I didn't see what happened. But one of the Free State soldiers might have seen me."

"You'll have to go into hiding. This is going to cause ructions. Boland is close to de Valera. You went to see de Valera too, didn't you?"

He looked thoughtful but said nothing.

"Anto is with the Republicans," I said. "He was in the Four Courts. But he escaped."

There must have been a catch in my voice because Jack looked at me closely.

"There's something you're not saying now," he said. "Is he in a bad way?"

"Why would I hide that?" I said quickly.

He waited a beat. "It is tough on him. He has lost his brother. May is heartbroken. Nancy too."

Tears sprang to my eyes. "This is a terrible war, Jack. Brother has turned against brother. Promise me you'll go back to the United States."

"Sure thing, Mollser!" He chucked me under the chin. "But not without Anto if he needs to escape this war."

I frowned.

He laughed in his light way. "I promise I'll do your bidding. But not in the way you might expect."

I shook my head. "When did you ever do anything that I'd expect?"

We turned to gaze into the deep dark night.

"What do you think Collins will do now?" he asked me.

I was surprised and somewhat flattered to be consulted.

"Dr. St. John Gogarty believes that Boland might have been arranging to see Collins when he was shot, to set up a meeting with de Valera. But the politicians aren't in charge now, are they? Not on the Republican side at any rate. Liam Lynch the Republican commander is a die-hard."

We stood side by side, watching the city curl asleep. The lamps were pinpricks of light among the dark outlines of rooftops, like strung gemstones.

Jack spoke. "The politicians need to talk to the gunmen."

I suddenly realised Jack, who had risked his neck in 1916 running messages, would be only too happy to be a go-between.

"Now listen here, Jack – if you think you can go gallivanting all over the country with all the eejits with guns about, you are out of your mind."

"Well, I'm not one of them."

"No, you're the gom running around with a bag of Russian Crown Jewels!"

This made him laugh.

I was curious. "Can I see them?"

"No."

I turned away for a second, hurt by his refusal. And before I could say anything else he was gone!

"*Jack!*" I roared into the night.

But there was only a high wind that snatched at my jacket, whipping my hair into my eyes.

It was only when I was lying in bed, turning all the day's events over in my mind, that I realised he had spoken of Nancy and May as if he had met them. I felt a pang of jealousy. He had tried to see Anto before me.

Oh Jack, I thought, you mad mad boy! What will you do next?

As much as I love having him here, I would rather he was safe in the United States. It comforts me that if I can

135

persuade him to leave you will do everything to help,

Your friend, always,

Molly

Chapter thirteen

The next letter was back to the Greek script. So we decided to ask old Stavros to take a break from chopping onions again after we'd met Patrick and Rachel at the lab.

We went through the main entrance to the lab in the Museum Building. Mal was a bit twitchy as we cut across the quad but I thought he was just doing his usual spy-at-large routine.

In the lab, Patrick already had the jewel set up under the powerful microscope. We took turns gazing at it down the lens It shone a most beautiful, warm, intense green, like no other colour found in nature.

"You can see why they call it 'green fire'," Rachel said.

It was mesmerising. We beamed like proud parents.

We bought them up to date on the information in Molly and Sanjay's letters – how Jack had come back with a second set of jewels. Patrick and Rachel exchanged a look of amazement.

Patrick then showed us a number of close-up 3D images of the jewel on the screen that was linked to the microscope. "We confirmed the salt damage that Rachel suspected." He zoomed in to show the surface of the brooch's metal setting. It resembled craters of the moon, pitted and dark. "The chemical profile is consistent with that."

"So it really could have been rescued by Jack from the bottom of New York harbour?" I asked.

Patrick nodded.

My stomach flipped with excitement.

"Have you worked out why the metal is twisted?" Mal asked.

"The settings and chain links are made of platinum which is an extremely rare metal. Twice the price of the best gold. Chewing it over with the metal-heads – I mean the metallurgists – we think it might have been hit by something at great velocity. Something that would damage it like that."

"Like a bullet?" I asked.

"Very possible. It might have been shot at. Or falling rocks."

"Oh gosh, I hope no one was wearing it – like Molly!" I gasped.

"It's still only a theory," Patrick reassured me. "Leave it with me. I need to run more sophisticated tests. I'm calling in favours to get the research done."

"We need to think about reporting it to the proper authorities," Rachel said.

Mal flashed her a look of annoyance. "We'll look like eejits if we don't have a bit more proof."

"I agree," Patrick said. "We should find out a bit more before we take any official steps. And find out where the rest of the necklace might be."

"Okay. Maybe there will be more clues in the letters," Rachel suggested. "When we have a more complete picture, we can report it to the right government agency."

We told them we were laboriously translating them with a small army of helpers and working out the codes and ciphers by ourselves without a computer.

Patrick was impressed at our ingenuity. "I might be able to help speed up the process," he offered. "I have a bunch of friends, other computer nerds. We call ourselves the 'Geek Squad'. We could help with cracking the codes and transcription?"

"We have one letter in Greek with us," I said, "but old Stavros – he's our one-man 'Greek Squad' – is helping with that. The other letters are back in the flat but we could bring them in. You could email the transcriptions to me?"

Both Rachel and Patrick nodded in agreement.

But Mal cut in. "We'll think about it."

We left then. Rachel stayed behind to talk to her boyfriend.

When we got outside, I was livid with him. "Why did you turn down the offer of help from the Geek Squad?"

Mal was offhand. "Do I have to explain everything?"

I was so angry I stormed off. I was kind of looking forward to getting some important mail. He soon caught up with me.

"Security," he said. "Think about it. If they really are the Crown Jewels, someone might blab about it. We don't want everybody interfering before we've got a chance to solve it on our own. And we don't want the translation on different computers that could be hacked."

I gave him a dirty look. "We already have about twenty people involved. Our library friends, old Stavros, Parvati, Patrick and Rachel —"

"You forgot about that Russian," he said. "I thought I saw him on our way in through Trinity's main entrance."

I groaned. "Then he might just follow us again. And don't you think we should tell Patrick and Rachel about him?"

"He's her customer!" Mal said. "And what are we going to say? We keep seeing this Russian tourist with terrible taste in hats?"

"Okay, I guess we don't want to sound like total dweebs if Patrick's doing us these favours and all," I said. "But we need to take more care. We don't want the Russian to follow us to Stavros's kebab shop."

Mal screwed up his face in concentration. "Okay. Let's be careful." He gave me one of his sweetest smiles and like that, we were friends again.

"At least I didn't have to tell them my email address," I said. "It's kind of babyish."

Mal considered. "Let me guess. Avaandfloppie@me.com."

"How did you know!" I blurted out.

He gave me an appraising look. "Lucky guess."

We took a roundabout route through town in case the

Russian followed us. Mal turned into Superspy. We hunched at the back of the bus. Then jumped off the first one to catch a second one. We were fairly confident that the Russian wasn't on our tail.

Old Stavros, who was working alone, was overjoyed to see us when we walked through the door. As soon as we produced the letter, he whipped off his apron and put the "Closed" sign on the door.

"Pah! the customers can wait. I want to see what this Molly was up to as much as you." He said something in Greek, then explained, "That means Molly is the dove among the crows of war."

I thought that was really neat.

We handed over the letter, which was a few pages long. He glanced over it quickly and told us to come back in a few hours. Then he gave us another two free kebabs and waved us out the door.

Mal went to collect it later in the evening and together we read it in our attic H.Q.

Chapter Fourteen

August 1922

Dear Sanjay,

Jack and I went to see Nancy and May last night. Despite my suspicions, it was the first time he'd visited them there.

"Howdy!" said Jack, lifting Nancy her off her feet in a hug.

He was wearing his light-green check suit with a check bow tie and two-tone brown-and-white lace-up shoes.

"Well, aren't you a sight for sore eyes!" she exclaimed, clacking the few teeth in her head. "And every inch the Yank!"

"Nope, I'm still Jack, ma'am," he said, hamming up his American accent.

Nancy laughed. "Would you listen to the craythur? You're too big now for me to box yer ears, like I did when you and our Anto were chisellers."

It was like a chill had entered the room at the sound of Anto's name.

Then she clasped his hand and became grave. "Will you make sure he comes out safely, Jack? He's got some wild notions, has Anto. Since he married yer one, all he wants to do is prove himself. She's gone back to her folks in Ballygobackwards or wherever she's from in Kerry."

Nancy didn't really approve of her daughter-in-law.

I glanced over at May and was surprised to see Jack and her exchanging glances. Like there was a taut wire between them.

"There is one person who might know where Anto is," Jack said.

We all looked at him.

"Countess Markievicz — or Marzipan as Nancy calls her."

"She's on the run too since the defeat at the Gresham Hotel," I said.

Nancy clapped her hands. "But she still goes around on that clacky bike of hers with the wonky chain," she said with a wink. "I'll ask the world's best secret service. Me fellow cleaners and charladies!"

She rushed out the door, and I swear she was only gone ten minutes when she came back with information.

"Minny next door said aul Marzipan is hangin' out looking after the Belfast refugees at the Kildare Club!"

We set out for the club with May, Jack kissing Nancy on both cheeks as we left, which left her looking ten years younger. He was more of a tonic than my own grim medicine.

The club is on the corner facing Trinity College and is a fine five-storey brick building oozing wealth and privilege. For it is an exclusive club for the "quality" — the grandest gentlemen in Ireland. No women or poor people allowed! Except now the anti-Treaty rebels have booted out the posh gents and set up a temporary hostel for Belfast refugees from the North who have been driven out by Loyalist extremists.

A glum-looking club doorman was still posted at the door in his tasselled uniform in case anyone stole the silver. He seemed to know Jack and tipped his hat to him.

"If we ever get rid of this lot," he said, "the only one happy about it would be Timmy who is a great one for helping the poor. But he doesn't have to live with them."

Jack laughed. "Next time you see Timmy give him my regards and tell him I might need to call in a favour." He winked at the doorman and gave him a shilling.

Jack explained that Timmy was a mysterious millionaire who loved racing yachts and who sometimes called in to the Kildare Club. He occasionally docked his yacht *The Emerald Isle* in Dún Laoghaire on his way to compete in a big race in America. He was also famous for his charity to the poor. Jack had got to know him in the States as he had a financial interest in the circus and loved show business.

Inside, instead of men with pencil moustaches smoking cigars there were small children screeching with delight as they slid down the plush red stair-carpet on a silver tray. The snooty portraits glared down at them from the green-painted walls.

The club had become a gypsy camp. The billiard room, the library, the fine drawing room with luxurious armchairs, had all been turned into accommodation. Many families were squashed together, three to a room, Jack told me. Everywhere wild children ran about the fine building with sticks — shooting at each other.

"Get them Staters!" roared one young fellow in his sharp Northern Irish accent. *"Up the Republic!"*

But the 'Staters' were having none of it and ambushed him by dropping over the bannister.

In the dining room, in the middle of it all, Countess Markievicz was in her element handing out blankets. She looked much frailer since I'd last seen her on sniper duty at the Gresham. Tall and slender, she must have been beautiful once. But now her sharp features stood out in her tanned face, all cheekbones and chin.

Jack delighted everyone by cartwheeling into the room.

"Well, what do you think of our Freak State?" the Countess asked in her grand aristocratic voice, fidgeting with the blankets, full of nervous energy.

Jack turned a somersault. "I can only make sense of this topsy-turvy world by spinning around too."

Madame shook her head. "Darling boy, it's lovely to see you and I had quite the time of it on my recent tour of America. The plumbing is a marvel!" She looked closely at him. "I take it you're not a spy!"

Jack lowered his voice. "Of course not! But I am seeking information about Anto Maguire. You remember him from when you ran the Fianna Boy Scouts? He was one of my band of brothers."

She smiled then. "Ah! So you're on the right side."

"I am always on the right side. Besides, I carry this in peace." He reached over to May and plucked from behind her head, as if out of nowhere, a leather pouch decorated with swirling triangles and circles.

The warring children gathered around, pressing in. There was a strong smell of tobacco from the pouch. They watched, opened-mouthed, as Jack produced a curious long pipe with an acorn-shaped bowl. It was made of greenish-blue clay and decorated with feathers, beads and fur.

"This, my friends, is a Native American peace

pipe. Made by the Cherokee out of river clay smoked over a fire." He spoke directly to the Countess. "Whoever carries the peace pipe is allowed to pass through enemy territory out of respect. Even showing it is enough to stop a battle."

"Let me see!" said one cheeky little fellow.

Jack presented it to the scruffy little boy and bowed low. The little scamp made a great show of passing it around reverently.

The Countess laughed.

"Then the tribes share a peace pipe and the smoke from the pipe carries their prayers up to heaven," Jack said. "Perhaps you saw one on your American travels?"

"I did not visit a reservation," she said. "But our true leader de Valera is now a chief of the Chippewa Nation. His Indian name is 'Nay Nay Ong a Ba', which means 'Dressing Feather'."

"My Cherokee name is Wa Ya Udo — which means 'Wolf Brother'," Jack said with a yowl like a wolf.

"Can I have a smoke?" asked a little urchin.

"Don't be silly," Jack said. "Only grown-ups can. They're the ones who start the wars after all."

"Smoking is very bad for the lungs!" I wagged my finger at the boy who stuck out his tongue at me.

"You would be better off with a shotgun," Countess Markievicz said. "That's the only

147

language the Staters understand."

Before Jack could contradict her, I cut in: "Anto has a foot injury that needs attention. I need to give him some bandages."

But the Countess just whistled and laughed as the children capered about. "Jack, you are half-cracked if think you can bring peace with that!"

"And you are full-cracked if you think you can force the nation to follow you into a Republic down the barrel of a gun."

Jack had spoken lightly but the Countess frowned.

"So you are pro-Treaty?" she asked, steely now, like I'd seen her as she aimed at snipers on Sackville Street.

"I am pro common sense. I think we should all stand together. We should have tried passive resistance — non-violent protests, civil disobedience, demonstrations — like Gandhi is doing in India."

"But that means everybody has to be brave," said the Countess.

"And so they should if they want a new country," said Jack. "You start with a small group. Soon it would spread. Good behaviour is contagious."

"Founding a republic is not child's play," the Countess said.

"There won't be any children to live in it if they kill us all," said one brave little girl.

"Why don't de Valera and Collins have a boxing

match and the winner gets his way?" suggested one little fellow with gappy teeth and a snub nose.

"I say give children the vote!" said Jack. And he delighted them all again by producing coins from behind their ears. Then he produced a handful of tin soldiers from his pockets and began to juggle, tossing them in the air and nimbly catching them. He threw one to me. It was like one of the larger, sturdy ones that he'd painted green and customised to smuggle messages during the Rising.

"Still playing with soldiers, Jack?" I asked him as I threw it back.

"You never know when they might come in handy," he laughed. Then, finishing his juggling with a flourish, he vanished them all into thin air!

The children shouted, "*Jack for President! Vote for Jack!*"

The Countess smiled and held him fondly by the hand as if he was a little boy. "Dear brave Jack. Quite unique. I have lost so many of my brave Fianna boys. At least promise me you will look out for those who are still breathing."

He raised his right palm as if swearing an oath. "I will consider it a sacred duty."

The Countess's beautiful eyes filled with tears of gratitude. But my heart filled with dread. Because for Jack this had the power of a binding promise.

"Ah, promise me 'honour bright', as they say." She looked intently into his eyes.

"I promise." He got down on one knee and handed her the peace pipe. "Someday we should smoke this together. No woman needs it more."

"Oh Jack, you are a tonic!" She threw back her head in laughter. A rare glimpse of the sparkling lady she must have been before politics stole her heart.

The children ran around us whooping like 'Red Indians' as Jack performed more tricks for their amusement.

As we were leaving the Countess took me aside. "I have terrible rheumatic pains in the cold weather. If you ever have some powders, let me know."

I said I would prepare something for her.

Then she lowered her voice. "A group of Fianna who escaped from the Four Courts is hiding out in the Dublin and Wicklow Mountains. With Daly. Ballinascorney. The password is 'Marino Casino'. That's all I can tell you."

As we left the building girls and boys were playing a skipping game in the grand entrance.

"Vote, vote, vote for de Valera
In comes Collins at the door,
He will shoot a gun
And we'll have a bit of fun,
And we won't have the Treaty any more!
Vote, vote, vote for Michael Collins,
In comes de Valera at the door!

He will throw a bomb
And sing a victory song.
And we won't want the Free State any more!"

"Only a second ago they wanted you for president," I said to Jack. "Now look at them."

"At least they're not fighting," he said. "New ideas take time."

I told him what the Countess had said. We agreed to search for Anto in the mountains first thing the next morning.

However, as I was having my breakfast early in the morning, Jack sent me a note saying he had some other business with "the Big Fellow" — that is, Collins — to attend to.

I went to Ballinascorney by jaunting car, alone but for the driver who was a friend of Nancy's, a stooped silent man with calloused hands. I was annoyed. Jack had seemed so anxious to see Anto. I thought it must be something big that had taken him away. I worried too that if he was carrying tin soldiers about he was back smuggling messages.

The jaunting car took me out of the city, through the small villages of Rathfarnham and Tallaght.

Towards lunchtime we reached the wild and deserted foothills of the Dublin Mountains with just the odd dwelling place scattered here and there. We looked for the cottage of a man called Daly in the townland of Ballinascorney and were told it was further up the mountain in a desolate spot. The jaunting car left me then at the bottom of the mountain. It would wait for me there.

I climbed the steep track, cursing my heavy doctor's bag and the provisions May had given me in case I found Anto.

Daly, an old farmer in his sixties, was working in the hayfield. He was suspicious to see a young female medical student until I gave the codeword "Marino Casino". I was led into a barn, where under some bales of hay there was an underground dugout.

It was an earthen room about ten by twelve foot. Inside was a group of ragged dirty-faced youths huddled around a paraffin lamp, scratching themselves like dogs. They were shivering. Not just from the cold, I thought, but from fear. Mail sacks and piles of letters torn open were strewn around.

One grinned at me. "We liberated these from the post office. Got a fair sight of postal orders and all!"

"'Liberated' is a fine word for stealing," I said.

They laughed then, like naughty schoolboys.

I took out my medical bag and soon I was dealing with their minor injuries — septic wounds, torn muscles, lacerated feet. God love them, they had hardly a pair of shoes between them. And they were riddled with lice and scabies.

After about an hour there was a rustle outside. We all froze, straining our ears. They doused the lamp. We were in pitch black, creatures in a hole.

Then we heard someone whistling, "The Croppy Boy".

"It's our own."

Seconds later, the hay bale was pulled back and the hatch opened. We came out, blinking to adjust our eyes.

It was Anto and a humorous-looking Dublin boy with a long thin mouth, called Frank Sherwin.

"Men, there's an ass and cart outside loaded with groceries," said Anto.

Glad for something to do, they went outside and brought in crates filled with the tea, sugar, biscuits and provisions that Anto and Frank had "liberated" in town.

Anto was limping badly. He ignored me as if I wasn't there.

As they sorted the provisions, I stood right in front of him, forcing him to look at me. I told him Jack wanted to see him. Would help him get away to America if necessary.

"So why isn't he here to give the message himself?" Anto said, a challenge in his voice.

"He's on some other business."

"For that traitor Collins, I bet," he said.

I insisted on seeing his foot. He winced at the pain when he took off his boot. The smell was terrible. I put iodine on the seeping wound and began to bandage it up.

"You need to have this dressing changed regularly," I said. "If you get septicaemia you could die of toxic shock."

"Is Jack with us in the fight?" he asked me.

"You know Jack," I said. "He has his own ideas."

"Turned into a cushy Yank," he said. "And what did he actually do in the Rising, flittin' about those rooftops on his 'special mission'?"

"You know full well he was gathering the funds for the widows and orphans left after the Rising," I said. "But he also saved your life when you got shot delivering messages. Who do you think pulled you into the doorway where I found you in Crown Alley? Who made sure your family had milk and food when they were trapped in Henry Place as the British Troops closed in?"

He looked away. "And am I to be eternally grateful for that?"

He was silent and sullen while I finished bandaging his foot. He winced a few times as I handled him a bit more roughly than I intended. I bit my lip to suppress my temper. Anto could always wind me up like nobody else — pulling my pigtails, goading me.

"How do you know he's not a spy?" he asked. "Did he send you up here to betray our position?"

I bundled away my things in a sudden fit of temper. "You might as well call me a spy so!"

There was an angry crackle in the air between us.

I was riled. "Why did I bother staying in

prison all those months last year? I could have spilled the beans about hiding places, betrayed people working behind the scenes then! But nothing is ever good enough for you True Believers!"

The other boys looked at me like I was a madwoman.

I hurried out of the barn in such a state that I forgot my hat. I turned round and caught sight of Anto struggling to put on his boot. He looked so tired and helpless, I felt bad about my temper.

"I never got a chance to give the locket to your wife," I said. "She has gone to her people in Kerry to have the baby."

His face softened then and he came out with my hat. "In the heart of the Munster Republic. It's where they've taken the fight. That's where I'll be goin' too. I'm just waiting for the order."

"Anto. Please don't let us part with bad feeling between us. In this terrible war, we might be saying goodbye for the last time."

It was as if the wind had dropped during a storm. All the anger went out of him.

We shook hands, oddly formal.

"Tell Jack I'm in for the fight. No runnin' away to join the circus for me." He went back into the barn.

As I struggled down the steep, stony path, Frank the young fellow came after me with the donkey.

"Take it, miss. It will help you get down the mountain. Tie it up at the blackthorn tree at the bottom of the path. The farmer will go down for it later."

Such kind boys really. Hard to believe they are also now robbers and worse. As the donkey staggered down the hill with me on its back, doubts came crowding in.

What if Jack was a spy? He'd used me before to spy on the GPO in 1916 and then gave the information so the rebels could cut the telephone and telegraph cables. What if all this stuff about peace pipes and passive resistance was a cod? As the donkey stumbled down the mountain, I could only hope we weren't all headed for the bog.

Yours, always,

Molly

✺

Later that night, as I was getting ready for bed, my mom came in with a bag of French fries or chips as they call them here. We made chip sandwiches with buttered bread and watched some dumb gameshow on TV. But it was nice – just me and Mom, hanging out like we used to. I rattled on about Molly's letters and about Anto going south to the heart of the Civil War.

But I should have known she had a reason to spend time with me.

"Has your dad been in contact?" she asked me.

I told her about his letter inviting me to the States.

She looked really sad. "Of course, on my cleaner's wages I can't compete with that."

"It's okay, Mom, I don't want to go," I said quickly. But once I'd said it I realised I really did. Just to see the old place and I really missed my dad. He hadn't hugged me for the longest time. Maybe even to get to cuddle Floppy and see if she was holding her own with the Babbitt cats.

We both stared at the TV screen. Mom's face looked haggard and she ate the chips and bread mechanically.

"You remember Nora, my old friend from university?" she said then. "She's given up her old life in New York as an attorney and she's now a yoga teacher in Kerry. She's invited us to visit her."

"Gee, that's great," I said.

"We could take a short vacation maybe," she said. "You could check out some of those places in the letters. And if you liked it you could stay longer on your own."

I considered it. "I'd rather stay here for a while. Mal needs my help with it all."

"Of course," she said. "But we can think about it. It might be fun."

"Maybe just a few days," I said.

But, as I brushed my teeth, I did think about it. It sounded like Mom wanted to get rid of me. I really didn't want to get left behind in Kerry, just as stuff was getting interesting back here!

Chapter Fifteen

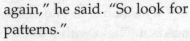

The next letter was a head-wrecker – a series of random numbers.

"Oh hell!" I exclaimed. "This is like the Enigma Code from World War II!"

But Mal surprised me again with his patient and persistent approach. He drew an alphabet wheel and a smaller number wheel.

"We can assume that the top line is 'Dear Sanjay' again," he said. "So look for patterns."

"Well, number 13 is 'e', I think. It's cropping up the most." I smiled. It was Open Sesame!

Mal adjusted the wheel and lined up e and 13. The whole pattern fell into place – Number 1 was "s" and 26, the last number, was "r". Easy when you know how!

"How on earth did she get the time!" I said. "I mean she was dashing off letters and then had to translate them into code!"

"They didn't have television then," Mal grinned. "Didn't Sanjay mention that luckily she and Jack used to do lots of codes and puzzles as children? I reckon she found it quite easy."

It was probably wise to be secretive, considering they were in a civil war.

We each took several pages. And then took turns typing it out on the clattery old typewriter. It took us the whole morning. I was glad of the distraction. I didn't want to think about my father's letter and my mother's proposal. But eventually the worries tumbled out.

"My mom is trying to pack me off to her friend in Kerry," I said. "She's pretending it's just for a few weeks, but actually I know she wants to get me from under her feet."

"My dad's trying to convince me to go the Gaeltacht in Cork. Those summer-holiday concentration camps where you learn Irish." He rolled his eyes. "Can you imagine me in the bog trying to talk Irish?"

"No. What are we going to do?"

"Concentrate," he said sternly, pointing at our work. "Let's see what happens to Molly, Jack and Anto."

August 1922

Dear Sanjay,

I am in County Cork in the thick of the Civil War. I know, out of the frying pan into the fire! But it's just as well because I desperately needed to come south. For not only Jack but Dan is caught up in the invasion of Cork by the Free State forces!

So you can see why I thought it was God's will when Doctor Dorothy asked me to bring her some necessary dispensary supplies down to Kilbrittain where she has a practice. It is a small parish, about thirty miles from Cork City, seven miles south of Bandon. She has rented the fine Harbour View House which is on the coast. It has a wonderful view of the sea. There is a grass garden and fields and cliffs nearby. The air is so bracing I wish I could bring Nancy here to cure her bronchitis. But instead I am once more in the thick of all the trouble.

Jack is still carrying on his secret business with Collins. He is keeping on the move because he is afraid that those who shot Boland saw him. But as soon as he heard from me that Anto was heading to Munster, he was anxious to be there too.

It's a guerilla war down here. Flying columns are going again, cars stopped, post offices raided. I hear the Republicans have even taken over the Port in Cork and are charging taxes from ships.

But I must confess it has been quite exciting for me. For Doctor Dorothy has insisted on teaching me to drive! She will be moving back to Dublin soon to take up a post at St. Ultan's Women's and Children's hospital. As it is, she makes frequent visits there to take clinics. I will cover for her while they find her replacement and during her frequent absences. She said it was important to be able to drive in case I needed it in an emergency.

She has an almost-new Ford, a black five-seater that she bought for £200 from some ladies in Bandon. It starts itself and has very good lights and a good hood, so I can keep very dry! Don't worry, I am very careful as I do not wish to smash up Dorothy's pride and joy. I have only once nearly bumped one cow when I was doing twenty-five miles an hour around a narrow corner on a boreen. You know how stupid cows are!

So let me tell you how Dan and Jack come to be in Cork. Dan's father, my Uncle Edward, finally got a job as a co-pilot on a ship, the cross-channel ferry *Arvonia* on the Dublin to Holyhead route. He signed up Dan as the cabin boy for a summer job. But, of all the ill luck, it was commandeered to take the Free State Army south to Cork in the first week of August!

Under no circumstances would my uncle have taken Dan straight into the heart of the war. But they only learned they were to transport not just supplies but a whole battalion of Free State troops when General Emmet Dalton turned up with hundreds of men! The Welsh crew was most reluctant. But you don't argue with a general with a gun.

Worse still, Jack was a stowaway on board with Dan's connivance! He hid the whole journey under the tarpaulin of a lifeboat. Thankfully most of the troops were too inexperienced and seasick to search the boat. Some of them spent the time dancing on the deck as a melodeon player perched on the 18-pounder gun. Dan said there were also some shady civilians on board, who he thought were spies.

As they came into Cork Harbour, on the 8th of August, the Captain, whose name was Roberts, advised General Emmet Dalton that there were mines laid in the Cork Harbour approaches and it was impossible to dock. But General Dalton held a gun to the Captain's head in case he tried to run the ship aground.

Dan was terrified but the Captain looked at Dalton coldly. "I am a professional. I will land the boat as I am paid to do."

They docked at the Dry Docks in Passage West, a port village about six miles south-east of Cork. My uncle managed to slip off the ship for a few hours and telephoned me at Doctor Dorothy's dispensary. I was given a message by the housekeeper. Could I come to the dock and take charge of Dan?

Doctor Dorothy drove me there. As we approached the harbour wall, I recognised the name of the ship. By the time we reached the dock, the soldiers had disembarked. They were proceeding into the centre of Cork City and fanning out to flush out the anti-Treaty resistance.

Sitting on a bollard on the dock was Dan. My uncle was busy filling out landing papers at the dockside offices of the Port authorities. Dan was quite shaken but it was more from seasickness than from his experiences.

Dan confessed to me about Jack being on board. He handed me a note. It was written in a childish code Jack and I devised as children. (It's very simple but somewhat laborious. You basically reverse the alphabet – so 'a' becomes 'z', 'b' is 'y' and so on.) Well, the note said he was carrying the peace pipe for the big C – Collins, of course. He was off to see DB – Dan Breen the notorious rebel – in Tipp, that's Tipperary – and then would catch up with Collins and possibly 'de big V' – de Valera – in Cork. He would get word to me in Cork to meet him. He asked me to use my local contacts to see where Anto was.

I wasn't happy about this one little bit. Cork was dangerous territory and Dan and I were lucky to have a quiet drive back with Doctor Dorothy to Kilbrittain. I didn't tell her about Jack's mission but asked her to put the word out about Anto.

Dan was actually thrilled to come to Kilbrittain. Doctor Dorothy dotes on him. She is about thirty and everyone around here calls her the "Doctoreen" meaning "the little doctor". She is a Protestant, went to school in England, but supports the Republicans in the split and is close to the Flying Columns. She is a brilliant doctor, a real live wire, and I learn a lot from her.

All day and night shadowy men arrived at the dispensary. We were also called out to tend the wounded in haybarns, remote cottages and dugouts. In hidden glens, down boreens, isolated godforsaken spots as armed cars prowled the countryside. But now they are hiding from their former friends in the Free State Army, not the British.

I was glad to have Dan staying with me. I love him so and we came through the War of Independence together. He has Jack's physical talent and is a brilliant footballer. But is more self-contained and careful. He is a great lad for running messages.

On the 12th of August he ran in when I was fixing a sling for a little girl. "Griffith's dropped dead!" he cried.

We were all shocked.

Doctor Dorothy immediately telephoned St. Vincent's hospital.

"It was a brain haemorrhage – probably brought on by stress," she told us then.

Collins was in Tralee town in Kerry, which the Free State has now reclaimed. He was rushing back to Dublin for the funeral.

I remembered Griffith's ashen face during the Battle of Dublin.

Shortly after the funeral we heard that Collins was coming back to the South of Ireland. It seemed crazy to come back to the area where the anti- Treaty 'Irregulars' were strongest.

A few days later Doctor Dorothy came back from a visit to a dugout and told me that all the top-ranking Republicans including de Valera, Erskine Childers, Liam Deasy and the commander Liam Lynch were meeting in the area. She knew a sentry who was guarding the remote cottage where they had gathered.

"He told me those boys mean to continue the fight."

"More bullet wounds and shrapnel," I said. "More shattered bones and shook nerves."

On the 22nd of August Doctor Dorothy had to go back to Dublin again and she asked me to cover her dispensary clinic. She gave me a list of the medicines to dispense and told me to refer any difficult cases to Dr. Welply in Bandon.

It was a busy day. There were two children with croup, a woman with leg ulcers and several labourers with bad backs.

Dan spent most of the morning kicking ball in the garden. But he got talking to some of the patients and learned that Collins was touring the nearby countryside.

"Yerra, 'tis a grand tour," one toothless old fellow told

him. "He left Cork at six o'clock in the morning. And he's been gallivanting to Bandon and all the way west."

"Will he go back by Bandon?" Dan asked excitedly. "It's only seven miles up the road, Molly. I could walk it."

"Don't be silly, Dan," I told him. "They might just drive through."

"He's sure to stop at Sam's Cross beyond Clonakilty," the old fellow said. "His brother Johnny lives nearby and his cousin Michael O'Brien owns the pub there. It's called The 4 All's. You'll get a laugh when you see why."

Well, that was that. Dan was determined to meet his old boss and he pestered me so much I agreed to drive him.

In truth, I was happy for any excuse to go for a drive. And I might get a chance to ask Collins how Jack was. Though it was unlikely he'd tell me much if it was a secret mission!

So, early afternoon, we set off for Sam's Cross which was about twenty-five miles away. It was a beautiful day with a slight chill in it, the sun shining on the ripening fields of corn dotted among the green fields where cattle grazed. A few white clouds scudded through a wide blue sky.

We reached Sam's Cross around four thirty and we were in luck. We saw a crowd gathered around a public house at the crossroads. I parked the car and we got out. There was a curious sign over the doorway and I soon found out why the pub was called "The 4 All's". It had a picture of a king exclaiming "I rule all" beside one of a soldier stating, "I fight for all". Next was an image of a bishop saying, "I pray for all". And finally, an annoyed-looking farmer declaring, "Ah! but I pay for all". It did indeed make me smile!

I knew we weren't far from the farmhouse where Collins

grew up – Woodfield, which was burnt to the ground in 1921 by the Tans.

It was quite an entourage. Four army vehicles were parked there. A Crossley Tender, a dark grey Rolls Royce armoured car, a buttery yellow open-topped tourer and a motorcycle. Dan gathered round the vehicles with a group of small boys, fascinated. A hard-faced officer stood guard and stopped the children piling over the fancy vehicles. Dan recognised him and pulled back in fright.

"That's Joe Dolan from the Squad," he said to me. "He has a terrible temper."

People were spilling out the door of the pub. All were in good spirits, like it was a party. Collins' cousin Michael was handing out free pints of creamy black stout to everyone.

"Come and try the Clonakilty Wrastler," he laughed. "The strongest drink in Ireland!"

Collins stood among them like the Sun King, all brass buttons and polished belt. Shaking hands with people, slapping backs and laughing. The Big Fellow.

Dan cut through the crowd and reached him. I followed. Up close, I was shocked to see General Collins' appearance. When I first met him in the GPO in 1916, he was a fresh-faced young man. But now that he was the boss, he had aged about ten years. His face was waxy, bloated and tired, with dark circles under his eyes. But he brightened when he set eyes on us.

"Mother of God, Dan, aren't you a sight for sore eyes!" He clapped his former messenger on the shoulder and then called over to me, "Molly, come here to me!"

I went up to him and he hugged me. His voice sounded thick with a cold, although he hid it well under his boyish high spirits.

"Molly, I am going to see that Dr. St. John Gogarty of yours to do something about my aches and pains!"

"Your stomach is troubling you again?" I asked. Dr. Gogarty had told me it was an old complaint of his.

"Yes, but I also have a dull pain here." He put his hand to the small of his back.

"You might have a kidney infection. And your cold sounds very bad and your throat is rasping. It might be pleurisy, an inflammation of the lungs. But I'd need to examine you."

"Now, don't be fussing. I'll be fine," he laughed, lifting his glass.

"You must have it seen to as soon as possible. But you have more immediate risks to your health." I glanced about anxiously. "There are a lot of Republicans in this neck of the woods."

"You're such a worrier, Molly." Then he turned to a woman about his own age, who he introduced as his cousin May and said, "At least no man will kill me in this, my part of Ireland."

"Some might disagree with you," I said. "De Valera and Dan Breen for example."

"I hear the Long Fellow, de Valera, is knocking around these parts." He swept his hand as though swatting a fly. "I'm touring the garrisons and hoping to bring the boys on the other side around. If not, I will have to get rough with them. I'm going to put an end to this bloody civil war as soon as possible."

"There might be fellas in the bushes waitin' to take a potshot at yeh," an old farmer said. "Especially if you go back the way yeh came."

"Sure haven't I got my men with me!" Collins said, gesturing to his Free State Army officers, all-imposing in their fine tailored uniforms and brown leggings. With all the drinking, they were beginning to become high-spirited.

More people arrived.

"Our new uncrowned King of Ireland!" an ancient old woman said. "Do you think you could get the bridge mended that was blown up near Leap?" She touched his jacket as if he were a holy man.

He bent his head to hers and said he'd see what he could do. He glanced over to me as if to say, 'See, I am loved here'.

I was just about to ask him about Jack when two of his men cut in and said they needed to speak to him urgently about their plans for the rest of the day. They walked a little way around the side of the pub and huddled in a spirited discussion but I couldn't hear what they were saying.

I walked over to the cars and asked one of the drivers where they were going.

He gave me a sly smile. "Looks like we'll be going back to Cork. Unless we get lost again on these terrible backroads. A stretch of the main road from Macroom to Bandon was blown up this morning and we had to come through some godforsaken place called Beál na mBláth where we had to ask directions. We'll go back the way we came. If we ever get out of here."

I looked over at Collin's entourage of vehicles. If they kept stopping off for refreshments their journey would take some time.

I wanted to call in to see Dr. Welply in Bandon, so after a cup of tea we left.

Just outside Bandon I slowed down to let a bread cart

turn into the road. The driver pulled up and jumped out, overjoyed to see me. It was Mickey Joe, an old fellow who was one of Dorothy's patients and a great man for the gossip.

"Molly! I was trying to find Dr Welply but he's out on house calls. A farmer I passed by on my rounds asked me to get the doctor for his wife who's having a baby. It's not her time but he said she's in a great lather as it's her first. It's in Gortnahague, in the valley of Beál na mBláth. Just up a boreen as the crow flies. Her husband wants to set her mind at rest."

That was where Collins' driver said they might be heading, if they made it out of the pub!

"I can show you the way after I drop off the 'ould bread cart at the bakery," Mickey Joe offered.

We set off together with Mickey Joe hunched in the passenger seat beside me, one of those old men as crooked as hillside trees who seem to go on forever despite all their aches and pains. He had brought us a welcome bag of fresh bread rolls and was all ears when we told him we'd met Collins.

"Yerra, Collins is being too cocky," he said, tutting as we drove along the winding country road. "People down here don't like the Big Fellow as much as he thinks. There were a lot of lads creeping around the hedgerows all day, and it wasn't pitchforks they were carrying."

I shuddered, thinking of all the pairs of eyes – and guns – behind every bush and hedge.

"Do you think Collins is really trying to make peace?" I asked him.

He made a sour face like he was gargling vinegar. "Maybe.

But it won't be easy. A lot of the fighters who escaped from Limerick are hiding here. They don't like these Dublin Free State boys, coming in lording it over us."

We passed several farmhouses, anxious people peeping out through windows. Then a woman on a bicycle flagged us down, saying she recognised Doctor Dorothy's car. She whispered urgently to me that her injured son was hiding out in a dugout under her barn. His leg wound was festering – would I take a look? I hesitated but Mickey Joe thought we'd be fine timewise as we weren't far from our destination. When she heard where we were headed, she told us we'd be better off taking the back route anyway as there were some roadblocks further ahead.

So cycling and pushing the bike ahead of us on the mucky stretches, she led us a good bit off the main road. I was terrified that we'd get stuck in a rut. Luckily we reached her farmhouse safely. It was a large stone building with several outhouses and a big cattle barn.

We found the young fellow sleeping in his dugout under the hay bales, curled up like a child. I cleaned out his wound. Told his mother to use iodine, or whiskey if that ran out, and to change the dressing every day.

She thanked me with a gift of cheese. "I think he's had enough of fighting," she confided in me. "But they don't know how to stop. 'Tis a terrible state of affairs altogether!"

She directed us to continue up the boreen, keep by the ditch, then turn right and come down to the cross of five roads at Long's pub.

We continued on our journey. The hedgerows were bursting with colour in the afternoon sun. We whipped past yellow furze and black sloe berries in the trees. I concentrated on the bendy road that corkscrewed around the slanting fields before me, terrified I'd plunge us into the ditch.

There were so many boreens, Mickey Joe got confused. "Yerra, I didn't come this way before," he said.

Then, more by luck than design, we came upon Long's public house at the junction of the five roads. So we went to ask for directions. The engine was also overheating and I needed some water.

We asked a serving girl, who was sweeping outside, for some water. When she opened the door to fetch a pitcher, I caught a glimpse of grim fellows inside. Voices rising then fading. A scrape of metal on a stone floor. Like the barrel of a rifle. Instinctively I pulled back.

We went back to the car.

The publican came out with the pitcher of water.

Mickey Joe told me he was called Denny the Dane, but didn't know why. Only that he was anti-Treaty to his core.

Denny was wary. But he relaxed when he saw the car and I said I was covering for the "Doctoreen" from Kilbrittain. She was trusted by all the local Republican brigades. He told us to travel just a little way along the road and look out for a track hidden behind a clump of trees. That way led down to the farm we were seeking.

"Did you see anything strange coming up the Newceston to Crookstown road?" he asked.

I explained we had cut up through the back roads. This seemed to satisfy him.

"You'd best be movin' on," he said, pointing to the road that led south at the crossroads.

We took the rutted track towards Gortnahague, so

narrow that hawthorn bushes scraped the side of the car. About four hundred yards down the road, we reached a little whitewashed cottage. Cattle were lowing in the nearby barn.

As we drew near, we heard the awful moaning of a woman mingling with the sound of the cattle.

We called out and knocked.

"Oh, Mother of God, come in!"

We entered the cottage.

The woman, named Deirdre, was on her own. She wasn't much older than me and was sprawled in the bed, heavy with child.

"Himself is gone out to bring home the cows," she said. "I thought I was just nervous. I'm not due for another few weeks yet. But something is happening! Please don't leave me!"

It was soon clear she was having contractions, signs that the baby was coming. I felt her stomach. The baby was the wrong way round. A possible breech birth, bottom out first. Very dangerous for the mother and for the baby.

I'd learned that you could sometimes turn the babies naturally with a special technique. I asked Mickey Joe and Dan to boil water and, taking a deep breath, I began to work, placing my hands in the right position to encourage the baby to do a somersault in the womb. But nothing budged. The baby stubbornly stayed in the same position.

At least my presence seemed to reassure Deirdre, which was something. But she was in a lot of pain. I tried to keep her comfortable, get her to drink water. Then I applied cold compresses to her ribs and hot compresses to her pelvic area. I tried again to gently encourage the baby into the right position, feeling the life pulsing under my hand. I kept this up at intervals, trying hard not to show my frustration.

Towards early evening a mist rolled in through the green fields and there was a light drizzle. Deirdre began to fret that her husband hadn't come back home with the cattle for milking. Mickey Joe went off to see where he was. Dan stayed to tend the fire.

Deirdre was struggling with exhaustion.

Suddenly around a quarter past seven, at sunset, shots barked out in the evening, then sounds like a mowing machine cutting hay. It was so foggy you couldn't see beyond the cattle shed outside.

"What in heaven? At this hour?" Deirdre said, her brow beaded with sweat.

My heart sank. I knew it was machine-gun fire raking through the air.

"*Dan, stay in!*" I shouted.

I helped Deirdre count her contractions as shots rang out. The gaps were closing now. More volleys of shots.

The baby was still the wrong way round. I was almost crying in despair, terrified that I'd lose both mother and baby. And all the time, the roar of gunfire. I wished I could drive her to Cork but the journey would be too much for her. And there was little chance we'd make it with the shooting and murky fog outside.

About half an hour later, the noise subsided.

Deirdre was now very weak from her labour. But then something miraculous happened. I applied pressure again to her belly, concentrating with all my might. The baby had turned round!

My relief was enormous.

I wondered what had happened to Mickey Joe and her husband and prayed they were safe.

Eventually I lost track of time. Then at last we heard the cows lowing outside and shortly afterwards Mickey Joe came in with her husband, both looking like they'd seen a ghost.

Shaunie, the man of the house, went to where his wife was sleeping fitfully.

Mickey Joe just stood there in front of me, tears running down his face.

"It's the Chief," he said. "Collins. He's been shot in an ambush!"

"But we just saw him earlier today!" I said. The news was like a body blow. "Can I go to help?"

"Too late. They drove off straight away," said Mickey Joe. "It took me a while to find Shaunie — he was up in the high field herding the cows to bring them down for milking. I helped him. And then the shooting started! We hid in a ditch."

Shaunie poured a large whiskey which he held out to Mickey Joe, then poured another for himself.

"Collins and his men came through here this morning," he said. "So the rebels decided to set up an ambush in case he came back. Didn't I see the anti-Treaty boys preparing it about noon when I was in the field with a cow that's due to calf. A fella came up with a four-wheel cart and horse from Bandon Brewery to collect empty bottles from Long's pub. They commandeered his vehicle and ordered him to drive it to a bend in the road. They used it to block the main road towards Cork and sent him packing."

"We missed it by coming up to you by a different road," I said. "That must be why Denny the Dane sent us up that terrible boreen."

Shaunie told us how mines containing sticks of gelignite were also buried in the road on the Bandon approach. Men were coming and going at their posts behind ditches and banks all day.

"Judging by their movements, I think they were going to call off the ambush when the mist rolled in at around seven o'clock," he said. "They didn't think Collins would be coming through after all."

"'Twas then I met you in the field," Mickey Joe butted in, "but wouldn't you know, Collins' lot did come through just as their enemies were calling it a day. The light was failing. The Republican fellows saw their chance. Some of them ran back and took cover behind a gap in a dry-stone wall."

"When the Free State convoy reached the part of the road with steep banks on both sides, they were ambushed. The rebels raked them with machine-gun and rifle fire." Shaunie put his head in his hands. "'Twas terrible."

His hands were shaking and I told him to sit, but he was restless, prowling around with nervous energy.

Mickey Joe took up the story. "We heard someone from Collin's convoy shout out 'Drive like hell!' But Collins, it must have been, roared, 'Stop! Jump out and we'll fight them!' They leapt from the car and took cover behind a rising mud bank on the left-hand side of the road. Collins and his four comrades were sheltered in the bank. But the Republicans, about twelve of them, were in a higher position on their left side and firing from behind the boreen fence."

"There was a hail of fire at the Republican fellas," continued Shaunie, his hands shaking. "Shure didn't the sloe berries of the blackthorn fall on their faces like snowfall in winter. Then there was a lull in the fighting after about twenty minutes and we crept closer. Collins jumped to his feet and went behind the armoured car, followed by Dalton, I think it was. The Republicans had started to creep away, thinking they were beat. Collins saw them turning tail and shouted out, 'Come on, boys, there they are running up the road!' He ran around a bend a good few yards up the road. The next thing was we heard more gunshot."

He paused, struggling to keep control.

"Collins must have been out in the open," he continued. "And someone further up the bank must have been a crack shot. Next thing I heard was one of Collins comrades call out 'Where's the Big Fellow?' Dalton shouted out 'He's around the corner!' They went after him – around the curve of the bank."

He paused again and took a long drink.

Mickey Joe took up the story.

"We heard someone shout out. 'The Chief is hit!' There was a lot of shouting. It was hard to make out what was happening then. But they must have dragged Collins back to the vehicles around the bend, while still being fired at. I think one of the other fellows was hit because someone else shouted out. The fight had only lasted half an hour even though it seemed longer."

Shaunie and Mickey Joe had stayed out in the field, cowering in the ditch, too terrified to move. Eventually they made their way down by Tullys' farm with the cows.

As they were passing the farmhouse they met one of Tullys' farmhands who was returning from a drink at Long's Bar. He was pumped up with all the news, Mickey Joe said, almost in hysterics.

"'This will be a night to be remembered,' he kept saying. 'The night that Michael Collins got killed.'"

"So he's dead!" I gasped.

"Far as we know, God rest his soul," said Mickey Joe. "He was shot in the head."

"Who did it?" Dan asked, tears coursing down his face.

"Rory the farmhand said he got talkin' to Denny the Dane," Shaunie said. "There was about twelve in the ambush, Denny told him. They swore an oath of secrecy never to reveal who fired the fatal shot. They'll all have gone into hiding now, for fear of reprisals."

My mind went blank. I couldn't think about any of this.

The woman Deirdre was crying out in her pain. But the baby had turned, she was young and strong and glad to have her husband back.

Around three in the morning, she gave birth. A baby boy – head first, thank God.

I slept then, fitfully, for two hours. I could hear Dan sobbing in the little cot they had pulled out from under my bed for him.

Towards dawn I rose from the bed, and went outside. Blindly I walked through the fields, where the swirling mist still hung. Over uneven ground, steep banks, scrambled up rocks on my hands and knees.

About one mile south from the tiny village of Béal na mBláth, no more than a rough cottage and the pub, I came to a bend in the road. There was a stream on the right-hand side with trees and scrub growth, a marshy field beyond. There was a mud bank about two feet high on that side of the road, a dry stone wall on the other and behind that rising ground. And a lot of blood spattered on the side of the earthen road.

I knelt down and said a prayer. For Michael Collins' soul and for the madness to stop. Then I heard a high mournful sound.

Across the way up a steep bank, a figure in the dawn mist was dancing and singing an unearthly song.

I took out my field glasses. It was like a gauzy figure glimpsed in a dream. He was wearing feathers in his blond hair as he shouted out a lament, the saddest keening I'd ever heard.

Jack!

I ran to him. "Jack, you mad fool!" I called out as I scrambled up the bank. "You'll get yourself killed!"

He continued his lament. When he finished, he lay down on the dew-covered ground.

"It's a native American song for souls passing over," he said. "The Chief is dead."

About five yards away something with brilliant green gems glinted on a stone amidst sparkling diamonds. It was dazzling like a constellation of stars fallen to earth.

Jack got calmly to his feet, bent down on one knee, the firing position, and raised a revolver. I stopped dead in my tracks as he uncocked the muzzle and took aim.

"*Jack, no!*" I cried out as he pulled the trigger. He fired several times.

The retort of the bullets rang out and echoed down the valley. Stones flew up in the air and shattered fragments rained down like hailstone. But he wasn't shooting at a person hiding behind the rock.

He was firing at the glittering necklace encrusted with jewels! Emeralds and diamonds. The one that had survived the Russian Revolution. That he had smuggled from America, rescued from the sea. Only to be destroyed on a lonely Irish road.

"Why have you destroyed that beautiful necklace?" I cried.

"Collins was right," he said. "It's bloodstained." He fired a few more shots and threw the gun away. "The last chance for a swift end to this madness died with Collins. They will be baying for blood in revenge."

I sobbed as I tried to gather up the shards of emerald, the scattered diamonds, broken bits of silver. "No, Jack. You mustn't destroy beautiful things. You must make it right." I clambered around on my hands and knees, sobbing hysterically, grabbing at twisted metal and broken gemstones. Some were still intact. Others were like needles. My hands began to bleed.

"Help me," I pleaded with him. "Help me!"

He dropped to his hands and knees and coolly searched the ground.

"The grass is so green here, the emeralds almost disappear," he said softly as he combed the blades of grass.

Soon, we had made a little pile. One of the tiers was almost intact. But I kept searching, searching for the damaged parts. He tried to lift me up and comfort me with a hug. But I beat his chest.

"No. Save all the necklace!"

He must have been moved by my anguish as he joined me again, hunting near and far for any overlooked twisted fragments of the necklace. We put the remains in the leather bag with the peace pipe.

He picked out a diamond-shaped piece from the necklace, set with a beautiful, unearthly emerald amidst a cluster of diamonds. It had a drop emerald pendant, so clear it seemed almost alive. He carefully detached the pendant and pushed both pieces of the necklace inside one of his tin soldiers. He parcelled up the soldier carefully in one of the little chamois-leather cloths he always used to wrap his larger soldiers in, and secured it with a thong.

He picked up the gun and went down to the roadside, to where the blood had been spilt. Using the barrel of the gun, he made a deep hole and buried the little parcel.

"A grave-marker. Poor old Michael Collins. His stepping stone of the Treaty has become his tombstone," he said. "I cannot bury the hatchet but I have buried these healing gems."

The sun was rising now and burning off the early morning mist.

"Someday perhaps these stones will speak. What will they speak of Molly – peace or war?"

"What mystical nonsense are you speaking now, Jack? No one will ever think to look for Russian Crown Jewels here!"

"I will leave a clue. Let me think. Boland said his Crown Jewels weren't to be given back until Ireland becomes a Republic." He paused, gazing at the rising sun as if for inspiration. "But how about when Ireland is at peace north and south of the border?"

"That might never happen," I shook my head.

"Then I will pass the clue on to the next generation. Or our children's children," he said.

"We must go – people will come along now it's first light," I said.

We walked over the hill. I asked him what he was doing

here, how he'd arrived. Of course, he was cagey as usual.

"That particular mission has died with Collins. But the message of peace hasn't," he said.

"Where will you go now?"

"I have a motor bike over the hill. I will look for Anto. I still have my promise to the Countess to keep. He is somewhere between here and Kerry. Will you help me?"

I hesitated. "I have to get Dan back to his father in Cork."

"Don't decide yet – think about it and I'll contact you in a few days."

I looked him square in the eye. "Jack, I love you. But you've gone mad. There's a war on. They'll laugh at you with your peace pipe and red feathers. Ireland has changed now. Changed utterly. There's an ugly, twisted genie unleashed from the bottle. They'll lock you up at best, shoot you dead at worst."

"Let them laugh," he said. "It's better than tears."

And with that he was away again like the will o' the wisp he is.

The farmer's wife, young Deirdre, has insisted the baby will be christened Michael. I hope he has a long and boring life.

My uncle was assigned to pilot the Classic, the ship that took the body back to Dublin. Dan stayed with poor dead Collins the whole voyage.

Dorothy went to the funeral. Four hundred thousand people turned up. People are taking comfort from the fact he died as he had lived. I heard George Bernard Shaw wrote to Collins' sister Hannie, who Dan and I stayed with in London during the Treaty negotiations, and told her not to mourn but to "hang up your brightest colours and be glad he did not die in a snuffy bed of a trumpery cough, weakened by old age".

Republican prisoner Tom Barry said that in Kilmainham Gaol he saw about 800 other Republican prisoners, men Collins had locked up, fall to their knees to pray for his soul.

And two days after his death, workmen began repairing the bridge at Leap village, fulfilling the promise he made to the old lady he met in Cork on the last day of his life.

At least one good piece of news. Clery's took advantage of the legions at his funeral to re-open in Sackville Street. May got a job as a shop girl. I hope she can get me a staff discount next time I need stockings.

I am making plans now to go further south. You might not hear from me for a while,

Your Irish friend,

Always,

Molly

⊷⊶

Mal telephoned his cousin immediately.

"We know how some of the jewels were damaged." He told her what we had discovered.

Rachel said she would pass the information on to her boyfriend.

Mal and I hurried to our incident room.

"Do you think that jewel could still be buried at Béal na mBláth?" I asked.

He said with a glint in his eye, "There's only one way to find out."

"Well, I suppose I could agree to my mother's proposal to visit Nora," I suggested.

Mal grimaced. "Okay, I'll have to volunteer to go to the Gaeltacht. At least that way we'd be in the same part of the country. Maybe we could take a day trip."

"But even if we got there it would be a needle in a haystack," I said. "We don't have much to go on."

"We could try a metal detector around the site where Collins was killed?" Then he went to the dusty tarpaulin he'd told me covered some of his stuff and pulled it off.

Underneath was a large rucksack. He unzipped it. Inside was a rickety contraption, a bit like a small vacuum cleaner, with dials and counters and a handle that folded up.

"This is my dad's old metal detector. Officially it's for his excavation work when he is on mineral exploration. But when I was a little kid I used to search for buried treasure on Malahide beach when we visited my gran during the holidays."

I laughed suddenly at the image of Mal with the metal detector, creeping around stones and bushes in his hoodie.

"It would help if we translated the rest of the letters," he continued. "At least we have a clue to the code they might have used for one of the letters. The simplest trick in the book: the back-to-front alphabet."

"Maybe Patrick's Geek Squad could help speed up the process," I said.

Mal smiled. "Miss Ava, you never give up. I'm still thinking about it."

"It's time for acting now," I said. "Providing of course we can get ourselves to Belly Blah or whatever it's called in County Cork!"

Chapter Sixteen

Our plan fell into place very easily, like it was fate.

My mom was overjoyed that I'd agreed to visit Nora in Killarney, in Kerry. She agreed that Mal could come too. Mal said his father had agreed to let him come with us on condition he went to the Gaeltacht later on.

I'd met Nora a couple of times in the States when she was a hotshot attorney in New York until she decided to go back home and give her life a makeover. I really liked her, even if she was always going on about veganism and chakras and energy fields and stuff.

So we were all set to go away for the weekend. But a couple of days before, my mother came home from her cleaning job and said we'd have to postpone. The cleaning crew was booked for a new weekend contract and if she didn't turn up she'd lose her job.

I was so bitterly disappointed I burst into big snotty tears.

"Oh, darling, I'm so sorry," she said, handing me a handkerchief. "But I can't help it."

"But I was so looking forward to it!" I said. "This time last year I was at summer camp with Cleeter!"

Her face fell and I thought she might cry. I felt bad immediately.

"Oh, Mom, I didn't mean it," I said. "I don't mind being here with you, truly."

But the damage was done. She walked into her bedroom and closed the door.

I slumped down on the sofa, feeling like a total creep.

But ten minutes later Mom came out, trying to smile brightly.

"You could travel down on your own with Mal," she said. "If I put you on the train, Nora could meet you. You're getting older. I need to let you have some responsibility."

So she discussed it with Nora on the phone. Who, from what I could hear, was all for the idea.

"She's nearly thirteen," I heard my mother say. "I suppose I should trust her."

Then she lowered her voice. I heard her say something about "baby" and "break-up" and guessed she was moaning about me being a baby after their split. That hurt, considering how she'd turned into a human crying-machine. But I figured at least she was doing something about it now.

I looked at the map and saw that Killarney was about an hour away from Béal na mBláth. So I went in and asked Mom if Nora would agree to give us a tour. Nora really liked the idea. I couldn't believe how everything was falling into place again.

The day before we left, Mal and I made another trip to the attic to check out that scuzzy old leather pouch. Maybe it was Jack's bag for the peace pipe which now we knew had once also held the jewels.

It was about the size of a medium packet of cornflakes, filthy with age and falling apart. The Native American markings must have had symbolic meanings. We did loads of stuff on their culture and stuff in the States. Like as if it was going to make up for killing them all.

Mal thought it might be deerskin. I touched it. I could almost feel Jack goofing around and taking out his peace pipe. The bottom and side were sewn with a red-leather thong which had become unravelled over the years. We searched but couldn't find any trace of a peace pipe in the trunk.

Then I decided to turn the pouch inside out. Just because I'm that kind of girl.

Inside, there was a drawing on the leather. Clear and strong, etched in red.

"Mal, look, it's some kind of map!"

"We have to open it out," he said.

So he unravelled the stitching around the sides. It was easy. The stitching was falling apart.

He stretched it out. Etched on the inside of the leather was a map of Ireland, with little crosses and numbers on it. Also, down the side, there was a series of numbers and letters.

"Maybe this was the clue Jack said he'd leave for his children when he met Molly at Béal na mBláth," I said.

Mal went down to his room and came back with a detailed atlas of Ireland. "I used to be in the Venture Scouts," he mumbled.

"Wow! A metal detector and a Boy Scout. I'm seeing a whole other side to you, Mal," I teased.

He ignored me – just scrutinised the map and the drawing.

I looked at the list of numbers and letters:

1. BnamB – 082222
2. YL – 082622
3. K – 030623
4. BS – 030723
5. CB – 030823
6. OCD – 031723
7. PD – 031723

Mal pointed to the cross marked Number 1 in West Cork. "That's Béal na mBláth, marking where Michael Collins died," he said. "And that corresponds to Number 1. with the letters 'BnamB' on the list. I'm not sure what the longer numbers are."

"I bet the first one is marking where Jack hid the emeralds in the tin soldier," I said. "Maybe the others are where he hid the rest of the necklace in the order he did it?"

"Woah! Let's take this slowly. The numbers are in sequence," he pointed out. "But that's not the date of Collins' death."

I squinted at it. "It is actually. But written in the American way. The month goes first and then the day. Jack must have picked up the habit in the States."

Mal's eyes lit up. "So we just need to find out what happened on those other dates."

It had been a few days since we'd visited the library.

We put the dates into the computer with the keywords "Irish Civil War". It was hard not to whoop when we saw the dates really did correspond to something. Even if they were really sad things.

"26th August 1922 – Yellow Lane, Whitehall. Two young Fianna men were picked up by Free Staters and murdered as a reprisal for Collins' death," Mal said.

Then Knocknagoshel – Five Free State soldiers blown up. Ballyseedy – a massacre of Republican prisoners, nine dead – and another five at Countess Bridge in Kerry.

We hit a blank on OCD and PD, which were somewhere in Dublin and corresponded to St. Patrick's Day 1923. There was no killing on that day.

"Apart from the last two, which are a puzzle, it looks like Jack recorded all these atrocities," Mal said. "The question is why."

"I'm guessing he hid a jewel in each place?"

"Hopefully the letters will give us more information and something about OCD and PD," Mal said.

"And even quicker if we get some help," I mumbled.

But Mal ignored me and we went back to the attic. He took no notice of me and just concentrated on the job in hand. I was sore at him but soon I was absorbed in the task of translating the next letter, which was dated soon after the last one. We worked on it for a couple of hours. It was simple – the backwards alphabet code. But I wouldn't talk to him and insisted on doing all the typing myself. Mal didn't seem to care much and ignored me back.

Stalemate.

5th September 1922

Dear Sanjay,

Just as I thought Jack and I were going south, he hightailed it back to Dublin! But I soon guessed why. Ireland was on a knife-edge after Collins' death though Mulcahy, the new General, tried to calm everyone's nerves by saying there should be no reprisals.

Yet within days, as the body of Michael Collins lay in state in City Hall, as shoppers went in for some bargains in Clery's and the world's press hailed Collins as a major statesman, a terrible act of revenge took place.

Free State forces picked up two Fianna boys and drove them to Yellow Lane in Whitehall, North Dublin. I was very busy and only read about it in the paper a few days after Collins funeral.

Nineteen-year-old Seán Cole and twenty-one-year-old Alf Colley were officers of the Fianna youth organization which had taken the anti-Treaty side. There were witnesses but that didn't stop the killers.

The newspapers reported that soon after 6pm a group of children and young people playing on Yellow Lane were surprised when a large Ford car came to a sharp halt. There were five or six men inside – Cole and Colley and their abductors. The two boys were forced out of the car while the crowd was held back at gunpoint. One of the Free Staters tried to open a gate to a field but it was locked.

The two young men were heard to cry out, "But what is it for?"

Cole and Colley were placed with their backs to the gate, and killed with revolver shots to the body and head. Their killers then drove away from the scene.

Sanjay, this senseless reprisal is the worst thing that could have happened.

I am very afraid,

Yours always,

Molly

❧

The terrible murders made me feel bad about a petty row with Mal. So I asked if we could be friends again. He smiled and gave me a high five. We went straight to the library to find out more about the murders.

"It says there's a memorial to the boys. Yellow Lane is now called Yellow Road and it's in Whitehall," I said. "Do you think Jack hid something there?"

"That's just up the road! Come on," he said. "There's only one way to find out."

So, next thing, we'd collected his old collapsible metal detector, in the rucksack, and a spade. Soon we were on our way on the couple of rickety bikes that we'd found in the attic, out to Yellow Road in Whitehall. It was a long quiet side road on an estate of small terraced houses with a large park nearby. Mal told me they were called "Corporation" houses as they'd been built by the local council.

We found the memorial easily enough. It was a small granite stone with the names of Cole and Colley, marking the spot, set into a wall. The street was all concrete and so were many of the gardens. But by a huge stroke of luck the storm drain in the road beside the memorial was being worked on. There was a sign saying "DANGER, PUBLIC WORKS" and a flimsy orange barrier. Quite a large hole had already been dug.

I was a bag of nerves just standing there.

"Just look like we are meant to be here," Mal said, all relaxed.

I felt like a right fool as Mal set up the metal detector.

"Glad to see you're going to finish that shore," an old lady called as she passed by. We nodded in agreement. She didn't notice we were rather young for a road crew! Or my look of bewilderment. Mal explained "shore" meant "drain" in Ireland.

Other passersby gave us some funny looks. But Mal was fairly expert at assembling the detector and familiar with all the knobs and dials. He put the earphones on so he could hear any pulses when the machine detected metal under the earth.

We stepped over the flimsy low barrier and set to work. Mal jumped into the hole and I handed him the detector.

It was our lucky day! Mal ran the sensor over the bottom of the hole and the dials leapt about as if it had found the goblet of fire from *Harry Potter* and a *Star Wars* light sabre at the same time!

We felt revved up.

"So we dig?" I asked. "What if someone sees us?"

Mal looked around. "We'll worry about that when it happens. Let's just get on with it."

A few women went by with pushchairs but once their toddlers didn't fall in they couldn't have cared less.

I passed Mal the spade.

Then a nosy old-timer buttonholed us.

"You're supposed to have a licence to use them yokes."

"Yokes" in Ireland could mean anything at all.

Mal put the earphones back on, pretending he couldn't hear him. But I gave Mr. Nosy a long yarn about our school project for archaeology.

He stuck his nosy old head in the hole and then gave an amused shrug. "You never know! You could find the Crown Jewels."

"Ha ha," I said. "You'll read all about it in the papers."

"I get all my news online, darlin'," he said as he ambled off.

But as soon as the old guy was out of sight Mal got back to work. I jumped down to help him. Soon the spade hit something.

It was a filthy little chamois-leather parcel bound in a leather thong, like a miniature mummy. Mal shook it and it rattled faintly.

I wanted to examine it but Mal thrust it into his pocket. "Not here."

We took turns shovelling the dirt back in and, with Mal wrangling the gear like a Chinese acrobat, cycled to the nearby park. We were both mucky, like a pair of gravediggers.

We rolled the bikes inside and left them on the grass. Then, in the shelter of a tree, we huddled together and Mal took out the chamois-leather package. He pulled out a pocketknife and cut the thong. Inside was a tin soldier. It was about three inches high, with a diameter of about an inch and a half. It stood on a little base and was crudely painted in green. It was like some of the larger ones in the trunk in the attic.

Mal examined it. At the bottom was a little spring lock. He poked at it with the pocketknife and the bottom came away.

It was hollow and inside was a slightly dented silver setting with an emerald gemstone! There were tiny diamonds studded around it, shining like small stars in the Milky Way. It was much better quality than the one we'd found in the chimney. But it didn't have a drop-stone.

For a nanosecond we were too excited to speak. Then we cheered like the Yankees had won the World Series!

"We're going to be rich! We're going to be famous!" I cried.

Mal, who was facing me, stared off into the distance like a dog that had caught a scent. He put his hand on my shoulder and then stopped dead. "We're going to be in trouble!"

I turned around to look. On a bench a good bit away from us, and half hidden by a copse of trees, was a man in a baseball cap. He was taking photos with a long-lens camera in our direction.

I screwed up my eyes.

"It's that guy again. Gee, couldn't he try a bit harder to disguise himself? He just tries a new hat."

Mal was still as a deer surprised in a forest. "We need to get our find to Patrick's lab." He turned his back to the Russian and slid the piece of necklace inside the zipped top pocket of his jeans.

"It will have to be today, as we're leaving for Kerry in the morning," I said.

His voice dropped to a whisper. "We don't want him to follow us."

"We can get away from him on the bikes."

"Shush, I'm thinking. It's better if we split up. You take charge of the spade and the detector. And I'll head into town. I know Dublin better than you. Try to get to the library to find out more about the next date."

"What? With the metal detector and a shovel, looking like a gravedigger!" I was grumpy, wondering how I was going to manage.

"Leave the shovel outside and ask to leave the metal detector at the desk. Come on, Ava! Use your initiative." Mal was losing patience with me.

He deftly took the metal detector apart and put it in its rucksack. It weighed a ton!

I glanced anxiously over at the "Russian spy" who

was peering at his mobile phone.

"We're going to play a game," said Mal. "Just act normal."

"That's really hard for me – particularly when I'm covered in mud." I said, trying to lighten the mood.

"Pretend we're having an argument," he murmured.

"But everyone will look!" I protested.

"Only for a second. Then they'll all look away in embarrassment. Trust me."

Mal returned the tin soldier to the chamois covering and tied it back up. Then he dropped the little packet on the ground and fell down on his knees.

He shouted at me real loud. *"Now look what you've done, you stupid eejit!"*

I was taken aback at first but then got into the spirit and gave as good as I got.

"Back off, loser!" I roared.

"Muppet!"

"Dork!"

He was right. People glanced over for a second. Then, when they saw it was some kids goofing around, they ignored us. I sure hope Mal never goes over to the Dark Side because he would make a great criminal mastermind.

Mal picked up the soldier and stood up.

"I want to see it!" I cried, trying to reach it.

He ran off a little way, launched the soldier into the air and then shouted at me. *"Catch!"*

I lunged and grabbed it and threw it back. We hollered and shouted. Mal worked us close to the Russian, throw by throw. Before he knew it, we were only a few yards away.

The Russian looked at his watch, then took off and dashed out of the park. I got a good look at him. The same pockmarked skin like a golf ball, the same deep scar down his left cheek. His head was massive. As he hurried off, he had a funny waddling gait, like a duck. And that distinctive smell of allspice lingered in the air.

"Quick, swop jackets and hats!" said Mal, ducking in behind the bushes.

I put on his hoodie. It smelt of wood smoke and pizza. He put on my cap and denim jacket which was way too small for him, the arms dangling just below his elbows. But if you looked quickly and carelessly or you were half blind, you might be fooled.

"You leave now on the bike and try to make sure he sees you," Mal said. "Then I'll head off in the other direction."

"What if he attacks me?" I asked.

"He won't. It's me he's interested in," he said, jumping on his bike.

"I don't suppose you'll tell me why."

"Someday. Now hurry and be a decoy or he'll make himself scarce. He doesn't want us to see that he's spying on us."

"See you tomorrow. If I'm still alive."

He gave me his laughing smile and sped off. Mal was enjoying this more than I was.

I heaved the rucksack onto my back. It weighed a ton! Then I found it impossible to mount my bike as I was lumbered with the spade as well. The only way I could manage was to balance the spade lengthways on the handlebars and the saddle and push the bike slowly along. I grumbled to myself. James Bond never had to make a getaway with a metal detector and a spade. Dressed in a ratty, smelly hoodie three sizes too big!

Outside there was no sign of the Russian but, as I was struggling with the bike on the wide footpath, he pulled up alongside in a car. He was driving a boring blue Nissan Micra. I had been hoping for a silver Merc with smoked bulletproof windows. Maybe even a gun turret. It made me think maybe Mal and I were bigging this guy up too much. He wasn't nearly flashy enough to be a proper villain. I couldn't tell if he clocked me as the sun was shining on his windscreen. But I hugged close to the railings. He drove away. Not fast or slow. Normal, like a dad. As he drove off I memorised the number plates – XOX 54J – just in case.

I took a shortcut down a narrow back lane and turned round to check. The Nissan Micra had doubled backed and was parking on the street. Oh no! Mal was onto something.

The Russian got out of his vehicle and crossed the street to the lane. He was headed in my direction. My heart skipped a beat.

I hid the shovel behind a low garden wall and, groaning with the weight of the metal detector on my back, struggled onto the bike and took off like a scalded cat. I pedalled through the lane and onto the main road as if I was in the Olympics. I managed to freewheel for about a hundred yards. When I saw the Number 14 bus,

I abandoned the bicycle at a bike rack and ran clumsily towards the bus stop, my heart knocking against my ribcage. The hood kept falling over my eyes. But I was the decoy so I couldn't pull it back. Nor could I see if he was following me.

I plunged into the centre of the bus queue, earning glares and muttered abuse. It was agony waiting for the world's slowest old ladies to climb onto the bus. They each had a thousand plastic bags and not one of them could find their bus pass. *Aaaaaaah!* I nearly gnawed my hand off in frustration.

I was next in the queue to pay when I realised my emergency money was in my denim jacket. I was about to jump out when a big crowd of teenagers surged on. There was so much laughter and kerfuffle with passes and change, the driver didn't notice one more hooded mid-sized human slink down the back. I looked out the back window but there was no sign of my Russian pursuer. Oh man! That was the most exercise I'd had since I came here.

The bus took me near the library and I got off as instructed by Master Spy Mal. I hoped he had gotten safely into town. I almost kissed the floor when I reached the library. Its cool interior and low buzz of activity made it a place of sanctuary. I caught my breath.

In the library, Betty and her posse of seniors were in the side room having their book-group session. When Karen the librarian saw me, the worried expression on her face made me think I was more beat up than I realised.

"Are you all right?"

I laughed through my wheezing. I took a few breaths through my inhaler.

"You wouldn't believe it if I told you!" I gasped.

I was very happy to dump the rucksack with Karen at the desk.

I stayed for about half an hour but I was too light-headed to concentrate on finding out anything about the next date. I gave up after the words on the screen started to swim before my eyes.

When I felt a bit better, I went back to retrieve the spade, which was just where I'd abandoned it in the laneway. Likewise the bike was still at the bike rack – too beat up for anyone to bother stealing it. There was no sign of the Russian. I began to relax and breathe normally again.

I went back home, really excited to see if Mal had been successful in his mission. But when I went to knock on his door, I heard the sound of raised voices. For a full ten horrific seconds I thought it might be the Russian come to cut his throat, but then I heard a door slam and then silence, and I guessed it was probably his mysterious dad back from overseas.

I went back to my room. Half an hour later, a note was pushed under my door.

"Hi, Pipsqueak, won't be joining you in Kerry. But you're in the right place to check out Knocknagoshel, the Ballyseedy Massacre and Countess Bridge in Killarney.

See you soon enough. All sorted with the cuz.

P.S. I had a chance to look up some stuff on my dad's computer when he wasn't looking. I crosschecked the other initials but I'm still a bit stumped on OCD and PD, the last ones. But will figure it out. My dad got a bit mad at me for using his computer, which is why I'm being packed off to the 'Jailtacht' next week. So sorry if you heard the shouting.".

Heck no! I felt hot tears prickle the back of my eyes when I read Mal wouldn't be able to come. And then he was disappearing off to speak Irish for the rest of the summer. Even if it wasn't his fault, I felt abandoned by my one friend. Now the trip would have to be postponed because Mom wouldn't let me travel on my own.

But, as I started to unpack my overnight bag, I caught sight of Robbie Robin pecking at his crumbs and thought of another plan. There was no reason I couldn't go. If I was already on the train and it looked like Mal was just late, I reckoned there was a chance my mom would leave me there.

I didn't sleep well, worrying that my act of rebellion would get found out. And somewhere in the depths of the night with the creepy branch banging on the window, I wondered why Mal's dad was so angry about him being on the computer.

Chapter seventeen

Pulling the wool over my mom's eyes was easier than I expected. When we got to the train, I told her to stop fussing over me like I was a baby, that Mal would meet me in the carriage. I made her say goodbye on the platform.

"Okay, honey, but you'll always be my baby." She smiled, fighting back the tears as she hugged me. I could feel her eyes burning into my back as I walked to the train.

I sank down low in the seat and slumped against the window as the train pulled out of the station. I left my bag on the seat beside me, praying nobody would sit down. A gaggle of noisy kids with a sweaty mother got on but she ushered them further down the carriage. Then a couple of nuns minced by, their necks stuck out like two geese. I was nervous. I'd never travelled so far on my own. But I sure didn't want to share my journey with a noisy kid, or a holy sister. Or a Russian with terrible aftershave and bad skin.

I was really sore at Mal. I wasn't sure I believed all that stuff about him having to go straight to Cork. I bet he just didn't want to be seen with a kid. I closed my eyes tight shut so nobody would disturb me.

"Is this seat taken?"

My heart jumped and my eyes flew open at the familiar gruff tones.

And there he was, large as life, stowing the metal detector rucksack in the overhead luggage shelf.

"I thought you weren't allowed to come," I said.

"Dad had a change of heart. Besides, someone has to keep an eye on you."

He sat down and tapped his knapsack.

"It's the lab analysis. We're on track."

"Yeah, whatever," I said.

"I only just made this train on time, you dope. I thought you'd be a bit happy to see me."

We sat in silence for a bit. Then a drinks trolley trundled by and Mal made a big show of buying me a lemonade and a chocolate bar as if I was his kid sister or something.

The chocolate bar cheered me up. He fished out a file from his knapsack.

"I sat up all night doing this. The Geek Squad are going to send the next instalments to your Ava and Floppie email. Hopefully your mother's friend will let us log on to her computer or we can go to an internet café. You are right. We need to move things along. Friends again?"

"Pinky promise," I said, offering him my little finger. I was touched that he had listened to me about getting help.

He linked his finger with mine. "Pinkie promise, kiddo."

I took the letter that Mal had typed up and read it as the Irish countryside whizzed by, a pure green streak.

November 1922

Dear Sanjay,

Months here in the south and no luck tracking Anto. The Civil War is turning even nastier. General Mulcahy met de Valera but they couldn't agree terms of a truce. The worse thing is the Free State government has an official policy of execution for bearing arms against them.

How can those who mourned their comrades executed in 1916 be so stupid and callous? Do they not realise they will be creating more martyrs for future conflicts? Even the hardline British leader Churchill said that grass would grow over a battlefield but never over a scaffold.

Jack still hasn't explained why he disappeared back off to Dublin recently. I'm sure it had something to do with the murder of those young Fianna lads that he knew as a boy. He was very mysterious about it and would only say, "The stones will speak." That is what he had said to me when he buried the jewels at Béal na mBláth.

It looks like nobody will be prosecuted, though several people saw Free State soldiers with trench coats over their uniforms.

Have to dash now as have been asked to attend to casualties in Kerry. It is the badlands, lots of rebel units hiding out. But I should be safe as a medic.

Always,
Molly

❧❧❧

"We were right about the Yellow Lane murders!" I exclaimed. "Imagine us finding the tin soldier and the jewels after all this time."

"It's Jack giving us a message from the grave, isn't it?" Mal said.

"The stones will speak," I said.

The next letter that Mal had done was very long and covered December 1922 and January 1923, written at intervals. It picked up on Molly's time in Kerry. It felt special that we were on our way there.

❧❧❧

December 1922

Dear Sanjay,
All over Kerry, little rough wooden crosses are springing up. Some not even bearing a name. They mark forsaken spots on the roads. Places where dead bodies were found in ditches. This is the war of brothers.

It is heartbreaking to see them in such wild and beautiful countryside. Soft lapping lakes are surrounded by lush tropical rhododendrons. Peaty boglands and stark blue-black mountains run to sandy beaches and inlets from the ocean. The air is so pure you could almost get drunk on it. Anto should be writing poetry here. Not creeping around hedges and squelching in bogs with a gun, murder in his heart.

We heard from one Republican unit that there was a red-haired Dublin man with a limp hiding out near Knocknagoshel about 20 miles north of Killarney. So we went there and were given lodgings by a farming family called O'Connor who were grateful for the money. Their son was with the Republicans as it turned out.

The cottage is large and comfortable but still the conditions are poor. I was asked to treat their uncle, a poor soul called "The Yankee," who lives in an adjoining barn. He is called that because he previously lived for three months in the United States.

He is half crippled with rheumatism. He told me some of the cures he has tried. Stinging nettles, porter, drinking yarrow tea and some fiendish device invented by a charlatan called Dr. McCaura who has advertised his cures in the newspapers and claimed he has healed the King of Prussia, if you please!

Of course, the real reason the poor old Yankee has rheumatism is that he sleeps in a damp room with a mud floor and water running in runnels down from the thatch roof. There is no ceiling, just old sacks nailed into the rafters.

It's a small farm with only eleven cows. But they have treated us with bounty. They killed a goose for supper on the first night. We had a fine soup for lunch a couple of days later. On enquiry I was told it was boiled curlew – a wading bird common in the fields. I nearly spat it back out! They give us the cow's milk. The family use goat's milk to colour their tea. The children go to school with a sod of turf for the teacher's fire.

One night Seamus, the rebel, came home. A slight bookish fellow wearing glasses, he had left Teacher Training college to fight for Ireland. Now he was on the run.

"We have nothing to lose," he told me. "That's why we keep fighting. The Free State is still part of the British Empire. Half a slave is still a slave."

This country is so impenetrable that fighters could hide out here for a long time. In vain, Jack and I have travelled around remote farms and mountain valleys in search of Anto. Jack sometimes disappears on missions of his own. He is very secretive about what he is up to.

But rumours came back to me as a steady stream of patients started turning up when they heard I was there. Children with the croup, farmers with festering cuts, old people crippled with arthritis. I heard of one raid on a cache of Thompson machine guns up near Listowel belonging to the Republicans. The firing mechanisms were destroyed and the ammunition removed but roses were placed in each of the gun barrels.

"Some brave craythur is trying to put a stop to them all fightin'," said an old woman, stooped from carrying wood.

I suspected it was Jack placed the roses in the guns.

There was another story of Free State ammunition in a barracks in Castlemaine being replaced by potatoes. And then a madman dressed as a 'Red Injun' standing on horseback in Milltown holding some kind of weird pipe.

January 1923

With Jack's absences getting longer, I became frantic. I had not seen him in over three weeks. Now I was looking not just for Anto but for him! I didn't know what to do. So I stayed in the area, hoping for a lead.

One night a motor car called to the house. It had been commandeered by a rebel friend of Seamus, called Con. They wanted me to go with them to help an injured comrade outside Tralee. Their normal doctor was being watched. A Republican fighter had shot a Free State soldier but his own leg was injured in the ricochet. It was a tense drive to the coast about twenty miles away. We barely spoke.

Then I was led over bogs and around rocky outcrops near a narrow inlet of the sea.

"What happened?" I asked Con.

"He – Mattie – shot dead the medical orderly who came out of Tralee on his bicycle but the bullet ricocheted and got his own leg," he said. "He came to me for help."

My heart filled with cold hate. Shooting at medics was a step too far.

I stopped dead. "And will you shoot me too, Con? I've a good mind to leave now. Or maybe your friends will just shoot me in the back!"

I turned around.

"Wisha, Molly, we won't hurt you," he said. "Please . . . Mattie's my best friend."

I relented and we carried on in the bitter rain.

We reached the dugout in a tumbledown cottage near the sea. I could see the rebel's leg was shattered. I automatically cleaned his wound, fished out the pieces of shrapnel. I gave thanks for the promise I had to make as a medical student to care for all. I could so easily have let him bleed to death. He cried out in pain. But my heart was still hardened. The worst part was when he held my hand in his fevered sleep. I administered morphine for the pain. Beads of sweat stood out on his forehead.

I gritted my teeth as I changed his bandage.

Towards morning his fever broke. His comrades decided to move on. They would take him to a hideout. They were very grateful to me for saving his life. So I asked them if they knew of Anto or Jack the Cat. But they shook their heads and went outside to bring in a makeshift stretcher they had put together.

Suddenly, as I tended to my patient, he grasped my hand.

His voice was weak and he could barely breathe the words out. "Jack the Cat. He was taken prisoner. Then we were told to take him away . . . me and the other Dublin fella that's with us . . ."

"Do you mean Anto, with the limp?"

He nodded his head.

"Where did you take him?" I urged.

His breath was ragged in his chest. "Where he wouldn't be found. Out in the bog. Near the valley of the Cloch Liatha . . . the fairy glen . . . no one goes there." His eyes stared out at me. "I left them there . . . haven't reported back to the boss . . . because of you . . . I won't tell where they are . . ."

"He's still alive? Is he a hostage?"

Mattie's voice was very faint. "I don't know . . . Anto might . . . better go quick . . ."

Then his comrades came back in with the stretcher and he fell silent, seeming to lapse back into semi-consciousness.

Jack a prisoner! I was beside myself with worry and couldn't wait to leave. Was it possible Jack was taken prisoner for destroying weapons? By Anto, his best friend? I didn't know if that was good or bad. What was he going to do with him in the bog? Shoot him? Was that what they were planning? "Where he wouldn't be found," Mattie had said. I shuddered. I couldn't bear to think about it.

It took a whole morning to get back. Con had arranged for me to be driven back to the farmhouse in a van that was going around the creameries.

I ran straight to the Yankee to ask about the fairy glen. He was applying ointment to his poor knobbled hands and I helped him.

"Yerra, Clocha Liath means 'grey stones' in Irish," he exclaimed. "It's a fairy fort! No one around here will go near it. They'd be more afraid of the Little People than the Staters!"

But Anto wouldn't be afraid, I thought. Nor Jack.

The young boy of the house, Kieran, agreed to take me for a shilling and carry a bag of food for the journey. As we set off, the farmer Dermot ran out and thrust a horseshoe into my hand.

"'Tis to protect you against their glamour, the way they do be makin' yeh see things," he said. "They don't like iron. Hold it up if they appear."

I promised I would.

We crossed over fields covered by gorse and blackthorn trees and surrounded by stone walls and hedges. Good cover for men on the run. All day we passed by boglands where turf was cut, in neat rectangles. Kieran pointed out grouse and snipe and woodcock. The pink mountain heather was green at this time of year.

The mountain was cut by several streams, all tumbling down rocks and over gravel beds, surrounded by bare willow trees waving in the breeze. We surprised a flock of wild duck that took flight like arrows. We crossed over another mountain with a stony path that cut through a ridge.

Finally, after carefully picking our way through a bog blooming with withered bog cotton late in the afternoon, we came to a remote flat valley. An empty space with the wind whistling through.

Large grey stones, the remains of what was once a stone fort, were scattered all around. Standing out among the grey flagstones was a sturdy old stone tower house, the top jagged and broken off. Tumbledown stone walls were completely covered in stunted yellow furze bushes and thorny briars. There were bent hazel trees dotted here and there. It must have been an ancient hill fort once, then a medieval castle but to the locals it was a sacred site of the Little People – the fairies who could do you good or ill. To enter it could mean enchantment or death.

Kieran, who had been growing in uneasiness as we approached the Fairy Fort, was now shivering in fear. "You can't go in. Them Little People will get you!"

"Nonsense," I said.

The boy shrank back.

"I'll go in," I said. "But please wait for me for a little bit. I'm not sure I could find my way home."

I felt sorry for him and gave him an extra shilling to console him. But as soon as my back was turned he ran, stumbling at first, then at full pelt, dropping the bag of food.

I picked up the bag and shoved it into my doctor's bag. Cursing him under my breath, I willed myself to be brave. In truth, my own hands were shaking in fear. I went onward, tripped over a rock, and fell forward awkwardly, gashing my hand. I was more shocked than hurt. I righted myself, then headed towards the stone tower, breathing hard now.

The old tower house was quite wide up close and several storeys high. There was a rough staircase, the stones worn and mossy with age, which snaked up one wall on the outside of the building. My curiosity overcame my nervousness. I intended to see if there was a vantage point where I could view the surrounding countryside.

Leaving my medicine bag tucked behind a rock, I mounted the staircase. I crept forward on the tips of my toes, afraid of making a sound. After about twenty steps up the slippery flagstone steps I came to a sturdy wooden door studded with nails in an archway in the wall. I pushed it in before I had time to think. I climbed through and found myself in a large hall. At the far end, there was another stone archway. I crossed the floor and saw there was a flight of steps leading to the next floor. The roof had caved in here and the stairway was open to the skies above, so I could see where I was going. I walked up and the broad flagstones led to another wooden door that was rotting on its elaborate iron hinges

As I drew nearer, there was the clang of raised voices. A shout. A curse. A bang. I froze and hunched down beside the half-rotten door. There was a gap in the wood, wide enough for me to see through.

I could see a large window across the room on the other side of the door. A sudden shaft of light flooded the room.

Through the crack, I saw figures swaying.

In the corner was Jack, standing but chained to the wall, his hands behind his back, his legs manacled. Brandishing a silver handgun at him was Anto.

"You're just a coward, Jack the so-called Cat. You don't even fire guns. All this talk of peace – it's because you're yellow." Anto spat the words.

"If you say so, Anto. Just put down the gun now and I'll disappear forever." Jack's voice, strong and measured.

"No chance. Not after the mess you've made. They know it's you who destroyed the Thompson guns. Just admit you're a Free State spy. Tell me who sent you. I have to . . . prove to them I'm not a spy myself."

"I'm not a spy."

"You're a fool. You were never a true believer, Jack. You just copied me and then it was all jumping off rooftops, showing off to the leaders. Getting all cushy with the bosses . . ."

I needed a plan fast. But my legs had turned to jelly. My brain wouldn't connect.

Anto cocked the gun and took a step closer to Jack. "Your lot were always lordin' it over me, thought you were a cut above. My mother skivvyin' for you . . ."

I clenched my fists. How dare he insult our parents! My good kindhearted mother who had devoted her life to helping people in the slums.

". . . and Molly, playin' at being a doctor. Kiddin' herself she's as good as a man."

I was shocked. And so was Jack.

"Take that back, you fool! Molly saved your life. Risked her neck and her only twelve!"

Anto laughed, a bitter grating sound. "For what though? So you can look down on me forever! I know you laughed at my poems. Jeered at my ambitions. But your kind won't always rule over the poor people. That's why I won't give up." His finger was poised on the trigger.

"Go on then, shoot me if you're so brave," said Jack.

I was glued to the spot in fear. I knew I had to act but didn't know what to do. Fear lurched up my throat.

I cast around for a weapon, a stick or a stone. But there was nothing.

Anto took a step nearer Jack. But he hesitated. This woke me from my trance. I tried to push the door further open but it was stuck. I opened my mouth to cry out but my throat was constricted. I couldn't make my tongue move.

"Come closer," said Jack, almost like an encouragement, still towering over his friend. "Make it easier on yourself."

Anto took a step closer.

"Look me in the eye." Jack had that laughing lilt in his voice.

"I will shoot you if it will keep you away from her," said Anto.

I couldn't stand by any longer. With an almighty heave, I pushed open the door.

"Jack, Anto, stop it!" I hurtled into the room.

A startled Anto swung round with the gun. Jack saw his chance. He head-butted Anto hard, then while he was dazed charged at him with his shoulder, rattling his chains. Anto lurched to one side and the gun flew out of his hand, clattering to the floor. I dashed forward and grabbed it.

"Molly, look out!" Jack cried out.

Anto came towards me to grab the gun. I fired a shot into

the floor, close enough to his feet to give him a shock. He sprang back and I was flung back by the recoil.

"Listen to me. Give me that gun!" Anto hissed.

"No, you listen!" I shouted, raising the muzzle. "I'm tired of your boys' games. Your silly quarrels like you're both still children. Both sides are insane. We'll have to work this out like grown-ups. Get you away from this madness. Go to America maybe."

Anto laughed again, mocking me. "Only cowards run away. And you saw what happened to Collins when he thought he could put us down."

"Watch him, Molly!" Jack shouted and rattled his chains.

Anto brazenly took a few steps even closer. My hands were shaking.

"Give me the gun," he said levelly. "I have work to do. There are at least two bullets left to kill enemies of the Republic."

My hands shook so badly I could barely hold the weapon, but I forced myself to spring the clasp of the gun.

I tried to take the bullets out of the cylinder.

"Molly, he's going to –" Jack shouted out.

Anto struck out and wrenched the gun from my hand. We wrestled. But he was stronger than me. He jostled me roughly to the ground and I went careening towards the wall. He recocked the gun and, laughing, aimed it first at Jack and then at me.

"Don't move!" he shouted.

"Go on then, take the coward's way out," I said, forcing myself to stand. "Killing comes easy to you since you could even kill your own brother in cold blood."

I saw the blood drain from his face.

"That sniper at the Four Courts. Remember?" I said. "You

were so keen to prove yourself. Well, you did. That was Jemsie. I was there. So was May. But she doesn't know it was you."

"You're lying," he said.

"I saw the trick you pulled with the cap, pretending you'd been hit. Jemsie fell for it."

He froze then. His face had the stunned look of someone who'd been slapped.

A short barking sound escaped from him. Then an unearthly cry of anguish. The gun hung limp in his hands. This time I didn't hesitate. I leaped forward and grabbed it. I removed the bullets, flinging them out the window, leaving the gun on the sill.

He gave me a stricken look. "You have hurt me more than a bullet would."

He ran towards the high arched window and scooped up the unloaded gun. Then he scrambled up to the sill and leapt out. I clambered up after him and looked down, afraid of what I might see. Considering the drop, he was lucky to be staggering to his feet. The ground was littered with rocks but very boggy in between and he'd had a soft landing. Still, it was a miracle that he was able to get up. I watched him reeling down the valley to God knows where.

"*No, the truth has hurt you, Anto! The truth!*" I shouted after him, my words snatched by the wind.

I climbed back down.

"He's all right," I told Jack. "He's gone off down the valley."

Jack was slumped down onto his haunches. He nodded his head towards another corner of the room. "The keys are over there."

I settled my nerves and retrieved a bunch of keys, then

opened the locks. Jack rubbed his wrists and stamped his feet to get the circulation going.

His hand was bleeding. I went back outside for my medicine bag and bandaged his wound.

He told me what had happened. After a few of his "escapades" as he called them, Anto was suspected of being in cahoots with him. Then he was taken prisoner. To prove his loyalty, Anto was told to question him, shoot him and bury him where he wouldn't be found. Mattie was sent along to witness that Anto really killed Jack and didn't just let him go for old time's sake. And in case Jack lived up to his reputation and got away.

But Mattie became jumpy. He went off somewhere, telling Anto to get on with the job and that he would be back shortly.

A sudden breeze made us shiver.

"Maybe Mattie just got spooked by the whole situation and the eeriness of the place," Jack said thoughtfully.

I told Jack that Mattie had senselessly shot dead a medical orderly, how he himself had sustained a ricochet and I had reluctantly treated him.

"Even though he should recover, we may never know what he was up to, or if he intended to come back here," I said.

Jack looked shocked. "Why did he shoot the orderly?"

"A nervous young fellow with a gun – who knows what he was thinking."

Jack shook his head, puzzled. "Well, in any case, Anto couldn't shoot me. "I'll give him that."

"You're not really a spy, are you?" I asked as I secured the bandage.

He gave me a hurt look. "You too, Molly?"

I had cut him to the quick.

"Please forgive me!" I cried.

He smiled. "Of course! You've saved at least two of my nine lives!"

We shared what little food I had – the brown soda bread and a flask of tea. But both of us were too tired to move. I was in shock, I think.

We set off down the mountain towards dawn. We agreed that I would go back to the O'Connor family. Hopefully, he could hide out in their barn. I urged him to think about returning to Dublin where he might be safer. But I knew better than to press him.

I looked out over the bog at the darkest hour before dawn. I saw pinpricks of lights moving, hovering in the air. I called Jack over. It was coming nearer, a yellow ghostly light.

"Could it be a raiding platoon come to get us?"

Jack smiled. "It's foxfire – phosphorescent light from the bog."

I laughed. "Of course! It's caused by decayed mushrooms faintly glowing in the dark. How silly of me!"

"Lucky for me, Anto and Mattie thought it was the fairies. It unsettled both of them, made it harder for them to shoot me in cold blood."

I was beginning to wonder whether I had been too harsh on Mattie. Maybe he'd been so spooked by the "fairies" that he'd shot the orderly by mistake? I prayed that he wouldn't betray us now.

We picked a path down by the stream.

"Why do you think Anto hates us so much?" I asked. "After all we have done for his family. Nancy scrubbed our floors but we love her."

"This long war has made him bitter," said Jack. "Deep down he knows he is fighting a lost cause. He's hurt inside."

I thought of how we visited Nancy every Easter morning with our gifts of eggs, sweets and money.

"But why he is he so angry at us? We were always kind," I said.

Jack looked thoughtful. "He's just lashing out at the injustice of the world. He resents that our family and others like us have more opportunities."

"Well, I've blown any chance of persuading him to go to America where he could have a fresh start." I bit my lip. "He'll never look me in the eye again since I'm the one who revealed to him that he killed his own brother. I should never have broken my own vow to keep it secret."

"You did the right thing," he said. "It brought him to his senses."

"Do you think he would have shot us?" I asked, half afraid of the answer.

"Maybe out of panic . . . but I don't believe so. Did you not see the way he was trying to work himself up to kill me? But he couldn't."

This gave me a little comfort. "Where will you go now, Jack?"

"I have made a vow to rescue him."

"But to Countess Markievicz? She's one of them! Was it she he asked you to keep away from?"

He coloured then. My mind reeled back. I saw the unearthly blue of a sapphire necklace glowing against May's white skin. A look between them.

"It's May!"

"I love her, Molly."

219

"But why hide it from me? I love her too."

He laughed then. With happiness. "I needed to make sure she felt the same. I think I loved her since I was a boy."

"But you've been in the US for six years," I said.

"During Easter Week, I dropped the milk to them all through the fighting. She used to wait for me. I'm not much of a writer but we've kept in touch while I've been away."

I shook my head. "And I always thought I noticed everything! I understand now why you were so desperate to get back."

When I asked him if May's sapphire necklace was a Russian Crown Jewel, he just smiled his mysterious smile.

Exhausted, we slept for a few hours before setting off.

It was a chilly but fine morning, a pale sun shining through the mist. My bones, cold and stiff from sleeping on a stone floor, began to heat up. I scanned the horizon and, as the mist rolled away, I thought I could make out a crossroads in the distance to the east. We had passed that way on our journey up the mountain. But Anto could be anywhere. No doubt he would head deeper into Republican territory. It would be a miracle if all of us came out of this alive.

We came to the open bog. In the cold light of morning now, it felt more exposed. On the other side were a few large boulders and a stand of trees.

Jack scanned the countryside. It had rained during the night so the ground was soggier than on my outward journey.

We picked our way over the bog like wading birds, careful where we put our feet. We were both relieved to reach the other side where there was firmer ground.

We continued down the foothill of the mountain.

By the ragged hazel trees there was a sudden movement behind a boulder. Jack tensed like a stag surprised. He swept his arm down and picked up a sharp rock.

"Get down behind me, Molly," he hissed.

But there wasn't time. For there before us was Anto, blood streaming from his shoulder, holding a gun.

He faced us, angry and tense. His eyes were red in his grimy face.

"No!" I cried out as Anto fired.

Jack sprang forward, rock in hand.

But Anto had aimed the gun away into the copse of trees. A crow rose, cawing loudly at the interruption. Jack's rock tumbled from his hand. The gun slipped from Anto's grasp. Within seconds Jack had placed his arms around his friend's shoulders, comforting him.

"I didn't know it was my own brother," Anto heaved as he tried to fight back the tears. Then, he was crying like a small boy.

Jack held him for what seemed like a long time.

I fished around and found a handkerchief and offered it to Anto.

He took it, collected himself and pulled away.

From beyond the valley came the bark of gunfire, the sound of car engines roaring down a road.

"There's a Free State patrol nearby," I said.

"If I go back, I can tell them I did it and buried you in the bog. But you must leave here immediately and never be seen again," Anto said to Jack.

"But if anyone sees or catches me, they'll know you lied," said Jack. "You'll be a dead man walking."

"I'm that anyway," said Anto. He winced in pain and clutched his shoulder. "I hurt my shoulder when I rolled to break my fall."

"It's a wonder you didn't break your neck, given the height you jumped from the window, you eejit!" I said.

He gave me a bleak smile.

"I'll need to see to that injury," I said.

He stripped off his filthy jacket and shirt. His shoulder was dislocated and his arm badly gashed from banging into rocks when he fell. He gasped in pain when I pushed his shoulder back into place and he bit his lip as I applied iodine to the wounds, then bandaged them. He had a lump coming up on his head where Jack had headbutted him.

Jack shivered and began to falter. He had managed well up until now but was weak from being tied up for so long. He coughed, like he was coming down with something. Anto too was struggling, his old foot injury bothering him.

Neither was in any state to go on for much longer.

"You both need to rest for at least a couple of days," I told Anto.

Jack scanned the horizon with my field glasses. "There's a lot of activity along the lanes and by-roads. It's not safe. We could both be picked up."

"There are some other hideouts but I can't go there with Jack," said Anto.

"Go back to the fairy glen while I work out how to get you out," I said. "The locals are still too nervous to go there and nobody knows yet that I've seen you. Do your comrades know you took Jack to the Tower House?"

Anto shook his head. "No. Only that we came – Mattie and me – with Jack to this part of the country. Where there is a deep bog to . . ." He looked away.

We knew he meant a deep bog to dump the body.

I told him what had happened to Mattie, how he had killed the orderly. But that he wouldn't talk – for now. Anto looked relieved for a second but then frowned.

Anto and Jack looked at each other, faces wary. Both were wondering if they could still trust each other. Then Jack smiled and placed Anto's jacket around his shoulders. Anto winced as it rested lightly on his injury. He murmured a quick thanks, looking away in embarrassment.

"We won't be able to stay here for much longer, Molly," he said. "Even if Mattie says nothing, my comrades will expect me to report back soon."

"I'll have to find another safe house," I said. "Or get you to Dublin."

Jack gazed at the horizon. "We might need to go farther away than that."

He meant they might have to go to the United States. Even though it was what I hoped for I still felt a twist in my stomach at the thought of losing him again.

Anto looked thoughtful. "My wife, Molly. Can you go and see she's all right? Her people are staunch Republicans and I will be seen as a traitor. But she might know of a safe place for us to move to. There are many good people here who help anyone. She lives above the draper shop in Tralee town – the Mall."

I nodded in agreement.

"Molly, if you could get us a few provisions every few days or so, that would be great. In case we are stuck here for a long time," Jack said. "But leave them here near these hazel trees."

As Anto limped ahead, I whispered quickly to Jack. "Can you trust him?"

"He couldn't kill me, Molly. Not in cold blood. Now that he knows he killed Jemsie, he won't kill anyone ever again."

I fished the horseshoe out of my pocket. "Take this just in case you meet the Little People'."

Jack laughed and ran to tell Anto. It gladdened my heart.

But now I had to work out a cover story.

cº©v

I looked up from the typed pages to Mal's eager face, almost surprised to find myself on a train hurtling towards the places mentioned in the letter.

"Sorry it breaks off there – that's as far as I got. It's in the hands of the Geek Squad now," Mal said.

"How could Anto hate his best friend? They were like family."

"You know yourself how families feud," Mal said.

My dad's face flashed through my mind. His sad voice on the few phone calls we'd had. All those torn-up letters. But that was different. Wasn't it? I pushed the big old mean thought away.

"But they patched it up," I said. "I hope Jack could still trust Anto."

"We'll soon find out if their friendship was strong enough," Mal said darkly.

"I'd trust you," I blurted out.

"Thanks, kid." Mal smiled but then he gazed out the

window. "Not many would."

But before I could ask him what he meant, the train pulled into Killarney. We couldn't see much of the famous mountains behind the thick curtain of misty rain.

Nora was at the station to meet us in a brightly coloured patchwork coat, her dark curly hair tumbling over her shoulders. She crushed me in a big hug and smiled warmly at Mal. She was just as I'd remembered her, smiling and serene. She seemed to float above the world. It must have been all that yoga and herbal tea.

She was impressed that we were so keen to visit Béal na mBláth and accepted our explanation that we were doing a history project.

Nora suggested we go there straight away, unless we were too tired. We assured her we were rearing to go. She chatted to us as she drove her new electric car, about her new vegetarian restaurant and teaching yoga in the local hotel. I liked the way she talked to us, as if we were equals. Not just a couple of kids.

We crossed into County Cork and drove through the traffic of the pretty little town of Macroom. The hometown of Patch, the boy Molly had rescued in the Battle of Dublin. Then we took the turn off to Béal na mBláth. There was very little traffic on this minor road. We drove past patchwork fields, past farms, little villages, herds of cows. The middle of nowhere. We turned right at the "Michael Collins" garage opposite the Diamond Bar. I guessed it might have once been Long's where the gunmen who shot Collins gathered.

We found the monument a few miles farther on where the road widened into a big gradual bend. We got out of the car. The monument was on the left-hand side. It was a large stone Celtic Cross, surrounded by railings with a little gate and built on a podium of painted red bricks. There were steps up to the cross, which bore Michael Collins' name in Irish and the date of his death. Behind the monument was a steep bank with a few trees bent by the winds. On the other side of the road, we could hear a stream gurgling, half hidden by bushes and scrub growth.

While Nora was examining the main monument, we went to look at a white bollard with a cross on it a few yards away.

"I guess this is where they think he was killed," Mal said. "We should get the metal detector out. But what are we going to say to Nora?"

"Maybe that we're looking for bullets?"

Mal didn't think this was a dumb idea. So that's what we told her when we asked to take the metal detector out of the car.

She obviously thought we were loco but said she'd go for a walk. She soon disappeared out of sight down the lonely road. A perfect place for an ambush.

We set to work. But we weren't having any luck around the monument or even by the bollard.

A woman went by with her dog and was keen to stop for a chat. We asked her if it was the exact spot.

"That monument was put up in 1924 but no one knew

where exactly he was killed. My grandfather, God bless him, said the road was very different in them days. It's been widened since. Then it was a narrow twisting road with a strip of grass down the middle. They say they put the monument in this spot and widened the road here to make space for cars and crowds on commemoration days."

"It must have been very confusing the day he died if it was misty," Mal said.

"I suppose you're hoping to find bullets," she said. "I wouldn't say you'll find anything. People have been souvenir-hunting all over this place since the moment it happened."

"With metal detectors?" I asked, alarmed.

"Not so many with them yokes, I'll grant you. You young people are more professional." Her dog pulled on the leash, eager to go. "But watch yourselves. The cars come flying round that bend like nobody's business!"

We relaxed. It was as good a cover story as any. She bid us good day. We watched her disappear round the bend.

"We could try the other side of the road?" I suggested. "Over by that stream. After all, Jack didn't know the exact spot either."

We ventured across the road as a bitter wind swept up the valley. After about fifteen minutes of tracking over the grass of the road verge, the counters went off and we started digging.

This time the packet wasn't very far down. We

unwrapped the grimy yellow chamois leather. Inside was a green-painted tin soldier. Mal opened it and tipped the jewel out into his palm. It was a beauty, and there was also the drop-stone, throbbing with life. Many of the diamond studs were intact, surrounding the emerald like a constellation. As I touched it, a wind whistled through the trees. It was like the ghost of Jack's lament for his lost leader.

It took us another hour's drive to get back to Killarney. Back through mountainous roads and winding valleys, covered with purple heather and patches of yellow furze blazing against grey and green rocks.

Nora lived on Countess Road, a long road that led into the centre of Killarney. A cute town with a tall steeple against a backdrop of purple mountains and blue sky. We could see it properly now that the misty drizzle had stopped. Nora told me you could call it a "mizzle". Her house was a two-storey converted stone coach house. At the time of the Civil War it would have been surrounded by fields, she told us. And guess what! It was rumoured Bram Stoker, Mr. Dracula himself, had once stayed in the inn next door! What a coincidence!

Nora was really good about letting us use her computer to check my account. We couldn't believe our luck until we found it had, like, the worst internet reception in the world. So we decided to go to bed and check again in the morning.

Chapter eighteen

Nora was doing an early morning yoga class at the nearby hotel. So Mal and I had breakfast together looking out at the mountain view from her kitchen. It was a living painting against the sky. You could spend all day just looking out the window. But I had some worries gnawing at the back of my mind.

"We should ask Nora to mind the jewels for us," I said. "Just in case the Russian follows us here."

Mal frowned. "The fewer people who know about this the better."

"You're so secretive, Mal. She's not going to reveal anything. And she's going to drive us all around the Civil War sites in her electric car."

The phone rang. Mal nearly jumped out of his skin. It was my mom. She was really happy that we'd arrived safely and Mal had caught the train. But I went stone-cold silent when she suggested that if I was really enjoying myself I could stay on.

When she kept going on about it, I asked her straight

out why she was trying to get rid of me. She got flustered.

"Because I could just go back to Dad in New York if you really want," I said angrily. I immediately regretted it.

"If that's what you really want," she said flatly. It was worse than if she'd shouted.

I said goodbye with a twist of pain in my stomach, feeling both mad at my mom and sad about how I always said the wrong thing.

Mal shook his head when I came off the phone. "You haven't learned how to talk to grown-ups, have you?"

I kicked the table in annoyance.

"You give them as little information as possible," he said. "That way they can't use your words against you."

"But I love my mom," I said, tears smarting in my eyes. "We never used to fight until we came to Ireland. She used to do that with my dad."

"I'm told it gets better with your parents when you are about thirty," Mal said. "Come on, let's check if the next part of the letter is in."

We went to the computer and logged into my account. And there, as if by magic, with one ping, we got the rest of the transcription of the letter from the Geek Squad to my old email address.

༄

I was hopeful that the easy ways of their boyhood could be restored for Jack and Anto. But I now had to deal with the problem of how to save both their skins. I grew more uneasy with every step I took away from them. For people would ask questions. Young Kieran was bound to blab something. I am not a great liar. It makes me feel bad. It is simpler to tell the truth.

When I got back into the farmyard, Dermot the farmer dashed out from the cow barn. "Yerra, they let you back!" he exclaimed. "I thought they'd take you too."

I was confused for a second.

"The Little People. Them Dublin lads have been taken. People around here saw the lights last night. Young Kieran and all."

I had been presented with a cover story. I did not lie. But I did not tell the truth either.

"I saw the lights too," I said. "Big as torches."

"Bedad! They're gone. Away with the Little People! It was my charm that protected you."

My silence was taken for a yes. The rumour escaped out the farmhouse door like smoke, and soon had a life of its own. I said nothing either way.

Many people seemed to believe the fairies had taken the lads. Others did not question too much, knowing the times that were in it. I was fearful the Dublin crowd would see through the lie if it reached their ears. They were far less likely to believe in yarns about the fairies though they had superstitions of their own.

The Free State Army now occupied most of the towns and garrisons but the rebel fighters for the Republic still ran free in the hills and remote valleys.

One night a rumour reached us in the farmhouse that the Free Staters were combing the hills looking for dugouts. I was frantic with worry as I was due to drop some food for the lads.

I set off early the next morning saying I had to visit some

patients. I found the route much easier this time. I knew what to expect.

I left the food with a note warning the boys to be careful, now that the Free Staters had vowed to hunt down all the anti-Treaty fighters.

I needed to contact Anto's wife Sinéad in Tralee. So I got a lift with a farmer going to town for the market. I would tell her that I had a locket from Anto and hoped that she would see me.

Tralee was tense, people hurrying about the streets to do their business, scurrying between shops like frightened mice.

After all I'd heard about her frostiness from Nancy, I wasn't looking forward to facing Anto's wife.

I arrived at her family's draper shop up on the Mall in the centre of Tralee, in the early afternoon. The shop below had the new smell of calico and lace and a warm fug from the hot irons used to press the fabric. There was a quiet bustle of women buying thread and needles, lengths of curtains and bright ribbons, red, gold, green and chalk-blue. The comforting sound of chatter. But a chill came over the room when I walked in. You could have heard one of their dressmaking pins drop.

"I am here to visit Mrs. Maguire," I said quietly. I could feel the prickle of suspicion around the shop at my Dublin accent. "I am a medic and a friend of her husband's." I showed my bag so they would think my visit was official.

People visibly relaxed and the chatter resumed.

The serving girl ran up the back stairs behind the counter to tell Sinéad, then came back down straight away and waved at me to follow her.

"We thought you might be one of dem Dublin spies," she said as she led me up. "'Tis shockin' what's goin' on. They've sent dem Dublin assassins to crush us. I want to get out of it meself and go to Boston to me aunty."

Anto's wife had her back to me when I entered. She turned to face me. She was even prettier than in her photo, her heart-shaped face slightly fuller now that she was pregnant. She struck me as being quite genteel.

"Anto asked me to give you this, in the Four Courts," I said, producing the little locket.

She stepped towards me to take it, her face flushed with hope. She was heavy with child, her stomach bulging under her stylish velvet dress.

She clutched the locket to her breast and held it close.

"I would be a proud mother to tell my child that his father died for Ireland," she said, her eyes awash with tears.

"My brother –" I began.

"God rest his soul."

"So you believe the rumours?"

She stared straight ahead of her and clasped her two hands tighter around the locket. "Word came back to me that your brother was taken prisoner and Anto was supposed to . . ." Her voice, nearly a whisper, trailed off.

I approached her and laid my hand on her arm. "Anto said you would know of a safe house."

She looked at me, full of hope.

"For both of them," I said. "Anto could not kill Jack."

Her eyes spilled with tears. Then she stiffened. "If Anto has not done the deed, it would be better if they think he is dead.

233

He will be when they find out." She gazed at the locket in her hands and put it in her pocket.

She walked away from me, wringing her hands. I was perplexed. Not sure if she was happy or sad that Anto hadn't killed Jack. I wanted to press her. But she was pregnant and wan. I didn't want to endanger the unborn baby.

"You need to rest," I said. "It is your first child and you will be tired." I saw that her hands were swollen and asked her if they pained her. She said they did at night. I told her to lie with her feet raised up and I made up hand splints for her to wear in bed.

"You should drink raspberry tea," I advised. "And nettle tea too. It's full of iron and good if you are nauseous."

She gave me a slight nod in gratitude but said no more. Meeting me had clearly been a huge strain on her.

As I went out the door, she called me back softly.

"Boyles' up near Farmer's Bridge is a safe house. They don't take sides. Or Moynihans' farm, out past Countess Bridge near Killarney going towards Kilcummin. They are staunch Republicans but are old friends who know how to keep their mouths shut."

I squeezed her hand in gratitude.

"Tell Anto I love him." She fought back tears. "I'm glad he spared your brother."

I left her then with another worry. Anto saving Jack had put her in danger too. They might think she was a traitor.

Next morning I went up to the stand of hazel trees with the food drop. I left a note about the safe houses, written in a code that Jack would know.

I could only risk going up every two or three days. On my

next visit up, I was stopped by a patrol of Free Staters but they let me go when they saw my doctor's bag.

There were more stories about strange occurrences. During a stand-off in Killorglin on market day, pigs were released onto the street. A flock of doves rose from a pen during a sniper fight, dazzling both sides and making it impossible for them to fire.

I guessed Jack was continuing his strange, reckless raids. But so far no one seemed to suspect it was him. For Jack could not be where he wasn't supposed to be. He was with the fairies. He had disappeared out of their imagining. But for me, all of these events had Jack's signature.

One lad I tended after he was badly beaten in Ballymullen Barracks in Tralee told me that most of the rebels assumed that Jack and Anto had killed each other and they were both buried in a bog. The more simple among them were convinced they were gone with the fairies. And the fairies were doing the mischief.

I am due to spend a couple of weeks working alongside a local doctor, Dr. Edmond Shanahan in Farranfore, so I can stay in the area. The first chance I get I will go to Boyles' farmhouse and then Moynihans' near Killarney.

Sanjay, if they make it to America, will you organise a safe hiding place for them in case anyone comes looking for them? We can't leave anything to trust in these fearful times.

I don't know if I will ever be able to repay you.

Except I remain your friend,

Always,

Molly

Chapter nineteen

When the next section of the letter arrived in Nora's inbox later in the afternoon, there was a note with the transcription. The Geek Squad hoped to have a few more bits of the letters with us before evening. But we were to call Rachel urgently.

Rachel's voice was steady and calm on the speakerphone.

"I have some bad news. There's been a break-in at the lab."

"Our emeralds!" I exclaimed.

"I'm so sorry," Rachel said. "We're trying to find out as much as we can. There might be some CCTV footage."

I could see Mal's face tense with worry. "And the police?"

"We can't involve them quite yet. You see, Patrick was doing that work without permission. The lab has recently tightened down on outside work. The thing is, they're the only thing that was taken. And there was no sign of disturbance."

"The Russian!" I gasped. "He must have followed us

there that day you thought you saw him, Mal."

We quickly told Rachel of our suspicions.

"Do you have any contact details for him?" Mal asked her.

"No, he was a cash buyer," she said. "He just told me his name was Yuri. His English was bad and he was a tourist. He might be on my CCTV. But that doesn't prove anything."

I burst into tears when we finished the call. "I feel like we've betrayed Molly and Jack after all they went through! I told you we should have warned Rachel and Patrick about the Russian! Patrick could have stood guard and kick-boxed him!"

Mal bit his lip. "We've still got the Béal na mBláth jewels and the rest of the ones to find on the map. We'll find a way to get the others back."

I dried my tears, trying not be such a wuss. "It makes it even more important that we track them down. I'm not letting that no-good, allspice, creepy guy with his terrible hats get the better of us."

Mal high-fived me. "That's the spirit. You can bet 'Yuri' is going to want the rest of the necklace. We'll smoke him out. Promise you."

I guess we are the ones setting the pace," I said, trying to look on the bright side. "Hey, you don't think he'll try to break into our flats?"

Mal laughed. "Old Lil has the place like Fort Knox and there's nothing but an attic full of rubbish. And the Geek squad have the letters now."

I laughed.

He frowned as something crossed his mind. "We'll ask Nora if the Geek Squad can send the next transcription to her account. It might be more secure to have it sent to a different email." He glanced quickly down through the printout. "It's all about Knocknagoshel! One of the places on the map, dated March 1923. I think we're in luck."

ↄঔৎৎৎ

March 1923

I was fast asleep in bed in the farmhouse in Knocknagoshel when there was an almighty bang in the distance! I ran out in my nightdress to the kitchen.

The Yankee was there, shaking. "There's been some sort of explosion. I think it was over near the woods!"

My head was still thick with sleep and the clock said it was after two o'clock in the morning. I ran back into my room and got dressed in a panic, scarcely able to close my buttons. Then I dashed back into the kitchen with my doctor's bag. I was scared senseless Anto and Jack had been discovered.

The farmer, Dermot, ran in panting. "You're wanted out near Baranarig Wood! There's been an explosion! They got five of dem Staters. But there's one fella who's still alive!"

He took me in a pony and trap to the wood on the edge of the village in the bitter cold. On the journey he told me what he knew. He had been up to Murphy's Forge earlier in the day to collect a new poker. There was some hugger-mugger going on at the forge. Dermot had found out they were making landmines and planning booby-traps against the Free Staters.

Later on, he'd called in to see about a bull in a farm near Baranarig Wood. He had stayed for a few drinks and was going to stay the night. But then he changed his mind. As he was setting off home, he heard the bomb go off near Burke's field on the edge of the wood out past Talbot's Cross.

The anti-Treaty lads had set a trap mine and lured the Free Staters there by giving them false information that there was an anti-Treaty dugout there. Five were dead – one was a local man from Castleisland.

"'Tis a shockin' story of revenge," he said. "Old Pat had a dugout on his land for the Republican boys. But he needed to get the hay in or the farm faced ruin. 'Twas a very bad summer here last year. But the lads wouldn't leave so he couldn't bring in other workers. Then back in December the Republicans looted the poor old fella. They took his boots, his leggings, his bike and cows and all. The son, Paddy Pats, was so mad at them he joined the Free State Army and became an informer."

Now Paddy Pats was blown to smithereens. But one of the other soldiers had survived.

We found him in a terrible state up at Burke's field, his legs and arms mangled. His name was Joe O'Brien and he was from Dublin.

I applied tourniquets to each of his limbs to stem the flow of blood. I had some morphine, which I gave him to quell the pain. A car arrived not long after to take him to the military hospital in Tralee.

"They will pay in blood for this," said a Free State officer with a strong Dublin accent. "We'll teach them a lesson! After this all mines will be cleared by anti-Treaty prisoners! We'll hunt then down in their foxholes. Every last one! We'll round them up in Ballymullen Barracks!"

I had to get word to Anto and Jack to move on. They would have to leave Kerry. I wrote to May to ask her to find some new quiet lodgings for me – knowing she would understand this to mean a safe house for them in Dublin. I went to the local post office and asked to use the telephone.

I telephoned to the Moore/McCormack Shipping line, the company based in Dublin that sails the trans-Atlantic liners to New York, asking if they could arrange tickets for two passengers, Mr. Adair and Mr. Twomey – I was using their mothers' maiden names. I asked for first-class tickets, thinking of Collins' advice to always hide in plain view. Though it did him no good in the end. I had no idea how I was going to pay for them but they agreed to allow for payment on boarding.

But my immediate concern was to check that the boys were still safe.

This time I went right back up to the fairy glen. The wind howled through the valley and a sudden rain lashed my face. I had an ominous feeling before I even set foot inside the tower.

They were gone.

Nora was really obliging about letting us have the Geek Squad send mail to her account and lending us her spade without prying. After lunch she drove us to Knocknagoshel, north of Killarney on the Limerick road. Mal and I were both gloomy and silent and once or twice Nora glanced back at me through the rearview mirror with a worried frown. I felt sick every time I thought of that Russian pawing our precious jewels. But as we got closer to Knocknagoshel, I got excited and went over the clues in my mind.

The monument commemorating the Free State soldiers who died in the booby-trap attack in Baranarig Wood was just up from Talbot's Bridge in a dip in the road on the outskirts of the village It was like a little grave in front of a steep field. To the right-hand side was a stream with a stony bed, surrounded by fluttering elder and ash trees, a tangle of ferns and blackberry bushes. A bed of nettles. A wide empty space, a lonely place to die. No wonder the noise had travelled for miles.

We reckoned from Molly's mentions of Burke's field that the explosion had happened up the steep hill. It now had a farmhouse built on it. Back then it must have been on the edge of the woods.

Nora was curious when we got out the metal detector and the spade again but soon lost interest when Mal started boring her with all the technical specifications. Mal gave me the thumbs-up as she walked off at a cracking pace.

"Bore them into submission," he laughed. "Works

every time with grown-ups."

There wasn't much to see on the dials immediately around the monument but when we ventured a little further up the road to the right-hand side of the field, the needle started going mental near a copse of trees. I looked around anxiously as I stuck the spade in the soil.

"This is right by somebody's farm," I said. "We might get seen, it might be part of their land."

It began to drizzle. I was glad we had worn our raincoats.

Mal took the spade off me and stuck the blade into a sod. "Relax, we're on the public highway on the boundary of the farm – eh, I think. We'll worry about that if they come."

I sweated every time a car went by. A couple of passersby glanced up the hill and gave us funny looks. But about a yard down in our digging, we hit paydirt! Another tin soldier wrapped in chamois leather. We hastily filled in the hole and tamped it down with our feet. It looked like a dog had been foraging for a bone.

Mal had put the little chamois-leather package containing the tin solider in his pocket. After the break-in, we were nervous. So neither of us wanted to risk taking a closer look at our find out in the open.

There was a sudden screech of brakes on the road. When we got back near the monument, a car drew up about fifty yards away and a couple got out. They looked like any other tourists in this rain-soaked part of the country. Bright red kagool anoraks with hoods on and jeans. They waved to us in a friendly off-hand way as they changed into their walking boots at the back of the car.

Nora came back from her walk.

Mal said, anxious at the appearance of the strangers, "We're expecting an email, Nora. Can you check your phone, please?"

Nora glanced at her phone. "There's no signal here. We'd better head to an Internet café. I know a nice one near the museum in Tralee and I'll leave you there to go shopping."

She glanced over at the couple, who were walking towards the monument and getting closer to us. Mal and I, carrying the equipment, hurried towards her car. The couple started taking photographs of the area. They didn't seem to be paying much attention to our departure. But I took a note of their car. A white Ford Focus with a KY – Kerry – number-plate. Maybe a hire car.

Nora drove us into Tralee, Mal in the front passenger seat. I watched anxiously out the back but no Ford Focus.

Near the Aquadome, on the outskirts of the town, we came up to a sign for Ballymullen Barracks. That was the barracks near where Sinéad's family had their draper's shop.

Then I saw the car again.

I prodded Mal's shoulder and when he looked around I made a slight nod backwards over my shoulder, hoping Nora wouldn't see me in the rearview mirror.

Mal looked and then gave a small nod.

At that moment, Nora's phone buzzed with an alert and she asked Mal to check.

"How's that for timing!" he said. "It's the next instalment of this document Ava needs right now for her history project. It will be about Ballyseedy."

"Gosh, you're a very diligent student, Ava!" said Nora.

I looked back. The car was on our tail. My mind galloped all over the place. Who were they? Were they working with the Russian? I didn't know how Mal was remaining so calm when we were in deep doo-doo. But he seemed to be paying a lot of attention to Nora's phone.

Nora took an abrupt left turn. "Sorry! Shortcut!" she apologised as we were jolted against our seatbelts.

The other car didn't follow in time and was caught in the one-way system. We had shaken our tail. I grinned from ear to ear in relief.

We found a parking spot near the Tralee museum, then headed to an internet café nearby. My eyes were on stalks looking out for a white Ford Focus. But there was no sign of it.

We enjoyed two hot chocolates and downloaded the next instalment while Nora went to buy vegetables.

❧

I was due to work with Dr. Shanahan in Farranfore on the 7th of March and had promised him I'd organise supplies at the

Tralee chemist's before travelling on. I also had to visit Sinéad. The farmer dropped me on the outskirts of the town.

I walked quickly down the Ballyseedy Road to the centre of Tralee. People were hurrying about trying to finish their business before darkness fell.

I passed a group of children playing a skipping game near a crossroads.

"*What's the news, what's the news,*
De Valera lit the fuse . . ."

They sang in time to their jumping feet, the rope whipping the air.

"*The Republicans' bomb*
 Up the Staters blew . . ."

Whirr, whirr went the rope as the children chanted in a sing-song rhythm.

"*Them Staters are dead,*
Their veins are bled,
Twenty bullets in your head!"

A covered Crossley tender carrying troops drove up and slowed to turn the corner, scattering the children about the road.

A young lad ran into the road after them, still singing.

"*They'll put a bullet in our head!*" he screeched, shaking his fists at the departing car, which had slowed to let a man with a donkey cross.

The car reversed back with a screech of brakes.

"*Go home, you young Kerry pup, or we'll have yeh!*" a soldier roared out the back.

The young lad was joined by a few others, rising to the challenge.

"What's the news, what's the news,
The Dublin Staters are confused . . ."

A sergeant stood with rifle raised on the back on the lorry. *"Stop that singing right now!"*

The boys and girls, terror-stricken for a moment, just stood there. The rhyme died on their lips.

"Run for it, you fools!" I shouted at them.

But they stood their ground.

The children, dirty and defiant, in tattered clothing, started to chant again, their courage coming back to them.

"The Staters shoot us with their gun
So we can't have any fun . . ."

A few of the soldiers stood up and raised their weapons.

"Fire!" shouted the sergeant.

A volley of shots erupted over the children's heads. The bullets clanged into a wall opposite, raising dust and whitewash. The vehicle roared off.

The children had dived into the roadside and were roughed up but unhurt. They even laughed with nervous excitement.

One little boy cried out. He had got shrapnel dust in his eye from a ricochet. I quickly licked out the debris, as I had seen Dr. English do at the Four Courts. He blinked and gave me a big gappy smile.

"Maybe you should see the doctor at the hospital," I said.

"No way. 'Tis full of Staters," he said. "And 'tis lucky I can now see 'em comin'!"

He ran off down a backstreet.

"Aren't they divils, those Staters! They were pelted with eggs in Ballybunion," a girl said. "By a Red Injun from America, they say. But I don't believe that."

Jack! He must still be in hiding round these parts. But how reckless of him to break cover in such a memorable disguise!

An old woman stuck her head out the doorway of a nearby cottage.

"They're after catchin' them two fellas that d'be doin' them things," she said.

"How do you know?" I demanded.

"Don't I be doin' the washin' up in the barracks?" she said. "I heard them with my own ears. They said they'd shoot that Cat boyo. For makin' a mockery of them. That his limpy rebel friend mustn't have killed him after all. They don't believe in the fairies. They said they'd get the both of them if they're still breathin'."

"Are you sure?" I pressed her.

"That's what they were sayin'. Or boastin' more like."

"Oh no!" My hand flew to my mouth.

I quickened my step and turned towards Ballymullen Barracks. But I forced myself to calm down, so I wouldn't scatter like a straw woman blown on the breeze. There was no proof they'd been captured yet. Only the threatening words overheard by an old washerwoman. But I was compelled to find out, to set my mind at rest.

En route, I passed by an old building that they were using as a gaolhouse because they had so many prisoners. A group of women in shawls were gathered outside.

A prisoner stuck his head out the window. He was a curly-haired boy of about twenty.

"I'll write tomorrow, Mother!" he shouted.

"Yeh will and all!" she shouted back, trying to be good-humoured in these grim surroundings.

"Have you seen any prisoners from Dublin, one with a shock of golden hair, the other red-haired with a limp?" I called out to him.

He shook his head again. "I'm not exactly in the know!" He laughed. "There's talk of more fellows being captured. We'll be ten deep at this rate."

"That's my Michael to a tee. As if there's ne'er a bother on him," his mother said to me as we walked on towards the barracks in Ballymullen. "He was picked up unarmed at a dance. Good lad he is too. He only joined the fight for Ireland's freedom so he would never be forced to join the British army."

She bid me good day as she took another road, warning me to be careful.

I dithered. I could make an official enquiry. But if they were captured and had given false names, I'd blow their cover. If they were still at large, I'd have alerted the army to their presence. I might even be tortured myself.

The wind howled round the town like a beast. I pulled my hat over my ears against the bitter cold. I walked by the old workhouse where injured prisoners were being kept. Sounds of groaning and clattering could be heard. Followed by a hollow silence. I saw a platoon of troops arriving with boxes of ammunition,

I met a nurse on her way home and asked her about the boys. But she hadn't seen them either.

Up near the marshes I came to Ballymullen Barracks. They were a group of low buildings surrounded by a big stone wall. A huge iron gate was guarded by a soldier on duty in a little gatehouse outside. Several women had gathered, all hoping for news of their loved ones. Some had parcels containing food and clothes.

As I tried to walk up further to the gate, I was stopped by the sentry guarding it.

I decided I needed to check inside. I would say I was on medical business.

"Halt! What is your business?"

"I need to see the Commanding Officer," I said, pulling myself up to my full height and looking him in the eye, even though my legs felt like jelly and my heart was thudding in my ears. It was bitter cold. I brandished my leather doctor's case. "I hear some of the prisoners need attention."

The sentry gave me a menacing look. "There's no call for you here."

There was a lot of activity. Lorries with prisoners arriving, troops jumping into patrol cars. The air was tense.

I pleaded with him in vain. He used rough language to me, called me names. But I was willing to bear anything for news of Anto and Jack. Through the gates I saw prisoners being taken to the guardroom. Some of them could barely walk. A couple had broken arms.

After about half an hour, I started to walk off. But then another sentry relieved the brutish one.

"You were the Doctoreen at Baranarig Wood," he said. "We heard you saved Joe's life."

"How is Joe?" I asked.

"He's in a bad way. But he'll make it. The surgeon who saw him said you did a good job."

I told him I needed to speak to Commandant O'Daly.

He looked nervous. But said he would do as I asked. He came back ten minutes later.

"An officer wants to question you."

My insides turned a somersault. This was what I wanted and yet I had a terrible sense of foreboding as I set foot in that place. It was worse than when I was arrested and taken to Mountjoy Gaol.

The young Free State soldier led me inside the maze of buildings. He was not much older than me. His uniform was too big for him and he walked on the back of his trouser hems. We went down a corridor with dark ugly walls oozing damp, peeling paint, broken windows. Men crying out in pain.

I passed by a guardroom where they were holding a group of ragged prisoners.

"And none of them have priests or nuns in the family?" I heard a Northern Irish voice say. "No people to make a fuss or make any noise?"

"We don't need to concern ourselves too much," said someone with a harsh Dublin accent. "We weren't asked to take kid gloves to Kerry."

I didn't like the sound of any of that.

"What are they doing with those prisoners?" I asked the young solider.

He looked shifty. "Putting them to clear barricades and mines," he said. "After they booby-trapped Knocknagoshel, that's the order."

"But those men aren't fit for anything. They should be in hospital."

The soldier didn't respond.

I passed a stable block. The door was slightly open and I glimpsed a row of rough coffins, just planks of wood nailed together. It was a terrible sight.

I was shown into an office. I faced an officer who did not give me his name. He had a hawkish face. An air of menace like a bird of prey about to strike.

I sat down. A Sam Browne belt and gun lay casually across the desk, I had walked into the lion's den. And nobody would come searching for me.

"Do you have any information about Anto Maguire and your brother Jack O'Donovan?" He had a strong Northern Irish accent but I wasn't sure if he was the same officer I'd heard in the guardroom.

My heart skittered. If he was asking me this, then they must still be free.

"I was going to ask you the same question," I said, brazening it out. "What do you want them for?"

"Don't get pert with me, young miss," he said. "Maguire is with the rebels. And your brother is facing charges of sabotaging arms and military operations."

"Jack is neutral in this war," I said.

"He'll be dead neutral soon enough." He laughed harshly.

"Have you arrested them?" I asked.

He curled his lip in a cruel smile. "Only a matter of time."

My mind was racing. They were still hiding out but not for much longer. They would be in grave danger if they were caught.

"I have asked my tutor Oliver St. John Gogarty to telephone

General Mulcahy on the matter. The doctor is a big supporter of the Free State."

I was dropping names so he wouldn't hurt me.

"And you? Where do your loyalties lie? 'Doctoreen'." His voice was thick with sarcasm.

"My loyalties are with my patients, sir."

"And would some of those patients be murdering Irregular traitors?" He grabbed the gun and bashed it down on the desk.

I jerked back in surprise.

"You were seen entering that draper's shop in town. A nest of vipers they are!"

"The daughter is with child – that's why I was there."

"Another rebel brat coming into the world. They need to watch themselves . . ."

I was aghast. Was he threatening Anto's wife?

"I was at Knocknagoshel too, sir. I tended to your injured comrade." My voice was wavering with fright.

His expression softened. "It is an offence to give any support to those criminals," he said but more quietly.

"I am planning to travel back to Dublin soon. I would be grateful if you forwarded any news of my brother to Dr. St. John Gogarty at St. Vincent's Hospital," I said. "Jack's very well known, you know, in the United States. He's a circus performer."

The officer stared at me hard.

Then another officer rushed in. I recognised him! His name was Niall Harrington and his father had been Lord Mayor of Dublin. My mother knew his mother from their charity work.

He was shocked when he saw me.

"*Get out of here!*" he barked.

I recoiled in fright.

My hands trembled as I picked up my doctor's bag. The first officer looked grimly at his colleague, annoyed at the interruption.

"You are to report to the guardroom," Niall told him.

The first officer stalked off.

When he was gone, Niall's expression changed. "Sorry. I didn't mean to frighten you. You need to get out of here as quick as your legs can carry you."

My legs shook as I left, walking past several lorries. I looked back. A party of prisoners were in the yard, tied together with ropes. Some of them could barely walk. One of them was the young curly-headed lad, Michael, I'd spoken to earlier, a dazed expression on his face.

I stayed in Benner's Hotel in Castle Street and was lucky to get there before the curfew. There was a message from Dr. Shanahan, confirming that he would meet me in the morning as arranged, after I visited the chemist's.

In the middle of the night, I awoke from a fitful sleep. There was a roar in the distance, like waves crashing against a shore. Or maybe a bomb. But I thought I was having a nightmare, turned back over and went back to sleep. I dreamed I was back in the GPO and then in the Four Courts.

I awoke, covered in sweat, feeling like I'd slept on a bed of nails.

As she served me my breakfast, the young girl asked me if I'd heard the explosion in the night. I nodded.

She leaned in, her expression grim, and lowered her voice to a whisper. "It was our lads made to clear a landmine out at

Ballyseedy Cross by the Free State soldiers, about three miles up the road."

"Oh mercy!" I breathed.

"I live near the barracks. I saw them head out last night. One of them was a friend of mine – Michael O'Connell from Castleisland."

"I just met his mother yesterday and spoke to him too in the gaolhouse!" I cried.

"Sure a couple of them could hardly walk. It's not landmines they should be clearing but lying in hospital beds."

"Was anyone injured?" I asked.

"You can be sure," she said darkly. "I'm in Cumann na mBan. And so is Dr. Shanahan's sister. His brother is one of us too. But the doctor will help anyone. We have a secret newspaper to record atrocities. They're out for blood since the Knocknagoshel booby trap."

As I walked through the town there was a strange atmosphere. People were milling onto the streets, heading towards the barracks. Small children crying, hanging on to their mothers' skirts.

There was a kind of madness in the air. Women calling out loudly, "Do you know who they took?" and "There's men killed!"

I rushed along with the crowd. Women were screaming now as we streamed towards Ballymullen. High keening sounds rent the air.

I stopped a man to ask what was happening.

"There was a group of prisoners blown to pieces out by Ballyseedy Cross," he said.

We reached the barracks and I jostled my way to the front,

terrified Anto and Jack were among the dead.

"Stand back!" ordered the sentry.

A group of Free State soldiers came out, arms at the ready. Then, the army band marched out and stood either side of the gate, on the inside, where they couldn't be touched. They played ragtime tunes – "The Sheik of Araby", a foxtrot. People's faces turned to stone at the disrespect.

There was a flurry of movement on the other side of the gate.

Shock was replaced by frenzy, with people pushing up against the gate. I almost lost my footing in the heave of bodies, but managed to clamber to the side.

A line of coffins was carried out through the gates with names on them. They were rough coffins. Little more than painted boards. The ones I had seen the day before. I counted nine. One of them bore the name of Michael O'Connell. Another of Stephen Fuller. I was relieved to see that none of them were Maguire or O'Donovan.

A woman cried out, "*But my son was six feet tall! How can he come home to me in such a small coffin?*"

The Free State soldiers would not let the mother open that coffin.

A madness spread among the crowd as families claimed the coffins. The Free State soldiers were pushed back. People opened the coffins in the street. Other people took them off to one side to a marshy area and pried open the lids.

The families' faces were terrible to behold. A mixture of shock, disgust, horror.

"*Sure they're all unrecognisable!*" someone called out. "*Blown to smithereens!*"

255

"*Destroyed all together!*" a young mother cried, clutching her child.

"*Torn limb from limb!*" An old woman nearly collapsed and had to be held up by her bent and crooked husband.

"*Murderers!*" an old man yelled.

The small boys and girls who'd been playing skipping yesterday picked up cobblestones and threw them at the Free State soldiers who retreated inside their barracks and closed the gates.

It was like a Greek tragedy. People wailing, women on their knees keening. Knots of people holding hands in anguish.

I went back into the centre of town. I was numb – sleepwalking. The chemist's was shut but when I knocked on the door the chemist opened up and ushered me inside. I told him what I'd seen and he gave me a strong cup of tea.

"They're saying it was a landmine planted by Republicans out at Ballyseedy Cross," said the chemist. "But sure, the Free State soldiers planted the bomb themselves. Someone up the town saw two officers preparing the bomb. You can't hide things in a small town like this."

He helped me load the bundles for Dr. Shanahan into a small cart. The young boy who had injured his eye the day before was there to help me carry back the loaded cart to Benner's Hotel where Dr. Shanahan was due to collect me by car.

"Is your eye all right?" I asked the lad.

"'Tis better than ever," he said, smiling.

I was glad someone could still smile in this place.

Dr. Shanahan was already waiting for me at Benner's Hotel.

He was a kindly youngish man with a warm manner. But his face was white as a sheet. He drew me into the sitting room.

"It's a horror," he said in his soft voice. "People in the neighbouring houses at Ballyseedy Crossroads saw the explosion. Nobody in the houses dared venture out. They knew they would be killed." He put his head in his hands. "I came down by Farmer's Bridge and saw where it happened. They were blown to bits. The crows in the trees . . ." He stopped talking and sobbed. "The crows were eating human flesh." Then he whispered to me, "But there's been a miracle. We must make haste to Hanlon's Cross."

❧⊙❧

We asked Nora to take us straight to the monument of the Ballyseedy massacre. It was about three miles down the N21 main road that led to Killarney.

We took the turn at the roundabout onto a wide main road with fast-flowing traffic. About a mile down the road, we reached a large monument. Nora dropped us off and we took out the metal detector and the spade. She went on to Ballyseedy garden centre to buy some plants.

The traffic roared past us. The monument was a large tableau. There were several figures carved in bronze – a mother holding a baby, a man walking away and another man, lying dying on the ground. An awful scene of war and suffering. There was a brick wall behind it and in front several plaques with names on them. I saw Michael O'Connell's name among the dead.

We combed the paved site with the metal detector. Then jumped over the wall to the field behind. We got nothing.

Then Mal had a brainwave. He checked his Road to the Republic book and gave me a thumb's-up. "The memorial is in a different site from the actual massacre. The farmer gave the land for the monument. But it happened further back towards town on the other side of the road near what was the old crossroads."

We crossed over to the opposite side of the road. It was terrifying dodging the cars. We jumped over a grey traffic barrier.

We saw a white wooden cross to someone else who had been killed during the Civil War and a large black sign for Ballyseede Castle Hotel. We could still make out the old disused road, now overgrown. Taking that, we headed deeper into Ballyseedy Wood towards Farmer's Bridge.

In among a copse of trees, the metal detector went ballistic. I was getting really expert at turning over Ireland's old sods. I wished my dad could see me, spade in hand. But I immediately banished that thought. I didn't want to think about that traitor.

The work was tiring as it was a warm day. But we took it in turns. And there it was in the dirt. A little chamois-leather parcel with the tin soldier inside, like a mummy.

After we found the soldier we went back to look at the monument. A crow alighted on it. It made me shudder.

Thinking of those crows in the trees after the massacre. But then a little robin hopped across the stones making me think of Robbie. And that made me feel better.

We had a closer look at the memorial. It was very moving. It said:

"From this day forth all who pass this way will know that the men of Kerry who fought and died for Ireland are not forgotten."

All fairly anonymous, no priests or nuns in the family, those that'll make the least noise, I thought. And yet their bones had cried out for justice.

It also listed the names of four other comrades who had died in the locality.

To think this busy junction not far from the town had been a killing field!

Mal concentrated intently on the sculpture. He seemed lost in it, wrapped in his own mist. His shoulders began to heave. He walked away and crumpled to the ground. He was sobbing, gulping for air.

I was shocked. Mal was usually so cool, seldom showing any fear or weakness. And here he was crying like a baby. I crouched down beside him, put my hand on his shoulder and handed him a none-too-clean handkerchief.

He blew his nose.

"It's really sad," I said. "But we live in different times."

He looked ahead, his face red from crying. "Do we? My mother was injured in a bomb blast when she was a kid. When I saw that sculpture of the mother with the baby . . . all the innocents who get hurt."

"But she survived to have you," I said, trying to console him, feeling my words were like little sticking plasters against a big wound. It was the first time he'd ever spoken to me about his mother.

"It was in Enniskillen in 1987 up in the North that everyone down here forgot about," he said. "The Irish Republican Army, or the Provos as they were known then, planted a bomb at a memorial service for Remembrance Sunday, the day those who died in the World Wars are remembered. My mother was with her grandfather. They were both hit by falling debris from the blast." He glanced over at the monument. "Eleven people were killed. Ten civilians and a police officer." He stopped and breathed deeply. "My mother recovered. Well, I mean her body healed. But she never got over it. Her wounds were on the inside. She drowned when I was ten. Her death was unexplained. I think she just wanted to finally wash away all the bad memories."

I wanted to hug him. But was too shy. Mal looked so alone in his suffering. He ran off and howled like a wolf under a full moon. Like a creature deranged. Then he stopped suddenly, his energy all spent.

I rooted around in my pocket for another hankie and found an old packet of mints.

I offered him a mint. He took it. Then spat it out.

"Yuck! It's covered in hair and lint from your pocket."

"Sorry, I just thought it would make you feel better." I

hung my head.

But he laughed then. "Thanks, Florence Nightingale."

He looked back at the monument.

"I bet the people who bombed my mother come here and plant wreaths. They use events like the Ballyseedy Massacre to justify their actions. It just led to more violence."

"That's so not cool," I said.

Mal laughed. "Sometimes you sound so dumb. You're just a kid. What would you know?"

I was glad he laughed at me but also a bit annoyed. "I know an eye for an eye and a tooth for a tooth is a really bad idea. Cos then everyone ends up eyeless and toothless. But it's right to remember this stuff. Some of the people who come here just want to pay respect to the lost ones."

A soft rain began to fall – somewhere between a mizzle and a drizzle. But Mal didn't seem to care, lost in his own pain.

"The worst thing is you can lose two parents. Not one," he said. "Like my dad. He buries himself in work. And gambling."

"Sounds a bit like my family," I said. "We're both kind of orphans."

The rain turned into a downpour.

"I guess Jack wanted us to remember so it never happens again. Come on, kid, we need to get out of the rain."

We ran at full pelt up to the coffee shop in Ballyseedy

garden centre. Nora was waiting for us. Mal felt much better after a huge slice of chocolate cake and he went looking for a computer to download the next instalment. The manager in the coffee shop was really kind and let him use the office facilities.

Mal's face was lit up when he came back with the printout.

"This really is miraculous!" he said.

⁓⊙⊙⁓

As we went in Dr. Shanahan's car he told me how the miracle had taken place.

"Nine coffins were sent back to Tralee, filled with the mangled remains of the prisoners of war. But in fact only eight prisoners were killed at Ballyseedy Cross," he said. "One of them, Stephen Fuller, survived. They sent for me to attend him. We're going to see him now."

We were both tense. So we talked of Dublin where he had gone to school in Castleknock College. And medical matters. If the survivor would be burnt or have broken bones. The best treatment for shock. I told him that one of our lecturers, who had been a doctor on the battlefields in the Great War, said there was a danger that bomb-blast victims could get swelling of the brain. Later they could lapse into a coma, even if they survived.

Up a boreen we arrived at a small farmhouse, belonging to a family called Curran.

A little girl dashed out.

"Kitty, where is he?" Dr. Shanahan asked.

"The burnt man is moved on already," she said. There were dark circles under her eyes. "I watched it all out our bedroom window. The moonlight was very bright, like day. I couldn't sleep after I heard shouting. There was an explosion, and the man Stephen was blown sky high."

"He was thrown quite a distance," said Dr. Shanahan, gazing across the field and to the road.

But Kitty had barely paused for breath. "So far he crossed the gate into our farm. I locked it myself last night to stop the animals getting out. He knocked on the window and Dada told him to come in. But he was too afraid to go and get help. The man's hands were all bloody and burnt. Mama washed them. His clothes were all blown off!"

"Did he have any other injuries?" I asked.

"Yerra, I don't know. But he couldn't sit down. She gave him a cup of tae so she did, my mama. Gave him some clothes. Then Dada put down a bag of hay and he lay down in the corner. He was twitching like a sick animal. But he didn't make a sound. 'Twas like he was in a trance."

Her father came out. "His friends took him out in a pony and trap to Billy O'Dálaigh's out near Knockane."

We drove to the remote hillside farm about twenty miles away, past Castleisland. Hidden behind a copse of trees there was a tent covered in leaves. Stephen was lying on his side with a sheet placed lightly over him, curled into a ball, moaning.

"Stephen, can you hear me?" the doctor said gently.

He winced when we took the sheet off him even though we

were gentle. A good-looking fellow in his early twenties, he was shockingly burnt.

He sat up then, his whole body quivering with nerves. We cut the shirt that the farmer had given him off his back.

His skin was black with gunpowder. Dozens of pieces of grit were embedded in his skin. Both his hands were burnt and there were pieces of metal embedded in them. His face was raw with the pain, his eyes squeezed shut.

"We'll give you something for the pain," the doctor said.

I prepared morphine in a syringe and the doctor gave him an injection.

Then I took out tweezers and iodine.

"This will hurt, Stephen, but it will be better in the long run," the doctor said. "Hold still while I take the grit out of your back, there's a good lad."

He nodded. But even though he was in agony, he wanted to tell his story.

I gave him a drink through a straw. His voice was husky, breathless.

"There was a log in the middle of the road. It had a landmine hidden under it. We were placed around it at about a two-foot distance from it. My hands, knees and ankles were bound and I was tied to my comrades by the hands. They left about a foot of rope between our hands and the next fella. They took off our caps. We all faced out."

"That's why the burns are on your back," I said.

"We said our prayers but I kept watching when the Staters withdrew. That's what saved me afterwards – I kept my wits about me. We said our goodbyes . . ." A sob escaped him.

"'Goodbye, lads' – each fella said it, knowing we were going to die. And then the blast. I went up with it of course."

A sudden noise outside made him pause. His eyes took on a haunted look.

It was only a rook cawing in the trees.

His breathing was laboured but he continued. "The explosion cut all the rope. The others were killed I've been told – eight of them. I was blown clear. The Staters had coffins with them."

"Hold steady there while I get rid of all this junk," the doctor said to him. Using the tweezers, he continued to pull out tiny bits of twisted metal, shrapnel and scraps of clothes from his skin.

"All my clothes were blasted off. But I was able to scramble away somehow."

He winced as I applied iodine to the wounds, the bright-red colour staining into his poor blackened, pockmarked skin.

"I made for the ditch and lay there," he said. "There were another couple of explosions. They were throwing in grenades to make sure everyone was dead."

"It's a miracle you made it," I said.

"It is. They opened rapid machine-gun fire then and I thought they were firing at me. I dragged myself on and reached the river – I thought about hiding in it but I forded it and kept going. To the house."

"Quiet now," I said as I applied iodine to his blackened hands.

He was brave. He didn't cry out. But he shook violently.

"We need to keep the wounds clean to prevent infection,"

said Dr. Shanahan.

I prepared a chemical solution to dress the wounds. This would dry to become a "second skin". We applied it to his back and hands.

"Will I live?" he asked me quietly as he moaned with pain.

"You survived a bomb blast. You can survive anything," I said.

He smiled then. A smile I shall treasure forever.

"But you must stay hidden," said Dr. Shanahan. "They will comb the area for you."

"I hope there will be no vengeance in my name," he said, a tear rolling down his cheek. "I forgive them. I hope this bitterness won't be passed on to the next generation."

I was moved by his words.

Dr. Shanahan told the woman of the house to give him plenty of broth and nourishment. To let him sleep for several hours but to send for help if he didn't rouse the next day.

"They will move him soon," Mrs. O'Dálaigh said. "To the Boyles' house. A Protestant family. They don't support the struggle but they are good people. He will be safer there for now."

My ears pricked up. Anto's wife Sinéad had mentioned the Boyles' as a possible safe house for Anto and Jack. Maybe they were hiding there.

But, as we got into the car, a boy ran up to us, breathless.

"There's been an explosion at Countess Bridge in Killarney! Just like Ballyseedy Cross. And one man blown free! He's at Jack Moynihan's where the Dublin fellows went!"

I gasped!

"How do you know about them?" I said.

"The Moynihans are my cousins," he said. "They told me to pass on the message if I saw the redheaded Doctoreen!"

⚬⚬⚭⚮⚬

We drove back to Killarney in a strange mood. We were shocked by the events of Ballyseedy. But also glad that we had recovered another tin soldier.

Mal was sitting in the back seat with me as Nora had put a big potted plant in the front that she'd bought at the garden centre. She was listening to her chanty music.

"If Jack was in hiding, how did he manage to bury an emerald in Ballyseedy?" I murmured to Mal. "Do you think he was nearby?"

"Maybe there will be an answer in the next letter," Mal muttered back. "The Geek Squad are really on the case."

Back at the house we checked our tin soldier. There it was – a beauty with a separate drop-stone this time, sparkling with its green fire. Jack's homage to the dead. We put it back in the soldier and parcelled it up again. We asked Nora to keep it safe.

Then we downloaded the next instalment from the Geek Squad. There was a letter from my father as well, that my mother had forwarded. I shoved it into my pocket, intending to tear it up later. Or maybe even read it. Mal's talking about his mother had had an effect on me.

"Why don't you open it?" Mal said.

"It's from my dad. It's radioactive."

"You won't know until you read it, cowardy custard."

I smirked at him and opened the letter. Something dropped out. Two return tickets to the United States for Mom and me. The letter said she had to go back to sign some documents.

And some other glad tidings.

He and Honey Belle were going to have an engagement party in Texas. They knew it would come as a surprise to me. And they had some other really exciting news, he said, something I'd always wanted. The words swam in front of my eyes. How did this all happen so fast? Did that mean we were never going home? I guess I'd been secretly hoping my mom and dad would get back together.

My peace of mind just went whoosh! I must have gone deathly pale because Mal looked funny at me.

"What's wrong with you?"

"Read it if you like. Then throw it in the garbage. Because that's what it is." I let out a low scream and then I fisted the letter into a ball and threw it on the floor.

Mal picked it up and read it.

"Woah! You've got a free trip to the United States."

"Are they insane! And the other 'good news'. Guess what? I bet they're going to have a baby. They both know I've always wanted a brother or sister."

"Hey, peace and love, Ava. This is how civil wars start," said Mal.

But it was going to take more than that to shake me out of my bad mood. "Come on, let's read Molly's letter. It'll take my mind off my own rotten family."

So we read about dark deeds right on our doorstep, a chill filling my bones.

⤬⤬⤬

I confided in Dr. Shanahan about my brother and Anto as we drove over to the Moynihans' farm near Killarney. He listened sympathetically. I could see why the Cumann na mBan trusted him.

There were a lot more patrols about. And after the boy spoke of the "redheaded Doctoreen" and my interview with Captain Ned, I was worried I was too conspicuous. So I concealed my hair under my hat and wore some wire-rimmed glasses. Dorothy had told me to keep some glasses in my bag in case I ever needed a disguise. I was glad I had now!

We were stopped by several patrols – Free State soldiers asking our business. Dr. Shanahan was polite and brief, saying that he was making house calls. One or two of the soldiers looked at me keenly but my disguise put them off the scent.

We drove on into Killarney. Such a beautiful town with the tall spire of the cathedral, surrounded by majestic mountains. We reached Moynihans' farm around midday.

The second incident was eerily like the first. Members of the Free State Army were based in the Great Southern Hotel in Killarney. Just hours after the explosion at Ballyseedy, five men were dragged from their prison cells in the barracks. The same cover story was used: the prisoners were to clear a roadblock, in case the rebels had booby-trapped it.

Among them was Tadgh Coffey who had been sentenced to death for possessing arms. In single file, they were marched by Free State soldiers across the fields from the hotel towards Countess Bridge less than half a mile away.

The prisoners were half-dressed and suffered in the bitter cold and biting wind. Some were bent double from beatings. At the sharp turn of the bridge, the five men were ordered to remove a barricade of rubble on the road. But there was a mine concealed in the stones.

The men, who had not been tied together, cautiously advanced. On a signal given by an officer, the mine was remotely detonated. Three of the prisoners caught the full force of the blast. Tadgh and his pal Jeremiah O'Donoghue were thrown to the ground but only slightly injured. The smoke and the dust cast a thick veil over the site. They could hear the groans of the dying men.

Tadgh tried to stand but his knee gave out under him. The soldiers threw grenades to finish the men off, then fired into the group of prisoners, bullets falling like hailstones.

Both men began to crawl away as fast as they could. They managed to get through the rubble to the other side of the bridge where there was a bend in the road before a burst of machine-gun fire rang out. O'Donoghue fell in his tracks, dead. Coffey risked standing and didn't buckle this time. He ran northwards, towards the Park Road. He jumped a nine-foot-high park gate, as bullets cut through his cap and clothes. He landed on his feet and ran to a clump of trees. Then he raced towards Kilcummin until his eyes were watering with the exertion.

When he thought he was out of range of the guns, he paused to regain his breath.

He knew of one safe house in the district, Moynihans', but he didn't know exactly where it was. In the distance, he could see a white house. Terrified, exhausted and hurt, he had to take a chance. When he reached it, he waited a few minutes to settle his breathing. Then he walked up to an open window and tapped lightly, casually asking the girl who peeped out for directions to Moynihans', hoping she wouldn't notice the state of him.

"This is Moynihans'," she replied.

Coffey was safe.

He wasn't as wounded as Stephen Fuller, though his hands and knees were lacerated from the crawling and he was covered in bruises. His left knee was also badly bruised. He trembled all over from the ordeal.

"The light was poor. The early-morning mist and the smoke from the blast saved me," he said.

We went outside to the barn to talk to Mr. Moynihan.

"Can you keep him safe for as long as possible?" Dr. Shanahan asked.

Mr. Moynihan was a decent man. "We'll have to move him to a long-term dugout. But first there's some lads from Dublin we need to move out. They ran foul of both sides. 'Tis easily done in these terrible times. But I know the wife's family in Tralee so I agreed to shelter them. Most people round here hide the lads, you know, no matter what side they're on."

My heart stopped. "Is it Jack and Anto? I'm Jack's sister."

He nodded his head and smiled. "I was thinking you might be the Doctoreen!"

"I need to get them to Dublin," I told Moynihan. "Can you take me to them?"

"I can. But there'll be search parties lookin' all over for them – both Staters and Republicans have a grudge against them," he said. "They're very recognisable fellows with the red and blond hair."

"Then they'll need to lose it. Can you bring a razor?" I asked. He nodded.

"But how are we going to get them out of Kerry alive?" I asked.

He winked at me. "We'll get them out easier dead! We have special deep coffins always at the ready. They have a false bottom and sliding panels at the side to get in and out of. And generally the soldiers show respect and don't like to look too close."

Dr. Shanahan drove us out the road past Muckross House and dropped us off near a bridge. He said he'd return in five hours and wait further up along the road where there was a lay-by sheltered by trees.

Moynihan took me trekking through the forest up to Torc Waterfall. It was a spectacular fall of water at the foot of Torc Mountain. Part of me wanted to step in, to wash away all the events of the day. But we had to climb the mountain.

The path was steep. There were some stepping-stones once the waterfall was behind us but the going was tough. A light mist blew in, like a veil. But it didn't stay and Mr. Moynihan pushed on. It took at least a couple of hours but he was confident leading the way and knew the terrain. Once we reached the summit, he pointed out a tumbledown old cottage covered in moss and ivy and surrounded by rocks and boulders. It was halfway down the other side of the mountain and you could miss it if it wasn't pointed out to you.

We picked our way down carefully as the ground was boggy in places. At the doorway, Moynihan let out three piercing whistles.

We went inside the wreck.

Towards the back, under a loose pile of leaves, was an old worn flagstone on the ground. Underneath was a cavity – just enough space for two men.

Two pairs of eyes peeped up at me. Anto and Jack, crouching in the hole.

"It's me – Molly," I said.

I was overjoyed to see them. They crawled out stiff and cold. But in good spirits, grinning with the pleasure of seeing me. Alive, blinking in the misty light.

"How on earth did you survive in there?" I asked.

"That's just the entrance," Jack said. "The cottage was built over a chamber in the rock that formed a natural basement. They used it for storage. It's quite roomy but I've had better lodgings. Besides, we're out and about a lot of the time."

I told them about the carnage that was happening. That they had to get away. That I had arranged passages to America for them. They nodded. They were willing to do whatever I told them.

I handed the razors to them. "Shave your heads. I'm going to organise your funerals."

Jack smiled. "I'm losing another of my nine lives."

Mr. Moynihan gazed at the length of Jack. "They're snug, mind. A bit of a squeeze for a big lad like you."

Jack grinned. "I've been in tighter spaces." He turned to me. "Give me one day, Molly. I need to mark these events."

I hesitated. "It's too dangerous."

"After these atrocities, there will be no safer place. They'll want people to see how far they will go," Jack argued. "We need to honour the dead." He bent down and retrieved something from the dugout. Two brown garments. He handed one to Anto and shook his out. Monks' cassocks with hoods. "And who will remark upon two holy brothers praying at the sites?"

I reluctantly agreed. It would take me at least a day to sort out our travel to Dublin. It was agreed. We set off to find Dr. Shanahan for our lift.

ഛംഔ

There was a note at the end from the Geek Squad, saying that that was the last of the transcriptions.

"But it's not fair! The story is left in mid-air!" I felt cheated. There wasn't even a signature. There must have been a page or more lost.

"We just have to sleuth a bit more," Mal said. "And at least we found out how he buried the jewel at Ballyseedy and his disguise."

"There must be another jewel at Countess Bridge just up the road!" I said. "It's the next initial and date on the map."

So we walked to the bridge, which was only about four hundred yards up the road from Nora's house. Mal lumbered along with the metal detector, while I carried a shovel borrowed from the garden.

It was an old stone bridge over the railway track on a dangerous, blind bend. You could see barns and beyond that a field of cows. On the other side of the bridge was a housing estate and across from that a parade of shops. Beyond that a roundabout, one of the roads leading to Tesco and other superstores. But the narrow bridge was in an isolated spot and surrounded by scrubby wasteland behind iron railings.

The monument was on the path by a lampost on the right-hand side just before the bridge. It was a simple stone gravestone. It had a crack but looked like it had been newly cleaned, commemorating the spot where four men were murdered by the Free State troops.

Near the monument was a little locked gate in a stone wall that led to some scrubland between the farm and the railway bank. We judged that to be the most likely place that Jack would pick to hide the jewel.

There were hardly any cars and no passersby. But we waited until the coast was completely clear. Then Mal jumped over the low gate. I passed him the rucksack and jumped in after him. Just beyond the gate by a spindly hazel tree and under a tangle of nettles and weeds we found a little packet wrapped in chamois leather, about two feet down in the mud. Inside the tin soldier lay a gleaming emerald encrusted with diamonds. We were elated.

Back at the house, Mal pored over the map inside the

peace-pipe bag, looking for inspiration.

"There are still those two more clues listed," he said. "OCD and PD, dated the 17th March 1923."

He turned the bag over, scanning it for any possible leads. Then he peered closely at it.

"Look!" he said, pointing.

I squinted at some faint markings on it in a circle, near the stitching. "It looks a bit like a cattle brand. I've seen it on a dairy farm belonging to a friend of my dad's."

The mark was worn with age. It looked a little bit like a cat.

"Whoever made this map did it after all these events," Mal said. "Who knows how long after."

"Maybe they ended up in Texas. That's cattle country," I said jokingly.

"Maybe they did," Mal said thoughtfully. "Maybe they did."

I looked at him sharply. "There's something you're not sharing."

"It's nothing. When I have something concrete I'll let you know."

He slunk off into Nora's study and went on her computer. When I looked in he got up and closed the door.

I sighed. No matter how much time I spent with him, Mal was never quite straight with me.

I went to stare out the window at the view. I thought of all those terrible things that had happened in this beautiful place not even a hundred years ago. I felt let down with the way we'd hit a dead end in the story, like a kid who didn't get what she wanted for Christmas. And hurt by the way Mal was shutting me out of whatever bright idea he had.

The phone rang briefly. Mal must have answered it.

He emerged out of the study, a bit agitated.

"Who was that on the phone?" I asked.

"Nuisance call," he said.

Nora came back at that point and, seeing our long faces, suggested we visit Torc Waterfall and climb the mountain.

Mal was more enthusiastic than I was. "Come on. It might make us feel close to Molly, Anto and Jack. To walk in their footsteps."

"I don't suppose you'll tell me what you're up to?" I said resentfully.

"It's on a need-to-know basis, for your own protection, kid," he said. "I'll tell you when the time is right."

Torc Waterfall was about ten miles up the road, just beyond Muckross House, a big stately home surrounded by lakes and a country park.

Mal kept taking furtive looks back along the road. I assumed he was looking out for the geography teachers.

Nora dropped us off and said she'd pick us up in a few hours.

The entrance just off the road was full of bustle and activity. In the car park there were jarveys with cartloads of tourists pulled by horses. Gaggles of foreign students clogged the way. We walked up the mossy footpath to the waterfall through the woodland, the river on our right.

Tons of people queued for pictures and selfies by the large boulders. Behind them the cascade of swirling water pounded into the river. A sparkling waterfall in a fairytale.

We continued up the gently climbing flat slabs of shale, then a steep ladder of steps, pausing now and then to look at the view. Glassy lakes below us, mountains meeting the sky. We crossed over by another car park. The ascent to the summit looked pretty rough. But luckily there was a boardwalk that zig-zagged up the mountain.

I puffed and panted but enjoyed the climb, feeling lightheaded and excited to be following in Molly's footsteps. Though Molly didn't have railway sleepers covered in chicken wire and a laid-out path to walk on. The higher we climbed, the fewer the trees, the ground covered by rough grass and rocks with patches of gorse. The sleepers gave way to a stony path and flagstones.

After about an hour of steady uphill walking we reached the summit. And, boy, was the view spectacular! All around lay a 360-degree view of mountains. Over towards the wooded parkland of Muckross House, the large splash of glittering Lough Leane. The mountains deep violet in the sun. Everything was like a picture book. The broken ruins of Muckross Abbey. Puffy clouds dancing across the wide sky.

Mal had the binoculars I'd borrowed from Nora and scanned for a ruined cottage on the other side of the mountain.

"Down there," he said, pointing.

I looked through the lenses. Tucked into the mountain was a tumbledown stone structure covered in moss and ivy, set among boulders and rocks. Just as Molly had described it.

We picked our way down to it, breathing hard. The ground was much rougher on this side and there was no path. We were far from any other tourists now.

We were glad to reach the cottage.

Inside was the large flagstone, with ivy creeping over it, just as Molly had described. With much huffing and puffing, we inched it to one side. Below us was the entrance to the dugout, about three feet deep and maybe two and a half feet across, with just enough room for two crouching down. Mal pulled a torch from his rucksack and shone the light inside. We peeked in. The entrance was lined with half-rotten sacking and planks of wood. Then there was a step down to a rock cave – the natural basement Jack had mentioned. It was hard to see but was about ten foot by ten foot and there seemed to be old mattresses and boxes in it.

"This was where Molly found Jack and Anto!' I said. "It's like a tomb!"

There was a sudden, loud thrum. A tocca-tocca-tocca sound. We peeked out of the cottage. Up above was a police helicopter, its blades whirring to stay static.

I looked through the binoculars. On the crest of the mountain a couple of Gardaí were combing the slope. Leading them were the two "geography teachers" who'd been following us around Kerry on our own unique tour of Civil War atrocities.

"They're looking for us, aren't they?" I said.

Mal nodded.

We didn't hesitate. Mal killed the torch and we dived down into the hidey-hole, and moved the flagstone cover over us with the flat of our hands, leaving a small gap so we could peek out.

Chapter twenty

We crouched down like two animals wanting to burrow into the earth. We didn't dare venture into the cave. I really didn't want to go there. Already I was claustrophobic.

Jack and Anto must have felt like they were buried alive. The entrance was bad enough – it was sturdy but despite the sacking lining it smelled earthy and like compost. The cold shot up from the bowels of the earth.

"Okay, shoot, laughing boy," I whispered. "You have about five minutes to tell me why two tourists who look like geography teachers and some Irish cops are on our tail." My voice cracked and my tinny laugh made me sound like a bonkers hyena.

"They're probably not geography teachers," hissed Mal. "I'd say they're Irish detectives. It's possible it's a joint operation with the FBI."

I'd say my eyes popped out of my head like Bart Simpson's. But Mal couldn't see me.

"So Suzy the creep from school was correct in saying

you were a criminal?" I hissed at Mal.

"I'm not a criminal. I'm a seeker for truth," he said. "Or a misguided loner as the psychiatric report said. Or a clever kid trying too hard to be cool as the judge decided. Or a stupid idiot who's a disgrace to the family name as my dad thinks. Take your pick."

I kicked against the bottom of his trousers. "And that tag around your leg isn't some fashion accessory."

"No, it's a tag that all the best criminals are wearing. I'm on probation. Banned from computers. Not supposed to leave home outside a twenty-kilometre radius. I thought I'd cracked how to override the system to come here. I tampered with the –"

"Don't tell me how they mal-function! Mr. Mal-function yourself!" I interrupted. "I don't want to be an accessory to a crime!"

"I left a note for my dad saying I was going to visit my aunt who lives just outside Dublin," he continued.

"Well, that was a pretty poor cover story," I said. "He'd work out you were lying with one phone call."

"Better than leading them straight here," he hissed. "Unfortunately my tag must have GPS navigation as well as radio frequency."

"Okay, start at the beginning," I told him.

"I was the 'Teenage Ninja Hacker'. You might not have heard of me but it was a big case here just over a year ago. I was thirteen. One of the youngest ever hackers to shut down several government networks including an FBI site in the US and, well, in China, Russia and a few others too . . ." He said the last bit with a little note of pride.

"Woah! This is hurting my head. You're some kind of loony hacker!"

"Nah. As the judge said I was just trying to be too clever. I got bored with *Dungeons and Dragons*. It started as a game. To see if I could. And I could. I was really, really good at it. I launched a cyber-attack on places that were mistreating animals. Then a few places where I thought they needed to tighten their security. And then countries that were involved in bad wars. Oh, and this café where they were rude to my gran."

"Mal, you're a computer genius!"

"It was easy really. I used Distributed Denial of Service, DDoS attacks for short, to cripple computer systems by bombarding them with data."

"Yeah, but you know little old me," I said. "I'm a good girl. I think that was real bad."

"Then the real hardcore hackers, the 'hactivists' and the anarchists began to pick up on what I was doing. They tried to reel me in but I got scared. Then the FBI tracked me down."

"So how come you're not in prison?"

"I pleaded guilty and I was real sorry. The judge said she was a bit disappointed because there was no trial and I'd deprived her of a really special case."

"That was her outside the Four Courts! Why did she take pity on you?"

"Judge Angela Wilkinson is her name. She said a

youth detention centre would destroy me. That I didn't realise the consequences of what happens in the real world when you do those things. Also my sad family history. Blah, blah."

"So why are these guys coming to arrest us?"

"Well, I got a two-year youth rehabilitation order and two-year supervision. That's why I have the tag. So the police can keep an eye on me. And why I'm always hot-tailing it to report in. The worst thing is they destroyed my computer and I'm not allowed to own one until my case is reviewed in a year's time. My dad banned me from all screens for good measure."

I nudged him in our tomb.

"So the geography teachers?"

"I think they're from the Computer Crime Investigation Unit," he said. "I couldn't help it. I started looking into documents to try to solve our mystery, first on my dad's computer, then on Nora's. I'd better tell you quickly. I think our guys Jack the Cat and Anto are linked to this ranch in Texas. Called 'Jack the Cat's'. The names don't quite tally. James Adair was the previous owner. That's as far as I got. And with the brand on the map –"

I gasped. "Remember! Adair was one of the mothers' maiden names Molly used to buy the tickets!"

"Of course! Well spotted, Ava!"

"But why didn't you tell me any of this before, Sherlock Holmes?"

"I don't want to get you into trouble."

"Thanks, pal. And the Russian?" I shivered. The cold

earth was penetrating my bones.

"That's an interesting one. Almost certainly he's stolen the jewels. He's some kind of bounty hunter. He has quite a few aliases – Gregor Aronovitch, Vladimir Nureyev, Jean Klampe. I wasn't able to crack the Interpol security system. But when he sees the incomplete state of the jewels, he'll be disappointed."

I desperately wanted to peek out to see where the cops were. I felt trapped in the tomb. It was getting noisier outside. The cops were closing in on us.

"Mal, you broke your court order to come to Kerry with me," I whispered.

He punched me lightly on the shoulder. "You're my friend. Watson to my Holmes."

I burst into tears. Quietly. It wasn't any of the other stuff. Just the word friend. "You're my best friend," I said. "But don't get too big-headed because you're my only friend."

We gave each other a very low five in the dark.

"So if we were in a movie, Mal, we'd have a shoot-out. But I think we've got to turn ourselves in."

Someone was saying something through a loud speaker. It sounded incredibly close and very far away at the same time.

"Mal and Ava. Can you show yourselves, please? You won't be in trouble," a man with a deep, musical Kerry accent shouted out.

And I almost believed him.

"Damn! They're able to pinpoint me exactly with the

co-ordinates!" hissed Mal, banging at his tag.

I whispered to Mal. "Are we in a whole heap of trouble?"

"I am. For the hacking bit. But I'll take the blame. I had to search for the Russian on the Dark Net – that's the hidden internet where all the bad people lurk – and that probably triggered the interest of the Computer Crime people. The FBI and Interpol too. I'm out of practice. I didn't cover my tracks properly."

"Wouldn't it be simpler to tell the truth? It's not like we've stolen the jewels. We were just waiting until we had them all. But I don't want to get Patrick into trouble at the lab. Or Rachel."

Mal was silent for a moment. I could almost hear the wheels of his mind whirring in the dark.

"The Russian is our trump card," he said. "He's on a lot of wanted lists. I tell them about him and they might be more lenient on us."

"Okay. I vote we just come clean. Agreed?"

"Agreed. But once they start these investigations, they take ages. And I still might be put away. You have those two tickets to America. Maybe you could go there and check out Jack the Cat's Texan ranch?"

"I'll consider it for your sake. But, tell me, why in heaven's name are they chasing us up a mountain? Couldn't they wait until we got back to town?" I knew it was a terrible situation but I really wanted to giggle. Nerves, I guess.

I could feel Mal blush in the dark. "The Gardaí

emailed Nora the other day, saying I was to come to the station. I deleted it. That was them on the phone just before we left the house, saying they were coming by to question me. I guess they think we've legged it. But it does seem like an overreaction."

That really did make me giggle for some strange reason.

There was the muffled sound of footsteps outside.

"Mal, Ava – come out now, please."

"Okay, partner, let's face the music," I said.

I'd always wanted to say that.

Chapter twenty-one

The sunshine of Texas stabbed my eyes after all that mist in Ireland. It felt really strange to be back in the good old US of A. Particularly as I was kind of a fugitive from justice.

Okay, I'm kidding. After our arrest and questioning, they realized I wasn't worth putting on a wanted list.

Mal was right. The geography teachers from the Computer Crime Investigation Unit were more interested in his hacking. And the police admitted they had gone over the top with the helicopter when they saw we were a couple of kids.

Nora's steely legal-eagle side came out and she said I could sue them for not following proper procedures. So they were super-nice to me. I cried a lot of snotty tears and told them everything. But Nora couldn't help poor old Mal. He was taken into detention in the youth centre for violating his parole and computer-fraud offences.

While he was waiting for his juvenile court hearing, we were not allowed contact. I'd written a long rambling letter saying that Mal was like a big brother to me, he only got involved with the jewel search for my sake and was really kind, blah, blah. I didn't expect it would do much good. But Nora said we had them on the back foot. He would be let out soon.

We handed over the jewels we found: the Beál na mBláth and Ballyseedy finds and the Countess Road one, which was also in good condition but without the drop-stone. At least neither Patrick nor Rachel got into trouble. In fact, Patrick's lab was only too delighted to be asked to run tests on our Kerry finds.

Mal was also right about the cops being so obsessed with the hacking that they didn't seem that interested in the jewels or the other clues in the letters. He also had another theory that they were pretending not to be interested in the jewels. But Nora said they were just focused on the computer stuff because that was their department.

The good thing was my mother promised the cops that she'd get her act together. I would get to see my dad. So she flew with me from Shannon to New York and then to Dallas in Texas where I would meet my dad for the engagement party. She travelled on separately to a retreat centre in the Arizona desert recommended by Nora. I would meet her back in New York to go back to Ireland – still couldn't think of it as home.

But I was hoping what I found in Texas would help me fulfil my promise to Mal and solve our history mystery. I wanted to find out what had happened to

Molly, Jack and Anto. And solve the last two clues.

I was dying to see my dad but I was also afraid. Of my own reaction mainly. The first time I saw him in the airport in Dallas in Texas I was kind of shy. There he was, all six foot two of him, with his shaggy hair and craggy face that formed dimples when he smiled. But within seconds I was hugging him tight. He was in tears. And if you knew my dad that would be a big surprise. He's not the emotional type. In a heartbeat, it was as if I'd never left. We were our old selves again.

But I wasn't quite so ready to embrace Honey Belle. To tell you the truth, it was a bit weird to think she was going to be my stepmom. My face ached from smiling inanely at her and Dad, pretending to be happy for them at their engagement party.

Some party. There was only the three of us. And Honey Belle's boring mommy who had insisted on us all coming to Dallas because she had some weird phobia about travel. Lorena ran a diner and spent her whole time pinching my cheeks. "Why, I could eat ya'all up," she kept saying. She only shut up when I told her that, had we both been alive during the American Civil War, we would have been on different sides. And, as a Yankee, I would have had to take her Confederate butt prisoner.

But even she couldn't stop me being super-excited to be in Texas. Because that was where Jack the Cat's ranch was, near Austin. I had no intention of leaving without checking it out.

Then something came up at his work and my dad had

to take a plane back to New York a day before I left. So I basically demanded that Honey Belle should drive me to Jack the Cat's on my last day. She was almost thanking me for asking her, she was so desperate to please me.

I was on a mission. I needed to find the last jewels listed on the map and some evidence of what happened to Molly, Jack and Anto. So I put up with Honey Belle telling me how much she loved me and how thrilled she was that I was going to be a big sister. Oh, did I mention the baby? Yes, as I expected, Honey Belle was pregnant. Yada yada yada. "I'm like so thrilled you're going to have another kid that you love more than me. Give it all the love you're depriving me of, why dontcha?"

No, I didn't actually say that but I felt like it. I wondered what Molly would have done. But I guess what with trying to save her brother and Anto and bring peace to Ireland, she wouldn't have minded about an itty-bitty baby. She'd have passed on smart advice like she did to Anto's wife – even though I don't think she liked her much either.

So instead of sulking and stropping as Honey Belle had to stop the car and throw up so much, I started to talk to her like Molly.

"You should try raspberry tea," I said. "Women in Ireland used to take it coming up to labour. And eat nettle soup. It's full of iron and stuff."

Honey Belle looked like she could have exploded with happiness. "I'll do that! Oh, I just know ya'all are going to be the best sister ever to Li'l Peanut."

The new baby had even taken my nickname! I used to laugh so much to be called "Pie-nut" in her Texan accent.

"Half-sister," I said. "You're not my mother. And you never will be."

"I know that, darlin'."

"And I'm not darlin' either."

Tears ran down her face. Despite myself, something moved inside me. My heart beat that little bit faster, remembering how much I used to love Honey Belle. I used to want her to be my big sister. But then I saw the engagement ring on her finger and it made me angry all over again.

So we rode in silence to the outskirts of Austin. I suppose I should have been really happy that she was driving me so far. Because it was about three hours away from Dallas. Texas is like HUGE! I'd had a vague idea I would get a bus there if Honey Belle hadn't obliged. But by the time we got there I realised what a dumb notion that was. No way could I have done it and got back for my flight that evening. No way would she have let me either.

A tingle ran up my spine when I saw the big sign – *Jack the Cat's Ranch* – tricked out in wrought iron over a big gate. There was also a figure of a cat and a symbol of a harp and a horseshoe! That wasn't just random.

The whole place was deserted. There was a "For Sale" sign on the ranch house – a large wooden house with two wings and a long porch. With peeling paint and a sagging roof it looked like it had seen better days. Big cacti were dotted around the house. There were lots of pens around the outskirts and barns, all empty of animals. Tumbleweed blew through the yard. It was a ghost house in a dust bowl.

While Honey Belle went off to throw up some more, I rooted around looking for signs of life under the blistering Texas sun. Just as I was about to give up, a man roared up on a buggy. He was Mexican, middle-aged, with a smiling face and snaggle teeth.

"This is private property," he said in his sing-song accent.

"And the owner, where is he?"

His eyes narrowed. "Why are you asking?"

I decided to risk a bit of spoofing, and a really bad Irish accent

"Mr. O'Donovan and meself are . . . sort of related, to be sure. I'm from the old country, so I am."

He smiled then. "Ah, Irish. But the owner is a Mr. Adair."

Jack's alias! I perked up. "Did you ever hear of Jack the Cat?"

He shook his head. "That is all I know. I am just a security man."

"So where is the current owner?"

The Mexican chuckled. "Jack Junior is over ninety! He is in Fairweather old people's home out by the lake."

Jack Junior Adair. He must have been called after his dad. I looked at my watch. Time was tight. But we could just squeeze it in and still make our flight if we dashed off now.

As we drove over, I did the Math quickly in my head. Jack Junior could be Jack the Cat's son if he was born around 1924. Honey Belle was too busy concentrating on driving to ask me any questions, which I was glad about.

Fairweather Retirement Home was a spruce new apartment block with some sprightly elders playing tennis and golf in the grounds. We parked right in front of reception as Honey Belle needed to make a quick dash to the bathroom. As we walked up the path to the entrance, one of the old folk lobbed a ball over the surrounding net and I threw it back. A woman came up to thank me. She was probably eighty but her face had the frozen plastic-surgery look, like someone had given her a new head on an old wrinkly body.

"Come to visit us seniors in our open prison?" she said gaily.

"I'm here to see Jack Junior – eh, I think his name is Adair."

"He's on a different wing to us," she said. "He can't get around none. Matron Masterson wraps us up in cotton wool. Just because we had that bug. Won't let anyone in either. Keeps the germs out."

The reception area was as sterile as a laboratory. But no amount of air freshener could disguise the old-people smell of boiled cabbage and wee. I knew the smell. My dad's mommy had Alzheimer's and ended up in a place like this. She was so kind, it hurts my heart every time I think of her.

While Honey Belle was in the bathroom, I asked the

receptionist in my best grown-up voice if there was a Jack Junior O'Donovan staying there. She smiled a big smile like she was advertising toothpaste as she checked on her computer.

"I'm sorry, hon. No O'Donovan. The only Jack Junior we have is a Adair."

I cursed myself. Trust me to say the wrong name. "Oh gee, that's him. I mixed him up with my other grandfather. Say, what are the chances of having two called Jack Junior!"

"How sweet of y'all to visit your – what must he be – great grand-daddy?"

I nodded inanely.

"And what is your name?"

"Ava eh Adair Kelly," I lied.

Tooth-advert receptionist toddled off into an inner office. But her face bore a look of disappointment when she came back.

"I'm sorry, hon, I don't have any record of y'all on our list."

Honey Belle came back then. "But Ava has come all this way from Dublin – that's in Ireland, Europe. We don't have much time. We have to get back to Dallas for her flight to New York."

"Gee, I'm sorry, hon. But it's our policy."

"Do I look like a thief?" I risked. I hoped I wasn't now on some FBI list like Mal.

"Can I please speak to the manager?" Honey Belle said.

"Matron Masterson won't be back for another fifteen minutes," said the receptionist. "But it won't change a thing."

"We'll wait," said Honey Belle firmly.

We sat down.

Then, just as I opened one of the Hershey bars Honey Belle had bought me, the chatty old lady in tennis whites wandered back in.

"They not lettin' you in, sweet child?" she asked.

I nodded.

"I'll be darned that they even let us in," she winked. She eyed my Hershey bar. "Doctor said I should cut down on sugar because of my diabetes and now I can't have anything sweeter than a crab apple."

The receptionist popped her head out of the inner office. Seeing it was one of the old folk, she buzzed her in. Honey Belle had another throwing-up emergency and dashed to the toilet.

But as soon as the receptionist turned her back, the tennis lady winked at me and held the door.

"Third floor, Primrose wing. Code is 2020," she whispered. "Watch out for Masterson. You can't miss her. Smiles like she has a pain in her large rear end!"

I handed her my Hershey bar. She grabbed it eagerly and hid it in her pocket.

I dashed up the stairs, figuring I'd have less chance of being detected. The Primrose wing was on the left of the top floor. Through the window of the security door, the corridor was deserted. I punched in the code and raced along the corridor. Most of the old people up here were lying in bed.

I panicked slightly that I wouldn't be able to find the room. But the names were on the doors, and I soon came to "Jack Junior" halfway down the corridor.

I went in. The room had a cold iron bed, one chair and a bedside cabinet, like in a hospital. Lying in the bed was a very ancient old man. His yellowish skin was so thin it looked like parchment and his veins stood out on his forehead.

My palms went clammy and my heart pitter-patted. What if I had given him a heart attack! But he snored slightly so I knew he was still living.

I looked at his chart. "Parkinson's and dementia," it said. "Liquids only."

Oh dear. That meant his brain was gone a bit wobbly and he'd forgotten more than he remembered. He might not be able to communicate much or make sense. I felt bad about crashing in on him. But he was my only hope.

There was a murmur from the bed.

"Who's there?" a frail voice called out.

I turned round. The old man's eyes were open. They were a startling shade of blue, like two pieces of the Texan sky. His eyes darted round, still full of life.

"I'm from Ireland," I said. "I want to know about Jack the Cat and his sister Molly."

The old man smiled. He must have been really handsome once, with high cheekbones and a straight nose like a ski slope.

He tried to speak and gestured towards the side of the bed. "Water," he said in a very faint voice.

I pressed the switch to raise the bed slightly so he was sitting up and brought a glass of water from the bedside table with a straw. He sipped and gave me a beautiful smile.

"Molly, how lovely to see you. And where are you now? So glad you made it that time. My father always spoke of you."

"No, I'm not Molly," I said. "I'm Ava. I live in Ireland and I'm trying to find out what happened to your aunt, her brother Jack the Cat and their friend Anto. They were from Dublin. They were in the Civil War in Ireland."

His vivid blue eyes opened wider and he sat bolt upright.

"My Aunt Molly . . . medicine woman." He spoke in a slightly slurred voice.

He gestured towards the wooden bedside cabinet. But when I tried it I found it was locked.

"Is there a key?" I asked him. My eyes darted anxiously about the room.

His hand flailed about wildly. He couldn't control it to point properly.

"You're an angel!" he suddenly exclaimed. "Get me out of bed!" He squirmed up out of the sheets, pushing them off, and tried to get out. I went to his side and helped him. He was in stripy blue pyjamas, and his poor old legs were withered and bent with age. But when he got to his feet he was still surprisingly strong.

"The window," he said.

I held his elbow and we moved forward, faltering step after faltering step towards the window which looked out on the front of the building. The small upper part of the window was open and some fresh air wafted into the room.

"Rode bareback until his eighties. Could have been in the movies but there weren't much call for a blond Injun." He broke into a wheezy chuckle that winded him.

"Are you talking about yourself or your father?" I asked.

But before he could answer, a crackling sound issued from an intercom box on the wall.

"*Mr. Adair, is everything all right?*" It was the fake-smiling receptionist.

"Never better!" he roared with sudden force. Then lowering his voice, he said to me. "In the box." He waved his gnarled old hand again.

I noticed a little jewellery box on the windowsill. There was a key inside.

I left Jack Junior leaning on the windowsill, enjoying the view outside and breathing deeply, while I went to the bedside cabinet. With fumbling fingers, I opened the locker.

The contents of the cabinet spilled out. Bric-a-brac, piles of framed photographs full of good-looking, smiling people. Family shots, graduation shots, group shots of ranch hands and horses.

Right at the bottom, there was a battered old leather

album. My heart leapt as I picked it up.

"Pa and Aunt Molly – all gone," Jack whispered from the window. "Finest folk you could ever meet."

I carried the album over to him and he touched it tenderly with his old arthritic hand.

I opened it. On the first page was a photograph of an old man riding a horse. Even though old, he looked like a movie star.

"Bareback until his eighties," he repeated.

"Was that your pa Jack the Cat?" I said. "And Molly?"

He gestured towards the album again.

On the next page was a black-and-white photograph of a sweet-faced woman in an old-fashioned hat.

"Mama," he said.

I scrutinised the image. She had dark hair and a kind face. "Is that your mother May?" I asked him.

He smiled broadly.

"Was her brother called Anto?"

But he just continued smiling.

"Could have been in Hollywood," he said. "But wouldn't shoot, or even pretend. Said he made some promise to never shoot a gun . . . maybe to his sister or my ma . . ." The memory got away from him. "And there wasn't much call for a blond Injun." He chuckled again and coughed.

I gave him some more water.

There was a lot of crackle on the intercom. "*Jack Junior, remain calm. We're going to send someone up to see y'all are just fine and dandy.*"

Oh no! I was so startled I nearly dropped the album.

"*I am fine and dandy!*" he called out with sudden force. Then he smiled at me and whispered "Shush!" like we were kids playing a prank at school.

"Were there ever any maps?" I whispered.

He nodded his head and tapped the old album at the back.

I turned it over and found a parchment paper and a couple of pages on flimsy paper tucked into the back sleeve. I took them out and glanced quickly. The two pages were covered in some kind of number code on both sides of the paper! It just had to be a letter. And the parchment was a replica of the leather map we had in Dublin. I put the map back in but held onto the coded pages for a closer look.

The intercom crackled into life again. "*Jack Junior, if an intruder comes into your room, remain calm.*"

Me an intruder!

Jack Junior tottered against the window frame, chuckling like a naughty schoolboy. He lurched forward on his spindly legs towards the pile of stuff from the cabinet. And with great effort nudged an old battered yellow tin with his foot. It said "*Jacobs Cream Crackers*" on it and was about half the size of a normal tin but deeper. The lid pictured a smiling dairymaid holding a milk pail.

The sharp clack of an electronic door pinging open. Voices rising and falling in the distance.

I froze, looking at the mess all over the floor.

He gestured towards the letter that was still in my

hand. I panicked. My hands went clammy. I was wearing shorts and a T-shirt and had no pockets.

Thump, thump! The footsteps were crashing down the corridor now. Voices calling urgently.

I floundered and pushed the letter under the pillow on the bed.

The footsteps were outside. The old man grabbed my hand with his gnarled one. But there was power in his grip.

"My angel," he said.

The door flung open.

"Young lady, you must not disturb the residents!"

The speaker was a plump woman in her late thirties accompanied by an unsmiling nurse and an embarrassed-looking security man. She smiled at me in a pained way, just like the tennis lady said she would. The badge in her starched white coat said, "Matron Masterson".

She turned her attention to Jack Junior. "Now back into bed with you." She had a thin grating voice. The nurse immediately escorted Jack back to sit on his bed.

Matron Masterson looked in horror at the mess on the floor.

"*Clear that up!*" she barked at the nurse. She grabbed me by the shoulder and thrust me towards the security man. "Search her!"

The man, a Mexican, already quite old himself, looked shamefaced and hung back.

"I didn't take anything," I said, shaking out my T-shirt and patting my shorts.

"All right, young lady, that won't be necessary," said Matron Masterson, glaring at me. "But we could still prosecute you for trespassing!"

There was the sound of rasping laughter. "Best fun I've had all year!" Jack Junior said with such glee even the grim-faced nurse smiled.

The Matron took a step towards me and, speaking through her teeth in a strained voice, said, "Now kindly get out of here."

"Could I come back some day?"

She lowered her voice. "You will have to apply through the proper channels. But given your flagrant disregard for the rules, I can't say I would recommend it."

She ushered me out of the room. I obeyed.

But as I went through the door, I thought I heard the old man murmur again. I bounded back inside the room and over to him.

"Bring my pa's ashes home," he whispered, nodding towards the biscuit tin.

The kind-faced security officer took me gently by the elbow and led me out.

When we got out of earshot, I spoke to him. "Can you please let Jack Junior know I was sure pleased to meet him. I'm sorry I left the letter he wanted me to have under his pillow."

The security officer nodded at me. "I'll do that right away. You make your own way out." He went back to the room.

On the walk back to the car, I gazed forlornly up at Jack Junior's window on the third storey. I caught the faint outline of a person and a hand waving. I waved back and turned towards the car.

But something flew before my eyes. A paper airplane floated on the breeze. I snatched it from the air.

I dashed to the car at the bottom of the path and leaped in.

"Drive!" I said to Honey Belle.

Clutched in my hand were the carefully folded sheets of the coded letter. Somehow Jack Junior had managed to throw them out of the window. Maybe the security man had helped him.

I tingled inside, knowing I had the final piece of our puzzle.

I couldn't wait now to get back to Dublin to discuss the latest developments with Mal. I was real hopeful the judge would let us have contact.

Honey Belle had one more surprise for me at the airport. We'd planned it so I would meet my mother at the departure lounge as she was catching a connecting flight from the Spa clinic in Arizona. Honey Belle and I went for one last cup of coffee. I was a bit grumpy because we had a full hour to sit staring at each other before my flight was called.

As I sat down with my smoothie, Honey Belle touched my arm and said, "There's someone here I think you should meet."

I looked up.

Well, if it wasn't ole Cleeter picking his way through the tables in that pigeon-toed way of his. His big head looking too heavy for his body like a tulip on a stem. He looked taller and I noticed a weedy little moustache creeping across his top lip. He broke into his big smile and it was infectious. I stood up, really pleased to see him. My silly heart skittering in my chest with the pure joy of it.

"Fancy meeting you here!"

He shrugged in that sweet dimpled way of his, like he'd been doing since nursery. But the smile died on my lips when I saw dumpy little Cookie emerging from behind him, trailing him like a vine.

They sat down opposite me. Cleeter, after his initial enthusiasm was now trying to look cool. Cookie hunched in to him like a limpet looking for her rock. Her tiny pale-blue eyes blinked in her white face as she wove a piece of her blonde hair around her finger.

I crunched an ice cube in my mouth. "Look, I'm literally breaking the ice!" I said. Cleeter laughed too loud. Cookie tittered behind her hand.

"Must be hard going back to Europe where I guess you don't have any friends. So I heard." That was Cookie's style. Say something innocent but with a mean little dig in it.

"Cookie, you heard wrong. I have made a really good friend."

"Me and Cleeter have been hanging out with Luciella and her posse since you left." Luciella was the coolest

305

girl in the class. And the meanest. Before I would have been dead jealous. But now I couldn't have cared less. No, really.

"My friend's name is Mal." I felt an inward glow as I said his name. "He's kind of like my big brother. He got himself into a whole heap of trouble just so he could help me."

Cookie rolled her eyes. But I could swear I saw Cleeter blush. Maybe he did feel bad that he hadn't been a better friend to me.

A thought that had been hovering burst into my mind. If Jack the Cat had made it to America, maybe Molly and Anto didn't. I felt a pang at the idea of the old friends separated.

"Hello, Ava! Have you been listening to a word I'm saying?" Cleeter's voice wavered. It was beginning to break.

"We're going to this really cool camp," Cookie said. "Cleeter said that drama camp you and he used to go to was really boring. With Shakespeare and all. Yawn!"

I raised my eyebrows. Cleeter used to love that camp.

"We're going to a pop music camp instead. You know how our moms are best friends. Just like me and Cleeter. They arranged it."

Cleeter's mom and my mom used to be best friends. Cookie was trying to stick the knife in. But I took a deep breath and sat back in my chair. For some reason Molly came into my head. Her sadness at good friends killing each other.

For once in my life I didn't take Cookie's bait. I looked hard at both of them. Cleeter who I'd known since I was a toddler. Cookie who I'd befriended in school and took under my wing because she was a new girl. She was funny and sweet most of the times. Before she got jealous of me. I had introduced them. They were the last two people I would ever have expected to be mean to me.

"I'm really glad you're making lots of new friends," I said. "I hope you will always make new friends. Good ones too, like I have Mal in Dublin. But just remember, Cleeter. I'll always be your oldest friend. No matter how long we live, you and me were really good friends for the first part of our lives. And you too, Cookie. I've known you since fourth grade. You can't make 'new' old friends."

Cleeter face lit up. He made the happy face we used to think was real cool – a thumbs-up either side of a big grin. It was an old joke between us since we'd played in the sandpit together in our local playground. I didn't want to leave Cookie out. So I high-fived with both of them. Then suddenly we were playing a clapping game we'd loved since we were eight. I felt good.

My flight was being called. It was time to go. As I walked towards the departure area, I turned back and waved. Cookie clinging onto Cleeter's arm, Honey Belle beside them. The three people who had hurt me the most in the whole wide world. I felt a pang. They looked so little from this distance.

Then I did something that surprised even me. I ran back to them and gathered them all in a big group hug.

"Hey, you guys! Don't be strangers."

Honey Belle burst into snotty tears. "I love you, Ava Kelly, don't ever forget that."

The intercom blared. "Would all remaining passengers for the flight to Dublin please make their way to the departures lounge?"

"And if you're passing my old apartment block, can you give Floppy a hug from me?"

I broke away from them and walked quickly towards the security barrier.

I had a curious sensation, like a big weight was falling off my shoulders with every step I took. Back in Dublin, there was Mal. And a mystery to solve!

I slept all the way through the flight home, slumped on my mother's shoulder. She was tanned and relaxed, more like my old mother. As I walked through the arrivals area of Dublin airport, I fumbled and dropped my bag. When I bent down to pick it up, I could have sworn I saw a swarthy-looking man in a beanie hat built like a garden shed, watching me from a coffee shop. But when I straightened up, he was gone.

Chapter twenty-two

The judge had been impressed with my letter begging for forgiveness and Mal was back home. He said the Rehabilitation Centre hadn't been too bad. So we got back to work untangling the mystery. We worked hard transcribing the letter I'd brought from America, hoping it would fill in some of the gaps in Molly's story. It was again a string of numbers in tiny writing on both sides of the pages.

On the top right-hand corner there was a little circle with the letter 'S' written above the number 7.

"It must be another letter/number substitution," I said.

Mal took our number wheel and lined up 7 and S to crack the code. Each letter now corresponded with a number, T was 8, U was 9 and so on.

I told him about seeing the Russian in Dublin airport.

"Maybe we can organise a sting," Mal said. "Smoke him out. On my dad's computer."

"Oh, not again, Mal," I said. "More trouble."

"Relax. I'm allowed half an hour a day. The judge decided a total ban was too severe and I hadn't actually done anything terrible. But let's do this transcription old style."

I was glad. I liked working on the code up there in the attic and typing it out on the typewriter that went "ping". It made me feel closer to Molly and the effort she must have put in.

＄⊙⊙＄

March 1923

Dear Sanjay,

The rebels have blown up many of the bridges and rail links. So we had to go by road for long stretches of the journey back to Dublin. I hired a horse and cart to transport the coffins. At some stages, we had to go off the road, where there were blockades. We finally caught the train at Mallow.

With great good fortune my friend Joseph was the train conductor. Dan and I had met him when Cork burnt down in 1921.

There were frequent stops, transfers to other lines. I sat with the coffins in the goods carriage for some of the time. I also had a seat in the next passenger carriage.

At Limerick Junction we had to transfer to another train. I went to the buffet car for some tea soon after and noticed there was a strange festive air on the train – a ripple of excitement with passengers looking out the window. When we pulled out of each station, there was a cheer. I assumed it was because people were so relieved we were travelling at all.

We'd only got as far as Athlone when a ragged group wearing trench coats held up the train at a signal point. I was sitting in the buffet car at the time. My hands went cold and clammy, heart pounded in my chest. Through the glass window I watched with dread as they advanced down the aisle of the neighbouring carriage. They looked wild, desperate, with bandoliers of bullets crossways around their shoulders, toting guns. They each had a kerchief over the bottom part of their faces, like gangsters, and made rough jerking movements with their guns. I was terror-stricken, not sure what to do.

"Hand over your money, food and valuables!" one young ruffian roared like a highwayman.

Without a word people began to take out coins, little parcels of food. They did it without panic. They were used to being held up at gunpoint. One rebel lad came through with a sack. To his credit he shook his head when an old or poorer-looking person offered something.

They were halfway up the carriage. I came to my senses, slipped out of the buffet car and got back into the goods carriage with the coffins.

I sat and waited. The ruffians barged into the goods carriage.

"Who's in dem coffins?" the leader asked. "Is it Staters or our side?"

My face was white. "Neither."

They moved towards the coffins. "Someone's been throwing flowers out the back of the train. Could be the same fellow who spiked our guns. Stand aside. We must check those coffins."

"We've been told to keep an eye out for a couple of renegades come from Kerry – some mad fellows," another rebel added.

"Go on, have a look," I said defiantly. "Admire the handiwork of this war."

311

One of the fellows came closer and saw that the coffin lids were nailed down.

Inside were old clothes and bones from the butcher's. I prayed they didn't investigate further.

Jack and Anto were in the false bottoms.

I was shocked when one of the rebels used the bayonet on his rifle to try to lever the lid off.

The game would be up any minute now. I was about to throw myself across the coffins when the young fellow who was holding the sack of stolen goods edged in front.

"Leave her be. She's a medical student. She saved my life and other Republicans too. I met her at the Four Courts in Dublin during the battle."

I recognised the voice, the soft lilting tones of West Cork. Patch. The young boy I'd saved in Dublin. I caught his eye. He gave me a warning look, but something else – a plea for forgiveness. I nodded to him.

They backed off and headed towards the door.

As soon as they'd gone, I collapsed in a heap.

The train started again. Twenty minutes later when we pulled into the next station, a Free State patrol boarded the train. They barged straight into the goods carriage and pulled up the window blinds. It was late afternoon and the light was poor.

"We have orders to search the train thoroughly," the officer said. "What's your name?"

"Elizabeth Adair," I said, giving my mother's maiden name. I held out my library pass and put my finger over my name. Luckily for me they barely glanced at it.

I stood in front of the coffins, trying to shield them with my body. But a soldier pulled me roughly away.

"Is it not enough to kill someone, that you have to dishonor the dead?" I cried.

They tapped around, looking for a false bottom. Another soldier tried to prise open the lids with the bayonet of his gun. I pushed in and threw myself over the lids.

Outside, under the gaslight, there was a group of women standing on the platform, countrywomen in shawls. They began to bang on the windows.

"Let the poor girleen be!" they shouted. "They're already dead!"

The officer gave me a hard look. "There are reports of white flags flying from every station this train has been on. And flowers strewn all over the tracks. It looks like the work of some troublemaker trying to steer things up. Do you know anything about this?"

I was astonished. The Republicans had also mentioned flowers. As far as I was aware Jack and Anto had been lying in the coffins the whole journey. I lowered my eyes and said nothing.

"That Jack the Cat won't escape this time," the officer said.

I stood stock still, making sure I didn't move so much as a muscle.

"There's no reason to keep him alive either. Him and his sidekick. You can't kill dead men," he said with a sneer.

His words sent a chill to my heart.

The women outside kept banging on the window, shaming the soldiers to leave me be, and to my utter relief the officer ordered his men to move on with their search.

After they left the train, I was gripped with worry. As soon as the train was in motion again, I pulled down the window blind of the carriage. Then I pulled back the fake sliding panels in the false bottoms of the coffins, to make sure Jack and Anto were safe. But they were both gone!

I was at my wit's end. How many times did I have to suffer the loss of my brother?

I slowed my breathing, counted to a hundred and tried to think it through logically.

Luckily my friend Joseph came by.

"Did you know about all these disturbances?" I asked him.

He smiled. "I thought you knew what was going on."

When I told him Jack had disappeared, he mounted the steps to the small hatch in the roof. He popped his head out and surveyed the length of the train.

Outside, the light was fading.

"They're on the roof!" he called down. He stuck his hand out and beckoned to them.

He came back down the ladder.

"You escaped by the skin of your teeth, Molly," he said to me. "But both sides might soon figure out it's you. And they'll rip those coffins apart. The lads can't get out in a station patrolled by soldiers. They'll have to jump off the train and reach Dublin another way. We're coming to a halting station soon."

He motioned to me to go up the ladder. Up I went and got a bad fright. As I stuck my head up, I saw the outline of a skull. But as the moon came out, I realised I was looking directly into Jack's face! I had forgotten he had no hair. In the pearly moonlight, he looked radiant and otherworldly. He was holding the peace pipe. I told him they had a few minutes before the next stop and that they'd have to get off the train.

He smiled in that easy way of his.

"Jack, they'll put a watch on all the ports," I said. "And both sides are vengeful. You could be looking over your shoulder for the rest of your life."

"Not if they think we're really gone," he said. "Do you trust me, Molly?"

314

I nodded my head.

"Tell May to pawn the sapphire necklace. We will need the funds. What date is today?"

I told him it was the 16th March.

"Come to the La Scala Picture House tomorrow. There's a boxing match there between Battling Siki, the world champion, and the contender McTigue."

"Battling Siki! I saw him in the cinema in the fight to win the world championship," I said. "The first black man to ever win the title. But I do not like this sport. I hope you are not now a fan of boxing, Jack?"

Jack's white teeth shone in the moonlight as he smiled. "No. But both McTigue and Siki are friends of friends in the entertainment world. Get word to Battling Siki that we will be making a very special guest appearance. And send Dan with a message to Timmy, care of the Kildare Club, to make the emergency arrangements with the yacht at Rogerson's Quay. Timmy will know what to do. I've already alerted him but couldn't tell him when we'd reach Dublin."

"But aren't you tempting fate?"

He bent over and kissed me lightly on the cheek. "I'll make sure they never want to look for me again with an escape act to end all escape acts! Now, most important – telephone the keeper at Dublin Zoo and ask him for the loan of a fish tank big enough for two people to stand in. He owes me a favour and will oblige. Also a black cloth big enough to cover it and eight chains and padlocks. May and Uncle Edward will be able to help you with them. Bring them all to the theatre and put them in the ring. Fill the fish tank with water and have a six-foot ladder beside it. Ask the theatre manager to get you some handcuffs."

"Are you planning a dangerous trick?" I asked him anxiously.

He laughed. "Depends on what you consider dangerous in the circumstances. You'll also need to organise some transport for us from the cinema to the quay."

"I'll go there on Red Cross duty," I said. "And ask P.J. to have an ambulance on standby."

"Make sure you have something to help us revive. We'll need a shot in the arm," he said.

"Revive! What do you mean to do, Jack? I'll not be part of something that may kill you!"

"Trust me, Molly, as you have always done."

I heaved a sigh. "I'll get some adrenalin and leave some with P.J. in the ambulance too," I promised. "It helps even with heart attacks. I might need it myself."

He calculated something in his head. "There's enough time. Do it at the yacht at Rogerson's Quay just in case we're stopped. If anything goes wrong, make your way separately and meet us at the yacht."

He kissed my cheek, took something from his pocket and handed it to me. It was one of the links in the emerald necklace. A diamond shape with an emerald gem in the centre. It was missing its drop-stone but the emerald was as glorious as God's green earth. I placed it in my pocket.

"Goodbye, dear sister. You're a heavyweight champion yourself."

When I got back down, the train began to slow coming into the halting station.

I raised the blind and looked out the window. The moon was playing hide and seek behind the clouds. The night was inky black one minute, bathed in light the next. As the train juddered to a halt, I saw two flickering shapes drop down by the side of the tracks. They disappeared off into the shadowy trees.

Joseph returned from checking tickets in the other carriages.

I told him Jack and Anto were off the train.

"I wonder if I will ever see them again," I said.

Joseph shook his head. "Dublin is like a tinderbox. The Free State government has executed seven Republican prisoners. There's shootings in the street, patrol cars everywhere. The Irregulars have said they're banning all forms of entertainment. They want to close cinemas and stop this big fight between Battling Siki and McTigue. They want everyone to mourn their dead."

"So the match might be cancelled!" I cried.

"But the government is determined it will go ahead. There are armed platoons all over the city making sure cinemas and theatres stay open. The eyes of the world are on Dublin because of this fight. The Free State government want to show that they are winning the civil war."

I wrote out the note to Battling Siki as instructed by Jack. But how could Jack's plan have any hope of succeeding with the city in chaos? But maybe with events see-sawing on a knife-edge, an audacious plan might be his only chance. I hoped that Jack the Cat still had a few lives left out of his nine.

When we got to Kingsbridge Station, Dan was there to meet me. A motor cab driven by a friend of Uncle Edward's was waiting outside.

We hung back until most of the other passengers had left in a clatter of luggage and loud voices. The station was now eerily quiet except for one or two stragglers.

Dan glanced towards the ticket office where a man with bad skin and a slouched hat was pretending to read the paper. "That man followed me here."

The hairs on the back of my neck prickled. We were being watched by other eyes. I scanned the station. Over in the far corner, a couple of corner boys were smoking cigarettes. Judging by the tell-tale bulge under their jackets, the nervous tic of touching the spot, they were carrying guns. Anti-Treaty spies, I figured.

"Dan, take the taxi to the Claremont Hotel in Howth. Give this to Battling Siki." I handed him the note.

"Really? I can meet him? There's supposed to be a hundred reporters in Dublin to cover the fight! People are even queuing up to watch him training!"

"Well, make sure the note is delivered. Everything depends on it, Dan. But we're being watched. I'll create a diversion so you can get away."

My luggage arrived. I winked at Joseph and quickly moved as close as I could to the corner boys. Skulking curs they were, people of the shadows. I dropped my doctor's bag, spilling the contents on the floor towards them.

"Could you please help me?" I said loudly and distinctly. There must have been something commanding in my manner because they did as I asked. "And you over there in the trench-coat, could you help?" I raised my voice.

The Free State spy dodged behind a pillar and melted away. It was enough. Dan was on his way in the cab.

First thing in the morning Dan and I met up. He was still flushed with the thrill of meeting the famous heavyweight who'd been only too happy to help.

Then Dan cycled with a message to May to pawn the necklace and with a rough outline of the plan. She said she'd manage it before going to her work in Clery's. He also dropped a note for Timmy the millionaire into the Kildare Club.

Dan and I spent the morning organising the props that Jack

had requested. I telephoned Dublin Zoo and once the keeper knew I was Jack's sister he couldn't do enough. He said he'd send the fish tank straight to the La Scala with two assistants to transport it by truck.

I telephoned P.J. the ambulance driver and he said he would be on standby to transport Jack and Anto away from the cinema. My Uncle Edward got us eight padlocks and chains from a ship's chandlers'. Luck was on my side. My old friend Mr. James who used to run the Waxworks display in Henry Street was now managing the cinema. When I rang him, he agreed readily to sort out the handcuffs and to help me in any way.

May also begged a loan of a large black cloth from the haberdashery department at Clery's. When I went to collect it from her, I squeezed her hand.

"I know about you and Jack."

She flushed a deep crimson. "I'm sorry I couldn't tell you."

"Do you realise that sapphire necklace might have been part of the Russian Crown Jewels?" I asked.

"Jack did say it would make me a real princess," she blushed. "But it's doing a better job now. I got £200 for it!"

I didn't want to tell her it was worth at least ten times that.

We embraced then. Like sisters. I had a thousand questions to ask her. But there wasn't time.

We reached the La Scala Picture House in Princes Street, alongside the GPO, in the afternoon. The streets were already thronged with people milling about hoping to go to the fight or just soak up the atmosphere.

"He's a fine-looking man, that Siki," I heard one fellow say as we ploughed the handcart with the black cloth, chains and locks through Sackville Street. "They searched him for weapons and his manager said 'Just feel his biceps!'"

"But will it be a fair fight?" his companion asked. "They don't like to see black men beating the white fighters."

What a terrible thing for those with darker skin, I thought. Why, it's just as nonsensical as thinking less of a person for having red hair and green eyes!

The cries of seagulls could barely be heard over the excited chatter of the swelling crowd. As we came nearer, platoons of soldiers in armoured cars were patrolling the streets. A cordon of soldiers surrounded the building. Two long lines of ticket holders wearing shamrocks in their buttonholes in support of McTigue were being forced into side streets surrounding the building site of the General Post Office.

Of course. How could I forget! It was Saint Patrick's Day.

A light drizzle fell from the sky. I glanced up the street from O'Connell Bridge and could not believe my eyes. Among the swelling crowds, I saw a lithe figure mount the statue of Daniel O'Connell. I took out my field glasses but he had climbed back down before I could make him out.

Before the crowds registered his action, he had crossed the street and shimmied up a drainpipe, scaling the rooftops along the eastern side of the street. My heart soared. It was Jack of course, running the old familiar routes of his childhood. I tracked his progress through my field glasses. He ran as far as the corner with Earl Street. Then he went out of sight. I guessed he was dropping down by the fire escape at the back of the building. He disappeared among the crowds around the ruins of the Gresham, only to reappear at Parnell's statue. This too he mounted. His cap fell off. I saw his gleaming bald head as he climbed up on Parnell's shoulders. I could have sworn he waved to me! Then he sat on his shoulders and seemed to be paying a lot of attention to Parnell's extended arm.

It wasn't the first time he'd clambered up those landmarks. Jack and I used to hide his tin soldiers everywhere in the curious game we played when we were children. It crossed my mind that he might be concealing something again. But I didn't have time to think about that.

We were jostled by the crowds as we hauled our props down Sackville Street and towards the La Scala Picture House which was in the laneway next to the GPO. CID officers were posted on the main door. I glanced at them in fear. But one of them smiled warmly at me and held up his hand. There was a faint scar on it.

"I'm still able to shoot straight thanks to you," the man said.

I smiled back in recognition. I had dressed his wound once when he was on the run during the War of Independence.

"There's rumours that the Irregulars are going to attack us to stop the fight," he told me. "The promoters tried to cancel it. But the government insisted it must go ahead. It was banned in Britain. They want to show the world that the Irish Free State can do what they can't."

He directed me around the corner to the Abbey Street entrance, which was down a laneway, and let me in through the stage door. A payback for once saving his hand.

Inside, at the office, I was overjoyed to meet my old friend Mr. James. He had the handcuffs for me but he looked worried.

"The detectives from the Criminal Investigation Department have taken over the cinema," he told me in hushed tones.

"But you will grant Jack's favour?" I asked, anxiety lurching up my throat.

"Both fighters have insisted," he said with a smile.

The auditorium was originally built as an opera house on the site of the old *Freeman's Journal* that had been destroyed in 1916. It was big enough to hold two thousand people with raked seating and balconies in the wings. At the far end there was a vast red curtain covering the movie screen. Before it was a fifty-foot stage, then an orchestra pit, where several musicians shuffled their musical sheets and tuned their instruments. Up above the orchestra pit, a boxing arena had been created on a raised podium on the stage. This area was surrounded by benches for VIP's and roped off from the main crowd.

The ropes around the boxing ring were the French colours of blue, white and red on one side. Battling Siki was from Senegal, which was a French colony. On the other side it was green, white and orange for McTigue. Soldiers with fixed bayonets were posted under the ropes. On one side were rows of tables with banks of typewriters manned by sports reporters from all around the world. Their little name-plates proclaimed *The Times* in London, *The Boston Globe* and even an Australian newspaper! They lounged around and chatted as they waited.

I went up onto the stage. "This is the weirdest fight I've ever been at," I heard an American reporter say. "There's more of a fight outside the ring than in it."

"Who do you think will win?" I asked him.

He pursed his lips. "Battling Siki is a war hero. He's twenty-six and in his prime. He's the world champion. McTigue is nearly forty. He's outta shape."

"I should be betting on Siki," I said.

"The Boxing Federation want a white champion," he said in his nasal accent. "McTigue is white and Irish too. There's soldiers with guns surrounding the stage. Draw your own conclusions."

I was shocked. "So you're saying it will be a fix!"

He gave me a big wink. "I ain't sayin' nuthin'."

There was a movie camera in position in one of the private boxes in the wings, with a commanding view of the stage. With a shudder I noticed several sharpshooters posted on the two balconies. Jack couldn't have chosen a more difficult place to escape. Nor Siki to defend his championship.

People, many in evening dress, were taking their seats on the racked seating that surrounded the ring on three sides.

I spotted Anto's younger brother and sister at the back of the theatre in their Sunday best. I wondered how on earth they had got tickets. But when I went to say hello, I saw they were selling oranges and monkey nuts to spectators.

"Does your mother know you're here?" I asked them.

Liam, who is a puny twelve-year-old, laughed and handed me an orange. "She was raging mad she couldn't get a ticket herself!" Alice, his ten-year-old sister, gave me a bag of nuts.

When May saw them, she decided it was best she take them home in case they were startled to see Anto. So they left, protesting, clutching an orange each.

While I waited for the manager, I joined the Red Cross Station near the ring with several doctors and nurses. The air was so fuggy I expected to deal with people passing out. But I told the other medics there that my brother was a warm-up act, which was high risk and if anything happened I wanted to attend him onstage.

The manager rushed up to me. "You have half an hour to set up Jack's act before we start the programme. We're going to show a film, *Peggy Puts It Over*. Then squeeze Jack in as a warm-up before the main event at seven thirty."

I told him we would have everything ready.

"I'll bring a large clock on stage too," Mr. James said. "So the audience can see how long it takes them to escape."

This brought the risk home to me and almost made my heart stop. But I concentrated on following Jack's instructions.

Despite my nerves, I caught the air of excitement that hummed in the theatre. There were hardly any spectators yet. Everyone was being searched on the way in. Those that made it through sat down stunned, overawed by the occasion.

I focused on our preparations. The tank was filled with water and a ladder was against it. The locks were lined up on a table. The black cloth was placed at the ready beside them.

Dan ran in. "The boxers have arrived!" he shouted. "Battling Siki came in an armoured car because someone sent him a death threat in Irish! That was a bit stupid. How was he supposed to understand it?"

"Any sign of Jack or Anto?" I asked.

He shook his head and went out the front to have a look.

The place was slowly filling up. But boredom was setting in among those already in their seats. People were tired of waiting. There were a few catcalls and boos. The lights were dimmed. A film flickered on the screen.

Peggy Puts It Over was a comedy about how a feisty young woman with an engineering degree was trying to rebuild her sleepy home town. I was most interested to see these modern women on screen. But I was too tense to concentrate.

After the film, the curtains closed across the screen and the auditorium went dark again. Then the curtains opened again and powerful arc lights shone down on the boxing arena, creating a strong daylight glare. The rest of the cinema became a dark pit. Here and there torchlights flickered like fireflies as ushers showed people to their seats.

"And now as our warm-up act," the manager announced, "all the way from Barnum and Baily Circus in America, the legendary Jack the Cat will attempt to escape from this fish tank. But this time not one but two magicians will face death! He will be joined by 'Amazing Anto', facing the tank for the first time. Will they emerge triumphant or sleep with the fishes?"

My stomach tightened as the orchestra played some ominous music. Jack and Anto in white dressing gowns climbed up the podium, dodged under the ropes and bounded into the ring. Jack, tall and broad-shouldered, Anto, smaller and wiry, limping by his side. Jack had the sheen of someone used to the limelight. Anto looked like a skinned rabbit, scared and lost. Both their bald heads gleamed in the glare of the spotlights on the boxing ring. The auditorium was so well designed, with its racked seating, that they were visible from every seat in the house.

Jack shrugged off his dressing gown, tossing it to the side. Anto, more timid, copied his friend but let his fall limply at his feet. They wore black swimming costumes from neck to knee underneath. In the stark silver light they seemed like characters from a movie stepped from the screen.

Jack bowed low and, smiling, walked towards the tank. He picked up a set of handcuffs and asked the manager to inspect them. An excited buzz ran through the crowd as the manager walked around the ring and, holding the handcuffs out over the ropes, requested the nearest people to take a closer look. Then he waved to some stagehands to carry on a large circular white clock with black hands, which was placed on a stand.

Jack ushered Anto forward and was about to lock the handcuffs into place when a shrill whistle erupted.

A voice rang out. "*Stop! Place these men under arrest!*"

A platoon of soldiers marched forward and surrounded the ring.

A man in a trench-coat, brandishing a pistol, dodged under the ropes and into the ring with four more soldiers.

Another group of soldiers surrounded the outside of the ring and pointed guns at the astonished press reporters.

"*It is forbidden to report on this arrest under martial law!*" the trench-coated man shouted out. His accent was distinctly Northern Irish.

I narrowed my eyes. It was the officer who'd interrogated me at Ballymullen Barracks in Tralee!

The soldiers, put off by the strong arc lights, froze in the spotlight. A hush went over the crowd.

"Here – you can even use our handcuffs!" Jack's voice rang out, languid and mocking.

He thrust the handcuffs towards the soldiers who were timid under the glare. The darkness did not like the light.

The audience held its breath. It was so quiet we could hear the ticking of the clock.

The manager stepped forward.

"Since the men will be wearing handcuffs, it wouldn't do any harm to let them finish their act," he said.

"Silence! We are here to do a job," said the man in the trench coat.

"*Ah, you' re as bad as them Irregulars! No fun in you!*" a man in the audience shouted out.

The mood turned. There were jeers and catcalls.

The soldiers turned their guns menacingly on the audience. An icy fear ran through the vast auditorium.

Jack's stood face to face with the arresting officer. "So, Captain Ned, we meet at last. Do you propose to kill all of the two thousand spectators in the audience? Not forgetting all the reporters from the international press? This trick is so dangerous not even Houdini has attempted it. At least give us a sporting chance."

Someone bravely shouted, "*Hear! Hear!*"

The cry was picked up by the crowd like a wave. "*Yes, let them try! Hear! Hear! Three cheers for Jack and Anto!*"

The arc lights raked through the crowd – fingers of light exposing braying mouths, pleading faces. It was like the baying crowd at a Roman amphitheatre, trying to convince the Emperor to spare a gladiator.

Captain Ned nodded at his soldiers and lowered his gun. The soldiers fell back.

"You have two minutes," he said.

A thunderous cheer raised the roof.

Jack raised his hand.

The whole auditorium fell silent.

"Perhaps the officer and his troops would help us in inspecting the locks and chains," Jack said lightly, with a wicked grin. He walked up and down, commanding the stage.

I marvelled to see him. Jack had left Ireland a wondrous boy. America had turned him into a star. All eyes in that tense auditorium were strained on him, watching his every move.

He waved the handcuffs under the officer's nose, who nodded grimly. Captain Ned took them and stepped back.

"*That fellow's locked plenty of people in handcuffs!*" someone bravely shouted.

"I want you to inspect them properly now, Captain Ned," Jack said. "As if you were about to use them on prisoners in a torture chamber."

I gasped at his brazen attack on the Captain who looked thunderously at him. He raised his hand as if to strike him. But Jack nimbly stepped aside and Captain Ned stumbled on stage. As he regained his footing, Jack magicked a feather duster out of the air and tickled him! Despite himself, Captain Ned laughed, a high-pitched nervous whinny. The crowd whistled and hooted their appreciation. General laughter broke out.

"*Come on now, Captain, don' t be shy!*" a wag shouted.

Jack picked up a chain in each hand. "I am, after all, asking you to lock us up!"

The audience went wild with laughter, cheering and stamping their feet.

To my astonishment, Captain Ned was brought to heel. He shrugged as if accepting his role in the play. He inspected the locks and chains with seriousness and attention, handing them to some of the other soldiers.

First Anto's hands were bound in handcuffs, then his ankles. He was trussed in chains from shoulders to his waist. He looked like he would rather face a firing squad.

"Can I ask two witnesses to step forward and verify that these are all locked tight?"

A thousand hands shot up. He invited an American reporter and a policeman to check. They peered closely, giving the locks a thorough inspection.

"As good as if I'd done it meself!" said the policeman.

"He ain't getting' outta that anytime soon," said the American.

The audience clapped their hands.

"Now it's time to truss me up, Captain Ned," said Jack.

With the help of the manager, Jack's shackles were put in place. First a brace was locked around his neck. Then the handcuffs were attached to the neck brace. A pair of cuffs chained together were clasped around his feet. Last, a large chain was wrapped over his shoulder. They presented much more of a challenge than Anto's chains.

"Before going into the water, Anto, is there anything you would like to say?" said Jack.

Anto's nodded his head. "I would like to recite a poem." He

voice was quavering with nerves. A thousand pair of ears strained to hear his words as he began.

"*Too many dead have been buried,*
Too many tears have been shed,
It' s time for the living to prosper,
Before all our dreams are . . ."

Anto's voice faltered to a whisper. He broke off, choked with emotion. Everyone waited, spellbound, while he found his voice.

"A dear friend once joked I would be Ireland's national bard. But I have spent my youth firing guns rather than craftin' words. Let me speak from the heart . . ."

His voice was reedy and thin but everyone strained to hear.

"I have been wounded for my country. I have even killed for my country and I will have that on my conscience until my dying day. Too much red blood has been spilt in our green emerald isle. Too many good lives wasted. I want my unborn child to live in a country of forgiveness. A country worth living for." He stood, staring out into the dark abyss of the cinema.

Jack's voice broke the spell. "Well said, Anto. There is an old Cherokee story that there are two wolves inside of us, which are always at war.

One is the good wolf of kindness, bravery and love. The other is the bad wolf of greed, hatred and fear. And which one wins? The Cherokees say it's the one you feed. So now in our country, where childhood friends have become bitter enemies, let us feed the good wolf."

Then he did something so brave and so generous that people gasped. He bowed low to the soldiers around him and stretched out his bound hands. They were so taken aback they responded and shook his hands.

"*Osyio, Wa Ya Udo* – that means 'Peace, Wolf Brother'," Jack said to each of them with a smile.

Only Captain Ned hung back and didn't take his hand. With a shrug, Jack moved back to stand beside Anto.

"Someday the stones will speak of our suffering and our wars. But someday the stones will heal. In the words of my wise sister: too many people have died for Ireland – it's time to try living for it instead."

Everyone cheered. He struck a fine figure. Strong and brave – a good wolf.

"We will now go into the water tank," he announced.

First Anto and then Jack was lowered into the water. They stood in the tank, completely submerged, their faces pressed against the glass. They were like some weird underwater creatures. The manager placed the countdown clock in the centre of the stage.

The lid was placed firmly down on the tank.

"*Countdown begins now!*" the manager announced.

I was mesmerised along with the rest of the audience.

Thirty seconds in, I watched their contorted faces as they struggled for air, trying to wriggle free. The seconds ticked by.

"One minute!" announced the manager.

The black cloth was placed over the box. But after thirty seconds Captain Ned shouted out. "*Take that curtain off! No trickery!*"

As they pulled the curtain back it was clear something was wrong. Anto was free of his chains and Jack had wiggled free of his. But both their eyes were wide open in their lifeless faces. They looked dead.

I struggled to get onto the stage.

"*Let me see them!*" I cried. "*Stop this act!*"

But, instructed by Captain Ned, the soldiers held me back at the point of their bayonets.

330

The lid was opened. Two lifeless bodies were lifted out of the tank.

Captain Ned, triumphant, felt their pulses.

"*Dead!*" he announced. A vicious look on his face.

I cried out in anguish. "*Let me through!*"

But my cries went unheard. There was a low rumble coming out of the walls. The whole theatre began to shake. Plaster dust fell from the roof. The spotlights juddered and veered drunkenly all over the place. The vast cinema was plunged into total darkness. People cried out into the void.

"It's a bomb!" somebody shouted out.

"*We're going to be killed!*"

After about a few minutes of sheer terror, the lights went back on again. I got my bearings and went towards the ring. It was completely empty except for the fish tank. The soldiers and Captain Ned must have jumped over the ropes in their fright at the bomb. The bodies of Anto and Jack had disappeared.

Within seconds two stagehands appeared and removed the tank.

The manager came back into the empty ring as two boxers stood in either corner. I picked my way through the spectators and headed towards the concealed side door near the screen that the manager had left open.

"*Please retake your seats. The bomb was down the street and will not affect our main event. Now get ready for the match of the century. Battling Siki versus Francis McTigue!*"

As I charged down the tunnel that led to the outside lane, I could hear the crowd erupting into a furious baying pack. Anto and Jack were already forgotten. They had disappeared out of their world.

Soon I was in the small lane that gave onto Abbey Street.

The scenes outside the cinema were just as astonishing as those within. Thousands of people still lined Sackville Street despite the bomb. I battled against the throng. As I was swept into the porch of a shop, I asked a man what had happened.

"The Irregulars planted a bomb and blew the doors off the Pillar Picture House in Henry Place," he told me. "But nothing is going to stop this fight!"

I rushed across O'Connell Bridge and on to Rogerson's Quay where Timmy the millionaire's yacht, the Emerald Isle, was docked. A sailor ushered me below deck.

Timmy, a kindly, dapper man, popped his head out of the cabin. He smiled faintly below his bushy moustache as I rushed to set up my medical supplies.

Anto and Jack were laid out side by side, their hair still wet from the fish tank. Their skin was blue and lifeless, marble to the touch. I took out my hypodermic needle and gave them each a shot of adrenalin in their arms.

I felt their pulses. Their heartbeat was so slowed it was easy to mistake it for death, as Captain Ned had done.

Anto came to first. "Oh my head!" he cried.

Seconds later Jack's eyes flew open. I hugged him tight.

"Ssso the old shhaman's herb did the trick," he said, slurring his words, still groggy.

I stood back and looked into his eyes.

"You mean you didn't actually know if it would work!"

He smiled his slow devilish smile, his eyes now swimming back into focus. "Relax, Molly. It's not every day your brother comes back from the dead."

Chapter twenty three

The letter ended there without a signature. There must have been a missing page. There were still so many questions unanswered. Like who won the fight for example. How did Anto and Jack escape from the cinema?

Mal examined the letter. It was torn on the edge but there was a faint stamp of Mountjoy Gaol in the right-hand corner.

"So Molly must have ended up in prison," I reasoned. "Oh, poor Molly!"

Mal consulted his pocket guide. "Francis McTigue won the fight. But lots of people thought it was a fix as Battling Siki did most of the punching and was much stronger."

"Maybe they arrested Molly when she came off the boat," I said. "You don't think they executed her?"

"For what?" Mal asked. "She wasn't even that interested in politics."

"Didn't look like they needed much of an excuse in those days."

Mal scanned his book and launched into a Betty-style rap.

"Seventy-seven anti-Treaty guys faced execution
So they realised the gun got no Republican solution.
Boss Liam Lynch was shot dead in April '23.
They surrendered, vowing to fight again
For all Ireland to be free.
So ended the Civil War, the Free State held sway.
But the bitterness it's lasted right till the present day."

"Mal, the History Rapper! Needs some work. But not bad for a first attempt." I gave him a round of applause and he bowed.

"But I feel down in the dumps about Molly," I said, "like I've lost a friend. We'll have to do a lot more digging to find out what happened to her."

Mal watched my face and gave me one of his rare smiles.

"Cheer up, junior. I think I know where two other pieces of the necklace are concealed. Molly watched Jack climb the statues . . . OCD and PD . . ."

"What do you mean?"

"O'Connell and Parnell, Dublin!"

"Oh my God! But surely someone would have noticed after all these years?"

"That remains to be seen. Lots of stuff slips through the cracks of history."

"But we've got ourselves into enough trouble down in Kerry!"

The ghost of an idea flitted across Mal's face. "The

judge said to ask for her help if any new evidence came to light. That she would help me stay on the right side of the law. Time to come clean about the jewels. Time to see if she's as good as her word!"

Two days later, Mal and I were at the centre of a sting.

The plan was that Mal and I would go into O'Connell Street and hang around the statues. Mal was going to be allowed to leak something on the internet. And they were going to plant a story in the newspapers about how the statues were getting a spring-cleaning. They would hint that they were also searching for a mystery object.

The police would mount a surveillance operation and apprehend the Russian if he took the bait.

I liked all this crime talk. Well, actually, I was scared as Floppy my old rabbit!

When I turned up to take the DART into town, I wore my mother's dark glasses, trying to look the part. Mal immediately pulled them off me.

"Are you mad?" he laughed. "You look like a spy out of central casting. As bad as our Russian."

"That's good coming from a guy who skulks round in a hoodie," I said.

We took our seats. I fidgeted the whole time, scrutinising every move of every passenger. I stared so hard at one large old lady wearing a suspicious-looking hat like a bowl of fruit that Mal had to kick me on the shins.

"*Ow!* He might be in disguise and have mikes in the

shape of a banana," I said, nursing my foot.

"You've been watching too much kids' TV drama." Mal shot me a piercing look. "Steady your nerves, Ava. We can do this."

I smiled inwardly. We were a team.

As the train pulled in towards Connolly Station I dared to speak to Mal again. "What if he has a gun?"

Mal looked me square in the eye. "This isn't the Civil War."

At seven o'clock in the morning, the set-up on O'Connell Street was so low key I was a bit disappointed. The street was eerily quiet. There was no overhead helicopter. No Special Ops team hidden behind doorways ready to leap out. No tough-looking guys with walkie-talkies pacing up and down.

But as we walked around O'Connell's statue on the central island, a few people were definitely not what they seemed. There was a mother with a pushchair who kept crossing from one side of the street to the other. When I looked into the pram, the baby looked suspiciously like a doll. The tramp who loitered around the base of the statue wore really clean trainers and looked like he worked out in a gym. Like how many tramps do you know who lift weights? I also saw the old woman with the fruity hat. There was something about her that bugged me.

I'd passed the O'Connell statue many times in the last few months. But I'd never really looked at it. Now standing at the base, it rose up about forty feet and was impressive. There were three sections of stone with bronze sculptures turned black with age. The bottom sections had four massive glum-looking winged angels.

Considering all the shooting in 1916 and afterwards, it's amazing the statue was still standing at all.

The angel strangling a serpent had a bullet wound in her right breast. Another had sustained a bullet in her left elbow. No wonder they looked grumpy! Above them was a circular bronze frieze with lots of folk. In the middle, some lady was holding a paper in one hand and pointing up at O'Connell (I hoped she wasn't making a rude gesture!).

"That's the Maid of Erin holding the Act of Catholic Emancipation," Mal told me. "It was passed nearly two hundred years ago through O'Connell's efforts, to give Catholics the same rights as everyone else."

"So who is this Maid of Erin with a bullet in her hem?" I asked.

"She's a symbol of Ireland," he said. "Like Uncle Sam for the United States."

The Maid was jostled by a bishop with some kids, a farmer, a labourer, important-looking guys in wigs. A few of them had bullet wounds too.

We loitered by the statue, hoping the thief would spot us. The cherry-picker arrived. It was a truck with a crane on the back – a steel extendable arm with a basket. A team of workers arrived and placed a cordon around the statue. The light traffic was reduced to one lane.

An efficient-looking woman, with a pulled-back

ponytail and wearing an overall, got out of the passenger seat.

"Hi, I'm Aoife," she introduced herself. "We're going to do this really quickly before rush hour. Mal and Ava, we'll just about squeeze both of you along with me into the basket."

I nodded, sick with excitement. But Mal looked a bit queasy.

"You go," he said. "Those flimsy things make me feel nervous." He was pale as a glass of milk.

"Aw, come on, Mal. We're the 'A' team! Face your fears and all that." I must have looked like a pleading puppy because he nodded reluctantly in agreement.

We were given hard hats, high-vis jackets and safety goggles. A man fitted us each with a harness. Aoife carried a small machine, like a miniature version of the metal detector. We were secured in the cage and the door was closed. Mal went green in the face and gulped the air. I squeezed his hand for reassurance.

The driver got back into the cabin and moments later the ground moved away from us as the cage began to rise.

"*Yaay!*" I cried, as excited as if it was a fairground ride.

Mal too relaxed as we began to ascend. We passed up by the angels and the Maid of Erin with her crew. As we went up Daniel O'Connell's wide chest, I saw he too was peppered with gunshot. I felt a bit like Jack must have felt on the rooftops – the freedom of the bird's-eye view.

The top of ole Daniel's head was less impressive. A

seagull perched on his curly hair and there were white droppings all down his face. But he had a nice smile and a funny pug nose. Behind him I could see the whole length of the street with its cute lollipop trees all the way to Parnell's statue at the other end. On the left was the grey stone GPO with its fine columns. The tops of some of the buildings on O'Connell Street were like fancy icing on a cake. Beyond us, the dark River Liffey flowed under O'Connell Bridge and made its way out to the sea. I looked straight up Westmoreland Street all the way to Trinity College. Everything, even the ugly things on the ground, looked beautiful from a higher angle.

But while I was busy looking around, Mal and Aoife were concentrating on the job. Aoife ran the device over the statue. Around old Daniel's solemn face, his bronze curly hair. She bit her lip in concentration. Mal looked at Daniel O'Connell's pudgy cheeks as if his life depended on it. But the dials on Aoife's little machine refused to budge.

Then, as we descended, something snagged Mal's attention.

"Try over by his left hand, where it's stuck into his jacket. Beyond the button and the tassel from his cloak – that larger bullet hole in his chest."

Aoife ran the device over it. The counter went wild!

She turned to us incredulous. "There's definitely something there!" Her eyes shining, she whistled. "They cleaned this statue up about ten years ago and put a thin layer of wax on it to protect against pollution. But luckily for you they left all the holes."

She reached into her bag and took out a long thin screwdriver with a slight hook on the end of it. A sudden gust shook the basket. Mal looked like he would throw up. But Aoife calmly waited for the wind to die down. She cupped her hand under the hole. She focused, as if she was performing keyhole surgery. Bit by bit, she pulled out a tiny rolled-up parcel no thicker than a pencil, sewn in tiny little stitches, like a sachet.

My stomach somersaulted. "Can we see?"

"Not yet. My instructions are to pretend to transfer them into a silver case for you to take to the next location, your cousin's jewellery design studio." She immediately placed them inside one of her zipped pockets. As we waited for the driver to crank us down, I looked across at the neighbouring buildings and caught the glint of a pair of binoculars through one of the windows. It was above the Starbucks Coffee Shop on the corner with Bachelor's Walk. I tugged Mal's sleeve to point it out. But all we could see was reflections on the glass.

Back on terra firma, Aoife placed the packet in a silver aluminium attaché case. Then we drove past the GPO and the Spire in the truck, and relocated to Parnell's statue on the north end of the street. Traffic was a bit heavier by now and there were more people about – office and shop workers mainly, on their way to work. A few even stopped to gawp. When asked, the workmen told them we were just cleaning the statue.

Parnell wasn't as elevated as O'Connell. There was a

massive big granite column shaped like an obelisk that Mal said was nineteen metres high – about 62 feet. But Parnell was standing near the bottom, his feet only about ten feet from the ground, like he didn't make it all the way to statue super-stardom. He was still trying to hail a taxi in his old-fashioned frock coat. He had a beard and looked a bit cross. Maybe those taxis just kept ignoring him! He was – a bit weird this – standing on a bunch of ox skulls. Aoife said they were popular classical symbols of farming and stuff. He too had a fair share of bullet holes.

The cherry picker was only up about thirty feet when we hit the jackpot. I spotted a bullet hole under the armpit of Parnell's extended right hand. I was a bit disappointed we didn't get to soar to the top of the obselisk but we were in a hurry.

Aoife set to work, long hooked needle in hand. Carefully she spiralled the little package of chamois leather free of its interior. The top was slightly blackened from pollution. But otherwise it was intact. Bingo! She put the packet in with the other one in the attaché case. Then she went into the back of the van and, out of sight, transferred the packages into a large leather wallet.

She came back out and handed me the empty attaché case.

"You are carrying the decoy," she explained. "Just in case he makes an attempt to steal it now."

My stomach fizzed with so much excitement it was like I'd eaten ten soda pops. Even ole Mal was revved up, although he tried to hide it by slouching more than usual.

A taxi pulled up outside the Ambassador Cinema to take us to Rachel's studio. But it was really a police car in disguise. We drove back down O'Connell Street, taking our time so the old Russian got a chance to eyeball us. Past the river, past the humpback of the Ha'penny Bridge. The real jewels were being transported by cycle courier by a different route.

"Do you think the Russian will take the bait?" I asked the police officer.

"Collectors are nutcases," he said. "They'll do anything to complete a collection. And if he's a bounty hunter, he'll want his reward."

The police escort dropped us off right outside the studio. Then he went to mingle among the passersby. He lingered in a doorway to make a call. A lookout.

The other attaché case with the wallet containing the real jewels had already arrived. Rachel's eyes glittered with excitement when she took out the packages. Patrick had brought along a powerful microscope hitched up to his computer.

With deft little movements, Rachel unstitched the first tiny package on a steel plate. She glanced up at our eager faces and gave us a little smile.

"I know it's like Santa's presents at Christmas, but it's better if you don't crowd me," she said.

We stood back.

"Why do you think Jack went to all that trouble to put

them in the statues of Parnell and O'Connell?" I asked Mal in a hushed voice.

"Maybe he wanted later generations to remember it wasn't all guns and glory. O'Connell and Parnell worked for a free Ireland through non-violent means."

"Or, since he left the map for his kids, perhaps he just wanted them to know it used to be his and Molly's playground," I said.

Rachel let out a gasp. We rushed over. Inside the first parcel were tiny little green gemstone fragments.

"The warm green of a meadow in spring," she said as she opened the second parcel. "Definitely emerald."

Patrick put them under the microscope and showed us the image with its tiny bubbles and cubes on screen.

"These are very pure fragments. They look like splinters from a cabochon. I'll have to get them to the lab urgently."

With great care he transferred each individual fragment into a clear plastic holder and labelled it. Rachel placed them in her safe. I glanced into her inner office. I got a shock to see a visitor. But Rachel nodded at him and I realised he was another plainclothes policeman.

Then she chose some gems and bits of silver filigree thread and put them in little padded boxes.

"These are the decoy jewels. Just paste and sterling silver. We don't want him stealing the real ones!" she explained.

She handed the decoys to Patrick who placed them in

343

the silver attaché case. Like straight out of a spy movie!

"Can we come with you?" I asked.

"The police said better not. We should do everything as normal. When we walk out the door we need to go our separate ways."

We went back into the Merchant's Alley passageway again. I saw the "taxi-driver" in one corner. Someone else ducked into a doorway. An old lady with a distinctive hat!

"It's him! It's him!" I tugged Mal's sleeve.

"Shush!"

"Why don't they arrest him?" I whispered.

"They can't just arrest him for standing in a doorway dressed as a woman in a stupid hat. They need evidence. It's out of our hands now."

We headed towards the Ha'penny Bridge to go back to Connolly Station for the DART. Just two ordinary kids again.

I grabbed Mal by the coat sleeve.

"If he's desperate, he's not going to wait," I said.

He shrugged his shoulders, non-committal.

But I didn't wait for Mal. I was off, across the road, cutting up along the river and then right towards Trinity College where Patrick was heading to the lab.

Then, as I stood at the traffic lights in College Green, I saw my worst nightmare in slow motion.

As Patrick raced across the pedestrian crossing and was about to walk through the gates of Trinity College, a large old lady in a funny hat barreled into him, grabbing the aluminium case. Patrick shouted out.

"Stop him!"

But people looked at him as if he was crazy. The "old lady" was already halfway across the road.

I stood, my legs wouldn't move. People milled around me as if I was a boulder in a stream. The plainclothes officers gave chase. But were snagged in the tide of people. Then two large buses rushed by.

The old lady ran with terrific speed and energy towards College Green.

The hat and wig hit the ground. There was no mistaking the bullet-headed Russian now. He was heading in my direction, bearing down so hard he cleared a path through the passersby who pulled back in fear.

Time stood still. My heart hammered in my chest. My eyesight became pin-sharp. I saw my chance. As the large Russian bore down on me, braced as if for a rugby tackle, I pulled back but stuck out my leg.

He stumbled forward like a barrel. Then crashed onto the sidewalk, and rolled into the gutter. The aluminium case bounced forward. Into the arms of Mal, who caught it in one deft move.

The Russian flailed around, somewhat comical in his terrible tweed suit and pearls, trying to get to his feet. He looked like he needed a shave. But the two plainclothes detectives were on him. Within moments he was pulled to his feet and the handcuffs snapped on him. He gave me a dirty look.

"You don't know who you're messing with!" he said to me with menace.

"You are under arrest for theft. You are advised that anything you say may be used in evidence against you," warned the detective.

The Russian spat as he was hustled in to a police car. The officer took the aluminium case. "Good work, kids," he said.

I grinned at Mal and looked him in the eye. "Hey, slow coach, what took you so long!"

Chapter twenty four

Mal's judge, Angela Wilkinson, was ecstatic. "Well, Mal, you cheated me on the internet case with your guilty plea. But you've certainly made up for it by handing me this complex treasure-trove case."

We were in the judge's office in King's Inn, at the centre now of a major international story.

I had been right all along to be suspicious about the Russian. He wasn't a collector but a bounty hunter, working for a shady Russian oligarch obsessed with collecting Russia's lost Crown Jewels. He was wanted on a string of other international charges of diamond smuggling, embezzlement, injury, affray. His only hope of a lighter sentence was to confess.

By a strange coincidence he had been in Fairview library that day, researching Harry Boland's story. He had come across the rumour that someone connected with Boland had retrieved jewels in New York harbour. That someone must have been Jack.

Then, when he heard us talking, he decided to hang

around and keep an eye on us. He found out about Mal's criminal record and couldn't believe his luck that we were operating in secrecy. He was patient. He let us do the work. He thought it would be like taking candy off a baby. He was wrong. He was forced to cough up the jewels he'd stolen from the Trinity College laboratory. Who owned them was now the subject of a big legal case.

But we were also in a whole heap of trouble. Guess what? For using a metal detector on national monuments!

"You didn't have a licence," said the judge. "Did you realise you could be fined €64,000 alone for using one unauthorised?"

"But it does have a licence," argued Mal. "My dad had it for his mineral exploration. In case he also finds archeological remains."

"Yes, but you are not your dad," said the judge sternly.

"But most of those monuments aren't technically archeological sites," I said. "They are memorials."

The judge smiled despite herself. "When you grow up I hope both of you put your sharp minds to some legal use. I do grant you these are extraordinary circumstances."

"You can't send Mal back to that reform centre," I said. "He would never have got mixed up in it if I hadn't asked him. Send me instead."

Mal shot me an appreciative look.

The judge shook her head. "I admire your loyalty, Ava. But, Mal, you are a young fellow who, even if he doesn't go looking for trouble, trouble finds him."

She stared at us both for a long time. Like she was measuring our souls.

"Technically you have both broken the law. Trespassed, illegally searched land, and in Mal's case broken the limits of his generous parole."

We didn't dare look at each other. My ears were burning. I could feel my mother's shame. I was afraid if I looked up the room would jump around the place.

"But the law is one thing. Justice is another. And it is justice that I have sworn to uphold. I would consider myself a criminal if I punished you two fine young people for so fearlessly seeking out the truth."

My head shot up. I looked at Mal who was grinning from ear to ear.

"Does that mean we're free?" I asked.

"You certainly are," the judge pronounced. "And what's more I will be recommending to the Department of Monuments that you are both rewarded for this find. It will take many months to verify if these really are the Crown Jewels but I don't see why a reward cannot be expedited."

Two weeks later two important items arrived in the post. The first was a cheque for €50,000 to be shared between us for our treasure trove. But the second, which arrived the next day, was even more of a reward. The parcel bore a Texan postmark, with the address of an Austin legal firm on the back.

In great excitement, I knocked on Mal's door. We carried it up to our incident room.

We unwrapped it to find another package and a letter. I tore the letter open. It was from a legal firm administering the estate of the late Jack Junior O'Donovan.

Dear Ava,

The executor of our client, his daughter Elsa, has asked me to forward this package to you in accordance with her late father's dying wish. The biscuit tin contains her grandfather Jack's ashes, which are now mingled with some of the ashes of our late client Jack Junior Adair. We request that you comply with his wishes to scatter them on the River Liffey in Dublin. And, please, if you could say a few words? We also enclose a photograph that Elsa says her father insisted on forwarding to you.

She wants you to know that her father died peacefully. After your visit Mr. Adair was transferred to his daughter's care, where he died among his family. She also asked me to tell you that she will contact you soon with more information.

With best wishes,
Victor Kildare
Attorney at Law

I was real sad to hear about Jack Junior. But glad that he'd been with his family at the end. Inside the package was the Jacob's Cream Crackers tin I'd last seen on the floor in Texas. There was also enclosed, in protective bubble wrap, a photograph.

I tore it open. It was a black-and-white photograph of a smiling woman in a doctor's coat. She might have been fifty or thirty – it was hard to say. She had frizzy hair pulled into a bun, freckles and a smile that could warm up the whole planet. She stood in front of a gleaming white building with a red cross on the front bearing the word 'HOSPITAL' and under it what we assumed was 'hospital' in Hindi. She was surrounded by a big group of Indian children, with beaming nurses and doctors in the background.

Molly.

Two weeks later a group gathered for a little ceremony by O'Connell Bridge at the corner of Bachelor's Walk. It was seven in the morning to avoid the traffic and crowds. Mal and I. His father, a tall thin man with a haggard face but Mal's piercing eyes. My mother. Even my father. There had been an icy moment when they met again. But both of them were behaving cordially for my sake. Nora came up from Killarney, with her good karma and kind face. And all our library friends, Betty, Bríd, looking frailer and yet radiant, and Karen the librarian. Rachel and Patrick. Young and old Stavros, both wearing their Sunday best. Old Stavros beamed at us like a kindly grandfather and smelled of rosewater. And Parvati too, glancing shyly at Mal.

I even asked Suzy and the Banshees. If they hadn't been so mean to me maybe Mal wouldn't have become my friend. It was good to see their eyes popping out of their heads! Angela the judge and the plainclothes policemen and Aoife the forensic scientist also joined us. And old landlady Lil who now claimed with a click of her teeth that she always knew "Benjy's old rubbish was real important"!

I would have liked a grown-up to do the job. But the letter said it had to be me.

As we stood by the water, the sound of seagulls pierced the air. One of them landed on Daniel O'Connell's head. I thought of Jack the Cat and his sister Molly and their friend Anto. His sister May, their mother Nancy. And all those brave people who had lived through those times. Someday I will find out more about what happened to them. If Anto's wife had the baby safely. How Molly really smuggled Jack and Anto out of the cinema and the country. How she ended up in India.

I didn't want to seem all holy or anything. But I had to say a few words.

"Thanks, folks, for all coming to say goodbye to Jack the Cat and his son Jack Junior. In a few moments all that is left of them will vanish into the water and into the air. Jack the Cat grew up here in O'Connell Street with his sister Molly, his best friend Anto and future wife May. He played his part in Ireland's road to freedom but had to leave. There aren't any monuments to Jack the Cat. But he stood for something. Peace, I guess. He was like the spirit of all that was good in Ireland. I hope we make it a better place than when he left." I glanced at my father and mother. "And I hope too we try to heal all the kinds of war you can have. In the world, against nature, even in our families. Because us kids don't start any wars. But we sure like to see an end to them."

My mother nodded at my father who smiled thoughtfully.

With Mal's help, I opened the lid and tipped the ashes towards the water. The ashes swirled for a moment. Then a breeze took them up and they fanned out towards the river. United for the last time and carried in the current towards to the sea.

My mother had organised breakfast in the Gresham Hotel at the other end of the long street. But as we turned towards O'Connell Street, past the statue of Daniel O'Connell, Mal had a surprise for me.

Out of side streets and from corners, hundreds of teenagers and young people streamed towards the Spire by the GPO and gathered around it. From the street where Battling Siki had fought and Jack and Anto had staged their disappearance. Past the building of Cleary's department store where May had worked as a shopgirl. Down from Henry Street where the rebels of 1916 made their last escape from the burning GPO under a hail of bullets. Tall teenagers in hoodies, beautiful girls in colourful dresses, some parents with little kids.

Several of the older teenagers were carrying white flags. All wore T-shirts. On each, the face and name of a child. *Muhammad aged 6 Syria. Khaled aged 16 Lebanon. Azima aged 11 Indonesia. Ali aged 8 Yemen*. Out they came from Abbey Street where Molly had rescued Patch.

Down Talbot Street where fleeing anti-Treaty fighters had escaped from the Hammam Hotel. Young people all bearing witness to other children less fortunate – those who were refugees or caught up in war.

Mal took off his jacket. He was wearing a T-shirt too. *Yasmin age 14 Gaza*. He handed me one: *Zada aged 6 Turkey*. Her large eyes smiling out from a beautiful face. Another child caught up in events she had not made.

"It's okay. The judge knows about it. She even gave me her computer to organise the flash mob."

I hugged him. We stood and faced the GPO for a minute's silence. Then on Mal's signal, everyone put in earphones. Mal shared his earbuds with me. The iPod was a gift from his father – a sign of trust. It was playing a fantastic rock version of my mother's old favourite "Molly Malone". As if with one body we all started dancing like lunatics.

"Alive, alive oh!
Alive, alive oh!
Crying cockles and mussels,
Alive, alive oh!"

As I gyrated around the Spire, a shaft of sunlight hit its shiny surface. I was blinded for a second. I blinked and saw the fleeting image of young girl with long curly red hair, freckles and a smile to dazzle the planet. "Molly," I breathed. We both held out our hands. I touched her fingers through the cold metal. I blinked and the image was gone. Only my own reflection looked back at me.

I made a vow to myself. When in life I have a choice between doing the big thing or the small thing, I will ask, what would Molly do? I will try to do the big thing. All those people gave their lives. It's the least I can do.

I was caught up back in the dance. We held hands, forming a circle around the Spire for all those children all over the world who don't have this freedom to dance and sing.

You might say it was my imagination, a trick of the light. But I saw what I saw. It doesn't matter anyhow. Molly and all she stood for is inside me now.

Always, dear Molly. Always.

The End

Civil War Timeline

Between 1919 and 1921 nationalists in Ireland fought a guerilla war against the British government – known as the War of Independence – demanding an independent Irish Republic. In July 1921 a truce was declared and Michael Collins led a delegation to London to negotiate a treaty. Key people and groups within the Irish nationalist movement opposed the Treaty and their opposition led to civil war.

1922

7th Jan – The Dáil approves the Anglo-Irish Treaty by 64 votes to 57. This creates an Irish Free State of 26 counties. The remaining 6 counties in the North stay part of the United Kingdom. The new elected representatives called T.D's (Teachta Dáile), have to swear an Oath of Allegiance to the British king.

Éamon de Valera and Cathal Brugha resign and join an anti-Treaty movement.

26th March – The Irish Republican Army rejects the Treaty and says they will not support the government. They set up their own army executive lead by Liam Mellows and Rory O'Connor.

14th April – A force of 200 anti-Treaty supporters occupy the Four Courts and other buildings in Dublin. Their aim is to restart the war against the British. They hope to provoke an attack by the British forces still in Dublin and force the pro-Treaty side to support them.

18th June - The pro-Treaty Sinn Féin Party wins the General Election. Over 75% of the Irish population votes for pro-Treaty candidates.

22nd June – Assassination in London of high-ranking Unionist and army officer Henry Hughes Wilson by IRA men in retaliation for attacks on Catholics in Northern Ireland. This causes British politicians, including Winston Churchill, to put pressure on Michael Collins to end the Civil War.

27th June – Collins gives a final ultimatum to the anti-Treaty forces occupying the Four Courts to surrender before they are attacked.

28th June – The Free State troops bombard the Four Courts with 18-pounder field guns borrowed from the British Government.

28th June – 5th of July – The Battle of Dublin takes place between the Free State Troops and anti-Treaty forces.

29th June – Anti-Treaty forces also occupy the Gresham Hotel and other buildings on Sackville Street. This is known as "The Block".

30th June – There is a massive explosion in the Four Courts, destroying the Public Record Office and the roof of its circular drum blows off. Many anti-Treaty fighters escape, including Ernie O'Malley.

3rd July – Anti-Treaty commander, Oscar Traynor, evacuates most of his troops, leaving an estimated 15 in the Gresham under Cathal Brugha.

4th July – Free State troops bring up a field gun and fire at point-blank range on "The Block". Incendiary bombs are also thrown.

5th July – the remaining fighters surrender or slip away. Cathal Brugha is shot dead refusing to surrender outside the building.

The casualties in the fighting in Dublin include 65 fighters killed (16 Free State and 49 anti-Treaty), 280 fighters wounded and over 250 civilians killed or injured.
The anti-Treaty Forces flee Dublin and continue the fight in what they call "The Munster Republic".

12th July Women's Peace Delegation meeting, Rotunda Round Room Dublin.

17-18th July – Free State Troops arrive in Limerick and Waterford to suppress Republican garrisons established there.

20th July – Fall of Limerick and Waterford.

31st July – Anti-Treaty activist Harry Boland is shot by Free State Troops as he is arrested in Skerries near Dublin. He dies of his wounds on 2nd August. He entrusts the Russian Crown Jewels to his sister Kathleen, instructing that they are to be handed over only when de Valera founds a Republic.

2nd August – Naval landing of 800 Free State troops in Country Kerry under the command of Paddy O'Daly. They fight their way to Tralee.

600 Free State troops engage 400 Republicans led by Dan Breen around Carrick-on-Suir. Free State troops take Carrick-on-Suir the next day.

8th August – Around 1000 Free State troops arrive in Cork by sea, led by General Emmet Dalton. After heavy fighting the Free State troops take Cork City on the **10th August.**

11th August – Liam Lynch, the anti-Treaty Republican leader, orders his fighters to abandon the policy of holding towns and to set up flying columns to wage guerilla warfare.

12th August – Free State President Arthur Griffith dies of a stroke brought on by stress. He is replaced by William T. Cosgrave.

22nd August – Free State Commander-in-Chief and architect of the Treaty, Michael Collins, is killed in an ambush at Béal na mBláth near his family home in Cork. Collins had been pursuing talks with anti-Treaty leaders to stop the fighting. He is replaced by General Richard Mulcahy who takes a harder line with anti-Treaty supporters.

26th August – Fianna members and anti-Treaty supporters, Seán Cole, Alf Colley and Bernard Daly, are abducted and killed in Yellow Lane, Whitehall, Dublin, by a special police unit of the Free State. Despite a verdict of "willful murder" at the inquest into their deaths, no one is ever charged.

31st August – Two Republicans are taken from a car in Drumcondra in Dublin and shot dead. An unarmed Free State soldier are shot in Athlone.

5th September. The Free State General Richard Mulcahy

and the political leader of the Republicans, Éamon de Valera, meet in secret. But they cannot agree a basis for a truce. Ambushes and skirmishes continue with loss of life.

9th September – Anti-Treaty fighters attack and take Kenmare in County Kerry. They shoot dead two local Free State leaders, the Scarteen O'Connors.

12th September – Republican forces loot and attack Ballina in County Mayo. Two civilians are killed in the fighting.

15th September – The Free State rules that the country is in a state of war and anti-Treaty supporters and fighters can be held prisoner without charge. As enemies of the state, they lose their rights under law.

19th September – Free State troops retake County Sligo. Six Republicans are killed on Ben Bulben, four it is alleged after surrendering. These include Brian MacNeill, the son of Eoin MacNeill who was the founder of the Irish Volunteers.

27th September – The Free State government passes the "Public Safety Bill". This sets up military courts and allows for the execution of men captured bearing arms or deemed to be aiding and abetting attacks on state forces. In total 77 anti-Treaty fighters are officially executed by the end of the Civil War.

3rd October – The Free State offers an amnesty to anti-Treaty fighters who surrender their arms and recognise the government.

7th October – Charlie Dalton, a National Army intelligence officer and brother of General Dalton, arrests three boys, neighbours of his, Edwin Hughes aged 17, Brendan Holohan aged 17 and Joe Rogers aged 16, for putting up Republican posters in Drumcondra. They are later found shot dead in a ditch in Clondalkin. Dalton was arrested but never charged with the offences.

10th October – The Catholic Bishops of Ireland issue a statement supporting the Free State and denying anti-Treaty fighters access to Holy Communion or Confession.

4th November – Ernie O'Malley, anti-Treaty IRA commander in Dublin, is captured in a shootout in Dublin. He kills a Free State soldier in the gunfight.

24th November – Former Treaty negotiator, British-born Robert Erskine Childers, is executed by the Free State. He was captured in possession of a pistol, which ironically had been given to him by Michael Collins.

30th November –anti-Treaty IRA commander Liam Lynch issues a general order for his forces to kill politicians who voted in favour of emergency powers to execute Republicans.

7th December – Pro-Treaty T.D. Seán Hales from Cork is shot dead in Dublin.

8th December – Anti-Treaty leaders captured in the Four Courts in Dublin, Rory O'Connor, Liam Mellows, Dick Barrett and Joe McKelvey, are executed by the Free State in revenge for the killing. This is considered an illegal act as all four were captured before the emergency legislation was passed.

10th December – Anti-Treaty IRA members burn down the house of TD Seán McGarry. His seven-year-old son dies in the blaze.

25th December – Anti-Treaty TD Joseph McDonagh, the brother of the Proclamation signatory Tomás McDonagh who was executed in 1916, dies on hunger strike.

1923

4th January – A Republican flying column under Tom Barry, recently escaped from jail, attack Millstreet in Cork. Two Free State and six anti-Treaty fighters are killed.

11th January – Anti-Treaty forces burn down Sligo railway station. The Great Southern and Western Railway release details of all their property damaged in the previous six months. These include 375 lines damaged, 42 engines derailed, 51 bridges and 207 under-bridges damaged.

11th February – The father of government minister Kevin O'Higgins is shot dead in County Laois. The family home is burnt down.

During the remainder of the month, a total of 37 houses of senators are destroyed by anti-Treaty forces. These include that of Dr. Oliver St. John Gogarty, a prominent Free State senator who also survives an assassination attempt.

18th February – Republican leader Dinny Lacey is killed and many of his column captured in an encircling attack at the Glen of Aherlow. This cripples the Republican cause in the Tipperary/Waterford area.

6th March – Free State soldiers including local recruit and informer Paddy Pats O'Connor are lured to a booby trap in Knocknagoshel, County Kerry. Five are killed. Another soldier is badly wounded. Commander Paddy O'Daly declares that all mines will now be cleared by Republican prisoners.

7th March – 9 Republican prisoners are blown up at Ballyseedy Cross in Kerry in retaliation. One man, Stephen Fuller, survives. A riot breaks out in Tralee when the troops bring nine coffins back to the town.

8th March – 4 more Kerry anti-Treaty IRA prisoners are murdered by a booby trap at Countess Bridge, Killarney. Again, one man, Tadgh Coffey miraculously escapes the massacre.

11th March – Republican Seamus Taylor is taken to Ballyseedy Woods, Kerry, and shot dead by Free State forces.

12th March – 5 Republican prisoners are blown up by a landmine in Cahirsiveen, Kerry, in a further reprisal.

13th March – 6 Republican prisoners are executed. The anti-Treaty leaders issue a ban on all public entertainment.

17th March – A major boxing match between Battling Siki and Mike McTigue takes place in Dublin under heavy Free State guard despite anti-Treaty threats. A bomb goes off nearby, injuring two children.

23rd March – 3 unarmed Free State soldiers are shot dead in a pub in Wexford in retaliation for the execution of Republican prisoners.

28th March – 5 Republicans captured in an anti-Treaty attack on Cahirsiveen are executed by firing squad.

1st April – Prominent anti-Treaty Officers are captured in the Knockmealdown Mountains in Tipperary, including Dan Breen and Todd Andrews.

6th April – Free State Troops in Kerry rescue an informer, a railway worker, Cornelius Hannifin, held prisoner by anti-Treaty fighters. 9 anti-Treaty fighters are killed in the skirmish.

10th April - Liam Lynch, Commander-in-Chief of the anti-Treaty forces is killed in a skirmish with Free State troops in the Knockmealdown Mountains in County Tipperary. This effectively marks the end of the Civil War.

15th April – The Free State claim that 9 Republicans are killed in a firefight in Glenvar, Kerry.

18th April – An anti-Treaty IRA column led by Timothy Lyons (known as Aeroplane) take refuge in caves from Free State troops on Kerry Head. 2 Free State soldiers are shot dead trying to storm the caves. After a three-day siege, 3 anti-Treaty fighters are killed by exploding landmines. Lyons is shot and drowns in the incident.

This is the last major engagement of the Civil War in Kerry. Around 180 people have been killed in the county – 85 Free State troops, 72 anti-Treaty fighters and 12 civilians.

30th April – Frank Aiken, the new anti-Treaty Commander, calls a ceasefire.

24th May – Frank Aiken orders the anti-Treaty fighters to "dump their arms" and return home. Éamon de Valera concedes military victory in the Civil War to the Free State.

17th August – Irish General Election. Pro-Treaty politicians win a majority of the votes. Cumann na nGaedhael, the new Free State party led by Cosgrave, wins 63 seats and forms a government. Republican Sinn Féin wins 44 seats and just under 30% of the vote. Cosgrave becomes the new Taoiseach, leader of Ireland.

There are no reliable figures for the number of dead during the Civil War. Estimates put the figure somewhere between 1,300 and 2,000 at a minimum: at least 730 Free State Army, 350-400 anti-Treaty fighters, and around 200 civilians.

About 12,000 anti-Treaty fighters and supporters were imprisoned during the conflict.

Source: Wikipedia, the free encyclopedia

Historical Characters

Michael Collins – guerilla leader during the War of Independence who negotiated the Anglo-Irish treaty establishing the Free State. General of the Free State. He was assassinated at Beál na mBláth by Republican forces.

Arthur Griffith – leader of Sinn Féin and first President of the Irish Free State. Died of a stroke brought on by stress during Civil War.

Éamon De Valera – former President of the Provisional Government who took the anti-Treaty side during the Civil War. Later head of Fianna Fáil political party, Taoiseach and President.

Ernie O'Malley – commander of anti-Treaty troops during the Civil War. Later a renowned author of books about the period.

Countess Constance Markievicz – founder of the Fianna Boy Scouts who took the anti-Treaty side during the Civil War.

Charlotte Despard – sister of former Lord Lieutenant Lord French. She rebelled against her family to support Irish freedom and was a staunch suffragette and political activist.

Maude Gonne MacBride – famous beauty who was married to John MacBride who was executed for his part in the 1916 Rising. She formed a women's delegation to lobby both sides for a truce. Later became an anti-Treaty supporter.

John MacBride – son of Maude Gonne and John MacBride. He supported the anti-Treaty side. Later he became a politician, a founder of Amnesty International and a winner of the Nobel Peace Prize.

Todd Andrews – reluctant supporter of the anti-Treaty side. He went on to become a head of the transport company C.I.E. and the Irish state broadcaster RTÉ.

Dr. Dorothy Stopford Price – pioneering doctor from an Irish Protestant family who tended to Irish volunteers in the War of Independence and who supported the anti-Treaty side in the split. She later played a key role in introducing the BCG vaccine to Ireland and eliminating tuberculosis.

Author's Note

The Civil War 1922-1923 – Ava's Diary is the final part of the trilogy that includes *The Easter Rising 1916 – Molly's Diary* and *The War of Independence 1920-22 – Dan's Diary*.

As in the previous books, the main protagonists are imaginary and are woven into a dramatic re-imaging of historical events. Otherwise much of the incidental detail and accounts of real characters is based on research.

In all cases, I have tried to remain faithful to the spirit of the times and the real events.

Harry Boland really did bring Russian Crown Jewels back to Ireland as collateral for a loan to the Russian Bolshevik government. They were kept up the chimney and sometimes in the pantry of his mother's house in Marino Crescent, Dublin, until 1948.

There is also an emerald necklace still missing from the Tsar's collection that had nothing to do with Harry Boland. Pulling these unrelated facts together, I have invented a second set of jewels coming to Ireland and spun a tale through the real timeline of the Civil War.

This is a work of fiction, so in other places I have taken some liberties where it doesn't take away from the historical narrative. There are accounts by rebel schoolmaster, Pat O'Connor of hiding out in a fairy fort in Knocknagoshel. I have expanded its dimensions and remoteness. Likewise the hideout on Torc Mountain is inspired by accounts of such structures but you wouldn't find it if you went looking. The character of Free State Captain Ned is a composite of David Nelligan and Ned Breslin and their troubling role in the Ballyseedy massacre – he took on a life of his own.

History is full of different versions. It can be hard to establish what really went on, particularly during a Civil War which many of those involved, particularly the founders of a new State, wanted to forget. But all inaccuracies are my own.

The Civil War is known as *Cogadh na gCarad*, the "War of Friends" in Irish. It was one of the most bitter and traumatic events in Irish history. But it is also fascinating as it contains so much of the seeds of our present. I have done my best to honour the memory of all those who lived and died in those turbulent times.

Acknowledgments

The Civil War 1922-1923 – Ava's Diary is the third book in the trilogy about Ireland's road to the Republic and I owe a big thank-you to Paula Campbell, Publisher at Poolbeg, who encouraged me to stay with my vision for the series. Also to Kieran Devlin for his support.

Round of applause to David Prendergast for his diligent typesetting of a text with enough challenges to send a lesser person cross-eyed. Also to Caroline Maloney for all her support and organization.

A huge bouquet to editor Gaye Shortland for her keen eye and deft touch. She has shown true dedication in the field. And I mean a real field. Even driving the route to Béal na mBláth to check out my description of the lie of the land!

And I extend my appreciation to illustrator Derry Dillon for his fine work on the front cover.

Thanks also to my eagle-eyed early readers – the Murphy clan, Neil, Stephen, Audrey, Ken and Karen. Patrick Collinson, and my nephews William, Senan, Cian, Daniel, Conor, Alex, Patrick and nieces Aoife and Isabella. They gave me invaluable feedback and reassurance.

Huge gratitude to my husband Marc and daughter Rosa who have shown great patience with a wife and mother who has spent a lot of her time in her head, down the side of a ditch in a dugout.

Special thanks too to Betty Cronin, my former history and English teacher, who has constantly cheered me from the sidelines. She is still teaching after fifty years in the job and is an inspiration to us all.

I would like to thank all the wonderful children and readers who have read my books and took Molly and the story of Ireland's journey to a Republic to their heart. Their response has been immense and their feedback invaluable.

I owe a lot to Ana Lucia McGrath and Mia Madden – their enthusiasm for books at a very young age is everything an author could wish for.

Special mention to Brighid Uí Almhain and Liam Ó hAlmhain for their warm support. Likewise Debbie Hutchinson from Near FM and the terrific girls of St. John of God's, Artane, who were a source of great inspiration. And a standing ovation to Joan O'Neill Kelly and all the boys and girls of Coole Harmonies in Kinvara.

Also to Brian Crowley from Pearse Museum whose conversation and perspective are always enlightening.

Many thanks to Superteacher Mr O'Hanlon and his great students at Saint Mary's Parish Primary School, Bryanstown, Drogheda. Likewise, to the staff and children at St. Fiachra's Senior National School Beaumont, St. Helen's Senior National School Portmarnock and Muire na Mainistreach, "The Mon", Killarney, County Kerry. I am indebted to their headteachers, Kieran Creaner, Mary O'Leary and Colm

O'Súilleabháin respectively. I am grateful too to teachers Louise McGarrity and Evie Price and the girls in Rosa's year at Oxford High School for their feedback and support.

Thanks to Orlagh Kelly at Wildwords Literary Festival in Carrick-on-Shannon and Leitrim Arts Officer Philip Delamere for the opportunity to present a historical fiction and creative workshop with terrific young participants.

I salute the libraries of Ireland, especially Tipperary, Dublin and South Cork who gave me such a warm welcome and allowed me to meet such inspirational young people.

I owe a huge debt to Dr. Tim Horgan, Ophthalmologist, author and local historian, who generously shared a wealth of detail and his invaluable insight into the Civil War in Kerry.

Thanks to the U.S. Geological Survey Library for permission to reproduce the photograph of the emerald necklace from The Russian Diamond Fund.

References and Sources

There is nowhere near the same level of primary sources available for the Civil War as for 1916 and the War of Independence. The Irish Bureau of Military History stopped short at the Truce, excepting a few instances where interviewees continued their accounts. But there are still some excellent books on the subject. I relied heavily on memoirs and biographies written by those who took part in those troubled times.

Memoirs and Biographies

Harry Boland's Irish Revolution by David Fitzpatrick, Cork University Press

Dorothy Stopford Price – Rebel Doctor by Anne MacLellan

Rosamund Jacob – Third Person Singular by Leeann Lane, UCD Press

Frank Sherwin – Independent and Unrepentant edited by Frank Sherwin Jr.

Kathleen Lynn – Irishwoman, Patriot, Doctor by Margaret Ó hÓgartaigh, Irish Academic Press

Prison Letters of Countess Markievicz, Virago Press

Terrible Beauty – A Life of Constance Markievicz by Diana Norman, Poolbeg

Constance Markeivicz – an Independent Life by Anne Haverty, Pandora Press

Charlotte Despard by Margaret Mulvihill, Pandora Press

Tomorrow Was Another Day: Irreverent Memories of an Irish Rebel Schoolmaster by Seamus O'Connor Anvil Books (out of print)

The Singing Flame by Ernie O'Malley, Mercier Press

Dublin Made Me by C. S. Andrews, The Liliput Press

Kerry Landing – August 1922 by Niall C. Harrington, Anvil Books

Overviews

The Green Divide – An Illustrated History of the Irish Civil War by Michael Barry. A brilliant collection of photographs and other visual materials. An excellent and engrossing introduction to the Civil War for all ages.

A City in Civil War by Pádraig Yeates, Gill and Macmillan. A masterful account of Dublin in the Civil War.

Bitter Freedom – Ireland in a Revolutionary World 1918-1923 by Maurice Walsh, Faber and Faber. A lively and pacy read, giving a good overview of the period.

The Republic – The Fight for Irish Independence by Charles Townshend. A scholarly work incorporating many viewpoints.

Vivid Faces – The Revolutionary Generation in Ireland 1890-1923 by R.F. Foster, Allen Lane. A beautifully written account of key players in the Irish revolution.

The Fall of Dublin by Liz Gillis, Mercier Press, a clear and concise narrative with great eyewitness testimonies.

Dying for the Cause – Kerry's Republican Dead by Tim Horgan, The Mercier Press. A detailed and emotional account of all 168 men who died in the period.

The Men Will Talk To Me – Kerry Interviews by Ernie O'Malley – edited by Cormac O'Malley and Tim Horgan, The Mercier Press. Fascinating interviews conducted long after the events.

The Irish Republic by Dorothy MacArdle, Merlin publishing. First published in 1937, this is a pro-Republican, pro-de-Valera account, enlivened by the fact that MacArdle knew many of the participants.

Tragedies of Kerry by Dorothy MacArdle, Irish Freedom Press. A short lyrical pamphlet outlining the atrocities in Kerry from a Republican point of view.

Michael Collins and the Irish Civil War by T. Ryle Dwyer, Mercier Press.

Green Against Green – The Irish Civil War by Michael Hopkinson, Gill & Macmillan.
Peace After the Final Battle – The Story of the Irish Revolution 1912-1923 by John Dorney, Merrion Press.

Further Resources

Ballyseedy – an RTÉ documentary 1997. A brilliant documentary researched over five years by broadcaster Pat Butler.

The Madness Within – RTÉ documentary 1998, presented by Brian Dobson.

The Wind That Shakes the Barley – 2005. Ken Loach's moving film about two brothers who end up on different sides of the Treaty during the Civil War.

Further resources and information are available on my website – www.patriciamurphyonline.com and follow me on twitter @PatriciaMurphy.

If you enjoyed *Ava's Diary* why not try
The Easter Rising 1916 - Molly's Diary

Here's a sample . . .

The
Easter Rising
1916

Molly's Diary

*E*aster 1916. *The Great War rages in Europe with two hundred thousand Irishmen fighting in the British Army. But a small group of Irish nationalists refuse to fight for Britain and strike a blow for Irish freedom. Caught up in the action in Dublin is twelve-year-old Molly O'Donovan. This is her diary.*

📖   📖   📖

9 o'clock, Saturday morning, 22nd April 1916 – MY BIRTHDAY!
My bedroom, 9 Sackville Street, Dublin, Ireland, Second City of the British Empire.

My name is Molly O'Donovan and I am twelve years old today. Hurray! My father is Chief Technical

Officer at the General Post Office (GPO for short) and makes sure everyone gets their telegraphs and telephone calls. My mother is called Bessie. She is a Quaker from Enniskillen in the North of Ireland. We live opposite the GPO in Sackville Street, Dublin, the widest street in Europe, in a tall thin house above a tailor's shop.

My brother Jack is two years older than me – and teases me something rotten!

I had hoped to fill my new diary with elegant words and clever thoughts but all I've had are constant interruptions. I only had to pick up my new fountain pen earlier at breakfast for Jack to make fun of me.

"Why on earth would a boring girl need a diary!" he jeered. "Dear Diary, today I broke a comb in my awful red hair, I played nurses with my silly dolls. Blah, blah, blah!"

Jack tried to swipe the diary from me but I held it out of reach.

"Die, Imperial Enemy! God save Ireland!" he cried and the eejit tried to bayonet my diary with his fork.

"Shush! I'm writing down EVERYTHING that happens. So you'd better stop jumping off roofs and marching with rebels!" I made a face at him but he made a worse one back and stabbed again at my lovely diary. "Hands off! It's the best present ever!"

It's true. It's vellum and hand-bound in leather with my name carved on the front. It has a little lock and all. Mother's friend, Addy, who works in Eason Stationers, made it.

Then our char Nancy Maguire chimed in. "Janey Mac! Would yeh ever stop actin' the maggot, young Jack," she scolded. She is quite old and crinkly and her face is sooty from cleaning the grate.

Jack mimed shooting at me with a rifle, the dangerous galoot.

"At least your sister's not hangin' outside old Fenian bomber's tobacco shops like you and our Anto," said Nancy.

Anto is Nancy's fifteen-year-old son, a messenger boy with buck teeth and sticky-out ears. Jack thinks the sun shines out of his scrawny backside.

"Nancy, who are the Fenians?" I asked.

"A shower of no-account troublemakers from way back who want to bomb us all into bein' an Irish Republic," she said, shaking her brush. "I'll give them the tail-end of this if they come too close."

Jack was going to rugby-tackle me so I jumped up on my chair to hold the diary out of arm's reach.

In all the rough and tumble we hadn't noticed that my father had walked into the room and heard what we'd been saying.

"What's this about Fenians?" he asked sharply.

"If I catch our Anto with dem bowsies marchin' around like tin soldiers," said Nancy, "I'll box his ears and theirs too."

My father suppressed a smile. He thinks Nancy is very funny.

"Lookin' for an Ireland Republic while my poor aul' husband Mossy and Jemsie me firstborn are fightin' the Germans," continued Nancy.

Both are soldiers with the Dublin Fusiliers in Flanders. So Nancy is one of the 'Separation Women' who wait to get money every week from the Post Office because their husbands are off fighting the Germans.

The Kaiser in Germany started the war. It's a long story. A madman in Serbia shot a duke and now everyone is fighting everybody. It all gets very confusing because some of the Irish, and not just the old Fenians that Nancy wants to wallop with her brush, won't fight for England against Germany and want an independent Ireland. Friends of Jack, I'll have you know.

"'We serve neither King nor Kaiser but Ireland!'" said Jack defiantly. He'd told me he saw this slogan on a big banner outside Liberty Hall down on Burgh Quay. It's the headquarters of the Trade Unionists who want the employers to give their workers more money and rights. They are yet another group who have their own army. There are so many armies marching about it's surprising they don't all bump into each other.

"I'm amazed you could even read that banner on Liberty Hall," I said to Jack. This was unkind and I immediately felt bad. Jack has problems with reading.

"If I ever see that Kaiser, I'll make him sit on his big pointy helmet – that'll put some manners on him," said Nancy.

"Nancy should be the Prime Minister," I giggled.

"And that fella Tom Clarke in the tobacco shop around the corner," she went on. "What that aul' Fenian bomb-maker says is more dangerous than the matches he sells. As for yer one, Countess Marzipan!"

"Countess Markievicz. Her husband is a Polish Count, though she herself is Anglo-Irish," corrected my father who is a stickler for accuracy.

"Whatever she's called, she's a bit of a consequence with her smokin' and trousers and big hats," said Nancy. "Turnin' all those young boys to devilment!"

"Isn't Anto in the Countess's Scouts –" I began, but Jack pinched me hard and looked daggers at me, so I bit my tongue. Luckily Nancy didn't hear me and was going on about how the Countess should stick to making soup for the poor.

"At the Post Office we maintain a neutral stance," said my father sternly to Jack. "I suggest you do the same, young man."

Jack kicked the chair leg. "I'll do as I please," he mumbled.

"Not when you're in my house," said Father. "Go to your room."

Jack skulked upstairs. My father hurried out. I was left standing on the chair, holding my Dear Diary, like a scarecrow. And my father hadn't even noticed!

I heard my father in the hall, taking his hat and umbrella from the hallstand, and then his exclamation of "Good God!"

He rushed back into the room and I thought I was in for it.

"Molly, I nearly forgot to wish you Happy Birthday!"

I jumped down and embraced him, for I love my daddy dearly and wish I could spend more time with him – but he is always so busy keeping the General Post Office going and says it is the most important building in Ireland. Not a telegram would be received nor a telephone call put through without my daddy looking after all the wires.

We heard a clatter at the front door. It was my mother arriving back with the delivery boy from the Dublin Bread Company, known as the DBC. As it's Holy Saturday it's closed for the rest of the day. The stout little boy was juggling several packages, including my birthday cake! His name is Tommy Keenan and he looks like he eats most of the cakes. He was wearing a little tricolour badge, the green, white and orange flag of the Republicans, so I think he is a Fenian too!

"Where's our wee Jack?" Mother asked anxiously in her soft Northern Irish accent. (Jack is heading towards six foot and is not at all wee!)

My father pointed up towards the ceiling, with an expression that indicated he had been sent to his room in disgrace. He kissed my mother on the cheek.

"The telegraph wires are always humming, holiday or no holiday," he said, heading for the door. This made me think of busy bees humming in a hive.

"Don't forget we're taking Molly to Bewley's Café when we come back from Howth Head," said my mother.

My father brightened up. "Make sure Jack goes to the sea. The fresh air will blow those silly notions out of his head."

"I'll write it all down in my diary!" I said excitedly.

"We better all watch our pee's and poo's so," proclaimed Nancy.

We all laughed. Nancy, of course, meant P's and Q's. Though I confess that doesn't make much sense either.

My mother gave her a bundle of old baby clothes and I helped her carry them to the door. I can't think why she needs baby clothes. Nancy is an old woman with lots of wobbly teeth and more like a grandmother – though I know she doesn't have grandchildren.

As she left Nancy whispered to me, "My Anto and Jack are good boys really. If Mossy were here, he'd tan Anto's hide to knock some sense into him."

"My mother won't let Father hit Jack," I said. It's because she's a Quaker and they are against war and violence, but Father would not like to do it anyhow.

"Yer da is as daecent as any man who ever wore a hat, and yer ma is a saint," said Nancy.

That is true for sure. Mother is always giving loaves of bread and stuff to old people in the slums, like in Moore Street.

Everything quietened down for a while after that but

Jack is wrong about my life being boring so, Dear Diary, together we are going to show him! I know one or two secrets about him and presently I may reveal them if he isn't nice to me!

But let me tell you more about myself and my family. I was christened Margaret but everyone calls me Molly. I am tall for my age with reddish hair and a dusting of freckles. My mother says my hair is "Titian" like the women in the pre-Raphaelite paintings. Jack says my hair is like rusty old springs and I look like I have the measles – that I am so ugly no one will want to marry me. But I don't care. There IS someone who wants to marry me – even if it's only Anto. Though I don't want to marry him. So Jack is wrong!

Find out more at poolbeg.com for
The Easter Rising 1916 - Molly's Diary,
The War of Independence 1920-22 - Dan's Diary
and other bestselling books.